W9-BZY-205

Angel Mine

Center Point
Large Print

Also by Sherryl Woods and available from
Center Point Large Print:

Sean's Reckoning
Michael's Discovery
Chesapeake Shores Christmas
Moonlight Cove
Beach Lane
O'Brien Family Christmas
Summer Garden

SHERRYL WOODS

Angel Mine

CENTER POINT LARGE PRINT
THORNDIKE, MAINE

This Center Point Large Print edition is published in the
year 2013 by arrangement with Harlequin Books S.A.

The text of this Large Print edition is unabridged.
In other aspects, this book may
vary from the original edition.
Printed in the United States of America
on permanent paper.
Set in 16-point Times New Roman type.

ISBN: 978-1-61173-720-2

Library of Congress Cataloging-in-Publication Data

Woods, Sherryl.
Angel mine : a Whispering Wind Novel / Sherryl Woods. — Center
   Point Large Print edition.
pages cm
ISBN 978-1-61173-720-2 (Library binding : alk. paper)
1. Actresses—Fiction. 2. Mothers and daughters—Fiction.
   3. Single parent families—Fiction. 4. Family secrets—Fiction.
   5. Life change events—Fiction. 6. Wyoming—Fiction.
   7. Domestic fiction. 8. Large type books. I. Title.
PS3573.O6418A83 2013
813'.54—dc23
                                              2013002170

For Kristi and Ron
And for Kerri and Tom

With more than a decade of marriage behind you,
may your lives continue to be filled with
blessings and joy and, most of all, love.

Dear Friends,

One of the most enjoyable things I get to do is plunk fictional characters down in a totally unfamiliar environment and let them try to fit in. Back in 2000 I was able to write the ultimate fish-out-of-water story, *Angel Mine*, about a big-city guy who suddenly finds himself in a tiny Wyoming town.

But if Todd Winston is completely out of his comfort zone in Whispering Wind, Wyoming, it's nothing compared to how he feels when his former girlfriend shows up in town with an angelic little girl who's unmistakably his daughter.

Overwhelmed by the demands of motherhood, Heather Reed has come for help from the man she once loved, but she stays to create a family.

While this unlikely trio find their way, you'll get to catch up with Megan O'Rourke and Jake Landers from *After Tex*, and all the inhabitants of Whispering Wind. If you missed either of these books the first time around, I hope you'll enjoy catching up.

And I hope you'll mark your calendars now for *Sand Castle Bay*, the first book in my new Ocean Breeze series, coming in May from Harlequin MIRA.

All best,

Sherryl

1

Despite her name, there was nothing the least bit angelic about Heather Reed's toddler, not when she was tired, anyway. And on this unseasonably warm early May afternoon she was exhausted *and* hot *and* hungry. Heather should have known that disaster loomed before she even considered taking Angel with her to the store. Not that she had any choice in the matter. She just should have antici-pated something like this. It was the way her day had gone.

Screaming as if she was being tortured, Angel threw herself onto the floor in the cereal aisle. Why? Because she was in pain? No. Because she was close to starvation? No. Simply to express her displeasure over her mother's refusal to buy her some sickly sweet product that was not only overpriced but would probably induce cavities after the first bite.

Heather debated what to do. She could snatch her up and run out of the crowded grocery store on New York's Upper West Side before anyone recognized her as an actress who'd spent a year as a hated villain on a popular soap opera. Or she could wait out her daughter's full-blown tantrum and endure the stares.

Embarrassment won. She'd taken enough abuse

from enraged fans over that soap role. If anyone recognized her, they'd likely assume she was being deliberately cruel to her daughter. Who knew where *that* could lead? Some soap fans had a hard time distinguishing between reality and fiction. By the time the truth could be sorted out, Heather's reputation would be in tatters.

Abandoning her half-filled shopping cart, she grabbed Angel and raced past startled shoppers and checkout clerks, not pausing until she was almost home. Setting her suddenly silent daughter on her feet on the sidewalk a block from their apartment building, she gazed down into tear-filled eyes and tried to feel some remorse over having been the cause of such apparent misery.

She couldn't.

Angel was the joy of her life . . . most of the time. But there were days—and today was definitely one of them—when Heather would have given anything for another adult to share the responsibility of raising her little girl, she thought as they walked the rest of the way home at a slower pace.

They had been in the stupid store in the first place because Heather had forgotten to pick up cereal the day before, and Angel had started the day with a breakfast of scrambled eggs, most of which had ended up smeared on her clothes and in her hair. That had necessitated another bath and a change of clothes before Angel went off to day-care and Heather headed for her waitressing job in a neighborhood deli, where the customers were only slightly less demanding and messy than her daughter. Her boss had docked her an hour's pay because she was five minutes late and warned her that the next time would be her last. Since her finances were already stretched to the limit, the threat carried a lot of weight.

To make matters worse, she'd gotten off early to go to a callback for a bit part in a new Broadway production, only to discover that the producer's girlfriend had been given the role overnight. Her acting career was in the middle of a frustrating lull of monumental proportions. Her self-esteem was slip-sliding away at an astonishing rate.

Angel's tantrum—nothing unusual in and of itself—had merely capped off a truly lousy day, but it was the proverbial straw that broke the camel's back. Plain and simple, Heather didn't see how she could do this single-mother routine much longer, not without losing her shaky grip on sanity.

She'd thought the worst of it had been the sleepless nights, when feedings had seemed to come every few minutes and colic kept Angel awake and cranky. Then the torments of potty training had replaced that. That accomplished, she'd been absolutely certain the rest would be smooth sailing.

Instead, she was discovering that the problems

never went away. They merely changed. Her admiration for single moms had increased by leaps and bounds in the past couple of years. In the past ten minutes she'd concluded she was simply one of those who couldn't hack it. At this rate she'd have high blood pressure and nervous tics by the time she turned thirty.

"That cuts it," Heather announced to no one in particular as she stood on the sidewalk in front of her apartment. "I cannot do this alone for one more day."

Once the admission had been uttered, an astonishing sense of relief spread through her. Independence was one thing. Foolhardy stubbornness was something else entirely.

She gazed at Angel, who stared back solemnly.

"We're going to find your daddy," she informed Angel as she brushed a stray wisp of silky hair from her child's forehead. "Let him figure out how to cope with you. Coping is what he does best," she said, fondly recalling all that cool competence. She figured he might be taken aback by the discovery that he was a daddy, but he would rally. He always did.

Angel's expression promptly brightened. "Daddy?"

It was a word that already fascinated her, even though she couldn't possibly understand its meaning. Angel automatically gravitated toward any male in a room, as if she sensed that he—or someone like him—was what was missing from her life.

"Yes, Daddy," Heather said firmly.

She knew for a fact that Todd was in Wyoming, working for media mogul Megan O'Rourke, who was giving Martha Stewart a run for her money in the world of TV, books and magazines. His promotion to executive producer of Megan's television show had been announced in all the trade papers a few months earlier. Heather hadn't been particularly surprised by the news. Todd always succeeded at whatever he set his mind to.

Of course, there had been a time when, like her, he'd wanted to be an actor. He'd claimed to want it with the same passion she did. He'd been good, too. Better than she'd been, she was forced to admit.

As much as Heather had believed in her own abilities, as much as she'd wanted desperately to be a star, she'd known she was likely to be relegated to bit parts in off-off-Broadway productions. Her skills ran to light comedic parts, not leading-lady roles. And while she could sing on key, she didn't have the showstopping voice for starring in musicals. She'd been willing to make do with that, because she couldn't imagine any other career, any other place to live. She loved the energy of New York, no matter how small a role she might have to take to stay there.

Todd, however, had been destined for stardom.

He'd just gotten sidetracked along the way by the lures of a weekly paycheck.

That had been one of the biggest hurdles they'd faced in their relationship. Four years ago she had been a free-spirited dreamer, willing to live on peanut butter and macaroni-and-cheese for her art. Todd had been steady and reliable and practical. He actually worried about having enough money for rent, decent food and vitamins. Over her objections, he'd let a temporary job with Megan O'Rourke turn into a full-time career. Heather had been disillusioned and saddened by his choice, by the sacrifice of their shared dream. Unable to accept his argument that he had done it for their future, she had split up with him soon afterward. On some level she had hoped that without his sense of obligation to her and their relationship, he might rediscover his old dream. He hadn't.

The breakup had come before she'd discovered she was pregnant. It was just as well, too. Todd would have wanted to do the *right thing,* even if it derailed both of their lives.

At the time she had been absolutely certain that she and her baby would both be better off on their own. She'd been taking care of herself— surviving—for a very long time. Struggling to be a working actress was second nature to her. Struggling to be a working actress with a baby would simply complicate things a little. It wouldn't actually worsen the struggle.

Or so she'd thought at the time.

Then, despite her optimism, practicality had set in. She'd had more trouble—more than she wanted to admit—putting food on the table. She might be able to survive on one meal a day at whatever restaurant she was working in part-time, but the baby couldn't. She'd taken jobs she'd hated— acting and otherwise—to make ends meet. Day-care costs were prohibitive and ate away at her paltry earnings. At night reliable baby-sitters were all but impossible to find at a price she could afford. Angel had spent more than her share of time in dingy backstage dressing rooms being tended by willing stagehands, who'd passed her around like a football as they went about their duties.

As a result, Angel was amazingly adaptable, but the constant demands were beginning to take a toll on Heather. She didn't need a man in her life, especially not a man as rigidly organized as Todd, but Angel could certainly use a father's influence. And much as she hated to admit it, they both could use additional financial support. She didn't want her baby suffering because she was trying unsuccessfully to live out a dream.

After a day like today, the prospect of sharing responsibility with Angel's daddy, something she'd vowed never to do, held an overwhelming appeal. She would have given almost anything just to have a single uninterrupted hour to soak in a bubble bath.

Not for the first time, she wondered what Todd would think of his daughter. They'd never talked about kids, so she had no idea where he stood on the subject. But how could he resist his own child? Angel had her daddy's stubborn chin, his brown hair and soft-green eyes the color of sage. Three now, she was healthy and strong, and her crooked little smile could brighten the darkest day.

But, oh, was she willful! She was definitely developing her own personality. Heather gazed at that precious, tear-streaked face and fought a smile. Angel had gotten that stubborn streak from her mama, no doubt about it. If Angel's temperament stayed true to form, Heather would never have to worry about her daughter turning into anybody's doormat. Just like her mother, Angel never hesitated to express her opinion about anything and everything. What she lacked in vocabulary, she more than made up for in volume.

Envisioning how Angel would undoubtedly disrupt her daddy's tidy, organized life gave Heather the most enjoyment she'd had in weeks. Todd might not be thrilled to see *her* again, but as rock-solid and dependable as he was, he wouldn't be able to turn his own daughter away. Heather was absolutely, one-hundred-percent confident of that.

Her decision made, Heather didn't stop to consider her plan beyond that. She figured if she gave up her apartment, which was no big loss, she'd have just enough money in the bank for a couple of plane tickets to Wyoming and a motel room. Maybe she'd even find a job and hang around for the summer, avoid the New York heat and humidity. After that, well, she'd play it by ear, the way she usually did.

But deep inside, something told her it was going to be the smartest investment of time and money she'd ever made.

The corner office at the new national headquarters of Megan's World Productions in Wyoming looked as if it had been plucked right out of midtown Manhattan. Todd Winston had worked incredibly hard to see that it did. He wanted every aspect of the decor to remind him of the city he loved, the city he'd reluctantly left behind when Megan O'Rourke had moved her media empire west and made him an offer too good to pass up.

It wasn't the money she'd offered him that had overcome his resistance. Oh, no. It was the way she'd turned those big blue eyes of hers on him and pleaded. She'd said she *needed* him, that she *couldn't live* without him, that he was the *best,* the *only* person she could trust. He was such a sucker. A vulnerable woman got to him every time, but Megan was about as vulnerable as General Patton. He'd remembered that belatedly.

Of course, there was no question that he was the best and that she did need him. So he'd stayed and done his level best to pretend he was still back East.

Modern art graced his office walls, along with framed posters of New York. In moments of real nostalgia, he could almost convince himself that those were the views outside the office. He'd actually framed one skyline scene behind an old window he'd found at a flea market. As illusions went, it wasn't half-bad.

Only rarely did he look outside and risk the sight of a stray cow peering back at him. That and the wide-open spaces reminded him all too vividly that he was a very long way from home and way, way out of his element. The sound of rain splattering on the refurbished warehouse's tin roof could shatter the illusion in a heartbeat. Fortunately it had been a dry few months.

In general, though, he thought he'd adapted pretty well. He owned a Stetson, cowboy boots and a pair of jeans. Much as he hated to admit it, he'd discovered the outfit was actually comfortable.

Recently he'd nearly decided to stop bugging Megan for hazardous-duty pay, but then he'd recalled the driving he had to do to get anywhere in this godforsaken, spread-out land. The thought of getting behind the wheel of a car had almost been enough to make him quit and head back to a city where it was possible to get everywhere on public transportation.

Over the years, though, he had prided himself on never giving in to panic, on doing what had to be done in any and all circumstances. He'd told him-self that this was just another role he had to learn to play. Only by distancing himself in that way had he been able to get his license.

Then he'd reluctantly gone car shopping. Megan had recommended an outrageously expensive but sturdy sport utility vehicle. He'd found himself gravitating toward something slightly less ostentatious, something a true Westerner would drive.

He'd walked out of the showroom with a great big, fancy pickup truck. That sucker could haul a lot of hay, maybe even a dead moose. Not that he had any intention of loading it up with either. As he'd driven off the lot, he'd been convinced he was doing a darn fine job of turning himself into the image of a rancher. Who would ever have thought it possible? Certainly not him, not in his wildest dreams. And while he would never in a million years admit it to his boss, he loved that truck. He just hated getting behind the wheel.

He glanced up at the television monitor in his office in time to see Megan and Peggy pull a perfect chocolate raspberry soufflé from the oven. His mouth watered. The town of Whispering Wind might not have the caliber of restaurants he'd frequented in Manhattan, but the recipes Megan and Peggy whipped up on their cable show almost made up for it. Unfortunately the show was taped and that soufflé was a distant memory. This week's tapings were heavy with summer salads, which were healthy enough but hardly appealed to his taste for the exotic.

"Can you believe how incredibly well that soufflé turned out?" Megan asked, walking into his office just in time to see the close-up of the finished product. "It never ceases to amaze me that I can actually cook when I put my mind to it."

"You don't cook. You let Peggy do all the tricky stuff," Todd reminded her with a grin. "Boiling water tests your skills. That's why you refuse to let the housekeeper out at the ranch retire. Whispering Wind doesn't exactly cater to your best culinary achievement—ordering in."

His boss frowned at him. "Have you forgotten who's in charge around here?" she asked with feigned indignation. "Besides, I was cooking all alone on the show for quite a while before we asked Peggy to take over those segments."

"All alone?" he repeated skeptically. "I seem to remember finished products being prepared by expert chefs so you wouldn't look like an idiot at the end of the show."

"Okay, okay, so cooking isn't my strong suit, which brings me to the reason for dropping in. What would you think of spinning Peggy's segment off into a full half-hour show? The response has been terrific. The audience is growing. Requests for recipes are up and that catalog we put together to sell gourmet ingredients is doing terrific business. Maybe we ought to capitalize on all that."

"How's Johnny going to feel about that? They're just beginning to get their marriage back on track. A show of her own will eat up a lot of Peggy's time."

Megan frowned at the mention of her best friend's rocky marriage. "It'll be up to Peggy, of course, but I think she needs to maintain as much financial independence as she can. It was only when Johnny began to see that she could walk away from him that he finally started to shape up. If you ask me, the relationship is still on shaky ground."

"Okay, so the ball is in Peggy's court on that one. How about you? Don't you have enough on your plate without starting up another television show?" Todd asked, even as the idea began to take hold in his imagination.

Megan's friend had turned out to be a natural in front of the camera. The viewers loved her. Advertisers clamored for the available commercial spots during her segments. Selling her show to the syndicator would be a breeze. And, to be perfectly frank, she was a whole lot less demanding than the woman seated in front of him. Peggy was a nurturer. Megan was a type-A control freak.

"It wouldn't be on my plate," Megan said. "It would be on yours. You're the executive producer around here."

"That's my name on the credits," he agreed. "But you're in charge. You still oversee every detail on the show and for the magazine. You vowed to let up once you married Jake, but I haven't seen any evidence of it."

"I'm letting up now," she said, an uncharacteristic blush on her cheeks.

"And I'm a full-fledged cowboy," Todd retorted, not believing her for a minute. Megan was far too obsessive-compulsive to give up any control of her empire.

"No, I *am* letting up," she insisted, then took a deep breath and blurted, "I'm pregnant."

Todd stared, then jumped up and let out a whoop as he scooped her out of the chair and spun her around. He was genuinely delighted for her. The ultimate career woman, Megan had taken a long time to realize that she was mother material. Thrust into the role when she'd assumed guardianship of her grandfather's illegitimate eight-year-old daughter less than a year ago, she'd panicked, then thrived, ultimately proving that she could handle career and motherhood without missing a beat. Over time she and Tess had built a better relationship than most kids had with their natural parents. She'd even found room in her heart and in their lives for Tess's biological mother, Flo.

"Congratulations! It's about time," he enthused.

"We haven't been married that long," Megan reminded him. "Just a few months."

"From what I've heard it only takes one night, especially if you're not planning on it. What does Jake think? Never mind. He's probably over the moon. How about Tess?" he asked.

"Still full of surprises. Jake and I worried how she would react, since she's just beginning to believe that I intend to be a real mother to her. Apparently, though, she thinks this is something we've done especially for her. She's looking forward to having a little brother or sister she can boss around. Says it'll be even better than all those kittens she's managed to sneak into the house." She surveyed him intently. "How about you? Think you're ready to be a godfather?"

Taken by surprise, his palms began to sweat. "Me? You can't be serious. I can't even remember the last time I set foot in a church. What kind of role model would I be?" he asked, dismissing the idea out of hand.

"Who else would we want? Jake agrees. You've been with us through thick and thin. We want to share this with you. And you can always start joining us in church on Sundays. You'll feel perfectly at home by the time the baby gets here."

Todd regarded her uneasily. As thrilled as he

was for her and Jake, this was definitely a twist he hadn't anticipated. It made his stomach constrict just thinking about it. How could he tactfully decline something most people would consider an honor?

"I'm flattered, really I am, but maybe you'd better think that over," he said carefully. "I haven't spent that much time around kids. I'd probably mess it up."

"You're wonderful with Tess."

"She's a real person. This would be a baby."

"Not forever," Megan pointed out. "We're counting on him or her growing up eventually."

On the verge of a full-fledged anxiety attack, Todd murmured, "Call me when that happens."

Obviously the depth of his uneasiness finally sank in. Megan studied him with that probing, take-no-prisoners look she usually reserved for tough on-air interviews. "You're serious, aren't you?"

"Like I said, I'm flattered, but I really don't think I'm the best candidate."

But Megan was not willing to let the subject drop. "I've known you for a long time. It's not like you to turn down a new project just because it's unfamiliar turf. You were on my case from the beginning when it came to Tess. You didn't let me back away from that challenge, just because I was scared out of my wits. So why should I let you?"

"This isn't a new project or a half-grown kid," he said tightly. "It's a baby, a helpless little baby. I'm telling you I can't do it."

"Are you sure?"

"Megan, how many ways do I have to say it? No. Not in this lifetime. Never. Forget it."

"Okay, okay," she said, backing down. "There's a long time to go. Maybe the idea will grow on you. Maybe you'll change your mind."

"I won't," Todd insisted, his gaze steady. Megan would simply have to understand that this time he couldn't be badgered or cajoled into giving in. There was only one thing he couldn't or wouldn't do for her and this was it.

"Find someone else, Megan."

"But—"

"I mean it. I love you. I respect you. I would do almost anything in the world for you or Jake. But I will not be godfather to your baby."

Her gaze narrowed, then turned speculative. "Why do I sense that there's more going on here than you've said?"

"Because you can't take no for an answer?" he suggested. "It's some genetic flaw, I think."

"I'm not giving up on you," she retorted, undaunted by his attitude. "It only took a few weeks to turn you into a cowboy against your will. The baby's not due for eight more months."

Todd sighed at the determined gleam in her eye. Megan on a mission was a force to be reckoned with. But just this once, he figured he was even more highly motivated than she was. If nothing else worked, he would resort to the truth. Then she wouldn't allow him within an arm's length of her baby.

2

Todd was living *here?* Heather gazed up and down the main street of Whispering Wind and wondered if she'd somehow landed on the set for *Annie Get Your Gun.* The downtown was no more than a few blocks long and dominated by a handful of old-fashioned storefronts, ranging from a diner and a general store to a hardware store and a feed-and-grain supplier. *Feed and grain?* Something told her that wasn't a gourmet grocery, catering to vegetarians.

The place did have a certain rustic charm, she supposed, but Todd, here? Todd Winston, the ultimate yuppie even when he hadn't had a dime, in a town that didn't have a Starbucks or department store in sight, much less a skyscraper? Where was he buying his designer shirts? Where was he going for sushi? Where were the theaters? Megan O'Rourke must have the persuasive skills of a hostage negotiator.

"Mama?" Angel tugged on her hand and gave her an imploring look. "Want ice cream. Now."

Now was Angel's second favorite word after *no*. It usually meant trouble was just around the corner unless Heather complied with her wishes. Since it was a tantrum that had brought them here, Heather was willing to do almost anything to avoid one now.

"In a minute, sweet pea," she said, trying to buy a few minutes to look around, to absorb not only the simplicity of the town, but the fact that the temperature seemed close to freezing even though it was already mid-May. She shivered and tugged her sweater more tightly around her, then checked the zipper on Angel's coat, which she had a way of tugging down.

"Now!" Angel repeated. "Want ice cream now!"

Heather sighed. She had barely had time to breathe since dropping their belongings off at a motel on the outskirts of town. Angel had been too excited to take her usual afternoon nap. This walk was supposed to settle her down, so Heather could have some quiet time to make plans, including coming up with a less expensive alternative to the car she'd been forced to rent at the airport.

On the flight to Laramie, she'd given more thought to exactly how she needed to handle things with Todd. She couldn't expect to drop Angel on his doorstep and simply walk away. Father and daughter were going to need time to get to know each other, time for Todd to accept the situation. Spending the summer sounded about right.

Surely after three months she and Todd could come to some sort of an agreement. Shared custody, maybe. Child-support payments. She wasn't sure exactly what was fair, which meant she probably ought to see a lawyer before making contact with Angel's daddy. She'd noticed a sign for an attorney—Jake Landers—right across the street. She doubted there was more than one in a town the size of Whispering Wind.

"Mama!" Angel's face was scrunched up, indicating that tears were on the immediate horizon.

"Okay, baby, let's get ice cream."

As they walked down the block to the ice-cream parlor Angel had spotted thanks to the colorful giant cone out front, Heather noticed the Help Wanted sign in the window of the diner. Now that she'd had a look around the town, something told her that waitressing was about the best she could hope to do here. It wasn't as if she wasn't used to it.

"Baby, let's stop in here for a minute," she said, turning Angel toward the diner.

Angel let out a wail that could have put a car alarm to shame.

"I'm sure they have ice cream in here, too," Heather consoled, for once undaunted by the building sobs. She hunkered down and touched a silencing finger to Angel's lips. "But if you don't stop that crying right this instant, you won't get any. Okay?"

The tears magically stopped. "Okay," Angel said agreeably, as if that had been her plan all along.

The Starlight Diner was spotless, but there was no mistaking the wear and tear on the red vinyl seats, the initials that had been scratched on the Formica tabletops, the jukeboxes in every booth that boasted hits from the sixties. It was the kind of place where generations of teens had probably courted, where old men came daily for a cup of coffee and local news. It had *tradition* written all over it. Some of the places she'd worked in in New York might have been fancier, but they had opened and closed faster than a bad Broadway play.

At nearly two o'clock in the afternoon, there was only a lone customer left at the counter, a man wearing a rumpled pin-striped suit and black leather cowboy boots. His gaze followed the waitress as she briskly wiped tables, but the woman seemed to be deliberately avoiding him.

Heather slid Angel into a booth, then sat across from her. The waitress, a tall, thin woman with short-cropped gray hair and a ready smile, came up with an order pad in hand. She grinned at Angel.

"Hey, there, aren't *you* a cutie. I haven't seen you in here before. I'm Henrietta Hastings, by the way," she said to Heather. "What can I get for you?"

"Ice cream for her. Chocolate, if you can bear

the thought of half of it winding up on the table or floor."

"Honey, you'd be amazed at how much winds up on the table or floor, put there by folks a whole lot older than this little one. Don't worry about it. Messes are just part of the business. Now, how about you? Ice cream, too? Although, if that's what you're after, I'd recommend you head on down the street. They have a fancier supply than I carry in here."

"I'll have coffee for now and maybe some information?"

Henrietta tucked her pencil behind her ear. "Sure. What can I tell you?"

"Do you know if the job's still available, and if it is, when I might be able to talk to the owner?"

The woman looked as if Heather had just offered her a million bucks. "The job's open and you're talking to the boss. Let me get that ice cream and coffee and we'll talk. It'll give me a chance to get off my feet. The lunch hour was a real bitch today." She scowled in the direction of the remaining customer as if he were one of the primary offenders. "Half the people couldn't make up their minds, and the half that could didn't like what they'd ordered when it turned up. We've got a new cook who keeps trying to gussy up the old standards. I almost had a rebellion when he tried to put avocado on the burgers. I should have known better than to hire someone whose last job was in southern California."

She went back behind the counter to pour the coffee and dish up the ice cream, still pointedly ignoring the man seated on a stool near the register.

"More coffee, Henrietta," he said.

"You don't need it," she retorted. "Besides, you've got court in ten minutes."

"They can't start without me, can they?" he shot back.

"Might be better if they did," Henrietta replied.

The man sighed heavily. "Okay, how much do I owe you?"

"Same as yesterday and the day before that. You're in a rut, old man. Just leave the money on the counter and don't bother with a tip. I don't want your handouts."

She marched past him with Heather's order. The man watched her starchy movements with a resigned expression, put a couple of bills beside his plate and left.

"Are you that way with all your customers, or is he special?" Heather inquired curiously.

"Foolish old man," Henrietta muttered, her gaze following him nonetheless. "He's a judge. Harry Corrigan. Thinks he's God. I'm here to tell him otherwise."

Heather hid a smile. "Interesting."

Henrietta turned her attention from the departing judge to Heather. "I haven't got time to waste talking about the likes of him. Tell me about you."

Heather gave her the short version, leaving out any specific mention of Todd. An hour later she had the job, a place to stay—in the rooms upstairs—and a new friend.

"This is just temporary," Heather reminded her.

"Girl, you've told me that half a dozen times. You'll go when the time is right and I'll be no worse off than I am today. Who knows, maybe you'll decide to stay. You could do worse than Whispering Wind. It's a nice little town for raising kids. And I imagine Buck over at the service station can find you a deal on a used car."

Heather knew with absolute certainty that staying wasn't an option, but she'd been as honest about that as she could be. "Thank you. You've been very kind."

"Kindness has nothing to do with it. You're bailing me out of a jam. I'm tired of working dawn to dusk, seven days a week. Having you around to share the load will be like going on vacation."

"Maybe so, but I can't tell you how much I appreciate it. I never expected to be lucky enough to find work on my first day in town."

"You want to run across the street and see Jake now, you go right on and do it," Henrietta told her. To her credit she hadn't asked Heather why she needed a lawyer when she'd barely set foot in town. "Business won't pick up for a while yet. I can keep an eye on Angel for you."

Heather hesitated. She hated taking advantage of a woman who'd already been so generous. "Angel can be a handful," she warned.

"Believe me, you don't know the meaning of the word until you meet the two hellions I've got living with me."

"You have kids?" Heather asked, surprised. She would have thought Henrietta was old enough for grandchildren, not little ones of her own.

"Oh, they're not mine, if that's what you're thinking. It's a long story and best saved for another day. They'll be along any minute once they've finished with their tutor. Both of them are smart as whips, but they missed a lot of classes a while back. They're getting caught up after regular school lets out. They can keep Angel company till you get back."

"If you're sure . . ."

"Go. You might as well get whatever's on your mind taken care of. Much as he tries to demonstrate otherwise, Jake's a good lawyer and a decent man. He'll do right by you."

"I won't be long," Heather promised. There was no need to reassure Angel about her absence. She'd already crawled into Henrietta's lap, where she was being rocked to sleep.

Maybe for once in her life, Heather concluded, she had done exactly the right thing. Not only was Angel going to gain a daddy, but it looked as if she was going to pick up an extended family, as well, something there had been little time for Heather to cultivate in New York.

And if the byplay she'd observed between Henrietta and the judge was anything to go by, the next two or three months would be downright entertaining.

The secretary in Jake's office regarded Heather with fascination.

"Honey, do I know you? You look real familiar to me."

"I doubt it," Heather said. "This is the first time I've ever been here."

The woman continued to stare, then snapped her fingers. "Wait. I know who you are. Hold it a sec. It's right here." She opened a file drawer in the desk and began tossing things out of it until she finally came up with an old issue of *Soap Opera Digest*, the one with Heather's picture on the cover. "I knew it. That's you, isn't it?"

Heather couldn't decide whether to be flattered or dismayed. She had played dozens of parts in her career, but it appeared that that particular one was going to follow her forever. Unfortunately there was no denying that she was the woman on the cover. "Afraid so," she said finally.

"Well, I'll be. What on earth are you doing in a one-horse town like Whispering Wind? I'm Flo

34

Olsen, by the way. If you're here to see Jake, he's out. Of course, he's usually out. That man works less than any human being I've ever known, and now that Megan's pregnant, he's impossible. He hovers over her like he thinks she's going to break. She keeps calling here and begging me to come up with some big emergency that'll get him into town and out of her hair, but I ask you, what sort of an emergency is a lawyer likely to have around here?"

Her expression brightened. "Of course, telling him that a famous actress is here to see him ought to do the trick. Just a sec. Have a seat. I'll track him down."

Heather sat. Since the only apparent reading material was the soap magazine, she had little to do but stare around at the office, which was surprisingly well-furnished for a man who supposedly did very little work. Suddenly what Flo had said clicked.

"Did you say his wife's name is Megan?" she asked Flo when the secretary had hung up, her expression triumphant.

"Yes. Megan O'Rourke. I'm sure you've heard of her. She's our very own local celebrity. Have to say she and I didn't hit it off too well at first. She's my little girl Tess's legal guardian. Tess's father was Megan's granddaddy. He was taking care of Tess for me when he died, and he speci-fied in his will that Megan was to take over."

A grin flitted across her face as she told the story. "Sounds like something that would happen on a soap, doesn't it? Leaving Tess with Tex O'Rourke wasn't one of my best moments, but everything's working out now. I get to spend a lot of time with Tess, but Megan and Jake are real good to her. I think things happen for a reason, don't you?"

"I do," Heather said, since nothing more seemed to be expected. This situation was getting increasingly fascinating. She couldn't help wondering, though, just how wise it was to spill her secrets to the man married to Todd's boss. She knew how much Megan relied on Todd. How would she feel about anything or anyone who upset the man's orderly existence? Just to protect her own interests, would she throw a monkey wrench into Heather's plan?

Heather was still debating what to do an hour later when Jake Landers finally came through the door, looking harried and nothing at all like a lawyer. Instead, in his worn jeans and chambray shirt, he fit her notion of a rugged cowboy to a T. Rugged and handsome, Jake exuded masculinity.

"What's the big emergency?" he asked Flo.

Flo jerked her head in Heather's direction. "You have a client."

Jake gave Heather a once-over, then focused his attention on Flo once again. "I thought I told you not to schedule any appointments without consulting me, not until this baby thing is wrapped up."

Heather stifled a grin at his naive belief that there would be a time in the near future when the "baby thing" would be wrapped up. Wasn't she here precisely because that never happened?

"Your wife is pregnant, not sick," Flo told him. "I'm sure she can spare you for a few minutes. Besides, this isn't just any client. This is Heather Reed."

When Jake failed to look impressed, Flo added pointedly, "Liza Whittington, you know, on *Heart's Desire.*"

Jake looked more perplexed than ever. "Excuse me?"

"On television," Flo said. "The soap. The one I watch during lunch."

Understanding dawned, though the man hardly looked as if he'd finally realized he was in the presence of greatness as Flo seemed to be implying. He shot an apologetic look at Heather. "Sorry. I don't watch a lot of daytime TV."

"It's okay. I'm not on anymore, anyway."

"Jason shot her," Flo said. "Good riddance, too." She regarded Heather apologetically. "Sorry, but you have to admit you were a real schemer."

"The worst," Heather agreed. It was what had made the part so appealing initially. It had been a chance to play against type. Usually she was somebody's perky sister. Only later, when she'd realized the ramifications with the fans, had she regretted the decision to take the role.

Jake appeared to have heard enough about the soap opera. After one last scowl at Flo, he motioned for Heather to follow him.

In his office, he gestured toward a credenza along the wall. "Coffee?"

She shook her head. He poured some for himself, then took a seat behind an impressive desk. That desk, combined with the bronze sculpture she recognized as a Remington, reassured her that despite his reportedly lackadaisical ways, Jake Landers was very successful at what he did. But could she trust him?

Right now he was studying her with what she supposed passed for an appropriately somber, lawyerly look, though on the soaps the men cast as attorneys rarely had such a twinkle in their eye.

"What can I do for you?" he asked. "I don't do a lot of entertainment law."

"I seem to remember that you played a big role in getting that syndicator to back down when he threatened to pull the plug on your wife's syndication deal," she said, recalling what she'd read in the trade papers at the time. She'd followed the story avidly, just as she did anything that might include a mention of Todd. Of course, if anyone had accused her of that, she would have denied it.

Jake grinned. "Let's just say that in that instance I was highly motivated."

Heather fiddled with her bangle bracelets, something she did only when she was nervous. Finally she said, "Look, maybe you should tell me about this lawyer-client confidentiality thing before we get started."

He nodded. "Okay. Anything you tell me, I am ethically bound not to repeat."

"Not to anyone?"

"Not to a living soul." He regarded her closely. "You haven't killed someone, have you?"

Startled by the question, Heather stared at him to see if he was serious, then caught that twinkle back in his eye. Normally, she enjoyed black humor, but at the moment she was way too tense to appreciate it.

"No, of course not," she said. "Nothing like that. It's just that you know the other person involved."

"I do?"

"Todd Winston."

Jake nodded slowly, apparently digesting that. "Is he in some sort of trouble?"

She grinned at his disbelieving expression. "I know. Hard to imagine, isn't it? Dudley Do-Right in trouble."

"Todd strikes me as a very ethical man."

"He is," she agreed, then took a deep breath and added, "He's also the father of my child."

Jake very nearly choked on the sip of coffee

he'd just taken. "Would you mind repeating that?"

"Oh, I think you heard me."

"Does he know about this?"

She shook her head.

"I see."

"Is this going to be a problem for you?" she asked, regarding him with concern. "I know how tight he is with your wife. That's why he and I broke up, in a way."

Jake held up his hands. "Whoa! Back up. What does Megan have to do with this?"

"Nothing, not directly, anyway. It's just that when Todd went to work for her and gave up the dream we shared to be on Broadway together, it pretty much ended our relationship. We split up."

"And you had his baby?"

She nodded. "After he'd left."

"And he doesn't know?" Jake asked again, as if he might have misunderstood her the first time.

"Nope."

"How old is this child?"

"She's three."

Jake whistled. "Does he know you're here now?"

"Not yet. I just got in. I took a room at a motel, but Henrietta gave me a job at her place across the street. She said I could use the apartment upstairs for as long as I'm here."

"You don't plan to stay?"

"Only long enough to settle things with Todd."

"Settle things how?"

Her bangles clinked noisily. "I'm not exactly sure. That's why I came to see you. I can't manage on my own anymore. Angel's the greatest blessing in my life, but she's a handful. And trying to be an actress doesn't exactly bring stability. She deserves to have more than I can give her. It took me a long time to admit that. It's not too late, is it?"

"No. I'm sure we can get you child support. Fortunately, I have an in with his boss." Jake allowed himself a smile. "I've seen the books. I know what she had to pay him to get him to move out here. You won't have any financial worries."

"That's not it," Heather said, leaning forward in her chair. "Not exactly. I know with money I could hire a nanny or something, but I want Todd to help out. Maybe shared custody. Angel needs to spend time with her daddy."

"Oh, boy," Jake murmured, but not so low that Heather missed it.

"What?"

"Nothing."

"You sounded like you don't think he's going to go for that."

"Really, I shouldn't have said anything. This is a different situation entirely."

"Different from what?"

"Never mind. Heather, let me think about this. Can you stop by tomorrow? We'll go over your

41

options and decide on the best course of action."

"Sure. What time?"

"Make it eleven. Megan's taping then, so I can get away from the studio for an hour and still be back to see that she eats a proper lunch."

Heather bit back a smile as she recalled what Flo had said about his hovering. "I'll be here. I won't have long, though, since I imagine Henrietta will want me to help with the lunch crowd."

"Folks around here show up promptly at noon, leave by one. You'll be okay."

"What about the judge? I notice he was there much later than that."

Jake chuckled. "The judge tries to snatch whatever private moments he can with Henrietta. His schedule drives everyone at the courthouse nuts. She doesn't seem to appreciate the gesture, though."

"I noticed."

"Did she run him off again today?"

"Pretty much."

"Henrietta has a stubborn streak, but so does the judge. He's been after her for years now. My bet's on him."

"Even though she's held out for years?" Heather said skeptically.

"Believe me, if Henrietta really wanted him gone, he'd be gone. She's just tormenting him."

"An interesting technique."

"It's certainly fun for the rest of us," Jake said.

"Now, as for Todd, if you run into him in the meantime, try not to get into anything with him just yet. We need a plan first."

"No problem. You'll probably see him before I will," she said.

He glanced toward the window, which faced the town's main street. "Oh, I doubt that," he said dryly. "Where's your daughter right now?"

"With Henrietta."

"Well, don't look now, but Todd is about to join them."

3

Todd always made it a point to stop by the Starlight Diner at the end of the day for a homemade meal and a chat with Henrietta. He'd developed a real fondness for her biting wit and her apple pie.

In New York he'd still be in the office at this hour, but out here he was on an earlier schedule. Because of the time difference, the New York offices of Megan's empire were closed. Jake had her out of the studio here and home by mid-afternoon. Todd wrapped up his West Coast contacts shortly thereafter, then ate between five and six. There had been a time not so long ago when he would have considered that a late lunch.

Afterward, thanks to his disgustingly barren

social life, he burned the midnight oil at home on the mountains of paperwork that never seemed to get done in the office. If it wasn't for the frequent trips he made back East, the situation would have been intolerable. But Megan regularly trumped up excuses for him to fly to New York, so he could get his fix of decent restaurants, Broadway plays and dates with some of the women he'd left behind. Not that any of them had a hold on his heart. They were little more than stand-ins for the one woman he'd dared to love.

Still, in some ways, his time in New York was better than it had been before he'd left. He made it a point to see people, rather than holing up in his office night after night. Apparently he was simply the kind of man who found a rut to fall into no matter where he lived.

Ordinarily the sameness soothed him, but tonight he felt restless, the way he often did when the air crackled with electricity just before a thunderstorm. The sensation was so intense, he looked at the horizon, but there was no evidence of a storm building. That must mean the restlessness was purely internal.

He hesitated outside the diner and considered changing his routine by going for pizza down the block, then shook his head. Who was he kidding? He enjoyed having Henrietta fuss over him, and the new cook occasionally tried out recipes for something besides chicken fried steak or meat loaf. Of course, the cook did it at his peril, since most of the customers hated the experiments and Henrietta only tolerated them because he was the best cook she'd had in years.

When Todd finally walked in, he was startled to find Henrietta with a bright-eyed toddler trailing in her wake and chattering a mile a minute.

"I know you're desperate, but isn't she a little young to be your new waitress?" he asked, after giving Henrietta a dutiful peck on the cheek.

The girl was dressed in denim overalls and a bright green T-shirt. Her little feet were clad in colorful sneakers adorned with daisies. The cheerful appearance was at odds with her solemn expression as she stared at him silently. She gave the disconcerting impression that she was assessing him. Apparently he passed muster, because before he could guess what she had in mind, she'd lifted her arms.

"Up," she demanded imperiously.

"You'd better do as she says," Henrietta advised, laughing. "She's only been here a couple of hours, but she already tends to think she's in charge. My kids actually volunteered to go off and do their homework, because they couldn't keep up with her. Her name's Angel."

Todd backed up a step. Why was it everyone was trying to foist kids on him lately? Granted, this one wasn't an infant, but he wanted no part of her. Just thinking about doing as she asked caused a cold sweat to break out on his forehead. She was still too little, too fragile to be trusted to someone like him. He never saw any child under four without thinking there was tragedy and heartache just waiting to happen.

"Sorry, I think maybe I'm coming down with the flu or something. I probably shouldn't get too close. In fact, I think I'll go on home. I'm not feeling much like food tonight."

Surely he could find something edible in his refrigerator. Hadn't he bought a half-dozen frozen meals the last time he'd gone to the store, just for emergencies like this? Of course, he usually relied on those when the special here was liver and onions, but tonight's turn of events was equally distasteful.

Henrietta regarded him with her typical motherly concern. If she was skeptical about his sudden illness, she didn't let on.

"Any fever?" she asked, touching his forehead with cool fingers before he could retreat. "Nope. I doubt you're contagious. Sit down and I'll get you some chicken soup. If there's anything wrong with you, that'll cure it."

"No, really. I'd better go."

"Sit," she insisted.

Filled with trepidation, Todd sat, keeping his wary gaze on the little girl who continued to stare at him with evident fascination even after

Henrietta had disappeared into the kitchen. She inched closer.

"You sick?" she asked, head tilted, her expression sympathetic.

He nodded.

"Want Mama to give you a hug?"

"No, thanks," he said, though he had to wonder about "Mama." Who was she? *Where* was she? Surely Henrietta hadn't taken in another stray. Folks in town were still talking about the way she'd adopted a pair of children whose parents had been killed. Henrietta hadn't hesitated, partly because she felt some misplaced sense of responsibility for the tragedy, partly because those kids deserved a better fate than living with their embittered paternal grandmother, but mostly because that was just the way she was: kindhearted and generous. All things considered, the children were doing well under her care.

Todd glanced at this child. The intensity of her gaze was disconcerting. Something about her eyes, probably. An unusual shade of green, they looked oddly familiar.

He was still trying to puzzle out the reason for that when the door opened and a woman breezed in, her gaze swinging at once on the little girl. She seemed to freeze in place when she realized that the child was with him.

In that single instant, a lot of things registered

at once. The woman had a mane of artfully streaked hair that had been tousled by the wind. He'd known someone once with thick, lustrous hair that exact color. She, too, had dressed unconventionally in long, flowing skirts, tunic-length tops and clinking bracelets. His gaze shot to this woman's face. Even with the oversize sunglasses in place, there was no mistaking her identity. He went into a form of shock, followed by an inexplicable lurch of his heart.

He'd been over Heather Reed for some time now, or so he'd thought until just this second. He'd dismissed the fact that she popped into his head with disturbing frequency. After all, she had started as an enchanting fling, a walk on the wild side when he'd first arrived in New York, fresh out of college and ready to take Broadway by storm. She'd touched the carefree part of his soul that he kept mostly hidden. He'd been drawn to her impulsiveness, her unpredictability, even as they had terrified him. She was so unlike any other woman he'd ever known, it was no wonder he couldn't quite forget about her. They'd stayed together for six years, long enough for her to become a part of him. Long enough to show just how ill-suited they were.

He was still reeling from the impossibility of her turning up in Whispering Wind when the toddler beside him raced across the restaurant and threw herself straight at the woman.

"Mama!" she shouted gleefully as if they'd been separated for days.

Everything after that seemed to happen in slow motion. Heather scooped the child into her arms, then turned fully in his direction. She seemed a whole lot less surprised to see him than he was to see her.

"Hello, Todd."

She spoke in that low, sultry voice that once had sent goose bumps down his spine. The effect hadn't been dulled by time, he noticed with regret.

He slid from the booth and stood, hating the way his blood had started pumping fast and furiously at the sight of her. "Heather," he said politely. "This is a surprise. What are you doing here?"

Henrietta picked that moment to return with his soup. "Ah," she said, beaming at them. "Todd, I see you've already met my new waitress. Just hired her today. Believe it or not, she actually has experience."

His gaze shot to Heather's face. He kept waiting for her to deny it, to say that she was only passing through, but she stared right back at him with her chin lifted defiantly.

Something was going on here he didn't understand, something that he had a hunch he'd better figure out in less than a New York minute. He latched on to Heather's arm.

"Can we talk?" he asked, already tugging her

toward the door. "Henrietta, keep an eye on her daughter for a few more minutes, will you?"

"Of course, but . . ."

Whatever Henrietta had intended to say died on her lips, as Todd unceremoniously escorted Heather from the restaurant.

"You don't need to manhandle me," Heather grumbled when they were on the sidewalk, safely out of earshot of Henrietta's keen hearing and well-honed curiosity.

"Why are you here?" he repeated, not at all pleased by the fact that on some level he was actually glad to see her. That was a knee-jerk, hormonal reaction, nothing more. Nobody on earth had ever kicked his libido into gear faster than Heather had. Apparently she could still do it. Reason, good sense, past history, none of it seemed to matter.

Of course, she was equally adept at annoying him with the unpredictability he had once found so charming, and right now he intended to concentrate on that.

"Well?" he prodded when she didn't answer right away.

Eyes flashing a challenge, she smiled at him. "You don't think it's pure coincidence that I showed up in Whispering Wind, where you happen to live?"

"Not in ten million lifetimes. I saw the look on your face in there. You weren't the least bit surprised to see me. You knew I was here."

"You always were brilliant. Good instincts, isn't that what the directors used to say? A real grasp of motivations."

He ignored the sarcasm in her voice. He knew how she felt about his decision to abandon his acting career. She'd made that very clear when she'd accused him of selling out, then flounced out of his life as if he'd failed her, instead of simply trying to keep their financial heads above water.

"Get to the point," he said now.

Though he wanted badly to deny it, he had a sick feeling in the pit of his stomach that he already knew the reason for her arrival. He also thought he knew now why that child's eyes had looked so disconcertingly familiar. He prayed he was wrong, but what if he wasn't?

If he was a father and Megan found out about it, Heather and Henrietta wouldn't be the only ones pestering him to do right by her. Megan would make it another one of her missions. She wouldn't let up until there had been a full-scale wedding complete with white doves and a seven-tier cake. She'd have him out of his cozy little bachelor apartment here in town and into a house with a white picket fence and a swing set in the backyard before he could blink. She would consider it just retribution for his role in forcing her to face her responsibility with Tess.

For some reason Heather's gaze strayed across the street to Jake's office, before turning back and locking defiantly with his.

"Okay," she said at last. "You want the truth, here it is."

Suddenly Todd didn't want to hear the truth, after all. He wanted to finish out this day in blissful ignorance. It was too late, though. Heather clearly had no intention of remaining silent now that he'd badgered her for the truth.

Her expression softened ever so slightly and her voice dropped to little more than a whisper, as if by speaking softly she could make the words more palatable. "I figured it was time you met your daughter."

Heather wished she'd been able to deliver her news in a less-public setting, wished she'd been able to wait as Jake had instructed her to do, but sometimes fate made its own timing. She'd pictured a dozen different scenarios for making the big announcement, but in none had she imagined blurting it out in the middle of a sidewalk while Todd stared at her as if she'd been speaking gibberish.

In fact, if Todd wasn't the strongest, most emotionally controlled man in captivity, she had a feeling he would have fainted right there on Main Street. He certainly looked as if he would rather be anyplace else on earth. Fortunately she hadn't counted on seeing a joyous outburst, so his stunned, silent reaction didn't cut straight through her the way it might have.

"Well? Aren't you going to say anything?" she prodded.

"Why should I believe you?"

Those weren't exactly the words every woman dreamed of hearing after she'd just told a man he was a daddy, but she'd anticipated little else. Todd was the kind of man who expected life to occur in a nice, orderly procession of events. He worked to see that it did just that. She'd skipped straight past any announcement of a pregnancy and delivered a three-year-old into his life. She held on to her temper, because she could understand the shock he must be feeling and knew she was to blame for that much, anyway.

"Because I don't lie?" she suggested mildly, refusing to be insulted by the question.

If she thought about it, she supposed it was natural enough for him to doubt her. After all, she hadn't told him the truth four years ago. In fact, she had deliberately avoided his calls—from the moment she'd learned she was pregnant, turning her back on their promise to remain friends after the breakup. She could have handled friendship with an ex-lover, but not under those circumstances. The baby had changed everything. Pride and a fierce streak of independence had made her determined to keep the secret.

She met his gaze evenly. "If you need one, have a paternity test done. Seems to me that a glance in the mirror would be enough proof, but do whatever it takes to make a believer of you," she told him with a shrug of feigned indifference.

He looked as if the suggestion made him vaguely uncomfortable, probably because he had been thinking about demanding that very thing and knew how small-minded it made him look.

"You want money, I suppose," he said, his voice flat.

Heather wished she could say no, wished she could throw the question back in his face and walk away, but money was part of what she needed, what Jake had just told her she deserved. Not for herself, but for Angel.

"That's only part of it," she said.

"And the rest?"

"I want you," she said. What had ever made her think she would savor this moment? Instead, she found she was getting precious-little enjoyment out of the stunned disbelief on his face.

"Just like that?" he asked incredulously. "After four years apart, after refusing to return any of my calls, you show up and claim you want me? Sorry, babe, but it just doesn't ring true. You'll have to work on your delivery if you expect me to buy that."

"It's true," she insisted.

He returned her steady gaze with blatant

skepticism. "What's the matter, Heather? Can't you cope with being a single mom, after all? Obviously you thought you could or you would have done the honorable, sensible thing and told me about our daughter a long time ago. Instead, you chose to cut me out of her life. Obviously you thought you'd both be better off without me."

The fact that he'd hit the nail on the head grated. He shouldn't be able to read her so well, especially not after all this time. She was supposed to be the unpredictable one, the one who kept everyone guessing.

"Oh, for heaven's sake, not for me," she snapped. "For Angel. She needs her daddy."

His gaze narrowed. "What do you mean, she needs her daddy?"

"She's a little girl. She needs you to be in her life, to know that there's somebody besides me she can count on. Over the last three years, I've realized how important that kind of stability is for a child."

Todd's complexion paled. "No," he said with a ferocity that stunned her. "Never. Get that idea right out of your head, Heather. You want money, okay. If Angel's mine, we'll work something out. As for the rest, forget it. It will never, *never* happen."

And before she could react, before she could challenge him, he simply turned and walked away. Fled, really, without once looking back.

"Well, that was interesting," she murmured as he disappeared from view.

It looked as if she'd finally found the one thing that could rattle Todd's almost scary composure. Obviously this was precisely the reaction that Jake had anticipated. The only question was why the most self-possessed man she'd ever known would be so terrified of one little three-year-old who was his spitting image.

4

Todd headed home in a complete daze. Heather's words echoed in his head, over and over in a deafening refrain.

I thought it was time you met your daughter.
Your daughter.
Your daughter . . .

At home, he tried to shut off the sound, but it was in vain. The words could even be heard over the music blasting through his small apartment. Not even work, which he'd become amazingly adept at using to block out emotional turmoil, helped this time the way it had when Heather had walked out on him in New York. The words on the papers he'd brought home blurred. The computer screen seemed far too bright, the blinking cursor an irritant, as if he was trying to view it with a blinding migraine.

She needs her daddy . . . she needs to know there's somebody in her life besides me she can count on.

Count on.

Count on . . .

How could Heather not know that he was the last person in the world that little girl could count on? True, he had never told her about the tragedy in his past, couldn't talk about it, in fact, but surely she should have seen how uneasy he was around the kids in the casts of the shows they'd done together. She should have known that he and any kid were a bad mix. But she'd either missed the signs or chosen to ignore them. The fact was, she was here and she had expectations.

For the first time in the four years he'd worked for Megan, Todd didn't show up for work the morning after Heather had stunned him with her news. He couldn't seem to make it out of bed. Not that he slept. Sleep eluded him like an artful puppy dodging its owner's reach.

He was tormented by images of the woman he'd never expected to see again. Worse, he was plagued by images of a bright-eyed toddler reaching out her arms, expecting him to pick her up. He'd rejected her, turned away. He'd refused her simple request, his own daughter. Would it have been any different if he'd known? Probably not.

Even so, she'd accepted him as generously and

unconditionally as her mother once had. A three-year-old with more kindness in her than *he'd* demonstrated.

Want Mama to give you a hug?

Her sympathetic words came back to haunt him. If only he'd known at the time who Mama was.

There had been a time not all that long ago when he'd craved hugs from Heather, when he'd responded to her free-spirited warmth and exuberance like a desert blossom suddenly exposed to a gentle shower. Now the arms that had once embraced him in passion seemed a lot more like a trap.

He should have known about the baby four years ago, when there were still options, he thought angrily. What would he have done if Heather had come to him then and told him she was carrying his child? He would have married her without hesitation, would have insisted on it, in fact. That was what a responsible man did under such circumstances, and he had spent most of the past thirteen years trying to prove how responsible he had become.

But he wouldn't have been one bit happier about the prospect of fatherhood than he was now, he conceded with brutal honesty. Indeed, he would have been terrified. But obligations were more important than terror.

Of course, the marriage would have been a disaster, just as the relationship had been. Maybe

Heather had been wise enough to see that. Maybe she'd sensed what he hadn't been willing to admit, that he was lousy husband material and an even lousier candidate for fatherhood. Maybe it had all turned out for the best.

That was then, though. Now Heather was here, needing something from him that he was no more prepared to give than he would have been if he'd had the usual nine months to prepare for it. What the hell was he going to do? The right thing? He didn't even know what that was. Based on his history rather than conventional wisdom, the right thing would be to steer clear of that little girl, protect her from the dangers of having him in her life.

Damn, this wasn't getting him anywhere. Anger wasn't solving anything. Recriminations were useless. He needed to sit down with a sheet of paper and methodically list all the options, then all the pros and cons for each. That was the way to tackle anything this complex—with cold logic and sound reasoning. He was a master of that. The prospect of breaking this down in such a familiar, practiced way reassured him, calmed him.

He showered, tugged on briefs and jeans, then headed for the kitchen and made a pot of very strong coffee to cut through the fog in his brain. He was seated at the kitchen table with a stack of paper, a neat row of sharp pencils and his coffee when the phone rang.

Grateful for the interruption, he grabbed it. "Yes?"

"Todd, are you okay?" Megan asked with the concern of a friend, rather than the anger of a boss whose employee had bailed out.

"I'm fine."

"Then why aren't you at work?"

Good question. An even better question was why he hadn't bothered to call to let anyone know he wasn't coming in. He didn't do things like this. He was always focused, always on task. Responsible. Today that word grated in ways it never had before.

"Something came up," he said finally.

"You're working at home?"

"Not exactly."

"Is everything all right?"

No! he wanted to shout. Nothing is all right. Nothing will be all right until there are hundreds of miles between me and this child who's apparently mine.

Instead, he said, "I needed a day off. If you have a problem with that, dock my pay."

Silence greeted his curt words, then Megan said quietly, "I'm coming over."

"Don't," he said, but he was talking to a dead phone line.

Terrific. Now he'd stirred up Megan's protective instincts. She would be all over him until she found out what had happened to turn the world's most reliable executive into an irresponsible, grouchy nutcase.

He should have hauled his sorry butt out of bed and gone to work as he had every other day. Even if it hadn't been the answer last night, maybe work was exactly what he needed today. Maybe if he simply ignored this whole blasted mess, it would go away. Heather would tire of Whispering Wind and go back East. She would take her daughter with her. And he could go right on living his life the way he liked it, alone and unencumbered.

Fat chance, he thought with a resigned sigh. Heather had never backed down from a challenge. Hell, the woman wanted to be a Broadway actress. She was steadfast and blithely determined to fight the odds against success. After all these years, she hadn't given up, even when he knew for a fact that she hadn't had anything closely resembling a big break. If she wanted him in her daughter's life, then she was going to make it happen or die trying. It was not a comforting thought.

Nor was it especially comforting that his front doorbell was ringing, suggesting that Megan had made it into town in record time. Before he could so much as budge, he heard her key turning in the lock. Giving her that key had obviously been a big mistake. It had been meant for emergencies, but it was apparent now that their definitions of that were at odds.

"Todd?" she shouted as if he might be either comatose or farther away than the next county, much less the next room.

"In here," he replied with a resigned sigh.

She appeared in the kitchen doorway with a frantic expression. She surveyed him from head to toe—probably looking for cuts and bruises from some accident he'd failed to mention—then finally sank onto a chair opposite him.

"Don't ever do that to me again," she pleaded. "My heart's still pounding."

"What did I do?"

"You stayed home. You didn't call in. And then," she said as if this last was the worst, "you snapped at me."

"Sorry."

"I don't want your apology. You were past due. What I want to know is what has you in such a tizzy that you are behaving in such a totally uncharacteristic way?"

"Why do I have to be in a tizzy, as you put it? Why can't I just be having a bad day? People have bad days all the time."

"Because you don't have bad days," she retorted. "You see to it that every day runs smoothly."

"Maybe I just see that *your* days run smoothly. Maybe mine are total chaos."

"No way. You'd never allow it."

He frowned at the suggestion that he was able to exert that much control over events, even though up until yesterday he had prided himself on doing just that. "In other words, I am totally predictable and boring."

"No, you are a treasure," she corrected him. "Twenty-four-karat gold. Solid as a rock. Dependable. That's why not finding you at your desk today was such a shock."

He wasn't especially reassured by the praise. It merely served as a reminder that he was going to have to do the *right thing* in a situation that he wasn't the least bit prepared to handle.

"Maybe I'm tired of being dependable," he said. "Maybe I want to be the guy dressed in black, the dangerous man no woman would dare trust."

"And the one every woman wants, anyway?" Megan suggested, gaze narrowing. "Is that what this is about? Are you in love? I didn't realize you were dating anyone seriously."

Now, there was a laugh. "Megan, the only women I've seen in the past year have been married, and I'm not about to tangle with the wife of some man who's likely to own a shotgun."

"Then what is this about?"

"It's private."

Megan laughed. " 'Private' never stopped you from meddling in my life."

"And now you intend to get even? I don't think so. This is my problem. I'll handle it."

She gestured toward the wadded-up papers he'd tossed on the floor, evidence of his inability to make one single rational list of solutions to the situation.

"Is that your idea of handling it?"

"Yes."

She reached for one of the scraps of paper, but he got to it first, crumpled it in his fist and kept it there.

"Stay out of this, Megan. You can't help."

"You don't know that. Try me."

"No," he said flatly, his gaze locked with hers. "Now go away and let me think."

She stood up with obvious reluctance. "Okay, I'll go," she told him. "But before I do, think about this. Not every problem can be solved by cold, hard logic. Sometimes you just have to go with your gut."

True enough, Todd conceded as she left. Unfortunately right this second his gut was all but shouting for him to pack his bags and get out of Dodge—or in this case, Whispering Wind.

A few months ago, he might have heeded that instinct eagerly. He would have seized any sign that encouraged him to head back to New York to a world he understood, a place he'd belonged. Ironically, he realized that going there would only put him right back in Heather's path, make it even easier for her to pursue this quest she had to involve him in his daughter's life.

More important, to his amazement, he realized that Whispering Wind had started to feel like home. He wasn't nearly as anxious as he once was to abandon not only his job, but his friends. Megan and Jake and Tess, Henrietta and Peggy, the people connected to Megan's show—they were like family to him, closer than the parents he so rarely saw. He couldn't see himself running out on them, not just because he was duty-bound to stay, but because he cared about them.

It was ironic, really. Thanks to this makeshift family—to say nothing of his deeply ingrained code of honor—it appeared he was going to have to stay right where he was and figure out how to deal with a *real* family, which until yesterday he hadn't even known he had.

That didn't mean he had to do it today, he thought as he grabbed a shirt and headed for his car. For once in his life he was going to be totally irresponsible and self-indulgent. He was going to run away—even if it was just for a day.

"What happened when you saw Todd yesterday?" Jake asked when Heather arrived in his office promptly at eleven. "I saw the two of you talking on the sidewalk. I imagine you told him."

Heather sighed. "I didn't see any way around it. He asked me point-blank what I was doing here. He'd already met Angel. I think he had a pretty good idea even before I said the words. You haven't seen her up close, but she's got her daddy's coloring and her daddy's eyes. Only a blind man would miss it. And believe me, Todd's vision is twenty-twenty."

"How did he take the news?"

"How do you think? He was stunned and angry. He didn't believe me. He wants a paternity test. He didn't come right out and ask for it, of course. He's far too polite. But when I offered, he didn't turn me down flat."

"You can't blame him for that."

"No, I suppose not," she conceded, though understanding that didn't make it hurt any less.

"There isn't any question about how it will turn out, is there?"

Heather stared at him, shocked that he even had to ask. "Absolutely not."

Jake nodded. "Okay, then. We'll do it right away. That'll be one less obstacle down the road. Have you given any more thought to what you want besides child support?"

"Some sort of custody arrangement," she told him. "Shared custody, joint custody, whatever you call it."

"Not just visitation?"

"What's the difference?"

"In one, the time would be pretty much equally divided. With visitation, Angel would only spend a set amount of time with Todd each year. The latter's more practical, if you intend to go on living in New York. Otherwise, you'll be completely separated from your daughter for half the year. She'll be dividing her time between schools, unless you put her in a boarding school. Even though that's down the road a couple of years, it's something to think about."

Heather shook her head. She didn't want to spend that much time away from her daughter. Boarding school was out of the question for the same reason. She hadn't even considered being separated from Angel when she'd started the process. She'd just wanted Todd to take over from time to time. If he'd been in New York still, this would have been simple, a matter of shuttling Angel from one part of the city to another.

"How would visitation work?"

"She'd fly out here at set times of the year. Summers, maybe. Certain holidays."

"I couldn't put her on a plane all by herself. And I can't afford to be flying back and forth with her."

"Then maybe Todd would come to New York to be with her. He makes fairly frequent trips there now. That wouldn't be a hardship."

"Then Angel would stay with him at a hotel for the weekend or something?"

"I think he still has his place there."

That could work, then, she concluded. If Todd would agree to it. After yesterday, she wasn't at all sure that was likely.

"What if he says no?" she asked hesitantly.

"Is that what he said yesterday?"

She nodded. "He was pretty adamant about it, too."

Jake muttered a curse. "I was afraid of that."

"I thought so. That was what you expected, wasn't it? What I don't understand is why you were so sure that would be his reaction."

"Never mind. Maybe he'll change his mind once he adjusts to the news. After all, this had to be a big shock."

She thought of Todd's bewildered expression, the panic in his eyes. "Yeah, you could say that."

"Give him time, Heather. Todd might be in denial right now, but we both know the kind of character he has. He's an honorable man. It'll be best if we can work all of this out amicably. You don't want to back him into a corner. You don't want him spending time with Angel just because he has to, do you?"

"No," she said at once, then added with a plaintive note, "I want him to love her."

"Then give him some time."

She thought of how vehement he'd been the day before. "How much time?"

"As much as it takes. After all, what matters here is arranging what's best for Angel, right? Or are you on a timetable I don't know about?"

"No, but I know how stubborn Todd can be. If he decides to dig in his heels, Angel could be in college before he changes his mind."

Jake grinned at her defeated tone. "I don't think

it'll take quite that long, not once my wife gets wind of this. Have you thought of letting her in on the secret?"

Heather figured that was just about the worst thing she could possibly do. Having Megan as an ally might have certain benefits, but the drawbacks were tremendous. Todd might never forgive her for dragging their personal business into the middle of his career, for one thing.

"I can't do that," she told Jake. "And you have to promise not to say a word."

"You know I can't. But I still think you ought to consider it."

"Ganging up on him won't work," Heather said. "You said it yourself. Forcing him into a corner isn't a good idea."

"Then we're back to time," Jake said.

Much as she hated to admit it, time was the one thing she had plenty of. It wasn't as if there were Broadway producers clamoring for her quick return.

"Okay, we'll wait him out," she said.

"In the meantime, I'll make the arrangements for the blood work and the DNA testing." He gave her a reassuring smile. "We'll work this out, Heather."

"I hope so." She regarded him worriedly. "I hope you're not too uncomfortable about keeping all this from your wife."

"It won't be the first secret I've kept from

Megan," he said. "The last one pretty much turned her life upside down and she forgave me, anyway. I'm not worried. There's no need for you to be, either."

Unfortunately that wasn't quite true. On her way out of Jake's office, Heather ran smack into Megan. They'd met only twice, both times right after Todd had first gone to work for her, but Megan had an astounding memory. It was why she was able to juggle so many details in her professional life. Head down, Heather murmured an apology for bumping into her and tried to move on, but Megan recognized her at once.

"Heather? Aren't you Todd's friend, the actress?" she asked, a speculative gleam in her eyes.

Heather paused, considered denying it, then finally nodded. "Hello, Megan, it's nice to see you again."

"What brings you to Whispering Wind? Are you on vacation?" she asked as if she thought she already knew the answer. In fact, there was a glint in her eye that suggested she had spent the past few seconds putting two and two together.

"Not exactly. I'm working here temporarily."

"An acting job? I wasn't aware there were any films being shot around here just now."

"There aren't. I'm working across the street."

Megan's gaze shot toward the diner, then up and down the block as if there might be some other business there, maybe even a theater she hadn't noticed before. "Where?"

"At the Starlight Diner."

"You're waitressing for Henrietta?" Her tone registered genuine shock.

"For the time being." Heather forced a smile. "Gotta run. It's almost lunchtime and I'm due back."

"Wait," Megan said, the single word a command that had Heather stopping against her will. "Have you seen Todd?"

Again, Heather forced that fake smile. Denying the meeting would only make it look more significant when Megan eventually discovered the truth.

"Yes," she said cheerfully. "I ran into him unexpectedly last night at the diner. It was great to see him again."

"Uh-huh," Megan said, her expression thoughtful. "You didn't know he was here in town?"

"I knew your show was being done somewhere in Wyoming and that he was wherever you were, but I didn't expect to be bumping into him. It's a big state." Well, she hadn't exactly lied. She really hadn't expected to bump into Todd on her first day in town.

"So, he didn't know you were coming?"

"Nope. Todd and I haven't spoken in years," she said honestly.

"I see," Megan said, as if those wheels in her

brain were clicking away, trying to process this new tidbit of information.

"Gotta run," Heather repeated. She didn't want Angel spotting her from the window of the café and running outside. For once Megan saw her daughter, she would leap to her own, probably very accurate conclusions. "Good to see you again."

"You, too," Megan replied distractedly.

She seemed so lost in thought Heather couldn't help wondering if she wasn't already engaging in some wild speculation. And since Heather had been leaving Jake's office when they bumped into each other, she figured her attorney was in for a fierce cross-examination. She could only pray he was as tough as he claimed to be and could withstand it without cracking.

When she glanced back one last time, she saw through the large, uncurtained window that Megan was now inside. Jake had pulled her into his arms and appeared to be kissing her passionately.

Heather grinned. An interesting technique for stalling, but she had a hunch Megan O'Rourke wasn't the kind of woman who could be put off for long.

But as long as it gave Heather time to win Todd's cooperation without interference, she certainly appreciated whatever sneaky skills Jake Landers used to keep his wife off the scent.

5

Todd spent two days in Laramie. He ate fast food, binged on movies, then lingered in a bookstore, immersed in scanning the bestsellers. For some reason he didn't care to examine too closely, he was especially drawn to murderous thrillers.

None of it, however, successfully pushed his situation with Heather from his head for more than minutes at a time. It was time to go back to Whispering Wind and face the music, he concluded on the afternoon of the second day. Postponing the inevitable wasn't his style. Quick and decisive were two qualities on which he prided himself.

Maybe he'd be lucky. Maybe Heather and Angel would be gone. Maybe it had all been some freakish dream that had seemed so real he could still feel the way Heather's skin had burned beneath his touch, still smell her once-familiar flowery scent, still hear the clink of those annoying bracelets.

And maybe there were no cattle in Wyoming, he thought with a resigned sigh.

He could handle this, he told himself as he approached the diner. He'd handled worse dilemmas, if less personal ones. Some of the egocentric, temperamental people he dealt with on a daily basis were a whole lot worse than one little girl and a mother with a determined glint in her eye.

Or maybe not, he thought, considering what Heather expected of him.

Still, if he wanted his life back, wanted to return to his safe, familiar rut, this was something he had to do. He was not going to be scared off by a pint-size human being who might or might not be his daughter. Maybe if he reminded himself often enough that Angel was just an innocent little girl with a shy smile, it would stop terrifying him so. Of course, that was precisely the point and that was precisely what terrified him.

He actually got out of his car in front of the diner, took several steps toward the door, then hesitated, his bravado vanishing. He glanced in the window. There was no sign of Angel, but Heather was talking to a customer, a wrangler from one of the nearby ranches, judging from the rugged, tanned looks of him. Her hand on his arm, she was leaning in close and laughing at something he said. What was she up to? If she was here to snag him as a daddy for Angel, what was she doing with another man? Looking for a substitute in case he held out? Jealousy streaked through Todd like a bolt of lightning.

One good thing about jealousy, he concluded. It could motivate a man to ignore just about everything else. He was through the door of the Starlight Diner without giving it another second thought.

As he passed by, he directed a scowl at Heather, then headed straight for his regular booth and grabbed a menu, even though he knew everything on it by heart. The specials were listed on a blackboard by the front door. He hadn't even bothered to glance at those. He doubted he'd notice if he was served a platter of sawdust.

Minutes later he heard the familiar, irksome tinkle of bangle bracelets and glanced up to find Heather regarding him with knowing amusement. He had to wonder then if she'd spotted him outside, then deliberately stood within view flirting with that cowboy. Such a tactic wouldn't be beyond her. She'd always known exactly the effect she wanted to create—on stage or off—and exactly how to make him crazy.

That was what made this current test of wills so dangerous. Heather had a way of sneaking past his defenses, of winning, despite whatever his intentions were. In the first year they'd dated, he'd told himself a million times to bail out because they were such an ill-suited match, but each and every time, she would sense his mood and find some clever way to change his mind.

"Something wrong?" she asked, studying him curiously.

"Nothing. Why should anything be wrong?"

"Just wondering," she said, her expression innocent, but her lips curved into the beginnings of a smile. "You seemed upset, the way you came striding through the front door. Looked like a man on a mission."

"Sweetheart, you've never seen me upset. This isn't it."

Her grin spread. "I'll keep that in mind. What can I get for you?"

After two days' worth of tacos, hamburgers, fries, popcorn and milk shakes in Laramie, the last thing Todd actually wanted was food. He was here because he wanted his life to settle into its familiar routine, and by God, he intended to see that it did.

"I'll have the steak," he said. He *always* had steak on Thursday night. "Medium rare. Baked potato. Salad."

"With ranch dressing," Heather said before he could, confirming that she had a long memory and that he was entirely predictable. Boring.

Just to prove she wasn't as clever as she thought she was, he said, "No. French."

"But you hate—"

"Not anymore."

"Okay," she said mildly, scratching out the original order and correcting it. "Coffee with cream, or has that changed, too?"

"Black," he said. "I like it black."

She shook her head. "If you say so."

"That's right. I say so. It's been four years. You don't know me, Heather. Not the way you think you do."

Suddenly serious, her gaze locked with his. "And what? If I did, I'd go screaming out of town, run back to New York, leave you alone?"

He nodded, relieved that she'd finally grasped the point. "Exactly."

"Sorry. I'm not buying it. Maybe things between us have changed, but you, the kind of man you are? Not a chance. Honor and integrity are as ingrained in you as your DNA. I'll be back with your coffee and salad in a sec."

After she'd gone, Todd felt his breath ease out of him, as if he'd been holding it the whole time they'd been talking. Somehow the purpose for coming here had gotten lost. His routine was still a shambles. He did hate French dressing and he liked cream in his coffee.

Maybe that's why he was almost relieved when Heather brought the dressing for his salad on the side—two kinds, French and the ranch he preferred. She also set down three tiny containers of cream for his coffee. She placed all of it on the table without comment and left him to make up his own mind about how far he intended to carry his stubbornness.

He was about to give in and spoon the ranch dressing onto his salad when he sensed he wasn't alone. He glanced down into green eyes that were unmistakably the exact same shade as his own.

"Hiya," Angel said.

Todd swallowed hard. "Hi."

"I gots a doll. Wanna see?" She was already holding up a plump baby doll with golden ringlets and a real child-size diaper that almost swallowed it up.

What was he supposed to say to that? Todd wondered. "Very pretty," he said finally.

"Her name's Leaky."

Leaky? Maybe that was the reason for that diaper, Todd concluded, surprised to find himself beginning to smile.

"Like my name," she explained.

"I thought your name was Angel," he said, confused.

She regarded him impatiently. "It is. Angel-leaky."

"That's Angelique, baby," Heather corrected her as she approached the table with the rest of Todd's meal.

"Ah," Todd murmured, understanding finally. "That's a lovely name."

"I read it in a book," Heather told him.

Suddenly Todd recalled her reading a set of dog-eared novels about a heroine named Angelique. He could remember the dreamy expression in her eyes, the deeply satisfied sighs when she reached the final page of each one.

"I remember," he said, wishing he didn't.

Because with those memories came others of the sweet intensity of their lovemaking when Heather had been off in some imaginary, romantic world for a few hours.

Her gaze honed in on his, as if she knew precisely where his thoughts had strayed. Her expression softened.

And then that blasted cowboy called out, "Hey, sugar, how about a little more coffee?"

The moment was lost. It was just as well, Todd thought. Tripping down memory lane was the last thing he needed to be doing. Cold, hard logic, he reminded himself firmly. That was the ticket.

"I sit with you?" Angel asked, startling him. "You looks lonesome."

Before he could reply, she slid in next to him, squeezing up against him until he shifted to make room for her and the doll she'd placed between them.

"Know what?"

"What?" he replied, reluctantly meeting her gaze.

"I'm gonna see my daddy," she confided, unaware of the impact her words were having. "Mama said." She leaned closer and patted his cheek. "I really, really need a daddy. I never had one."

Todd's gaze shot to Heather, who was still chatting with the cowboy. What the devil had she been telling Angel? Apparently she hadn't identified him as the daddy in question just yet, but clearly it was only a matter of time if she was already prepping Angel for the big introduction.

Suddenly his appetite, not all that great to begin with, vanished.

"Let me out, Angel," he asked, his voice choked. "I have to get going."

Angel stared at his plate, wide-eyed. "But you didn't finish your dinner. Mama says I can't leave the table till I eat every bite."

"And that's a very good rule, I'm sure, but I'm not hungry."

"Mama's gonna be mad," Angel predicted, still not budging.

Too impatient to wait for her to do as he'd asked, Todd awkwardly circled her waist with his arm and scooted Angel, Leaky and himself out of the booth, then set Angel back on the bench.

"I'll leave your mom a big tip. That should improve her mood," he said wryly, tossing bills —way too many of them—on the table.

He sidestepped Heather in the aisle, ignoring her surprise as he aimed straight for the door and the air he suddenly needed.

Apparently defiantly clinging to his routine wasn't going to be quite the snap he'd hoped it would be, not with Heather and his daughter right smack in the middle of it.

"Was that Todd I saw charging out of here?" Henrietta asked when she came in to help Heather close up.

"It was."

"He didn't clean his plate," Angel informed them both. She gazed up at Heather. "Maybe he should go to his room."

Heather grinned. "He's a grown-up, baby. He doesn't have to eat if he doesn't want to. Besides, my hunch is that he's already headed for his room."

Probably to make one of those infernal lists of his, she thought. If it couldn't be quantified or analyzed or broken down into pros and cons, Todd wanted no part of it. Her arrival in town with Angel in tow had to be driving him nuts. She had to confess to taking a certain amount of pleasure in his discomfort. One of her favorite pastimes when they'd lived together was to rattle his sometimes scary, intimidating composure on a regular basis. Of course, nothing she'd done back then came even close to this.

Henrietta was still staring at the door with evident concern. "That's two nights this week that he's disappeared without eating. Last night and the night before, he didn't come in at all. Something's definitely wrong. Normally that man is here like clockwork every night and he has the appetite of a horse."

Heather wasn't about to enlighten her about what was likely wrong with Todd, but Henrietta was regarding her speculatively, clearly linking her arrival and Todd's abrupt change in behavior.

"This all started when you showed up here the other day," she said slowly, her expression thoughtful. "I know I introduced you, but he latched on to you like a man with something on his mind. You two already knew each other, didn't you? How well?"

"That probably depends on which one of us you ask," Heather replied, thinking of Todd's insistence that she didn't know him at all.

"How well?" Henrietta repeated.

"We dated for a while."

Henrietta's eyes narrowed. "How long is a while?"

"A few years."

The older woman's gaze shot to Angel. Then she sat down in one of the vacant booths. "Oh, my. Don't tell me . . ." Her voice trailed off.

"Maybe we shouldn't talk about this just now," Heather said with a pointed look at Angel. Her daughter didn't appear to be listening to the grown-ups, but with Angel you could never tell. She'd repeated an awful lot of things Heather would have sworn she hadn't heard.

"No, I suppose not." Henrietta regarded Heather sternly. "But we will talk about it. Make no mistake about that."

Heather winced at her tone. Henrietta had been kind and generous, taking Heather and Angel in without giving it a second thought. But it was obvious that her first loyalty was to a man she'd known for months, a man she clearly liked and respected.

"I'll explain everything," Heather promised. If Henrietta was going to continue letting her work here, maybe she did deserve to know the whole truth about what had brought Heather and Angel to Whispering Wind. She didn't belong in the cross fire, at least not without understanding what was going on and deciding for herself if she was willing to be a party to it.

"I'll explain tonight, if you want," Heather offered. "I'll get Angel into bed and come back down."

"Tomorrow will be soon enough," Henrietta said, then glanced at the remaining customer. "Looks as if Joe would like more coffee. If you'll see to that, I'll close out the register and get the bank deposit ready."

Heather wasn't particularly anxious to serve Joe coffee or anything else. He was a friendly, nice-looking young man. With his coal-black hair curling over his collar, the chiseled planes of his face and his piercing blue eyes, he was every woman's fantasy of a rugged cowboy, in fact, but she wasn't interested.

He, however, clearly was. He'd been sweet-talking her the past two nights in his shy, gentle way. While the attention had been flattering, she was very much afraid he was starting to hope for something more than good service in exchange for his tip.

"Why don't you sit down and join me for a bit?" he suggested when she'd filled his cup.

"We're about to close. I need to help Henrietta."

"Henrietta's been managing this place just fine on her own for a long time now. She can spare you. Come on, sugar, sit down and tell me about yourself."

"Sorry, I can't. As soon as we're finished, I have to get Angel up to bed. I don't like her to get in the habit of staying up late." Even when she'd carted her to the theater, she'd tried to make sure that she was asleep in the dressing room by eight when the show went on, so the stagehands would only have to peek in on her while Heather was on stage.

"Looks as if she's found herself a napping place in that booth over there," Joe pointed out with a lopsided, engaging grin.

Sure enough, Angel was curled up in the space Todd had just vacated, sound asleep, her doll snuggled next to her. Heather seized on the excuse.

"Then I'd better carry her up right now."

Joe stood at once. "She's too heavy for you. I could take her for you."

The man was solid muscle beneath his clean white T-shirt and snug-fitting jeans. He seemed like a genuinely nice man. She wondered why she wasn't even the slightest bit attracted to him. Maybe, regretfully, it was simply because he was nothing at all like the man who'd once been the love of her life.

Todd had changed some since he'd come to Wyoming. Knowing him, she realized he'd begun adapting to a new role, just as he did when cast in a play, just as he had when he'd first gone to work for Megan. They were subtle changes he probably wasn't even aware of making. His hair was a little longer, for one thing. And he had a light tan from being outdoors more. But there was no mistaking the eastern polish and sophistication that had drawn her to him years ago.

"Thanks for offering," she said. "But I can manage."

Joe nodded and, to her relief, backed off. "Another time, then." He dropped a generous tip on the table, then strolled over to the counter and paid Henrietta, pausing long enough to flirt outrageously with her until she laughingly told him to get out so she could lock up.

When he'd gone, Henrietta regarded Heather intently. "You know, if you were looking for a fine husband and a daddy for Angel, you could do a whole lot worse than Joe Stevens. You're the first woman I've seen him take an interest in since his wife died."

"He lost his wife?" Heather asked, shocked. She ignored the suggestion that he could be a stand-in for Angel's real daddy. "He can't be more than twenty-eight, twenty-nine. How old was she?"

"He's thirty-one, actually, but Marilee was only twenty-five when she was diagnosed with ovarian cancer. It took her in less than a year. That was about two years ago. Joe's stayed to himself since then. For a time he was like a lost soul. We were all worried sick about him. He was doing some hard drinking, but from what I've seen he's pulled himself together and sobered up now."

"What does he do? For a living, I mean," Heather asked.

"He's a rancher. Has a spread west of town. He's been buying up land, expanding the ranch he inherited from his family. He's breeding some of the finest horses in the state. He caters to the rodeo circuit. He spent some time busting broncs himself. Has a couple of championship buckles, but he gave it up to marry Marilee.

"I have a lot of respect for that boy. He married her after she was diagnosed with cancer. Stuck right by her side. Wouldn't let anybody else come in to help him nurse her. Wore himself out during that time. I think he blamed himself for not marrying her sooner, for taking the time to go off on the rodeo circuit the way he'd dreamed of doing since he was a boy. He made up for it, though. The way he loved her was something to see."

"How awful that they had such a short time together," Heather said.

"Not so short," Henrietta replied. "The marriage was short, that's true, but Joe had loved Marilee for as far back as I can remember. The expression 'childhood sweethearts' could have been coined for the two of them. They used to come in here when they were barely into their teens. They'd sit in that same booth where he was tonight, drinking sodas and laughing, planning their future. He was going to be a big rodeo star, then settle down with Marilee and raise horses and babies. I wondered if I'd ever see him in here again after she died, but he's been coming back real regular the past few weeks. Until you came along, though, I hadn't seen him laugh much."

"He's such a hunk, I'm amazed some woman around here hasn't snapped him up."

Henrietta chuckled. "Oh, believe you me, they've tried. One night he sat here and told me some of the tricks they've pulled. Said his freezer was still filled with all the casseroles and cakes they brought him. That's normal enough, I suppose, when a man's a widower, but they were offering a whole lot more, and some of them none too subtle about it. In my day, any woman who dared to go after a man so blatantly wouldn't have been called a lady, that's for sure."

Heather began to get Henrietta's own none-too-subtle message. "You told me all this so I won't do anything to hurt him, didn't you?" she guessed.

"Exactly. Like I said, Joe hasn't shown any

interest in another woman until you turned up. I wouldn't want to see his heart broken."

"I'll make sure he knows that I'm leaving," Heather promised.

"Either that," Henrietta advised, then added pointedly, "or tell him your heart's already taken."

"But—"

"You can't fool me, girl. Whatever history there is between you and Todd, it's far from over."

Heather prayed Henrietta was wrong, but deep inside she couldn't help wondering if the older woman hadn't gotten it exactly right.

6

Todd hadn't scheduled so many back-to-back meetings for himself and Megan since they'd moved the company's headquarters from Manhattan to Whispering Wind. He was determined to fill every waking minute with work. Since paperwork left his mind free to wander, he'd concluded that meetings that forced him to focus on the subject at hand were safer. So far everyone was tolerating the shift in routine without comment, but both Megan and Peggy had started giving him speculative looks every time they walked through his office door. Right this second, Peggy was doing it again.

"What?" he snapped finally.

"Something's up with you," she said. "Want to talk about it? I know when things were real bad for me and Johnny, talking helped."

That almost drew a full-fledged smile. The woman was a chatterbox. "I'm not surprised," he said wryly.

"Okay, I know I babble sometimes, but I'm talking about real serious talk, you know? The heart-to-heart kind. Megan let me go on and on till I worked things out in my head. I'd be happy to listen to you."

"The only thing I want to talk about is Megan's idea for this cooking show," he said adamantly. "Are you sure you're up for it?"

She regarded him with obvious disappointment, but finally shrugged. "Okay, let's talk about the show. I think the better question is whether you think I can do it. You're the expert."

"Peggy, there is not a doubt in my mind that you could handle this and be wildly successful. The real question is do you want to?"

"You're worried that Johnny's going to have a cow, aren't you? Well, the truth is, he might, but you know what? That's okay, because it's something I want to do. For a long time, he expected me to get used to his running around with other women. That may be over, but it's my turn now. He'll have to get used to this."

Todd barely resisted the urge to chuckle at her defiant tone. "It's hardly the same thing."

"No, but since I never wanted to run around with other men, it will have to do."

He regarded her worriedly. "Peggy, if this is some sort of payback, if you're not going into it with wholehearted enthusiasm, it's a bad idea."

"To tell you the truth, it scares me to death. The whole idea of carrying a nationally syndicated show all on my own, who would have thought it? I am so grateful to you and Megan for giving me this kind of an opportunity. I won't let you down. I promise."

"You can give it a hundred percent?"

"Whatever it takes," she said firmly. "I'm not afraid of long hours or hard work." She grinned. "Besides, it won't hurt Johnny to spend a little more time looking after the kids. It'll keep him out of trouble."

"An interesting marital philosophy," Todd observed.

"I'm learning as I go," she admitted. "A year ago I wouldn't have given you two cents for our chances to turn our marriage around, but we have. Almost, anyway. I think the biggest lesson we both learned is that you can't take a relationship for granted. You have to work at it, especially when it hits the rough patches."

"Something tells me you and Johnny will make it," Todd said, all too aware that Heather had bolted at the first sign of difficulty. Now he was about to do the same thing.

"If we do, maybe we ought to launch a marriage-counseling program. Goodness knows I could have used some down-to-earth practical advice the first time I found out he was cheating on me."

Todd chuckled.

"You think I'm joking, don't you? I'm serious," Peggy declared.

"If you keep this up, you'll be the one with the media empire," Todd told her.

"Not me. I'm just an average Wyoming house-wife."

"Peggy, there is nothing average about you," Todd said, wishing he had the nerve to let her take a shot at counseling him. But he wasn't prepared to let the world—or even this one kind, decent person—know about the situation in which he'd suddenly found himself. Years ago he'd been taught that a man faced his troubles all on his own. So what if he'd only been seventeen at the time? It was a lesson he'd never forgotten.

Despite the chill in the air, the sun was shining brightly and the breeze had a belated hint of spring in it on Friday afternoon. Angel was down for her nap, so Heather pulled a chair onto the sunny landing outside the upstairs apartment and settled down with a bottle of nail polish and an old issue of *People*.

She'd just finished putting the first coat of bright pink polish on her nails when she realized she wasn't alone. She turned her head to find Sissy Perkins standing halfway up the steps and watching her solemnly.

It seemed to Heather that Sissy was way too serious for a ten-year-old. Although she was a beautiful girl, with her red hair, flawless skin and delicate features, she rarely smiled and she never laughed. In fact, she was just about the quietest, politest and most sedate child Heather had ever seen. When Heather asked Henrietta about it, the older woman said only that Sissy had been through a lot in the past year.

Henrietta had adopted Sissy and her younger brother, Will, but that was about as much as Heather had learned. She figured Henrietta would reveal the rest when she was good and ready. She already knew that was Henrietta's way, operating on a need-to-know basis, whether it had to do with customer idiosyncrasies or the location of extra creamers. She was talkative enough when she chose to be, but those times could be few and far between.

"Hi, Sissy. Is school out?"

The girl nodded and crept up another step. "Am I bothering you? Henrietta said not to bother you."

Heather smiled. "Nope. I'm just doing my nails." She glanced at Sissy's nails, which had been chewed off practically to the quick. "Want me to do yours?"

Sissy hid her hands behind her back in obvious embarrassment. "No, thanks. I bite mine."

"Maybe if they were a pretty color, you wouldn't want to bite them," Heather countered.

Sissy considered that, then sighed. "It probably wouldn't matter. It's a nervous habit, that's what the shrink says, anyway. He says I'll stop when I'm ready."

Heather was startled by the casual reference to a shrink, but she didn't pursue it. If this child needed a psychiatrist at her age, it was none of Heather's business. That didn't mean she couldn't try to be Sissy's friend.

"So, what are your plans for the weekend?"

Sissy shrugged. "Nothing special."

"You're not going to see any of your friends?"

"No. I guess I'll help Henrietta around the house. And I'll baby-sit Will." Her expression brightened a little. "I could baby-sit Angel, too, if you want. I'm real responsible."

"I'm sure you are, but you should be doing something fun. What's your favorite thing to do?"

"Reading, I guess. You can go anywhere in the whole world you want to go in a book."

Heather heard a wistful note in the girl's voice, as if she longed to be someplace else. It was a longing no ten-year-old should be feeling. She should be living in the here and now, surrounded by friends and family and laughter.

"What about outdoors?" Heather asked. "Do you like any sports?"

Sissy shrugged again. "I guess so, but I'm not very good. Nobody ever chooses me for their team."

"Then how about something you can do on your own? Cycling, maybe." She was struck by a sudden inspiration, something she could share with this obviously lonely child. "How about in-line skating?"

Sissy looked intrigued, but she shook her head. "I don't know how. Besides, I don't have any skates."

"I could show you," Heather offered. "And I'll bet my skates would fit you. We might have to stuff some paper in the toes, but they'd work. If you like it, we can talk to Henrietta about getting you your own skates."

"Really?" the girl said, a spark of excitement in her eyes.

Heather seized the moment to try to do something to wipe that sad expression from Sissy's face. "I don't see why not. Let's give it a try right now."

She went inside and grabbed some tissues, which she wadded up, and the in-line skates she'd brought from New York because they were her favorite form of exercise. She'd already discovered that the sidewalk along Main Street was nice and level and mostly deserted, perfect for blading. She'd been out at dawn several times this week already, drawing stares at first, but friendly waves of greeting ever since.

Outside on the landing, she handed the skates to Sissy. "Let's go downstairs and you can try them on."

"What if Angel wakes up?"

"The door's open. I'll hear her. Angel makes a lot of racket when she's ready to get up. She's always afraid she might be missing something."

Sissy nodded. "Will was like that, too, when he was little," she said, then fell silent. Her lips quivered and she added in a low voice, "Till Daddy would get mad."

As she spoke, a tear tracked down her cheek, followed by another and then another. Obviously Sissy had touched on something almost too painful for her to bear. Heather stared at her helplessly, then reached out to gather her close. At her touch Sissy froze for an instant, then released a shuddering sigh. She relaxed in Heather's arms and gave way to noisy, gut-wrenching sobs. The sound brought Henrietta running.

"Oh, baby," she murmured, taking over from Heather. "What is it?"

"She said something about her dad, and then she just started crying." Heather had rarely seen such a heartbreaking display of anguish.

"I'll explain later," Henrietta mouthed, then led Sissy away.

Heather stared after them, shaken by the child's misery. Her own childhood, in upstate New York, had been happy, if a little dull. She had considered her parents too strict from time to time and maybe they hadn't been as supportive as she'd wanted them to be of her acting career or her decision to raise Angel on her own, but all in all, she'd had no experience with the kind of torment that Sissy was evidently going through. Even the wild mood swings of adolescence hadn't brought anything like Sissy's tears.

She recalled the bleakness in Sissy's eyes when she'd mentioned her father. And those tears, they hadn't been about sorrow, but something deeper. Suddenly it struck her. There had been anger, maybe even hatred, in that outburst. Could a ten-year-old child experience that kind of rage?

Later, after the diner had closed for the night, Henrietta poured two cups of coffee and beckoned Heather to a booth.

"After what happened earlier, you must have a lot of questions," she began.

"It's none of my business, but obviously I did or said something that set her off. Maybe I should know at least enough so that I won't inadvertently do it again."

Henrietta nodded. "Here it is in a nutshell. It's not pretty. Sissy lost both her parents a few months back. The long and short of it is that her daddy had been abusing her mama for years. One night he started after Sissy. Her mama stepped in and shot him. Lyle survived, but at my urging Barbara Sue left him and she and the kids moved in with me. Lyle just couldn't handle that. She was working for me here. As soon as he could get around, he came over here with a gun. Jake tried to stop him, but Lyle shot Jake in the leg, then killed Barbara Sue. The sheriff shot Lyle. That's how I wound up with the two kids. I figured I owed it to Barbara Sue, because I was the one who all but forced her to finally take a stand."

Heather was horrified. No wonder Sissy's impulsive mention of her father's anger had brought terrible memories flooding back. How many violent episodes had she witnessed? One would have been too many for a young, impressionable girl. And even at six, Will must be devastated.

As for Henrietta, she was clearly living with a burden of pain that shouldn't be hers. Heather reached across the table and clasped her hand, giving it a squeeze.

"Don't you dare blame yourself. It certainly wasn't your fault," Heather said. "The blame lies totally with that awful man. How could you possibly have known it would turn out the way it did? You told her what anyone would have, to get out and protect herself and her kids."

"Yes, but . . ." Henrietta sighed. "I suppose you're right." Then her voice took on a trace of anger. "But there was no way to protect her, not really. It seems as if there's not a damned thing the system can do until it's too late!"

The door opened and the judge walked in just in time to overhear Henrietta's last remark.

"You're blaming the system for one fool's misdeeds," he said. "No one could have stopped Lyle Perkins. He was a mean kid and a rotten adult."

"And everyone, including the sheriff, turned a blind eye to it," Henrietta countered, scowling at him. "Oh, I don't know why I waste my breath trying to talk to you about this," she said, and headed for the kitchen.

The judge sighed and slid into the spot she'd vacated. "I doubt she'll ever stop blaming herself," he said sadly. "Or me."

"What did you have to do with it?" Heather asked.

"Since Lyle was never brought into court, nothing. That doesn't stop Henrietta from thinking I should have come swooping in and locked him up, anyway. Barbara Sue never filed charges, so how could I? My hands were tied. And the one time Barbara Sue did try to defend herself by shooting him, she wound up in my courtroom. I was tough on her, said she couldn't go around shooting people just because she thought they deserved it."

A rueful smile settled on his face. "You should

have heard Henrietta. She stood up in the middle of that courtroom and blasted me from here to kingdom come. I could have held her in contempt and tossed her in jail right then and there. Probably should have, just to keep some decorum in the courtroom, but what she said had some merit. I took it into account when I let Barbara Sue off with probation. We got a restraining order against Lyle, too, so he couldn't go near Barbara Sue when he got out of the hospital."

"But that didn't stop him, did it?"

He shook his head. "There's no way to stop a man who's determined to get even, not unless he messes it up the first time and gives us reason enough to throw him in jail. Unfortunately, Lyle didn't mess it up. There's not a minute that's gone by since that I don't ask myself what I could have done differently, but I have yet to come up with an answer."

"Henrietta must understand that your hands were tied legally."

"In her head, yes. In her heart, I doubt she'll ever forgive me." He gave Heather a wry look. "Not that there's anything new in that. Henrietta's made it her life's work to hold a grudge against me."

"Why?"

"Because I foolishly let her down once, a long time ago. The woman has a good memory."

"But you keep coming back," Heather pointed out.

"So I do. Somebody told me once that persistence is a virtue. Henrietta might take exception to that, but I figure one of these days I'll wear her down."

"And then what?"

"I'll marry her, of course, assuming we've both retained enough mental capabilities by then to repeat the vows," he said wryly.

Heather chuckled. "Maybe you need a new strategy."

He stared at her. "I'm listening."

"Flowers, maybe. All women love flowers."

"Henrietta's allergic. She claims she sneezed for a week the first time I sent roses. That was thirty years ago and she's never let me forget. Said I was trying to kill her."

"Candy?"

"Won't touch it. Says she gets all the sweets she needs in her own pies and cakes."

"Is there something else she's fond of? Does she collect anything?"

"Henrietta lives and breathes this diner. It's as much her home as that place she lives in a couple of blocks from here. The customers are her family. She fusses and fights with 'em like they were, too." He shook his head. "No. I'm afraid the usual courting would be wasted on her. Not that I haven't given it a try from time to time."

"Well, there has to be something," Heather said, undaunted. "I'll think about it."

The judge regarded her curiously. "Now why would you do that, young lady? You barely know me or Henrietta."

Heather patted his hand and gave him a wink. "I'm a romantic. I like happy endings."

His expression brightened. "I'll be much obliged if you can figure out how to go about getting one for the two of us before we're both too danged old to enjoy it."

Todd didn't set foot in the diner all weekend long. Henrietta was about to storm over to his place to check on him, but Heather managed to talk her out of it.

"Give him some time," she begged. "He needs to wrestle with this news I've dumped on him. It just hit him out of the blue, but he'll adjust. That's what Todd does. He accepts facts, searches for solutions and moves on."

But when he hadn't surfaced by midweek, even she began to get concerned. Since the ever-busy Starlight was the last place she wanted to confront him, she decided a drive to the studios might be in order. She could explain her presence simply by saying that as an actress, naturally she was curious about the production facility Megan had created.

Wisely, though, she opted to leave Angel with Henrietta. The two of them were already thick as thieves. Heather couldn't help thinking what a shame it was that Henrietta hadn't had kids of her own years ago. But she was making up for it now with Sissy, Will and, lately, Angel.

Angel trailed " 'Retta" around like a little shadow, mimicking her activities. She insisted on helping to set the places at the booths—all of which had to be reset the minute her back was turned—then carried a "coffeepot"—an empty plastic milk jug that Henrietta assured her was better for little hands—from booth to booth, pretending to pour. She chattered away at her imaginary customers as she went.

When real customers came in, she was often the first one to reach the table, greeting them with her sunny smile and asking, "Take your order?" as if she could actually do it. Fortunately Henrietta was never so far away that she couldn't step in and actually write down whatever order the grinning customers gave.

"Where you going?" Angel asked when Heather headed for the door.

"Just to run an errand," Heather told her. "You're going to stay and help 'Retta."

"Okey-dokey."

She turned and toddled off to find Henrietta without a backward glance. After all this time being Angel's primary caregiver, Heather wasn't at all sure how she felt about such ready abandonment. Today, however, it suited her purposes.

Following Henrietta's carefully written directions, she drove to the outskirts of town, where she had no trouble at all finding the production facility. Unfortunately the first person she ran into was Jake.

"What are you doing here?" her lawyer asked.

"I thought maybe I could see Todd."

"Not a good idea."

"Why?"

"He's grumpier than a bear with a thorn stuck in its paw, for one thing. For another, Megan's protective instincts have kicked in. She knows something's wrong and she's pretty sure you're the cause of it. She won't welcome you and I won't have her upset."

The door to the facility opened and Todd looked out. "Jake, what's up?" He spotted Heather and the color seemed to drain from his face. "I'll handle this," he said tersely.

Jake hesitated uncertainly, then shrugged. "Whatever you say."

When he'd gone, Todd scowled at her. "What are you doing here?"

"I just thought I'd take a look around."

"It's not a tourist destination, Heather. It's a place of business."

"Believe it or not, I know my way around a studio, Todd. I know not to talk when the red light is on. I know to stay out of camera range. I even know how to tell which camera is live at any given moment."

He winced. "I know that. I just meant—"

"You just meant that you don't want me anywhere around you."

"Not at work."

"If not at work, where? You haven't been by Henrietta's in days. She's about to send out a search party."

"I'll get by sooner or later."

"She's worried about you. Worse than that, she's blaming me because you're staying away. She's figured out what's going on, Todd. I didn't say a word. She's seen us together, knows we've known each other longer than a few days. All it took was a good long look at Angel for her to figure out the rest."

"That's all I need," Todd muttered. "Henrietta's like a pit bull once she gets a notion in her head."

"Then stop by and ease her mind."

"Okay, okay. I'll make it sooner rather than later."

When she didn't take that as his final word and simply go away, he jammed his hands in his pockets and stared at her. "What? Is there something else you wanted?"

She started to say yes, that she wanted him to be a part of his daughter's life, but he already knew that. That was exactly why he'd been giving the diner a wide berth.

"Angel's been asking about you, too," she said, instead, trying to gauge his reaction.

Surprise flitted across his face, then disbelief.

"Why would she ask about me? She doesn't even know me."

"She's afraid we really did send you to your room for not eating your dinner that night last week. She thinks we locked you in. And if we could do it to you, we could do it to her. She's worried." It was only a slight stretch of the truth. Angel *had* expressed concern that night.

"Tell her I'm just fine."

"She won't believe me. She needs to see you for herself." Admittedly it was a sneaky tactic, but she told herself it was only a tiny fib, and if it got Todd and Angel together again, it was worth it.

His gaze narrowed. "You're making that up just to get me back to the diner, aren't you?"

She regarded him innocently. "Would I do a thing like that?"

"In a heartbeat," he retorted succinctly.

"Well, I guess the only way to find out for sure is for you to come in and check out her reaction for yourself."

"Heather—"

"Think it over, Todd. Are you willing to give a little girl sleepless nights, just because you're a coward?"

"Jeez, Heather, you are shameless," he said, but amusement tugged at his lips. "Using that little girl—"

"You work with what you've got." She grinned unrepentantly. "See you, Todd."

"Tonight," he agreed finally.

Impulsively, she rested her fingers against his cheek, then stood on tiptoe and touched her lips to his. "I knew you'd see it my way."

Before she could step away, he captured her hand and held it in place, then slowly turned his head and pressed his own kiss to her palm. A shudder swept through her. Her gaze flew up and clashed with his.

"What was that for?" she asked.

His hands were jammed in his pockets again. He shrugged. "Old times, I suppose. Why'd you kiss me?"

More shaken than she cared to admit, she couldn't seem to find her voice at first. "Old times," she finally echoed in a whisper.

"Maybe old times for us are best forgotten," Todd suggested.

"Never," she said vehemently. "Because of those times, we have a beautiful little girl."

"Something you're not likely to let me forget," he retorted.

She regarded him with dismay. "Is that what you want? Now that you know she exists, could you really forget about her? Even if we left, would you be able to get the image of your daughter out of your head?"

"I could try," he said, a plaintive note in his voice.

"But why would you want to?"

"Because it would be for the best."

"You're wrong," she told him. "I might have made a mistake in not telling you about Angel from the very beginning, but if you turn your back on her, you'll never forgive yourself."

Before she could say more, before she could express her disappointment in him, she turned away and headed for her car.

"I'll see you tonight," he said quietly.

"Whatever."

She noticed as she drove away that he was still staring after her, his expression troubled.

7

Todd stood outside the studio for several minutes after Heather had driven away. The woman was going to be the death of him. He'd caught sight of her driving up, guessed her intentions and bolted from his office, hoping to intercept her before she came inside. The last thing he wanted was for Megan to spot her and link Heather to the funk he'd been in. It was just bad luck that Jake had gotten to her first. Seeing the two of them with their heads together had been enough to make his stomach churn. If Jake was already in on the secret, then Megan would surely pry it out of him sooner or later, ethics be damned.

Oh, yes, Heather was going to turn his life

upside down, no doubt about it. She was going to keep right on poking at him until she got her way. If the stakes hadn't been so high, the risk so great, he would have given in now, accepted a role in Angel's life and been done with it.

But he couldn't and that was that. He would fight her as hard as he had to.

When at last he walked back inside, he found Jake waiting for him in his office. Since Jake was seldom far from Megan's side these days, Todd guessed the man had something serious on his mind. It wasn't all that difficult to figure out what it was.

"You want to talk about Megan's schedule again?" he asked, hoping he was wrong and that it was something that simple and impersonal, something professional. He charged ahead, assuming that he'd gotten it right. "I've made it as light as I could and still keep her on the air. She's champing at the bit because the pace of the tapings has slowed down. She seems to think we should be taping more, not less, so she'll have shows in the can when she takes time off to have the baby. She has a point. Unless you want her maternity leave to last less than a week, we need a backlog of shows."

For once, Jake didn't pounce on the suggestion that Megan return to a more demanding schedule. "This isn't about Megan," he said mildly.

Todd's hand stilled over the taping schedule

he'd been about to pull from its place on the wall behind him. "Oh?"

"It's about Heather," Jake said, then added, "and your baby."

Todd sank into his chair. "You know, then? I was afraid of that."

"I'm representing her. I thought you should know."

"So much for loyalty," Todd groused. "Isn't there a conflict in there somewhere?"

"I don't see one."

"Megan might," Todd suggested, hoping that would be enough to get Jake to drop the case.

"I don't discuss my cases with my wife. And even if I did, are you so sure she wouldn't want me to help a mother get what she deserves from her child's father?"

To be truthful, Todd wasn't sure of that at all, but he did know that Megan would at least listen to his side of things before jumping into the fray. That was more than he could say for Jake, even though he considered him a friend—particularly these past few months when he and Jake had been united in saving Megan's syndication deal and making her life easier.

"Are you so desperate for clients that you have to take on a case that puts the two of us at odds?" he asked.

"You know better," Jake replied quietly. "Heather came to me with a legitimate legal matter. If there had been another attorney to send her to here in town, I would have done it." His gaze narrowed. "Are we really going to have a problem over this? It's not personal, Todd. It doesn't have to turn into a fight. I know the kind of man you are. You don't walk away from responsibilities."

"It seems damned personal to me. And believe me, if this is about me taking legal custody of that little girl in any way whatsoever, there will be a fight. It's not going to happen, Jake."

"Todd, be reasonable. The girl needs a daddy. You'd make a fine one. I can't see why you're so all-fired set against it. How much time have you actually spent with Angel since the two of them got to town? You haven't even given the idea a chance, have you?"

"It doesn't matter why I'm against it. I am, so let's just start from there when you're working your legal magic. You prove she's mine and I'll fork over whatever child support seems right. Beyond that, I won't agree to anything. And since you're Heather's attorney, from here on out, I don't think you and I should be discussing this at all."

Jake seemed taken aback by Todd's unyielding attitude, but he nodded slowly. "Okay, you're probably right about that. Once you hire an attorney, I'll go through him."

"I have no intention of hiring an attorney."

"But—"

"Like I said, if Angel's mine, I'll meet any reasonable request. I don't need to have an attorney making this any more complicated than it is already. I'll make my offer to Heather. She can run it by you if she wants, then we'll sign whatever papers are necessary."

"She wants more than money," Jake reminded him, despite Todd's vehement insistence that anything else was out of the question.

Todd felt besieged, especially since he knew that what Heather wanted was not an unreasonable demand. If he'd been a different man with a different past, he wouldn't fight her. He'd *want* to spend time with his child.

But there was no point dealing with what-ifs. He was who he was and there was no forgetting the past. God knows he had tried every way he knew how, but it was always with him. Every time he was behind the wheel of a car, it came back to him.

"She's not going to get it," Todd said flatly.

"Okay," Jake said. "Let's go about this one step at a time. I'll schedule the blood work so we'll know exactly what the situation is. Then we can go from there."

"You do what you have to do," Todd said, just as Megan walked in.

She stared first at Todd, then at her husband, clearly sensing the tension in the air. "What's wrong?"

"Nothing," Jake said, leaping up to usher her

into a chair. "Sit. You shouldn't be on your feet."

"Jake, will you please stop it," she begged with evident frustration. "If you two are arguing over my schedule again . . ."

"We aren't," Todd said, inadvertently opening the door for more questions.

Fortunately Jake stepped in. He whipped a sheet of paper from his pocket. "The doctor said you should take it easy. It says so right here."

Megan scowled at the paper. "Give me that." She snatched it from his hand, balled it up and tossed it to Todd. "Burn that."

Todd grinned. "With pleasure."

Jake frowned. "I have more copies."

"I don't doubt it," Megan said. "I'm going to find the entire stash and burn those, too. And just for the record, it also says on there that I should continue to get a moderate amount of exercise, or have you conveniently forgotten that?"

Jake shrugged. "I must have missed it," he said without apology. "We'll go for a walk later, if it's not too chilly."

"Let's get back to what was going on in here before I walked in," Megan suggested. "Tell me the truth. Were the two of you arguing?"

Todd knew better than to head down that path. "Nope."

"Just talking," Jake agreed.

"About?"

"This and that," her husband said. He latched

on to Megan's hand. "We've got to run. I'll take care of that matter, Todd, and let you know the particulars."

"The particulars of what?" Megan asked, trailing after him reluctantly.

"Nothing for you to worry your head about," Jake told her.

Megan rolled her eyes. "I'll see you later, Todd, and be prepared. Whatever you two are up to, I will find out."

"Duly noted," he told her. He knew he'd been living on borrowed time from the moment Heather set foot in town. Despite Jake's claim to ethical considerations, his own determination to keep the matter private and Heather's promise not to let word get out, too many people already knew—or had accurately guessed—the facts. Megan was not the kind of woman to stay out of the loop for long. Well-placed sources and timely leaks were how she kept her magazine and her TV show one step ahead of the trends.

To her credit, she hadn't asked about Heather's presence in Whispering Wind, and by now she had to know about it. It was a small town, and Heather's soap role would have brought her instant attention. But as far as he knew, Megan hadn't caught so much as a glimpse of Angel. It was only a matter of time, though. Todd shuddered when he thought of what would happen when she finally honed in on the secret.

・・・

Heather was on pins and needles waiting for Todd to keep his word and show up at the diner. Every time the door opened, she glanced over, then sighed with disappointment when another of the regulars entered.

"You looking for somebody in particular?" Henrietta asked.

"No."

"You're a terrible liar, girl. Which man is it you're hoping will show up?"

"Which man?"

"I notice Joe's not here tonight. He's been making himself scarce the last few days, same as Todd. You chase off any more of my customers, I'll be out of business."

Heather winced. She certainly didn't want Henrietta to lose business because of her. "Sorry."

"I was joking," Henrietta soothed. "Must not be much good at it. Look around here. The tables are filled. I haven't seen this many ranch hands in here in years. Word must be getting around that I have a pretty new waitress."

Yes, Heather thought, there did indeed seem to be an awful lot of men crowded into the booths tonight. Young, rugged cowboys with friendly smiles and twinkling eyes. She'd been so busy serving heaping plates of Henrietta's spaghetti, she hadn't paid much attention to the gender of the customers. None of them was Todd, that was all she cared about. She'd finally sent Angel upstairs with Sissy, who'd promised to read her a story and then watch her favorite video with her for the umpteenth time.

The door opened again and Heather's gaze shot to the latest arrival. It was Joe Stevens. He stared around in surprise at the crowd.

"You giving away food in here tonight?" he asked. "Can't think of anything else that would get these motley ranch hands to leave the comfort of the bunkhouse and their nightly poker games."

"They're all paying customers," Henrietta assured him. "You'll have to join one of these gangs or sit at the counter. Unless you want to wait."

He shook his head. "The counter's fine." He slid onto a stool and grabbed a menu.

"You take his order, Heather. I'll get these plates over to table seven," Henrietta said.

Heather nodded, poured Joe a cup of coffee and set it in front of him.

"Where have you been?" she asked.

"Miss me?" he asked with a grin.

"Henrietta did," she corrected him.

"Had to take a run down to Denver for a few days," he said, then studied her with that impudent grin still firmly in place. "You sure you didn't miss me even a little bit?"

"I'm sure. But I was worried you might have

taken offense the other night," she told him candidly.

"Sugar, it would take more than a brush-off like that to keep me away from Henrietta's food." His grin spread. "Maybe I'll try again one of these days and you'll be in a more receptive frame of mind."

"Joe—"

"One of these days, Heather. No need to dig in your heels now. It'll just make it harder for you to change your mind later."

She laughed. "Your ego's obviously tougher than I thought."

He winked. "Keep that in mind, why don't you."

Just then the door opened and Jake's secretary came in, took one look around at the mostly male crowd and silently whistled. She took an empty seat at the counter, which hiked up her tight skirt, and grinned at Heather. "If I'd known you were going to start pulling in every bachelor in town, I'd have been over here sooner," she teased.

"They're here for Henrietta's spaghetti," Heather insisted.

"Yeah, right," Flo said. "Henrietta's been serving that same spaghetti since I came to town and I've never seen a crowd like this."

Joe's gaze settled on Flo as if he'd never seen her before. Heather seized on that promising flash of masculine interest and introduced the two of them.

"Are you both having the spaghetti?" she asked.

"Suits me," Joe said, without taking his gaze from Flo.

He was looking at her as if she were some sort of fascinating exotic bird, Heather thought. Given Flo's short skirt and snug sweater, Heather had a very strong feeling that she wouldn't need to worry about Joe's unwanted attention anymore.

"Me, too," Flo agreed, equally distracted.

Heather headed toward the kitchen to place the order and ran into Henrietta coming out with a loaded tray.

"Matchmaking?" Henrietta inquired.

"Not intentionally, but it sure looks as if it might work out that way." Something in Henrietta's expression suggested disapproval. "What do you think?"

"I think he could do better," she said succinctly, then turned right around and went back into the kitchen, food and all.

Heather followed her. "You don't like Flo?"

Scowling, Henrietta put the tray down. "I didn't say I didn't like her."

"But you don't approve of her for Joe, right?"

Henrietta sighed. "They're both grown people. They'll do what they want without my say-so." She paused, then added pointedly, "Same as you."

"What does that mean?"

"Take it however you want," Henrietta said as

she grabbed up two more salads, added them to the tray and left Heather staring after her.

"Now, what on earth was that about?" she asked.

"She gets riled up when things don't go to suit her," Mack answered as he expertly flipped burgers. "It'll pass. I ought to know. She spends most days riled up at me about one thing or another. If I experiment with some spice she hasn't personally okayed, you'd think I was trying to ruin her business."

Heather chuckled at the cook's disgruntled expression. "Remember the clientele," she said. "These folks can't take a lot of change all at once. You have to ease 'em along. Henrietta knows that."

"Henrietta's worse than the whole lot of them." He shook his head. "Talk about being set in her ways. But like I said, her moods pass."

Henrietta being riled up was plain enough, but what had set her off? Flo Olsen and Joe Stevens? Was she irked because she'd wanted something to happen between Joe and Heather? That didn't make a whole lot of sense. Hadn't she warned Heather to stay away from him since she intended to leave Whispering Wind? Or was it simply Flo she objected to?

Well, standing around in the kitchen wasn't going to get dinners served or solve the mystery of Henrietta's mood. Heather picked up salads for Joe and Flo, then went back to serve them—only to discover that Todd had joined them at the counter. From the way Todd and Flo were chatting, it was obvious that they were well-acquainted. Heather suspected she had the same scowl on her face that was plain on Joe's. Damn, but working here was getting complicated. There was more intrigue going on at the counter tonight than there had been on that soap opera.

Fortunately it was so busy, she didn't have time to dwell on any of it. It was eight by the time the crowd eventually thinned out. The three people at the counter, however, hadn't budged. Henrietta had joined them. Heather suspected she had deliberately scooted onto the stool between Joe and Flo to keep them a safe distance apart. That left one stool for Heather, next to Todd. She was too exhausted not to take it. She was also too tired to do more than pick at the food she'd brought with her.

"You have to eat more than that," Todd advised. "Otherwise, you'll insult Henrietta."

"I notice you cleaned your plate. Your appetite must be back. Did that have something to do with the fact that Angel was already upstairs when you got here?"

Rather than admit that the absence of his daughter had been a relief, Todd frowned. "Who's watching her?"

"Sissy. They're looking at *The Little Mermaid.* It's Angel's favorite."

"Sissy is too young to be baby-sitting," he said,

on his feet at once. "What the hell were you thinking, Heather?"

Even as the angry words left his mouth, he headed for the door. She shot after him and caught up with him on the sidewalk. "Todd, Angel is perfectly fine with Sissy. Henrietta and I are both right downstairs."

That didn't seem to appease him. He bolted for the stairs, not slowing until he was at the screen door and could see Angel and Sissy in front of the television.

As Heather reached his side, she noticed how pale he'd gone. When she touched his arm, he jerked as if he hadn't even realized she was beside him.

"Todd, what was that all about?" she asked in a low tone that wouldn't be overheard by the two girls.

He turned away and braced his hands on the railing. He drew in several deep breaths before meeting her gaze. "I just don't like the idea of Angel being left with a ten-year-old, even if you *are* nearby. If there was a real emergency, Sissy might be too upset to come and get you. She's just a kid. You shouldn't forget that."

"I'm not forgetting it. But Sissy is very responsible, and I explained before that Henrietta and I are both within shouting distance. We could be up here in seconds."

That clearly didn't pacify him. His expression

set stubbornly. "If you're not going to keep her downstairs with you, then hire an adult to watch her," he insisted.

"Baby-sitters cost money. Why waste the precious little I'm making when Sissy is willing and Angel adores spending time with her?"

"I'll pay for it."

"Todd—"

"I mean it, Heather."

"Maybe you'd like to come over here and spend time with her," she suggested. "It would be the perfect opportunity for the two of you to get better acquainted."

"Absolutely not."

Heather knew there had to be more going on here than Todd was saying, but for the life of her she couldn't figure out what it was. For a man determined to have no role in his daughter's life, he was awfully insistent on how she should be cared for in her mother's absence.

Was that instinctive paternal protectiveness surfacing? If so, maybe it was a promising sign. Maybe when push came to shove, Todd wouldn't turn his back on Angel. Maybe he would become part of her life by default, one tiny step at a time.

If only he could do it enthusiastically, Heather thought, biting back a sigh.

When she glanced his way, she saw that he had turned back toward the door, just enough so that he could see Angel reciting the dialogue from memory, and periodically bouncing with excite-ment. He seemed to watch her with total absorption.

"Does she know every word?" he asked eventually.

"Pretty much. I probably know most of them myself from watching it so often."

"If she's that good at learning lines, maybe she'll grow up to be on stage like her mother."

"And her father," she pointed out.

He scoffed. "I'm an executive, not an actor."

"Just because you work in an office doesn't mean your talent dried up and went away," she countered. "Talent like yours is as ingrained as breathing. You just turned your back on it."

"Let's not go there, okay?"

"I wasn't judging you. You made a choice you had every right to make. It just makes me sad when I think about what you gave up."

"You mean lousy pay and bit parts in bad plays?"

"You were one step away from getting a big break and you know it. That one producer all but promised you the lead in the next play he did."

"Promises don't pay the bills."

She eyed him skeptically. "So you're totally content with the decision you made?"

"Totally. Working for Megan is challenging. I'm in television, even if it is on the production side. I couldn't be happier."

"You know I almost believe that," she said, after studying him intently. "But maybe that's because you always could deliver a line with just the right degree of sincerity."

He frowned. "It's the truth, Heather. I don't look back."

She sighed. "No, you probably don't. You always were able to live in the moment, accept the hand you were dealt. I envied that. I was the romantic, the dreamer, and I was always butting up against reality."

"Is that what brought you here? Reality?"

She nodded, opting for total, unvarnished honesty, since the mood seemed to call for it. "I couldn't do it alone anymore, just as you said the other day. I wanted to. I wanted to make good as a mom and an actress without taking help from you or anyone else, but the truth is, I was at my wit's end. My parents weren't willing to help out. Like you, they thought I should have told the father. Of course, they assumed I would have gotten the help I needed from him."

She paused significantly, then continued, "I discovered all too quickly that it's almost impossible to work two jobs to make ends meet, go to auditions and raise a baby, not and do any of it right. I knew I had to make Angel the priority, but I was afraid I was going to start resenting her if I couldn't take the kind of risks for acting that I needed to take."

"Maybe you should have gone to your parents again," he said. "Told them what a tough time you were having."

"Pride almost kept me from doing exactly that, but I finally broke down and tried a few months ago. They said they'd help out, but only if I'd give up my silly pipe dream, as they called it, and come back home." She shrugged. "I wasn't willing to sell out, not yet."

"Then coming to me was the lesser of two evils?"

She nodded.

"What if I can't give you what you need, either? What will you do?"

"Can't or won't?"

"Either one. They add up to the same thing."

She met his gaze evenly, stared into those pale-green eyes that had once mesmerized her, and allowed a smile to slowly spread across her face.

"I'm the romantic, remember? I believe in happy endings."

He shook his head. "Not this time, sweetheart," he said with what almost sounded like regret. "I can't give you one this time."

She reached up and rested her hand against his cheek, saw the once-familiar flash of heat in his eyes. "We'll see."

"Heather—"

She cut off the protest with the press of a finger against his lips, then stood on tiptoe to replace finger with lips. The kiss lasted no longer than a heartbeat, was gentler than a breeze, but it was enough to convince her that her faith in this man was not misplaced, that the feelings they had once shared were as alive as the pulsing streaks of electricity flashing in the distant night sky. She might not understand why he was fighting her so hard on this, but he would come around eventually. She was certain of that much.

8

The image of Angel sitting in front of the TV reciting lines from *The Little Mermaid* stayed with Todd for the next few days. Every time it popped into his head, he found himself grinning. The kid was a natural. Maybe Heather was right about it having to do with her genetic makeup.

Learning lines had always been a breeze for him and Heather. How many nights had they curled up at opposite ends of the sofa and run lines from either his latest script or hers? How many times had he gone to see her in a play and been able to mentally recite every line from every scene in which she appeared?

But even as that image of Angel continued to amuse him, the stark reality of her being upstairs alone with a ten-year-old baby-sitter made his stomach churn. The fear that Heather wouldn't listen to him, that she would send Angel off with Sissy again, made his visits to the diner assume a certain urgency.

When Megan tried to catch him on his way out of the office one night, he brushed her off in a way he never would have done in the past.

"We'll talk about it in the morning."

She regarded him thoughtfully. "Big plans tonight?"

"Just going to dinner, same as always."

"And you can't put it off for five minutes?"

"No," he said very firmly.

"Not even to talk about the suit against Dean and Micah?"

Todd was tempted. Those two had almost destroyed Megan's syndication deal. Although Dean Whicker had ultimately been pressured to keep the deal in place, Jake had insisted that Megan consider suing them both. Todd had agreed, though his desire for revenge had a lot to do with his own sense of betrayal; he'd been infatuated with the beautiful Micah Richards, his predecessor as producer. Her attempt to sabotage Megan with the syndicator had been a bitter blow on several levels.

But that was then and this was now. He had something more important on his mind: Angel's safety.

"No," he said again, just as firmly.

"Is it because Heather's there?" Megan asked

point-blank. "I know how deeply she hurt you when she walked out right after you came to work for me."

"You knew about that?" he asked, surprised.

"I'm observant. If anyone should know that, it's you. Are the two of you getting something going again? Is that why she's here? Have you been seeing her on your trips back East?"

He shook his head. "Never even thought about it," he said honestly. Until Heather had shown up in Whispering Wind, he'd considered their relationship long over.

Now, though, he couldn't help thinking about that kiss on the landing. It was hardly passionate, nothing at all like kisses they'd once shared, but there had been the promise of something in it. He was very much afraid that he didn't want to know exactly what.

Megan studied his face. "Are you sure?"

"Absolutely," he said more fiercely than he'd intended.

Megan grinned. "What's the old line about protesting too much?"

"Don't even go there. I'm just hungry, that's all. I missed lunch."

"And whose fault was that? You're the one who scheduled a meeting at lunchtime, then ignored the sandwiches that were sent in."

He chuckled. "Ignored them? They vanished before I could even reach for one. Pregnancy has

127

definitely improved your appetite. Jake's, too."

Megan laughed at that. "I know. We're both going to be as big as houses if we keep this up. He swears it's sympathy hunger pangs, but I notice he's not the one craving pickles with ice cream. Doesn't mean he doesn't eat it to keep me company, though."

Todd shuddered at the thought. "It's true? Women really do crave those things?"

"Disgusting, isn't it?"

He wondered suddenly if Heather had had such cravings when she was pregnant, and if so, who had been around to run out and get whatever odd food she longed for. Or had that been another of those things she'd insisted on handling for herself? He couldn't seem to decide which bothered him most, that she might have been all alone or that there might have been someone doing the things he should have been there to do.

"Hey," Megan said. "Where'd you go?"

"I told you. My mind's on dinner. All this talk of pickles and ice cream has made me even hungrier."

"If you say so. Go, then. We'll talk in the morning." Her expression brightened. "Unless you'd like me to come along? We could talk about this over dinner."

Talking about Micah would definitely ruin his appetite. Worse, though, was the thought of Megan at the Starlight where she might get a good look at Angel. That was enough to make him cringe.

"No," he said sharply. "Morning's soon enough. Go home to your husband. I'm sure if you're not there right on time, he'll send out a search party and I'll catch the blame."

"You're probably right. I never thought I'd say this, but all this attention is very trying. I've got Flo practically begging him to come into the office and Tess trying to lure him into going riding with her, just so I can have a few minutes to myself."

"To do what?"

"Think," she said wistfully. "With Jake trying to anticipate my every whim, I never even get to think for myself, it seems. I'm not sure I've had a new idea in weeks."

Todd tapped his briefcase. "I have the paperwork in here to prove otherwise. Your creative juices are flowing just fine. Go home, put your feet up and let your husband pamper you. Enjoy it while it lasts. Once the baby comes along, my hunch is you're going to be playing second fiddle to his heir."

Megan sighed. "You're probably right about that, too. I'd better get home and claim my share of his attention now."

The mention of heirs reminded Todd that he'd heard nothing from Jake about the blood test he'd promised to schedule. The minute he got in the car, he punched in Jake's number on his cell phone.

"Have you scheduled that blood test yet?" he asked without preamble.

"First of next week. Why?"

"I don't want to waste any more time. I want this over with."

"Why?" Jake asked again. "Is there a problem?"

Just fear, Todd thought, but didn't say. Heather was a beautiful, desirable woman with a mission. It was a dangerous combination and he was no more immune to it than the next man. He wanted her—and Angel—back in New York before he acted on impulse and did something all of them would live to regret.

"Just take care of it, Jake. Move it up, if you can."

"I'll see what I can do."

"Thanks."

"No problem. One of these days, though, we probably ought to talk about what you're so afraid of. Despite what you think about my having taken this case, I am your friend and I'm a good listener."

"Then listen to your wife. Let up on her before you drive her nuts."

Jake chuckled. "She's complaining about the hovering again?"

"You've got it."

"I'll try, but I'm not promising anything. Meantime, remember what I said. I'll fight for

Heather because it's my job, but Megan and I also want what's best for you. We both owe you. Right now you're obviously tied up in knots."

Apparently he wasn't nearly as good at hiding his emotions as he'd thought, Todd concluded. He found it especially annoying that Jake was the one who could see through him so easily. Men were supposed to be oblivious to nuances and undercurrents. Since Jake seemed no more insightful than the next guy, that must mean Todd's panic was plainly visible to anyone who cared to notice.

"I just want my life back," he said tightly. "Make it happen."

"I'll do what I can, but I work for Heather, not you," Jake reminded him.

"Believe me, this is to your client's advantage," Todd assured him.

The sooner an agreement was reached, the better for all of them.

Todd was barely seated at the diner when Angel climbed into the booth beside him, a book in hand. This was a development he hadn't figured out how to handle. It was one thing when she stood beside the table or slid in opposite him, a nice, safe distance away, but having her snuggled trustingly up against him made him yearn for things that couldn't possibly be, reminded him of things he'd hoped to forget.

"I been thinking," she told him.

"Oh?"

"I really, really need to have a story." She gazed up at him with a hopeful expression. "You gots time to read to me?"

Praying for a reprieve, he patted his briefcase. "Sorry, kiddo. I've got papers to go over."

"It's not a very big book," she said, shoving it into his hand. "It's gots lots of pictures. See?" She opened the book and began turning pages. Sure enough, there were a lot of pictures and very few words. The little minx seemed to know most of them because she recited them from memory as she flipped the pages. When she'd reached the last page, she shot him another hopeful look. "See? It's not very long."

"Sounds to me as if you know that story by heart," Todd said. "Why do you keep reading it?"

She regarded him as if that were the silliest question she'd ever heard. "Because I like it."

"Good reason."

"So will you?"

"Will I what?"

"Read it to me," she said with a hint of impatience.

Todd was beginning to feel claustrophobic, even though he was in a large, well-ventilated room. Maybe if he read her this one story, she would be satisfied. Maybe she would take her wistful smile and big eyes and go away.

He sighed in resignation. "Okay," he said.

He took the book and began turning the thick pages, reading the simple words about a bunny. Before he'd turned the third page, he felt Angel snuggle closer—and something deep inside him melted just a little. He waited for the panic to follow, but it was slower in coming and not as severe.

As he read "The end," he felt someone else's presence. He looked up to find Heather standing beside the table, his dinner in her hand and an unreadable expression on her face.

"I see Angel shared her favorite book with you," she said as she made room for his plate amid the scattering of papers.

"Quite a story," he said. "I couldn't wait to see how it turned out."

She grinned. "The plots will get a little more complicated in a few years."

"I can't wait."

She gave him a questioning look. "Does that mean you've decided to stick around for those?"

"Absolutely not," he said fiercely, realizing that his dry rejoinder could have been interpreted exactly that way.

As if she sensed the sudden tension between the adults, Angel squirmed to get down. Looking as if she was about to cry, she ran straight for Henrietta, who scooped her up and shot a scowl in Todd's direction. He knew he'd hear more from her later about upsetting Angel. Henrietta had added Angel to her flock, protecting her as fiercely as she did Sissy and Will. There was only one way he could think of to avoid it.

"Can you put that into a take-out box?" he asked Heather. "I'll eat at home, so I can actually get some work done."

"Can't handle the heat, huh?"

He frowned. "Meaning?"

She grinned. "I saw that look in Henrietta's eyes."

"What look?"

"The one that said you're in for it, pal, for upsetting Angel."

"Oh, *that* look."

"You can finish your meal," Heather said. "I'll protect you."

"I can fight my own battles with Henrietta," he said. "She doesn't scare me."

"But a sweet little three-year-old does?"

"I can handle Angel, too," he insisted, though there was definitely some question about that. She'd manipulated him pretty easily a few minutes ago.

"Then I must be the one chasing you off."

"No one is chasing me off. I have work to do and I can't get it done with all this commotion."

"What commotion? Five minutes' reading about a runaway bunny?"

"Exactly."

"Must have been pretty disturbing stuff to rattle

you like this. Maybe I'd better take another look at that story. Could be it's too scary for Angel."

"You know, Heather, you have a really smart mouth."

She laughed at that. "Clever, too. Want me to demonstrate?"

Memories of her lips on his slammed into him with the force of a freight train. Oh, he wanted her to demonstrate, all right, just not here and not now.

Not *ever*, he corrected himself with his one remaining functioning brain cell.

"Another time," he said lightly.

"I'll keep that in mind."

She left his dinner right where it was and walked away with a provocative sway to her hips that was obviously meant to inflame him. It worked, too. He felt as if the temperature in the restaurant had climbed at least twenty degrees.

He loosened his tie and opened the top button of his shirt, then took a long swallow of his iced tea. It soothed his throat, but didn't do a blasted thing to cool the blood throbbing in another part of his anatomy. There was only one way to relieve that, and she had just sashayed over to flirt with that same cowboy who'd been hanging around here way too frequently lately. Stevens, that was it. Henrietta had introduced them at the counter. If it wasn't for the way he looked at Heather, he might have actually liked the guy.

Todd glanced across the room and saw Henrietta watching him with a knowing glint in her eyes. That nosy old woman saw too damn much for her own good. Todd forced his attention back to his rapidly cooling meal. If he didn't eat every bite, Henrietta would draw her own conclusions about his lack of appetite. She was already storing up a lecture regarding Angel. He didn't need another one on the topic of Heather or his dietary habits.

When he'd eaten the last bite, he crammed his papers into his briefcase, left a hefty tip on the table, then stopped at the register to pay his bill.

"Everything okay?" Henrietta inquired cheerfully.

"The food was terrific as always."

"And the company?"

He leaned closer as if to confide a secret. "You know, Henrietta, if you start meddling in my life, I might just get it into my head to start encouraging a certain judge in his pursuit of a certain diner proprietor. I know a few things that might help him out. For instance, I know that she is not nearly as immune to him as she'd like him to think. I know that if he were to take an interest in Will and Sissy, spend a little quality time with them, it just might work in his favor."

She frowned at his warning. "I am not the least bit interested in that old man."

"I know better."

"You don't know anything about it."

136

"Care to test me?"

"You cannot blackmail me, Todd Winston."

He laughed. "Don't look now, but I just did."

"You tried. That doesn't mean it worked."

"I guess we'll see about that." He glanced toward the door. "Why, there's the judge now, right on time. I wonder if he'd like a little company for dinner."

Color flamed in her cheeks. "You stay away from him, you hear me?"

"And you'll steer clear of my relationship with Heather?"

She looked torn, but finally gave a curt nod. "As long as you don't do anything to hurt her or that little girl."

He nodded with satisfaction. "Deal."

He turned to go, but Henrietta put her hand on his arm to catch his attention.

"If you send them away, it's going to hurt them, Todd."

He sighed heavily. "Not half as much as I would if they stayed."

The diner had pretty much cleared out when Flo came in for a cup of coffee and a piece of pie.

"You're late," Heather said. "Joe's already come and gone."

"I know. I was watching from across the street."

Heather gave her a sharp look. "Why? I thought the two of you hit it off the other night."

137

"We did. He's a terrific guy. That's the trouble. He's not going to be interested in a woman like me, not when he knows my whole story."

Heather glanced around, saw that Henrietta was with the judge, who was the last customer, and that Angel was curled up and fast asleep in a booth. She poured a cup of decaf for herself and took a seat opposite Flo. Over the past few days, she had developed a real fondness for the flamboyant, plain-spoken woman who was only a few years older than herself.

"Tell me," she suggested. "What's so awful that it would make Joe not care about you? He looked pretty interested to me."

"He is. At least, he said he is. He called me at Jake's and asked me out the other day, but I turned him down. It's one thing to sit in here and flirt with him. It's another to let it progress to anything more. He doesn't deserve someone with all my baggage."

"What baggage is that?"

Flo stared at her untouched pie, looking miserable. Her usually flawless makeup was smudged and her eyes were red-rimmed, as if she'd been crying. It was such a contrast to her usual devil-may-care demeanor that Heather was concerned.

"Flo, tell me. I promise I'll just listen. No judging, no advice, unless you ask for it."

"I told you the other day. I've got a kid," Flo

said finally, as if that were some sort of character flaw.

"So? Why is that a problem? A lot of men aren't put off by single moms."

"It's not that," Flo said. "It's because she lives with Megan and Jake, instead of me. I glossed over it the other day, but the truth is I pretty much abandoned her."

"But you're back in her life now," Heather reminded her. "Isn't that what you told me?"

"I know, but that's gotta look weird to Joe. If somebody else is my kid's legal guardian, he must think it's because I was really lousy at it. And the truth is, I was."

Her expression turned sad. "I don't know why I didn't appreciate Tess more when she was with me. I guess I just felt overwhelmed all the time. I hadn't told her father a thing about her. We were close for a while, but I was living in Laramie, and he just stopped coming around. When I found out I was pregnant, I never called him up and told him. I figured it was *my* deal, right? I should have been more careful."

Her story was all too familiar. Heather could empathize completely. "I know exactly how you felt," she said at once.

"You do?" Flo said, staring at her. "You don't think I was awful, not telling him?"

"I pretty much did the same thing with Angel's daddy," Heather admitted. "I'm trying to make it right now, but it's not working out the way I thought it would."

Flo blinked, her eyes widening as understanding registered. "Todd?" she breathed in a hushed tone. "He's Angel's daddy?"

Heather hesitated, then nodded.

"Oh, boy. No wonder he looks shell-shocked most of the time these days. That's why you were in to see Jake, isn't it?"

"Yes. So you see, I do know what you were going through."

"But you never walked out on Angel."

Heather hesitated. "In a way, that's what I was planning to do when I came here. Not for good. Just to get a break. I couldn't handle doing it all on my own anymore."

"That's exactly how I felt, like I was going to do Tess more harm by keeping her with me than by giving her up."

"Have you considered fighting for custody now?"

"Once in a while I think about it, but I'm not really ready. Tess is happy. I think she's finally forgiven me for walking out on her. She's real lucky to have so many people in her life who care about her. And I'm finally getting the rest of my life together. Megan made Jake hire me, mainly to drive him nuts, I think. I'm actually turning out to be a pretty decent secretary, though. Not that he has that much for me to do."

Her expression turned despondent again. "Anyway, you can see why a man like Joe, a man who stuck it out with a woman through the most terrible time of her life, no matter how it hurt him, would never understand that I walked out on my own kid."

"Maybe you're not giving him enough credit," Heather suggested. "He strikes me as a pretty decent guy, who'd try to see your side of things. For all you know, he's already heard the whole story. It must have been a hot topic here in Whispering Wind for a while. Why not just be up-front with him and let him decide, rather than making the decision for him? You might be surprised by how things turn out."

"You really think so?" Flo asked hopefully.

"I think it's always better to take a chance and know for sure than to do nothing and spend the rest of your life wondering."

"Are you going to take a chance with Todd?"

Was that what she wanted? Despite all her claims, did she want him back in her life for herself as much as she did for Angel?

Maybe so, she admitted to herself. Unfortunately the decision wasn't up to her.

"I don't know," she told Flo honestly.

"Sounds to me like you're pretty good at handing out advice, but not at taking it."

"You could be right," Heather conceded.

But Todd was here and her life was in New

York. Maybe it wasn't much of a life, but it was the one she wanted. Why start working on something that didn't stand a snowball's chance in hell of being successful? Better to concentrate on bringing him and Angel together and leaving it at that.

"But you can't recapture the past or dwell on past mistakes," she told Flo. "You can only move forward. And that's advice both of us would do well to remember."

9

Over the next few days, Heather found herself settling into a surprisingly comfortable routine in Whispering Wind. She'd always been adept as a waitress, but she'd never particularly enjoyed it before. But here it was as if she were at the hub of a very small universe, in which the customers were rapidly turning into friends. The pace was leisurely. She had time to pause and chat, to ask about their families, to fill them in on Angel's latest skill.

And while most of them knew by now that she'd once been on a television soap opera, they were more curious than awed. Even the ones who'd recognized her from the show accepted her as a friendly newcomer to town, rather than the villainess she'd portrayed on TV.

Equally important, Angel loved being the center of attention in the diner. And though she apparently hadn't made the leap to the conclusion that Todd was her daddy, she always gravitated toward him whenever he was around, much to his obvious discomfort.

Even though there had been no real sign that his resistance was weakening, Heather was determined to wait Todd out. Sooner or later, he would come around and do the right thing. That was what Todd was all about. Pressuring him would accomplish nothing. She also thought the blood-test results would go a long way toward hastening his acceptance of the facts. He and Angel had been tested on Tuesday and preliminary results were due back anytime.

Since she knew exactly what the results would show, there was no anxiety for her during the wait, as there clearly was for Todd. Each time she saw him, he looked like a man awaiting sentencing for a felony, but at least he no longer stayed away from the diner.

In the meantime, she was finding the slow-paced rhythm of small-town life oddly satisfying, a welcome break from the struggles and frenetic pace back in New York. Because Henrietta was a morning person and Heather wasn't, Henrietta took the early shift most days. Heather had time then to feed Angel, bathe her, take her along while she skated to the park, pushing Angel's stroller in front of her. There Angel spent time playing on the swings and feeding her beloved ducks, before Heather went to the Starlight at eleven to get ready for the lunch crowd.

The park was where Jake found her on Wednesday morning. He sat down beside her on the bench.

"Nice day," he observed.

Despite her faith in those test results, her stomach churned, anyway, at his unexpected arrival. "You didn't come out here to talk about the weather, did you?"

"Nope."

"The preliminary results are in?"

"Yes."

"And?"

"The blood types are compatible."

Of course. "I told you they would be. Have you told Todd?"

"I'm heading out to the studio to tell him in person. Do you want to come along?"

She shook her head. "It's better if you do it. He'll believe you. He still doesn't trust me. A part of him desperately wants to believe I'm trying to put something over on him. I wish I understood why, but I don't. Not really. It's not like him to be so cynical and suspicious."

"I think a part of him knows the truth and it scares him," Jake suggested. "That's why he's been so blasted tense. If he accepts the truth, then he has to deal with the guilt. Even though you made the decision to keep the pregnancy from him, he'll find some way to blame himself for not knowing about it, for not being there to help you through it."

"If that's true, if this is just about guilt, what do you think he'll do when he knows for sure?"

"Heather, you've known him longer than I have. What do you think he'll do?"

She wished that what she *wanted* him to do matched what she *thought* he'd do. "He'll insist on doing the right thing, or at least what he sees as the right thing. He'll start throwing money in my direction." She regarded Jake despondently. "Whatever it is, it won't be enough. Angel needs her daddy. Jake, you should see her with Todd. I haven't said a word, but she clearly senses a connection. She doesn't let his cool responses put her off. She crawls into his lap whenever he'll let her. If I give them enough time, I just know she'll break through that reserve and he'll come around."

"How much time are you willing to give? Can you stay here indefinitely?"

She'd been thinking a lot about that the past few days. The urgency to get back to her life in New York had faded. Although she missed being on stage, missed the adrenaline rush of going to auditions, she didn't miss the struggle just to stay financially afloat. Here she and Angel had every-thing they needed without her feeling as if she had to work two jobs.

With people like Henrietta and Sissy pitching in to spend time with Angel, she no longer felt overwhelmed. With a good friend like Flo, who understood what she was going through, this was turning out to be exactly the break she needed, much more like a vacation than what she'd envisioned when she'd made the plans to come.

She *could* stay awhile. It wasn't as if she was abandoning her dream. She was just getting her batteries recharged. She would go back to New York revitalized, take Broadway by storm.

"Through the summer, anyway," she said, making up her mind. "This is too important to rush."

Jake nodded his approval. "Good. Then when Todd starts making offers, I'll tell him that the terms for settlement include some form of custody."

She'd been telling Todd exactly that since she'd arrived. He didn't seem to be getting the message. "What if he flatly refuses?" she asked Jake. "I can't very well *make* him spend time with her."

"We'll cross that bridge when the time comes," Jake said. "For now, let's just see where these preliminary test results and a little patience get us."

Angel spotted Jake just then and came running over from the edge of the pond.

"Hiya, Jake!"

"Hey, sweetheart. How are the ducks today?"

"Hungry. I needs more bread, Mama."

"You've already fed them all the stale bread Henrietta gave you. That's enough for today. Otherwise they'll get so fat, they'll waddle."

Angel giggled. "Mama, that's what ducks do. They waddle."

Jake winked at her. "You are so smart. I hope when my little boy or girl gets here, he or she is as smart as you."

Angel looked intrigued. "You gonna have a baby?"

He nodded. "In a few months."

"How long is that?"

"A long time, sweetie," Heather told her, thinking that Megan wasn't even showing yet. She had to wonder if they would even be here when the new baby arrived in the fall.

"Can I hold the baby?" Angel asked as she crawled into Jake's lap.

"Of course you can," he said. "You can come out to the ranch and play with the baby any time you want."

Her eyes widened. "You gots a ranch?"

"Yep."

" 'Retta told me 'bout ranches," she said, surprising Heather. "You gots horses?"

"Lots of horses."

She patted his cheek. "I come see, okay?"

Jake laughed. "Anytime." He glanced at Heather.

"In fact, why don't you drive out after work tonight? It'll still be daylight in case that rattle-trap you bought conks out on you."

Heather hesitated. "I don't know." She glanced pointedly at Angel. "Megan might . . ." She didn't finish.

"If you ask me, it's time to call in the big guns," he said, clearly guessing her worry. "Besides, Todd is coming over for dinner at six. Maybe the two of you can spend some time talking about the latest development while I take Angel to meet the horses."

"Please, Mama," Angel begged, clinching it.

"Okay," Heather agreed, lured by the prospect of some time alone with Todd away from the diner. "I'll try to get off by seven, which should get us out there by seven-thirty, right?"

"That's perfect. Todd will have time to let his food and this news digest before you get there. Shall we save you some dinner?"

"No, thanks. I'll grab something during my shift at work. Angel, too."

Still holding Angel, Jake stood up, then put the little girl back on her feet. "I'll see you later. If anything comes up during my meeting with Todd, I'll let you know, so you won't be caught off guard tonight."

"Thanks, Jake."

Although she hadn't been anxious while awaiting the test results, Heather had a feeling she was going to be a wreck by nightfall, until she could gauge Todd's reaction to the news firsthand.

Todd had almost backed out of going to Megan's for dinner. Jake's news about the blood test hadn't really come as a shock, not after all these weeks of gazing into Angel's green eyes. A part of him had been trying to face the possibility for some time now. But knowing with almost absolute certainty that he was a father shook him more than he cared to admit. He wasn't sure he wanted to spend an entire evening with Megan surrep-titiously studying him the way she'd been doing at the studio lately.

Unfortunately he'd realized that trying to get out of the dinner at the last second would only stir up her suspicions more. So he'd gone.

Now he sat at the dinner table, enduring more stares, trying to make strained small talk with Jake that didn't involve a pint-size person. If it hadn't been for Tess's excited chatter about her plans for the last week of school and her upcoming summer vacation, it would have been a very tense evening.

When the doorbell rang at seven-thirty, he was almost relieved, though he found it somewhat worrisome that Jake didn't seem to be the least bit surprised.

"That must be Heather," he announced. "I'll get it."

As soon as Jake left the room, Todd frowned at

Megan. "I didn't know you'd invited Heather out here."

"I didn't. Jake did."

"But you knew?"

"Not until just before you arrived." She regarded him with feigned innocence. "Why? Does it bother you? I thought you two were old friends."

"You know perfectly well we were more than friends, the operative word being *were*."

"And now?"

"And now we're not," he said flatly, even as he wondered about the truthfulness of that. On some level, didn't he want more, even though he knew the potentially disastrous consequences of such a desire?

Before Megan could question him about his claim, Jake led Heather into the dining room. Todd hadn't thought things could get any more complicated, but then he spotted Angel tagging along in her wake. She caught sight of Todd and ran to his side.

"Up," she demanded.

He reached for her instinctively, settling her on his lap. He realized as he did so that he'd almost gotten used to holding her, that the baby-powder smell of her had gotten as familiar and as much a part of his visits to the diner as the rich aroma of Henrietta's coffee.

Megan's gaze shot from him to Angel, then

back again. "Oh, my," she mouthed. Aloud, she asked, "Now, Heather I know, but who is this?"

"I Angel," his daughter announced.

"Well, I'm Megan," his boss responded. "And I am very glad to meet you."

Megan's eyes glinted with sudden determination. "Tess, why don't you take Angel out to the barn? I'll bet she'd love to see the horses."

Clearly fascinated by the undercurrents, Tess balked. "What about dessert?"

"We'll have it when you come back." Megan glanced at Heather. "Would you like to see the horses, as well? Jake?"

It was less question than command. Jake dutifully stood. The traitor was probably anxious to be gone when the inquisition began.

"Come on, Heather," Jake said with a rueful glance at Todd. "I think we've all been dismissed."

"Maybe I'll come along, too," Todd said.

But before he could even stand up, Megan's gaze locked with his. "Sit."

Not another word was spoken as everyone except the two of them left the room. Then Megan turned to him with a fascinated expression. "Well?"

"What?"

"She's yours, isn't she?"

Todd sighed. He saw little point in denying it. "So they tell me."

"What do you intend to do about it?"

"I'm putting a financial settlement together."

"And then what?"

"They'll go back to New York," he said, desperate to believe that was the way it would turn out.

"And then what?" she persisted.

"Nothing."

She stared at him, her eyes wide with shock. "That's it?" she asked indignantly. "You'll just cut your daughter out of your life except for a monthly check she and her mom will get in the mail?"

Todd winced. She made it sound so cold-blooded, so completely uncaring, when the opposite was true. He was protecting Angel. "It's for the best," he said defensively.

"Says who? Is that what Heather wants?"

"Not exactly." He frowned at her. "This really isn't any of your business, you know."

She beamed at him, clearly undaunted. "Maybe not, but that's never stopped either one of us before. That's why we make such a good team. We don't back off when we believe in something."

"Megan, I will work this out."

"Just like you always do," she scoffed. "With logic and reason."

"Exactly."

"I'm here to tell you that logic and reason don't have a thing to do with the emotional ties at work here. If you doubt that for an instant, take a good long look at me and my history, first with Tex and now with Tess. Stop fighting what your heart is telling you to do."

He scowled. "How the hell do you know what my heart is telling me to do?"

"I just know, okay? I saw it in your eyes when those two walked into the room. Listen to your heart," she repeated, then stood up, clearly satisfied that she'd delivered her message and that he'd heard it and mentally filed it away, as he always did with her commands.

"Now, why don't we take a stroll to the barn and join the others?" she said, perfectly aware that the barn held all sorts of dangers he preferred to avoid.

"I'd rather eat dirt," he muttered, even as he trailed after her.

"I heard that."

"I meant for you to," he retorted.

It was no huge surprise that within ten seconds of their arrival at the barn, everyone except him and Heather had disappeared. Megan was better than any director he'd ever worked with at getting people on and off stage. He wasn't even sure how it had happened, but here they were, facing each other, neither of them quite sure what to say.

"So you know now," she said finally.

He nodded. "But I don't want to get into this tonight, Heather. I need to think."

A smile crept across her face. "Yes, you do like to think things through, don't you? Take your time. We're not going anywhere."

Unfortunately that was precisely what he was afraid of. And the longer they stayed, the more complicated this was going to get. He had to find a strategy that would get them out of town, and he had to do it fast. For Angel's sake, he reminded himself nobly.

"We'll talk about this tomorrow." In fact, tomorrow wouldn't give him time to make as many lists as he'd like, but time was of the essence.

"Where?" she asked.

"My place. I'm not playing this out at Henrietta's with the whole town looking on and choosing sides."

"Fine. When? I'm not off until eight."

"Eight will be fine."

"Angel will be with me," she said, clearly testing him. "I don't want to ask Henrietta to keep her. She's done too much for me already. She has enough on her plate with Sissy and Will without me coming to rely on her, too."

Though he understood and appreciated her concern for Henrietta, Todd felt as panicked as if she'd announced she'd be bringing along a cobra. He swallowed hard. "Whatever," he said, then gave her directions.

She gave a little nod of approval, as if he'd passed some sort of a test.

"We'll be there, then. I'll look forward to it."

She said it as if he'd invited her for tea, rather than a heart-to-heart about their daughter's future. His pulse thudded dully. He could feel the jaws of that giant trap tightening around him.

"Okay, what will it take to make you go away?" Todd blurted when Heather was sitting across from him in the living room of the small apartment he'd finally rented six months earlier when it had become clear that he was in Whispering Wind to stay. He hadn't intended to get into this quite so directly, not with Angel within hearing distance, but he didn't like the way he felt with her and Angel in his place. Rather than being appalled by their intrusion into his space, he had a sinking feeling it wouldn't take much for him to ask them to stay. He just had to phrase his words so Angel wouldn't grasp what he was discussing with her mother.

Heather ignored the question, just as she had always ignored any topic that didn't suit her. She stood up and wandered around the living room, examining the artwork on the walls and the few personal items he'd brought from New York. Pausing in front of the fireplace, she picked up a small marble carving of a woman from the mantel, staring at it in wonder as she ran her fingers over the smooth curves.

"I remember this. You bought it at that flea

market in the country one Sunday." Her gaze locked with his. "You said it reminded you of me."

He remembered that day—and that comment—all too well. In fact, he had to wonder if that was one reason he hadn't left the carving behind in his New York apartment. Had he subliminally wanted something with him that reminded him of Heather, even though she'd been out of his life for so long? Even his brief infatuation with the beautiful, traitorous Micah hadn't completely wiped away the memories of the woman watching him so intently right now. Emotions he'd thought long forgotten churned inside him.

Fortunately there was nothing he could do about them with Angel in the room. His gaze strayed to the little girl, who was sitting on the floor engrossed in one of the bagful of picture books Heather had brought along for her. Despite the panic that never quite left him whenever he caught sight of Angel, he was undeniably fascinated with her. *His daughter.* It was terrifying. Awesome, though, too. He couldn't seem to take his eyes off her.

Heather, however, was another matter. She rattled him every bit as deeply as their daughter did. He knew with every fiber of his being that they were still wrong for each other. He knew that renewing their relationship, especially now, courted disaster. And yet he couldn't seem to

156

stop thinking about her. He only prayed he could get her to go back to New York before he did something about it.

He tested his first offer on her, a settlement that most sensible women would have grabbed in a heartbeat.

"Very generous," she commented, her attention distracted by a picture on the wall, also from New York. "But no."

He topped it by another hundred dollars a month.

The amount caught her attention, but she shook her head. "I don't think so."

He made another half-dozen suggestions, each one more desperate than the last, but she stood right in front of him and kept on saying no without even considering them. After a while, his gaze locked on her mouth like a heat-seeking missile. Every no became a challenge, a dare.

And finally, because there was no other way to keep her silent, no other way he could think of to end this negative streak she was on, he kissed her. Maybe once they got this out of the way, she would be reasonable.

Once their lips touched, once hot, swirling heat slammed through him, however, he recognized his mistake. Heather had been like a drug to him once. He'd been addicted to her, desperate to have her, even when he realized how ill-suited they were. It was the same now. Not even Angel's presence could stop him from finishing the kiss, from savoring it.

This was no casual peck, no light brushing of his lips over hers. This was a no-holds-barred, been-alone-too-long kiss. This was a reclaiming. His blood roared. Her soft curves fit snugly against the hard planes of his body, reminding him of the way they had come together in his bed—impatiently, hungrily, naturally. He had never expected to have such totally uninhibited passion in his life, but she had stirred it in him. Obviously she still could.

His brain, which was supposed to keep him out of just this kind of trouble, finally kicked in. Reason—and the awareness that Angel was very much with them—overruled lust and he stepped away.

After all, Heather was still free-spirited, still doing outrageous, impulsive things. Showing up in Whispering Wind with a baby she had kept a complete secret from him for years was proof enough of that.

He was still compulsively organized, obsessively concerned with routines and commitments and duty.

And then, of course, there was Angel, who would be very much a part of anything that happened between him and Heather.

Logic—his favorite weapon for keeping his life on course—told him it would be a grave error to ignore those differences, to pretend they didn't matter, an even graver error for him to forget about the past and another little girl he should have kept safe.

But somehow, after that kiss, he knew it was going to be a whole lot harder to get Heather to go.

10

Heather was still thrown for a loop days after Todd's kiss. She hadn't been able to get that brief moment of insanity out of her head. All he had to do was walk into the diner and her body heat escalated. Worse, the only thing that had been resolved that night was that the chemistry between them was still as volatile as TNT. Two smart people would let their attorneys do the talking from now on. Except Todd didn't have an attorney and continued to refuse to get one.

"We'll work it out," he'd insisted every time she'd raised the suggestion since that night in his apartment. "Jake's a great guy, but I do not intend to discuss this matter with him."

"You couldn't even if you wanted to. He's my attorney." At least for the record, she amended silently. She hadn't exactly fired Jake, but the morning after her encounter with Todd, she'd told the attorney that maybe Todd was right. They could settle this between them . . . eventually.

"Any chance of a reconciliation?" Jake had asked her when she'd told him to give Todd some breathing room. "That would be the best thing all around."

"Absolutely not," she insisted, but was that really true? After that kiss, she had to wonder. A reconciliation had been the last thing on her mind when she'd traveled to Whispering Wind. She'd been after a daddy for Angel and a little free time for herself. Nothing more.

Now, however, she was going a little crazy wondering if Todd would try to kiss her again. She wanted him to, even though he appeared to be giving her a wide berth as if he feared that very thing. How had she managed to forget that when the ever-cautious, ever-defensive Todd let down his guard, he could rock her to her very soul?

Okay, so it was evident that the chemistry was still there. But that was it. It had to be. Loving Todd now would mean not only accepting that he was no longer an actor, but would require her to stay right here in Whispering Wind. She wouldn't even consider such a thing.

"I've lost my mind," she muttered when she realized that for one brief second she actually had considered that very thing. "Obviously I have lost my mind."

"What was that?" Henrietta demanded, taking her by surprise.

Heather sighed. "Nothing."

But she very much feared it was everything, that she was well on her way to proving that she didn't have a grain of sense left in her head. She didn't need Henrietta's take on the situation to confirm it.

"More coffee," the judge called out, trying to snag Henrietta's attention.

The interruption suited Heather just fine. Henrietta turned away with obvious reluctance and crossed to the judge with a scowl. Heather lingered over her chores, just to listen to the expected fireworks. They were getting to be a nightly occurrence and provided more live entertainment than anything else in town.

"You've had enough," Henrietta told him predictably.

"Woman, I am old enough to decide how much coffee I want," he grumbled, just as predictably. He tapped the rim of the cup. "Fill it or I'll go back there and do it myself." His gaze narrowed. "And while I'm there, I just might decide to kiss that sassy mouth of yours."

Color bloomed in Henrietta's cheeks. She grabbed the pot and practically raced over to pour more coffee for the judge. He grinned at her.

"Thought that might do the trick."

"It worked once," she warned him. "Won't work again. I'll ban you from the premises."

"You can't. It's a public place."

"It's *my* public place and I'll damned well keep out anybody who's proving himself to be a nuisance," she informed him.

"Which one of us do you think has a better grasp of the law?" he retorted.

"Who's talking about the law? I've got a broomstick in back that'll do my talking for me."

He chuckled as if he found her feistiness delightful. "Damn, Henrietta. There is no one like you."

"And don't you forget it, Harry Corrigan," she snapped back. "Heather, I'm going to the kitchen. If this old man gives you a hard time, call the sheriff. Maybe a night in a jail cell will remind him of his manners."

Heather winked at him. "Oh, I don't think that will be necessary. You're the only one he gives a hard time to."

"More's the pity," Henrietta lamented. "You'd think a smart man, like he claims to be, would have wised up by now and would stay away from here."

"Hell, woman, our little chats are the only things that keep my blood pumping," he countered.

Henrietta rolled her eyes and disappeared into the kitchen.

Heather gave a last swipe to the booth she'd been pretending to clean, went over, propped her elbows on the counter and grinned at the judge. "I think you're making progress."

"Maybe so, but at this rate, I won't live long enough to savor the victory," he said with a sigh. "That obstinate woman is going to be the death of me."

"Have you ever considered just asking her out?"

"For twenty years I asked her out once a week, like clockwork. She turned me down every time. It was enough to discourage a lesser man. For the past ten years I've settled for coming in here every day and night and counting it as a date. What she doesn't know won't hurt her."

"Sounds to me like turning you down was just a habit she got into and didn't know how to break. Maybe instead of coming here, like she counts on you doing, you should start showing up at her house, bring dinner along or a game to play with the kids. She won't turn you away. It wouldn't be polite."

"Since when was Henrietta polite when it comes to me?"

He had a point. Sometimes her words had a sharp edge to them that wasn't done in jest. Since Henrietta struck Heather as the fairest, kindest woman she'd ever known, there had to be a story behind that.

"What happened all those years ago to throw you two off course?" she asked.

He regarded her with uncharacteristic uncertainty. "You really want to hear all that old history?"

She nodded.

"The long and short of it is, I took her at her word and married somebody else."

"Oh, dear," Heather murmured. "That would do it."

"Well, how was I supposed to know she didn't mean it when she said no?" he grumbled. "When she told me I was not going to bully her into marrying me, I took it as her final word. Violet Jenkins was available. She wasn't as pretty as Henrietta or as . . . difficult, but I was ready to settle down and she was willing. We had a whirl-wind courtship and married a couple of months after we'd started seeing each other."

"And Henrietta's never forgiven you?"

"Never. Acts like I betrayed her, when she was the one who sent me away. Wasn't till after Violet and I were married that I found out it was Henrietta's daddy who was behind the refusals. He thought I wouldn't amount to anything, threatened to disinherit her if she got mixed up with me."

"She chose money over you?"

"Wasn't money she cared two hoots about. It was this place. Her heart was in this restaurant. Her daddy would have sold it right out from under her or closed it down. Least that's what he claimed. When I heard how little he thought of me, I took Violet and went off to law school, set up practice here in town, then became a judge, all to prove him wrong. I suppose I owe my whole career to that old fool who stood between Henrietta and me."

"If it was her father who came between you, how can she go on blaming you?"

"She thought I should have fought harder. Made her madder than sin that I went on and made something of myself after I'd married another woman, instead of doing it before when it might have made a difference for the two of us."

Heather had to admit that Henrietta might have a point about that, but it was all so long ago.

"What happened to Violet?" she asked.

"Now, that was the real tragedy in all this," he said, looking suddenly tired. "She was a real delicate woman. When she got pregnant, she took to her bed. She died in childbirth. We lost the baby, too. That was thirty years ago. Last thing she said to me was that Henrietta wouldn't have messed it up like she had. You see, she always knew where my heart was."

He sighed, his expression filled with sorrow and long-held regrets. "Hasn't been a thing that's happened to me before or since that made me feel worse than knowing I let that sweet woman down. Violet was the innocent party in all this. I spent a lot of years nursing my guilt before I woke up and realized I was still alive and so was Henrietta and that we'd already wasted too much time. I've been pestering her ever since, but she nurses a grudge like no one else on God's green earth."

"And in all this time, she never married?"

He shook his head. "Not that there haven't been men who were interested. A half-dozen or more would have married her for her fried chicken alone, but she never gave one of them the time of day."

"Maybe she wanted them to love her for herself and not for her talent with a skillet," Heather said wryly.

"Oh, that goes without saying," he said, as if startled that she would think otherwise. "Henrietta commands a lot of respect and admiration in this town."

"Then maybe she's afraid," Heather suggested.

"Afraid?" he scoffed. "Henrietta? There's nothing that scares that woman."

"Risking her heart again might, especially with you."

"There's no risk involved," he insisted. "I've told her how I feel every way I can think of. Coming in here day after day and putting up with her abuse ought to make it clear enough, don't you think?"

"Maybe she just sees that as proper penance," Heather teased.

He chuckled. "You know, she probably does. Well, I'll think about that idea of yours. Time was when she liked Chinese food right well. Maybe I'll pick up some egg rolls and chow mein one night and take 'em by the house. Maybe I'll even slip my own fortune-telling note into the cookies to get her thinking along the right lines."

"It's worth a try," Heather said. "If you'll tell me what night you plan to do it, maybe I could keep Sissy and Will with me for the evening. Take them out for ice cream or something to give you two some privacy."

He seemed touched by the gesture. "You'd do that?"

"Absolutely."

"Henrietta may not thank you if she guesses what you're up to," he warned.

"I'll take my chances."

He gave a little nod of satisfaction. "You're a good girl. Remind me of Henrietta, in fact. You've got spirit. I'll get back to you about that dinner."

"I've got the late shift tomorrow," she told him, anxious to see this scheme of theirs set in motion. "No point in wasting time."

"Right," he said, suddenly looking as eager as a teenage boy. "Tomorrow it is. I'll go make the arrangements right now."

"And I'll talk to Sissy and Will," she promised.

There was a new spring in the judge's step when he left. There was also a hint of disappointment in Henrietta's expression when she came back out from the kitchen to find him gone, but she was quick to mask it.

"I see the old man finally had sense enough to leave," she said.

167

"He said something about some plans he had to take care of."

Henrietta's gaze shot to Heather. "What plans?"

Heather innocently returned her gaze and shrugged. "He didn't say."

"You sure about that?"

"Not a peep. Must be personal. Why? Would it bother you if he had a lady friend?"

"Of course not!" Henrietta snapped, but the color had faded from her cheeks. "Wouldn't be the first time."

With that she turned around and stalked back into the kitchen, spine rigid. After that, the pots and pans seemed to be taking more of a beating than usual as she put them back in place. Heather listened to the banging and grinned. Phase one of the mission had been accomplished.

"Henrietta, why don't you take off early?" Heather suggested the next night. "I'll keep Sissy and Will here with me. As soon as I close up, I'll take them with Angel and me for ice cream, then bring them on by your house."

"Please, Henrietta," Will begged without coaching.

"Say yes," Sissy pleaded.

Angel turned her big eyes on Henrietta. "They gots to go with us, 'Retta. Please."

Henrietta regarded all of them suspiciously.

"Why are you so blasted anxious to get rid of me? It's not my birthday, is it?"

"No," Sissy said solemnly. "Your birthday is months and months away. I'm going to bake a cake, remember?"

"True enough. Well, if that's not it, maybe I'll just wait right here and come along," Henrietta suggested. "Ice cream sounds like a great idea. Summer's finally turned up in spades. It's been a scorcher out there today and there's not a storm in sight to break the heat."

"You can't," Heather said urgently, then winced at Henrietta's sharp look. "I mean, it's the perfect chance for you to have some time to yourself. Don't you want to pamper yourself for a change, maybe take a nice bubble bath?"

"Now, why on earth would I want to do that?" Henrietta asked briskly. "Who has time to waste soaking in a tub?"

"That's the point," Heather countered. "This is your chance. You deserve a break."

Henrietta still looked as if she didn't quite get it, but she finally relented. "Okay, since it's obviously so all-fired important to you, I'll go." She opened the cash register and pulled out a twenty. "But the ice cream is my treat."

When Heather started to protest, the older woman frowned. "Either take it, or I come along."

Since Heather wasn't about to risk ruining the judge's surprise, she took the money. She would put it right back in the register after Henrietta left.

Of course, it took another half hour to actually get Henrietta out the door. Todd watched the entire exchange from a booth in the back, his expression increasingly curious. It was obvious he suspected something was up, but, thankfully, he kept his questions to himself.

After Henrietta had gone, he beckoned Heather over. "Okay, spill it. What was that all about?"

"The judge is surprising Henrietta at her place with dinner," she told him.

Todd's eyes widened. "Whose idea was that?"

"Partly his, partly mine."

"Mostly yours, I imagine. It's been my experience that Harry Corrigan is a straightforward kind of a guy without a sneaky bone in his body. You, however, thrive on this kind of backdoor intrigue."

She ignored the jibe. "The point is the two of them will finally have a night together to work out their differences."

"I don't suppose it would do any good to mention that they've already had years to work out their so-called differences. Maybe what you describe as *differences* are actually deep-rooted problems."

Heather couldn't honestly argue with that, considering what had happened between them all those years ago. Even so, she countered, "They can't solve anything at all if they don't talk."

"Don't you think if that was what Henrietta wanted, it would have happened by now? Just because you're a notorious romantic who believes in happy endings doesn't mean you can manipulate them into happening."

Her gaze narrowed. "Are we still talking about Henrietta and the judge?"

"Yes," he said. "Since we both know there's no happy ending in store for the two of us, right?"

"Right," she echoed dutifully. "Want to come with us for ice cream?"

"I'd rather die," he said, but without much rancor.

"Do it, anyway," she told him. "It will be good for you to expand your horizons."

"Expand them how? Thanks to Megan, every time I turn around I'm being hit with some new trend. Whatever happened to stability, sticking with the tried and true?"

Heather laughed at his despondent tone. "You're working for the wrong woman, if that's what you're after. Now, stop grumbling and come with us. You might be surprised by how much fun it is to see the world through a kid's eyes."

He grumbled about it, but he didn't refuse. He looked a little startled when Angel tucked her hand into his as they walked down the street. Heather held her breath waiting to see what would happen, but he didn't reject the gesture.

Sissy apparently noticed the same thing, because she inched a little closer and shyly took his other hand.

"What kind of ice cream you gonna have?" Angel asked him.

Vanilla, Heather predicted. Bland, ordinary vanilla. He'd always loved the basic flavor and refused to gussy it up with so much as a scattering of nuts, much less hot fudge or whipped cream.

"Vanilla," he said.

Heather chuckled.

"What?" he demanded.

"Just once, why not be daring? Try strawberry."

"Why should I when I like vanilla?"

"I like chocolate," Angel confided. "You can have some of mine."

"But I don't . . ." His voice trailed off in a sigh. He glanced over at Sissy. "How about you? What kind of ice cream do you want?"

She seemed to be stunned that he'd asked. "Vanilla," she said at once, as if to back him up.

"Good for you," he said approvingly.

Sissy beamed at the praise.

"Well, I'm having mocha fudge," Heather declared.

"And I want strawberry," Will chimed in just as they reached the ice cream parlor.

"Is that everybody's last word?" Todd inquired. "No last-minute changes? No need to look in the case and see what other flavors they have?"

"I wanna look," Angel said, reaching out her arms to be picked up so she could see.

Todd seemed to pick her up without thinking, then gave her a startled look as if he wasn't quite certain how she'd gotten into his arms. Everyone else confirmed their original order, then went with Heather to grab a table in a corner of the crowded room. Sissy stared at Heather with her big, solemn eyes.

"May I go with Todd and Angel? I could help him carry the ice cream. Angel won't be any help."

"Of course," Heather said, concluding that Todd had just acquired an admirer. Given what she knew of Sissy's father, it was little wonder that she was gravitating toward the soft-spoken Todd. She had to wonder, though, how Todd was going to react to being the object of her hero-worship. Truthfully, though, he didn't seem to get that same panicky expression on his face around Sissy as he did around Angel.

Heather kept her gaze on the trio at the counter, grinning at Angel's obvious indecision. She couldn't hear the words, but could tell Todd was trying to coax her into making a choice. Sissy finally took the cones for herself, Will and Heather and brought them back to the table.

"Angel can't make up her mind," she told them.

Heather considered going over to rescue Todd, but so far, he didn't seem to be losing patience with the process. She could have told him that just as he always ended up with vanilla, Angel would invariably end up ordering chocolate. This was just her way of claiming a little extra attention for herself. Sure enough, five minutes later Todd left the counter with his vanilla cone and Angel trotted at his side with a chocolate one.

"Trouble deciding?" she asked innocently when they reached the table.

"There were a lot of choices."

"I seem to recall hearing vanilla and chocolate mentioned before we ever walked in the front door," she teased.

"Angel almost went with the pistachio," he retorted. "She thought it was a pretty color."

"Yeah, I got taken in with that, too. She took one taste and dumped it on the ground, then demanded chocolate. How did you talk her out of it?"

"It was a snap, really," he said with evident pride. "I pointed out the rainbow sherbet, which was next to the chocolate. Once her favorite snagged her attention again, it was all over except for getting the scoop into the cone."

"Very clever," she said with admiration. "You're good at this."

His gaze narrowed. "At what?"

He was clearly fearful that she was going to mention "parenting" in front of Angel, but she knew better than that. One of these days soon, Angel would have to be told that Todd was her

174

real daddy, but not until he was ready to take an active role in her life. He might be with them here tonight, but he was a long way from accepting fatherhood.

"Hey, Todd?" Angel said, practically sticking her cone into his nose. "Wanna taste?"

He instinctively licked at the dripping chocolate before it could fall onto his pristine designer shirt, then encouraged Angel to hold it over the table.

"You like it?" she asked, clearly concerned.

"Very good," he conceded.

The cone wobbled precariously in his direction again. "You wants more?"

"No, thanks," he said. "You eat it." He glanced across the table and caught Heather watching him.

"What?" he demanded.

"You liked it, didn't you?"

"Liked what?"

"The chocolate."

"I said I did."

She chuckled. "No, I mean, you really, really liked it."

He scowled. "So what if I did?"

"Nothing."

"Heather, if you have a point, just make it."

"It just seems that if you can open yourself up to chocolate ice cream, there may be a whole world of possibilities you'll be open to trying next."

His frown deepened. "Cut it out."

"The world won't rock on its foundation just because you try something different."

"I'm always open to new ideas," he said defensively.

"Since when?"

"How do you think I ended up an executive assistant to someone like Megan?"

"Default," she suggested.

"I am not discussing this with you," he said.

Heather heard the determined edge in his voice and apparently Sissy did, too. She looked as if she were trying to make herself invisible. Todd apparently noticed it the same time Heather did, because he forced a smile and winked at her.

"How about one more scoop of vanilla, Sissy? These other people don't know what they're missing."

She glanced nervously at Heather. "Is it okay?"

"Absolutely," Heather told her, well aware that the girl was asking about more than ice cream.

A half smile flitted briefly across Sissy's face. "Okay," she said to Todd as she slipped from her chair. "I'll get it."

"I'll help," her brother said, scrambling after her.

"Me, too," Angel chimed in, dumping her own dripping cone onto the table.

Todd gave Sissy the money, then watched with concern as the three children darted over to the counter. Then his gaze returned to Heather. "I wasn't thinking," he apologized.

"I know. Neither was I. Obviously she picked up on the tension. I think Will did, too."

"Every time I think about what those kids endured, it makes me furious. That father of theirs deserved to die, but Barbara Sue didn't, and Sissy and Will surely didn't deserve to lose both parents."

"At least they have Henrietta," Heather said.

"Yeah, thank God for that. The woman's as rock-solid as they come."

"I wonder how she and the judge are getting along," Heather said.

"Probably well enough, assuming she let him in the door."

"Shall we go over there now or give them some more time?"

"Worried about your scheming?" Todd asked. "Are you afraid Henrietta might have scratched his eyes out?"

"No, I'm concerned about their privacy," she replied. "I vote for a stop in the park. Let the kids run off some of this energy before we take Sissy and Will home. You can help push them on the swings."

In the end, though, the kids didn't want to swing. They played some game of their own invention that required a lot of screaming and giggling. Heather sat on a swing, instead, idly pushing herself back and forth until she felt Todd come up behind her and put his hands on her waist.

That simple touch sent a shiver through her.

"How high do you want to go?" he asked quietly.

Suddenly she was taken back to another night, when he'd asked the same question, though under very different circumstances. His clever fingers had been at play on the most sensitive parts of her body. It had been like standing on the edge of a cliff, wild with anticipation, a little desperate.

She answered him now, as she had then. "I want to touch the stars."

Then she felt the briefest brush of his lips against her neck, before he sent her soaring.

11

"Is it true you used to be an actress?" Sissy asked Heather as they sat on a park bench some minutes later savoring the pleasant evening temperature and the star-filled sky before going to Henrietta's. Judging from the girl's awestruck expression and hesitant tone, it was a question she'd been waiting days to work up the courage to ask, Todd concluded, drawing in a deep breath of the sweet air as he awaited Heather's reply.

Though it was nearly mid-June, it felt as if spring had just arrived in Whispering Wind. Todd tried to recall the last time he'd spent a relaxing evening outdoors like this in New York. He couldn't. Most nights he was either working late or dining out or simply too frazzled at the end of a long day.

"I'm still an actress," Heather said, obviously unwilling to suggest that she'd given up on the profession even temporarily.

Sissy looked confused. "But you're working at Henrietta's."

"That's just for the time being," Heather said. "I'll go back to New York one of these days, as soon as I take care of some business I have here."

Todd didn't like the way his stomach plummeted when she said the words. Maybe it was just because of that kiss days ago and that fleeting moment earlier when they'd reconnected in a way that had nothing to do with Angel and everything to do with the way things had once been between them—carefree and practically crackling with sparks. He knew she'd felt it, too. The awareness had been in her eyes when she'd stepped off the swing and turned to face him. Fire and passion had burned in her gaze, just as they must have in his.

"You're not going to stay in Whispering Wind?" Sissy asked accusingly, as if Heather was betraying her.

"Not forever, no. I have to go back to New York."

"Why?" Sissy demanded, her eyes suddenly bright with unshed tears.

There was no mistaking the attachment she had formed to Heather in a few short weeks. To a girl like Sissy, Heather must seem like some sort of exotic creature, just the way she had once seemed to him.

"Why do you have to go?" she asked in a voice that wobbled precariously.

"Because the acting jobs are in New York."

Apparently she, too, was aware of Sissy's distress, because she tried to distract her by announcing that Todd was an actor, too. For now, the ploy worked. Sissy's gaze widened with such astonishment it would have been insulting if Todd hadn't long since stopped thinking of himself as an actor.

"You are?" Sissy asked. "Like, a real one?"

"I was," he corrected her. "A long time ago."

"Not that long ago," Heather countered with a pointed glance, then confided, "He was good, too. Really good."

"Did you sing?" Sissy wanted to know, clearly fascinated. "Were you ever in one of those big Broadway musicals, like *Lion King* or something?"

"Just one musical, but it wasn't a big hit."

"Did you dance, too?"

"Not very well," he said ruefully. "I've got two left feet."

The comment snagged Will's attention. He stared solemnly at Todd's feet in the Italian loafers he favored over the local preference for cowboy boots. "It don't look like two left feet to me," the boy declared, looking puzzled. He stuck out his own feet, then gazed back and forth between his feet and Todd's. "Yours look just like mine, 'cept bigger."

Todd laughed and scooped him up. "It's an expression, slugger. It just means I wasn't a very good dancer."

"Show me," Sissy pleaded. "Do something you did in a play."

"I don't think so," Todd said.

"Oh, come on," Heather said, not helping him out at all. She was obviously enjoying this forced trek down memory lane. Or maybe she was just taking satisfaction in provoking him. "You used to thrive on performing before a live audience. It gave you the same adrenaline rush it gives me."

"But not in the middle of a park," he protested.

"Must not be able to remember his lines," Heather confided to Sissy in a stage whisper.

"You are not going to make me do this," he told her.

Angel chose that moment to give him a sleepy smile. "Please," she said. "Wanna hear."

Todd wanted to resist her, not just this second, but in general, but she was sneaking past his defenses. Between her and Heather, it was becoming clear that he needed to maintain a much tighter rein on his emotions. How was he supposed to protect them if he didn't?

"One song," Sissy pleaded.

His gaze met Heather's. "Only if you'll sing with me."

They had met when they both had second leads in one memorable show during its pre-Broadway engagement in Boston. They had done a duet in the second act, but it had been cut before the show reached Broadway. Todd heard it was because the leading actor had protested, through his agent, that the two of them were stealing the show. The producers had caved in, because they needed the star to keep the show's financial backers on board.

The musical had ultimately flopped, ironically because it lacked a real showstopper in the second act, according to one well-respected critic. It had hardly mattered to the two of them, because by then, just like their characters, they had fallen in love. No doubt that was what had made their performances so compelling, why audiences had loved them.

Though Sissy and Angel sat between them, Todd reached across the back of the bench to rest his hand on Heather's shoulder. Caught up in a sudden wave of nostalgia, he locked his gaze on hers and held it as he hummed the opening notes of the song. She regarded him with surprise.

"Okay, whatever," she finally relented, then launched into the opening bar of the love song.

He'd always thought she had a sweet, if not powerful, voice, and it rang out in the night air.

His lower tones blended with hers, teasing and taunting as the once-familiar words came back to him. In a gesture that had once come naturally, he stroked her cheek in a tender caress, then withdrew because it made him want more. Too much more.

When the final notes drifted away, he felt a sense of loss he couldn't explain. Was it the character's loss of a lover? Or the ending of a dream he had once shared with this woman? Was it because Heather had changed in ways he hadn't wanted to see? She was more responsible now, devoted to her daughter, the kind of woman he'd always thought he'd end up with, but with flashes of the impetuous, daredevil woman he'd loved.

He had no idea and there was no time to think about it, because Sissy, Will and Angel were applauding and laughing, keeping him very much in the present.

"Shouldn't you kiss her now?" Sissy asked hopefully. "I'll bet there was a kiss when you did it in the play."

There had been, but there was no way in hell Todd was going to willingly walk down that particular path again tonight. Too much nostalgia was a dangerous game.

"There was," Heather said with a teasing, dare-you glint in her eyes.

"Do it," Sissy begged, echoed by Will and Angel.

Todd was torn between his own suddenly rampaging hormones and reason. He told himself he could have ignored the challenge in Heather's eyes, listened instead to his head, but Sissy so obviously craved a happy ending he had no choice but to do as she asked.

It wasn't as if it could turn wildly passionate the way their earlier kisses had. The kids were right here, snuggled between them. It would be no more than a peck to satisfy a girl's yearning for evidence that sweet romance did exist, contrary to all the violence and heartache she had witnessed in her young life.

Todd leaned forward, brushed his lips across Heather's and retreated.

"Oh, yuck," Will declared, even though he'd been one of those clamoring for just such a kiss.

"You are such a *boy,*" Sissy countered, as if that were the worst insult she could think of. "It was beautiful."

Safe was the word Todd would have used to describe it. He gathered from the amusement lurking in Heather's eyes that she thought the same thing.

"Okay, show's over," she declared, letting him off the hook, anyway. "Let's get everybody home and in bed."

Todd suddenly experienced a flash of inexplicable longing so intense it rocked him. Surely he didn't want to have more nights like this, nights reminiscent of his own childhood before his world had turned upside down, nights when he and his parents had been close and the air had rung with shared laughter.

Despite the mental denial, his mind experimented with the vision. He imagined going home with Heather, taking Angel and the other children they would have up to their beds and tucking them in. It was so real he could almost feel their arms around his neck, their sticky kisses on his cheek.

Then he crashed into reality. It wasn't going to happen. Not ever. If he had to remind himself of the risks a thousand times a day, he would. If he didn't, his father certainly would on one of those rare occasions when Todd spoke to him. Accepting that, he forced the tempting images from his head, picked Will up and started toward Henrietta's, not even waiting for Heather, Sissy and Angel to catch up.

He'd gone a whole block before he finally slowed to wait for them. He glanced at Heather, saw the questions in her eyes, but ignored them with the mental excuse that they could hardly discuss his thoughts with Sissy, at least, listening avidly to every word.

Something told him, though, that Heather wouldn't let the matter rest.

Fortunately she was distracted by the appearance of the judge out on Henrietta's porch. Though he was partly hidden by the shrubbery, it was possible to see him holding out his hand. Henrietta placed her hand in his, rose slowly from the porch swing and took a step toward him. As she neared, he bent down and touched her lips with his in a tender gesture not unlike the kiss Todd had just shared with Heather.

"Thank you for a lovely evening," the judge said, his words carrying to where Todd and Heather stood frozen in place with the silently gaping children. "I'll look forward to another one."

"We'll see," she said, sounding as tart as ever.

"You're not going to give an inch, are you, Henrietta?" the judge asked.

Todd could hear the amused exasperation in his voice. He could also imagine the smile that Henrietta would find equally annoying.

"If I give an inch, you'll take a mile, same as always," she retorted.

"Would that be so bad?"

She hesitated for so long Todd thought maybe she wasn't going to answer, but then she said with apparent reluctance, "No, I suppose it wouldn't."

As if she'd granted him a long-withheld reprieve, the judge's arms went around her and he twirled her in circles until she was giddy with laughter.

"Stop it, you old fool!"

"Only if you'll agree to have Sunday dinner with me in Laramie this weekend."

"You're pushing your luck, old man."

"Henrietta," he chided.

"How can I? The restaurant—"

"Heather can handle it, I'm sure."

"The children—"

"Can come along," he said at once. "They'll enjoy a change of scenery."

"You wouldn't mind?" she asked, clearly skeptical.

"Why would I mind? They're wonderful children and they matter to you."

Henrietta reached up, hesitated, then rested her hand against his cheek. "Thank you for saying that. We would love to have dinner with you this weekend."

"Sunday, then."

"Sunday," she echoed as if she couldn't quite believe she'd agreed.

The judge strolled off whistling, still unaware of his audience.

"You can come out of the shadows now," Henrietta said dryly when he was some distance away. "I suppose you all got yourselves an earful."

"We didn't mean to eavesdrop," Heather apologized. "We just didn't want to interrupt."

"I can see why that would bother you since you went to so much trouble to set the whole thing up," she said, then glanced at Todd. "I suppose you were in on it, too."

"Don't look at me. I'm a totally innocent bystander. I had no clue what was going on until after you'd left work. I just got roped into the ice-cream excursion."

"Did you have a nice dinner?" Heather asked anxiously.

"Not as good as my own cooking, but nice enough. Did you know he remembered that I liked Chinese?"

Heather grinned. "He mentioned that."

"Wonder what else he remembers?" Henrietta murmured, more to herself than to either of them. Then she caught sight of Will sound asleep in Todd's arms.

"My goodness, what am I thinking? I have to get these two up to bed. It's way past their bedtime." She reached for Will.

"I'll carry him up," Todd volunteered. He glanced at Heather. "You'll wait? I'll take Angel and walk you home."

"I'll wait," she said, settling into the porch swing with her sleepy daughter cradled in her arms.

Todd followed Henrietta and Sissy up the stairs, then deposited the still-sleeping boy in his bed. He would have turned and gone, but Henrietta snagged his arm.

"How was your evening?"

"Fine."

"That's it? Fine? What kind of an answer is that?"

"An honest one."

She shook her head. "At this rate, it will take the two of you longer to get together than it has the judge and me."

"Henrietta, there's nothing in the cards for Heather and me."

"Then you're a damned fool. The woman's crazy about you. And you share a daughter. If that's not enough for a starting point, I don't know what is."

"Henrietta . . ." he began in a tone warning her to steer clear of this particular topic.

"Don't waste your breath, young man. I know what I'm talking about. Now, you think long and hard before you turn your back on Heather and that little girl. Believe me, nobody knows more about regrets than I do."

Todd couldn't argue with her. Thanks to a long-ago tragedy, he'd been living with regrets for most of his life. He knew better than most that the ones he'd have if Heather left were nothing compared to the ones he might have to face if she and Angel stayed and he took a chance on becoming a part of their lives.

Todd's mood was bleak when he came back downstairs from carrying the little boy to bed. Heather cast surreptitious glances at him all the way back to her apartment. Finally she couldn't stand it any longer.

"Okay, spill it," she demanded. "What happened while you were upstairs with Henrietta?"

"Nothing," he said tersely.

"Don't tell me that. You were cheerful enough

when you carried Will up those stairs. Now you look as if you've just lost your best friend."

He turned his head slightly, looked over Angel's head, which rested on his shoulder, and asked, "Isn't that what's about to happen? You said it yourself, you're going back to New York anytime now."

She blinked in confusion. "Wait a minute. I thought you wanted me to go. In fact, you've all but offered to pack my bags and drive me to the airport."

"True," he admitted, "because it's for the best. That doesn't mean I have to like it."

"Whose best?" Suddenly she recalled the way he'd phrased his distress a moment earlier, the admission he'd all but verbalized. "Are you saying that despite everything, you still think of me as your best friend?"

"You were once," he conceded.

"I could be again," she said, trying not to sound too eager. "I want that, for Angel's sake, if not for ours. I want us to get along, Todd, the way we used to."

"Darlin', we can't go back to the way it was. Too much has happened. Besides, your life is in New York. Mine's here."

His attempt to simplify their differences in such a way totally exasperated her. "That's a cop-out and you know it. This isn't about the two of us being geographically unsuitable. We could make it work if we wanted to. Your life was in New York once. It could be again."

She waved him off impatiently when he started to respond. "Besides, this isn't even about striking up some hot romance between us again. It's about our daughter and what's best for her."

"I agree," he said.

She stared at him in surprise. "You do?"

"Of course I do. Which is why it's even more important for you to go back to New York now. Make this break before she finds out who I am and develops an attachment to me."

A knot formed in her stomach. "Obviously, we still disagree about what's best for Angel."

"She needs a mother who's not struggling financially, who's working at a profession she loves. She needs to be able to go to a good private school when the time comes and have a nanny in the meantime. I can give her all of those things," he said.

"You forgot one thing," Heather retorted.

"Name it."

"You, Todd. She needs her father."

"She doesn't need me," he insisted. "You'll meet another man one of these days who'll be the father she needs."

"And that wouldn't bother you at all, knowing that your little girl thinks of another man as her daddy?"

A flash of something that might have been pain

flitted across his face, then was gone, replaced by that stoic expression she had come to detest.

"It's for the best," he said. "Name any amount you want and we'll settle this right now before things get too complicated."

She regarded him furiously. "Is that what Angel is to you, a complication? An inconvenience? Write a check and it'll go away?"

"That's not what I said."

"Well, it sure as hell sounded like it to me. She's a child, Todd, your child. She's a wonderful little girl, and you're missing out on one of the greatest joys there is. What I don't understand is why you're being so stubborn about this. Is it because I didn't tell you years ago when I first found out I was pregnant? Are you taking it out on her because you're angry at me?"

"Don't be ridiculous. This isn't some childish game of revenge."

"You could have fooled me."

"Dammit, Heather, I am trying to do what's right. I am trying to protect Angel in the only way I know how."

"Protect her," she echoed, startled by the fierce conviction in his voice. It was evident he believed what he was saying. "From what?"

"From me," he said bluntly, then whirled around as if he feared saying more and left.

Stunned, Heather stared after him. What had he meant by that cryptic remark? How on earth could he possibly see himself as a danger to their child? What kind of threat did he think he posed? She knew Todd as well as she knew anyone on the face of the earth. She knew with every fiber of her being that he would never harm a living, breathing soul.

Maybe it didn't matter what she thought, though. It only mattered that he believed it, and until she knew why, nothing would change. That was another thing she knew about Todd: he was a man of his word. Ironically, just this once, she wished that wasn't so.

12

"How are things going between you and Todd?" Jake asked when he stopped by the diner for coffee late the next afternoon.

"Not good," Heather said, wondering if she should tell Jake what Todd had said the night before about perceiving himself as a danger to Angel. Maybe she'd made too much of it, but then again, it was clear that Todd was taking the claim to heart. If there really was some danger, how could she ignore it?

She gave herself a mental shake. No, it was ridiculous to think of Todd as anything other than the kind, gentle man she'd always known him to be.

When she didn't respond, Jake regarded her worriedly. "Okay, sit," he ordered finally, gesturing to the seat opposite him. When she glanced around, he added, "There's not another soul in here. You can take a break."

Once she was seated, he leaned back and waited. Heather concluded it was a technique designed to make a client eventually start babbling just to end the silence. She was as susceptible to it as the next person.

"Maybe I shouldn't get into this with you," she began.

"I'm your attorney, even if you do have me on a short leash at the moment. You can tell me anything, then we'll both decide if there's any action required. Has Todd said or done something?"

"His position hasn't changed," she admitted. "He wants the two of us gone. But last night he said something . . ."

"What?" Jake prodded when she didn't finish.

She took a deep breath, then said, "He's worried that he might put Angel in some kind of danger."

Jake's reaction was as stunned as her own had been. "Todd? You've got to be kidding."

"That was my reaction, but, Jake, he clearly believes it. What if there *is* something?"

"Such as? Did you ask him what he was talking about?"

"I couldn't. He left as soon as the words were

out of his mouth, and I was too startled to go after him."

"I suppose I could do some checking," he began, but Heather cut him off, horrified by the idea of an investigator putting the most decent man she knew under some sort of a microscope.

"No, absolutely not," she said adamantly, already regretting mentioning the incident. "I don't want you to hire someone to go digging around in Todd's past."

"But if what he said has any truth in it . . ."

"I said no. I'll get to the bottom of it. Maybe he's just worrying about nothing. A lot of new fathers think they're going to be totally inept." She regarded him knowingly. "I can think of one in particular who's obsessing over everything and the baby's not even here yet."

Jake clearly recognized the description. "No point in leaving anything to chance," he said, not the least bit chastened. "Okay, I won't do anything unless you say the word. I have to admit, I can't imagine it being anything serious where Todd's concerned. I'd bet the ranch that he's a good guy."

Heather smiled at the conviction in his voice. "I would, too."

Still, as the day went on, she couldn't shake the feeling that, real or imagined, there was something behind Todd's fear. She believed in him completely, knew exactly what kind of a father he could be, but it was evident he didn't share that faith.

She watched for him all during the dinner hour, but he didn't put in an appearance. She was disappointed but not surprised. How many men would make such a revelation, then come back to face the obvious barrage of questions likely to follow? But that didn't mean she couldn't go to him.

Just as Henrietta was about to leave for the night, Heather asked, "Could you do me a huge favor? I hate to even ask, but—"

"Don't beat around the bush, girl. Just ask."

"Could you keep Angel for an hour or so? There's something I need to do as soon as I close up here."

Henrietta studied her intently. "If it's important, don't put it off. Go now. I'll close up, and of course I'll keep Angel. She's no trouble at all. You can pick her up at my place when you're done." She regarded her knowingly. "If it gets to be too late, just call. She can spend the night."

"It won't be late," Heather insisted, despite the color that Henrietta's suggestion put in her cheeks.

"Whatever. Just give me a call so I don't wait up."

Heather gave her a kiss on the cheek. "Thanks. You're a saint."

Henrietta laughed. "There are some who'd disagree with that."

"Not anyone who knows you," Heather said, taking off her apron and hanging it on a hook behind the kitchen door. "I'll call if anything changes."

Not that she expected it to. It was too much to hope that Todd was going to let down his guard, especially if she started the encounter by challenging him on his parting words of the night before.

When she got to his apartment, it was dusk, but there were no lights on inside. Nor did she spot that rugged pickup he drove to work. Judging it a wasted trip, she was about to leave when one of his neighbors arrived home, a young woman who did accounting work for Henrietta and stopped by the diner from time to time.

"Are you looking for Todd?" Rachel asked.

Heather nodded. "Have you seen him?"

"Not more than five minutes ago, he was sitting across from me at the pizza place. That's where I left him."

Heather wasn't quite sure what to make of that. Apparently the woman read her mind.

"We weren't together, if that's what you're thinking. We just ran into each other. He looked as if he needed company, so I joined him. Turned out the only company he really wanted was a bottle of beer."

Heather gaped. "Todd was drinking?"

Todd never drank, or at least only rarely. Once

in a long while he'd have a glass of wine with dinner if they were celebrating something, but otherwise he never touched alcohol. Since they hadn't had money to waste on it, anyway, she'd never questioned the fact that she almost never saw him drink. This woman was obviously suggesting that he was doing more than having a single beer with his pizza.

"Drowning his sorrows, I'd say." Rachel shook her head. "It surprised me, too. I tried to give him a ride home, but he said he wasn't ready to leave, said he wasn't numb enough."

Heather couldn't decide whether to be shocked or worried. Either way, she had a feeling she was somehow responsible. Her mind racing, she gave Rachel a vague smile. "Thanks. I'll check on him."

"He won't thank you for it," she warned. "He got downright testy with me."

"I'll handle it," Heather told her. "You handle enough surly customers, 'testy' gets to be a breeze."

The woman laughed. "Good luck, then."

Heather wished she felt as confident as she'd sounded. This was a wrinkle she definitely hadn't anticipated when she'd set off to find Todd tonight.

She found him tucked into a booth with a half-eaten pizza in front of him and a row of empty beer bottles lined up on the table. He gazed at her with bleary eyes, tried to muster up a fierce expression, but failed miserably. She settled into the booth opposite him.

"Don't you make a pretty picture," she observed. "Any particular reason you decided to tie one on?"

He frowned. "You just walked in. You saying I'm drunk?"

"I don't know. Are you?"

"Not yet, but I'm working on it." He waved over the waitress. "Another one and something for my friend here. You want a beer, darlin'?"

"I think there's been enough beer served here. How about coffee?" she suggested instead. "Two coffees."

"Not for me," Todd protested. "Never touch the stuff."

Heather rolled her eyes, then gestured for the waitress to bring the coffee, anyway. "One with cream."

After the woman had brought the coffee, Heather leveled a look straight into Todd's eyes. "Care to tell me what's going on?"

"Nothing going on," he said. "Just having an evening on the town."

"Must not be that much fun. You've already scared off one woman."

He squinted at her in apparent confusion. "I did?"

"Your neighbor," she reminded him. "Rachel."

"Oh, yeah. Said she had to go."

Heather wondered if she could use his muddled state to her advantage and get some answers he might be unwilling to share if he was stone-cold sober.

"Todd—" she began, but he reached across the table just then and grasped her hand, lifted it to his lips and kissed it.

"You're beautiful, you know that?"

"Thanks. Todd, I—"

"Why'd you go away, Heather?"

Despite his earnest tone, she doubted he was interested in a serious discussion of the past.

"We had a disagreement," she reminded him. "It's not important now. I'm more interested in what's going on with you tonight."

"Just having a couple of beers," he replied. "No big deal."

"It's more than a couple and it is a big deal. It's not like you to run away from your problems, not like this."

"Is that what you think I'm doing? Running away?"

"Aren't you?"

"Can't run from this," he said, his expression sad. "Stays with me all the time."

He sounded so despondent her heart ached for him. "What stays with you?"

He shook his head. "Can't talk about it. Too tired." Still holding her hand, he put his head down on the table and, practically before she could blink, fell soundly asleep. She spotted his car keys on the table and confiscated them.

"Now what?" Heather murmured just as the waitress returned to see if they needed refills on the coffee. Todd's first cup was still untouched.

"Too late, I see," she said sympathetically. "I can get the bartender to help you get him to your car if you like."

"If you don't mind, let's let him rest right here a few minutes. Then I'll try to wake him up enough to get some coffee into him."

"Fine by me. Just holler if you need some help."

When she'd gone, Heather sipped her coffee and studied the man across from her. There had been no mistaking the pain in his voice a few minutes ago. Something was weighing heavily on his mind, something he'd been desperate enough to forget that it had brought him here tonight.

She thought again of Jake's offer to look into Todd's past, but recoiled from the idea. Whatever was torturing Todd, she wanted him to tell her himself. She listened to his steady, even breathing and concluded that whatever the answer was, she wouldn't hear it tonight. The best she could hope for was to get him home in one piece.

She reached across the table and brushed a lock of hair back from his face. His brown hair was longer now than it had been in New York, where he'd taken pride in maintaining a starched, preppy look, complete with glasses she knew for a fact he hadn't really needed. It was as if he'd carved out a role for himself and made himself over to fit it. She thought maybe she liked this look better. It made him seem more accessible, which was ironic since he seemed dead-set on making himself as inaccessible as possible.

Her fingers strayed to his cheek, where stubble darkened his skin. That was new, too. The Todd of old shaved twice a day to maintain his clean-cut image. Maybe he was slowly conforming to the different standards of the rough-and-tumble West.

Of course, the new look faltered a little when she got to his shirt. It was still a designer dress shirt in a blend of silk and cotton. If his sleeves hadn't been rolled up, she was pretty sure she would have found his monogram on the cuffs. Todd was only likely to bend his sense of style so far to blend into his new surroundings.

She hadn't realized she was stroking his cheek until he awoke suddenly, blinked, then covered her hand with his.

"What's going on?" he murmured. "Where'd you come from?"

She smiled. "I've been here for a while, chum. Do you have any idea where you are?"

"Of course I do," he claimed indignantly. "Right here, with you."

"And here would be?"

He lifted his head, did a slow survey of the room, then groaned. "Please tell me I did not crash in a restaurant."

"Sorry. No can do. You've been out like a light

for the past fifteen minutes, and we are definitely in a restaurant."

He straightened gingerly, then caught sight of the empty beer bottles. "Mine?"

"Every one of them."

"No wonder my head is pounding."

"Offhand, I'd say it's going to get worse before it gets better. Want some coffee?"

She slid the cup in front of him. He reached for it eagerly, took a long swallow, then sighed.

"Care to explain what brought this on?" she asked for the second time.

He started to shake his head, then clutched it as if he feared it might fall off. "No," he said tightly.

"It's not like you."

"How do you know? You haven't been around for years. Maybe I've changed."

She met his gaze evenly. "Have you?"

He returned the look with a surprising touch of defiance for a man whose head probably ached like the very dickens, but eventually his gaze slid away.

"Have you?" she persisted.

"Time doesn't stand still, Heather."

She chuckled at this bit of philosophy. "That is the most pathetic attempt to evade a question I've ever heard."

"What do you expect? I'm not myself."

She grinned at that. "I rest my case."

He blinked at her triumphant tone. "Huh?"

"You just admitted that this isn't exactly a nightly or, I suspect, even a yearly occurrence."

"I did?"

She shook her head. "If Megan could see you now, she might question why she ever hired you. You're not exactly quick on your feet, mentally speaking."

He scowled at her, then took another slug of coffee. "You're enjoying this, aren't you?"

"As a matter of fact, I do find it rather encouraging to discover that you're not perfect. Not that I'd be thrilled if you decided to make a habit of this."

"Would you take Angel and go away if I did?" he inquired with a faint trace of hopefulness.

"Todd, I am not going to be responsible for driving you to drink, even temporarily. Besides, you can't get rid of me and Angel that easily. It's going to take some heavy-duty negotiating and a lot of compromises." She leaned forward and propped her chin on her hand. "Want to start now? Something tells me you'll agree to just about anything tonight just to get me to shut up."

"I may be slightly drunk—"

"Slightly?"

"Okay, a lot drunk, but I am not stupid. I am not negotiating anything while I'm in this state."

"Then let's go back to my original question— why are you in this state?"

"Because life's a bitch."

"That ranks up there pretty close to the 'time not standing still' line. You're going to have to do better than that."

"Not tonight." He struggled to his feet. "I'm going home."

He wobbled, then sank back down. "In a minute."

"Have some more coffee. When you're a little steadier, I'll drive you."

He shook his head. "Don't want you to. You'll just keep pestering me for answers."

"True, but it's a long way home and I don't think you're in any shape to walk it."

"Give me a few minutes. I'll be sober enough to drive myself."

"I don't think so. Not anytime tonight, anyway."

He frowned. "You going to stop me?"

"Yep."

"How?"

She dangled his keys in front of him, then in a provocative gesture of defiance slipped them in the front of her blouse. The metal was cold against her breasts, but she figured they were safe enough there. Even in his inebriated state Todd would think long and hard before venturing after them. Unfortunate, she thought with a twinge of real regret, but true.

To her surprise, he peered at her with a suddenly fascinated expression. "Do you really think that would stop me? Seems to me like you just upped the ante."

The amusement in his voice made her a little less certain. "You wouldn't dare."

He beckoned to her. "Let's go outside and see."

A shiver of anticipation danced down her spine. "I don't think so."

"We have to go out eventually if you're going to take me home," he pointed out.

"And then what? You're going to pounce on me, wrestle me to the ground and steal back your keys?"

"Maybe."

"I'd like to see you try."

A grin spread across his face. "Would you really?"

That shiver turned into a blast of heat. There had been a time when teasing like this would have led directly to bed. Sometimes, they hadn't even made it to a bed. They'd tumbled onto the sofa or the floor, or—on one memorable occasion —onto a blanket on the sand.

"Todd," she began in a choked voice, prepared to warn him off, to remind him that this wasn't the time or the place or the circumstances.

"Yes, Heather," he said so soberly she had to wonder if the coffee had truly kicked in with a vengeance or if he was just displaying that masterful acting skill of his.

"Don't mess with my head," she said quietly.

He seemed startled by the request with its edge of desperation. "Is that what I'm doing?"

She nodded. "You're sending out so many mixed signals it could cause a train wreck. You've told me a thousand and one times we can't go back to the way things were. I believe you mean it. I can even accept it, but not if you're going to say things like that or look at me like that."

"Like what?"

"As if you'd like to strip me of my clothes right here and now."

"Now, there's an image designed to bring me to my senses," he said wryly.

"You started it," she reminded him, then regarded him intently. "Todd, there is going to be no stripping."

"If you say so," he said agreeably.

Perplexed by his attitude, she asked, "Are you saying that you want to get me out of my clothes?"

"I'm a healthy male. You're a sexy female. Of course I want to. That doesn't mean I can't control my hormones. Been showing admirable restraint ever since you hit town, haven't I?"

Now, there was news. He had definitely been very good at hiding any evidence that he wanted her. "Good," she told him approvingly, though she didn't think it was good at all. Her body was all but vibrating with need. Every nerve ending was alive. If he had so much as skimmed a finger across her knuckles, she would probably have thrown herself across the table and straight into his arms.

Because she was so blasted ready for anything, she made herself look straight into his eyes. "That settles that, then. We'll leave here. You will make no attempt to steal back your car keys. I will drive you home and we'll say good-night politely in the parking lot. Agreed?"

He laughed. "Since when did you turn into such a planner? I thought you were the spontaneous, unpredictable one."

"Usually I pride myself on it," she said. "But when you're around that seems to buy me nothing but trouble. I've decided to reform."

His gaze locked with hers. "Bet you can't."

"Of course I can," she replied indignantly. "I can do anything I set my mind to."

"We'll see," he said.

The challenging tone set her teeth on edge. He stood up more steadily this time and held out his hand. She ignored it and stood up, too, maintaining a careful distance between them. She wasn't allowing him within an inch of any part of her anatomy. Too risky. She might have reformed —very recently—but she was no saint. And Todd's touch right now, no matter how innocent, would be like dousing a fire with gasoline.

Outside, he dutifully followed her to her rental car, climbed into the passenger seat and buckled up. So far, so good, she thought.

He continued to behave himself all the way to his small apartment complex, but when she pulled up beside the building and would have left the engine running, he reached over and turned off the ignition.

"Todd," she warned, swallowing hard as he leaned in her direction.

"Yes, Heather."

"We agreed . . ."

He shook his head. "I didn't agree to anything. Now, if you don't mind, I think I'll just get my keys back."

Her breath caught in her throat. His fingers brushed the curve of her breast before she could bat his hand away. Her nipple instantly tightened in response.

"I'll get them," she said, her voice uneven.

His gaze met hers. "Let me," he said quietly.

She thought she shook her head, but he must not have seen it, or else he simply chose to ignore it. The pad of his thumb grazed her skin. If she thought for a single second this was actually about the blasted car keys, he quickly disabused her of that notion. With a frown of concentration knitting his brow, he traced the curve of her breast at the opening of her blouse, then undid the top button to give him even easier access. Her breath snagged, cutting off the protest that had formed in her mind, but never made it past her lips.

The front clasp on her bra came undone with no effort at all and the keys spilled into her lap. Todd ignored them as his gaze feasted on the sight of her bared breasts, which were responding as if he'd been caressing them. One touch, one faint whisper of a touch, and she knew she'd come completely undone.

"Todd," she murmured, part command, but mostly plea.

His mouth—moist, hot, wildly clever—surrounded one aching peak, sending shock waves ricocheting through her. Her back arched and he deepened the suckling until delicious spasms of pleasure made her wonder why she'd ever protested against anything so wonderful.

"You are—" he moved to the other breast, his tongue circling the nipple until it was swollen and sensitive "—incredible."

"Sweet heaven," she whispered on another breathless gasp.

Then, just when she was ready and willing to go along with anything he asked, he backed away. He hooked her bra, then closed her blouse, each movement jerky but deliberate as if he was struggling with himself. His expression had turned stoic.

"Todd—" she began.

"Go home, Heather," he said, his voice harsh. The longing in his eyes took the edge off, but there was no mistaking his determination.

Shaken, she simply nodded, then clutched the steering wheel tightly while he nabbed those damn keys and exited the car. He stuck his head back in the window as she fumbled to restart the engine.

"You're okay to drive?"

The question, given the reason she was behind the wheel in the first place, might have been funny, if she wasn't feeling so thoroughly unsettled.

"I'll manage," she told him. "How will you get into town in the morning to pick up your car?"

"I'll hitch a ride in with Rachel."

Heather nodded, then shifted into gear. He backed off as she hit the accelerator, lurched forward, then hit the brakes. *Calm down,* she silently instructed herself.

The next time she stepped on the accelerator, she moved smoothly out onto the street. She pulled off what she considered a jaunty wave in the direction of the man who still stood watching her.

Though she was satisfied that she had managed the departure without any further evidence of her inner turmoil, she had a hunch it was going to be a long, long time before she could follow her own advice and truly calm down. Tonight's test of wills had sparked desires she thought might take a lifetime to quench.

13

Wanting Heather was settling into Todd's routine as regularly as his morning cup of coffee or his 10:00 a.m. meeting with Megan. He woke up in a state of arousal, directly attributable to the dreams he'd been having about her, dreams that resurrected the first days of their wildly uninhibited infatuation. He detoured past Henrietta's just to catch a glimpse of her. He explained a hundred times a day—to himself and to the ever-curious Megan—that he was no longer the least bit interested in Heather, that this was some temporary aberration caused by his lack of a love life.

He grumbled as much to Jake, when he saw him a few days after that fateful encounter with Heather. "Is it any wonder Heather looks so blasted good to me? Oh, well, when she goes away . . ."

Jake regarded him unsympathetically. "She's not going anywhere, Todd, not until you resolve this custody issue. Frankly, I'll be just as relieved when you do, because Megan's fretting and pestering me for answers I don't have or can't give. I don't want her worrying. It's—"

"Not good for her or the baby," Todd interrupted, automatically completing the thought with the refrain he'd heard at least a million times.

Leaning back in his chair, he regarded Jake glumly. "How do you resolve something like that with a woman who won't listen to reason?"

"Get a lawyer and haggle it out in court," Jake suggested.

Todd knew that was the logical thing to do, but his distrust of lawyers was deep-rooted. They'd circled like vultures years ago. Putting a price tag on tragedy had just added to the strain his parents were already facing.

"No," he said vehemently. "It will just get more complicated."

"How?" Jake asked. "How could it possibly get any more complicated than it already is? Look, I'm in no position to advise you, except to tell you that getting your own lawyer would be the smart thing to do. You need somebody objective in your corner. I can't begin to understand where you're coming from, probably couldn't even if it were ethical for you to explain it to me. Looks to me as if you've just been handed one of God's greatest gifts, but then again, I've always wanted kids."

"No kidding," Todd said dryly. "You mean you're excited about this baby Megan is carrying?"

"Wiseass," Jake muttered.

Todd didn't let up. "Wasn't that you I saw carting an armload of baby books home from the library the other day?"

Jake frowned. "It's important to be prepared."

"You're not just going to be prepared. You're

going to be ready for a degree in pediatrics."

Unperturbed, Jake merely said, "We're getting away from the point here."

"Which is?"

"Angel. How can you look at that little girl and not want to be a part of her life?"

Todd sighed. Jake was right about one thing. When he thought of kids in the abstract, it was easy enough to say he wanted no part of them, easy enough to give in to the raw fear that just being in the same room with a small child instilled in him. But when he put a face to it, a sweet little face smeared with chocolate ice cream or orange Popsicle, it was a whole lot harder to do.

He picked up a proposal for the new cooking show he'd been hammering out with Peggy for the past couple of weeks. She'd come up with some intriguing ideas he'd promised to consider. "I've got work to do," he said, hoping his brusque tone would send Jake away.

Of course, the man hadn't won over Megan without possessing a healthy trait of persistence. He didn't budge. He just sat there and waited until Todd finally glanced up again and met his gaze.

"You're not the kind of man who can turn his back on his own daughter," Jake said quietly. "If you do, you'll regret it the rest of your life."

He didn't wait for Todd's response to that. He left the office with the observation still hanging in the air. Todd muttered a harsh expletive he rarely used, then tried to force his attention back to the proposal in front of him. The words swam on the page.

"Damn it all to hell," he muttered, tossing the proposal aside and grabbing his jacket on his way out of the office. He had to put a stop to this. He'd never allowed any problem to fester, never allowed anything to interfere with his work.

Until now.

He wasn't certain exactly where he was headed until he found himself pounding on the door of the apartment above the Starlight Diner. He made quite a commotion, but he got no response for his efforts. He finally sank down on the top step and tried to decide what to do next.

A moment later, Sissy crept up the steps and sat down hesitantly beside him, not breathing a word.

"Hi," Todd said eventually.

"Hi." She regarded him shyly. "I heard you knocking."

"I imagine the entire block heard me knocking." In fact, he'd been half-surprised that Henrietta hadn't charged out and told him to cut out the racket.

"Heather's not home," Sissy said.

"So I gathered."

"She's probably in the park with Angel," she told him helpfully. "They go every morning."

That was news to him. It sounded an awful lot like a routine, which must be something new for

Heather. She'd always done her level best to avoid anything at all that smacked of sameness. It was just another sign that she'd changed.

"Sometimes I go with them," Sissy added.

"But not today," he noted. "How come?"

"I gotta see my shrink," she told him matter-of-factly. "Henrietta's gonna take me in a little while."

Todd knew all about the psychologist who was helping Sissy to deal with the trauma of her parents' deaths. He'd never put much stock in the idea of talking things over with a total stranger, but in Sissy's case he could see why it would be important. She must have all sorts of conflicting emotions churning inside her that would be too much for a ten-year-old to sort out alone.

"Is the shrink helping?" he asked, since she seemed comfortable enough mentioning the sessions. He knew that Henrietta thought it was important that Sissy not be made to feel that there was anything wrong with seeing a psychologist.

She nodded. "It's easier to talk to him than it is to somebody around here. He just listens to me, you know? He didn't know my mom or my dad. Henrietta's been real good to me, but she hated my dad for what he did to my mom, so I can't talk to her about loving my dad. She gets real quiet and sad. And my grandmother blames my mom for everything that happened. She says it was her fault my dad went crazy." She gave Todd a plaintive look. "How could it be her fault that he shot her?"

"It wasn't," Todd said, as sure of that as he was of anything. Domestic violence was never that simple.

Sissy nodded. "That's what the shrink says, too."

Todd began to see why Jake wanted him to have an unbiased third party intercede in his case. Maybe it would give him some comfort to have an outsider tell him that what he was feeling wasn't just selfishness. Maybe what he needed wasn't a lawyer, but a shrink. Keeping silent about the past had gotten him nothing but criticism from everyone he knew, but he hadn't wanted to air his secret.

But just the thought of confiding in anyone, even a stranger, made him feel sick and ashamed, just the way he had years ago, just the way he did every time his father reminded him what a no-good, lousy son he was.

So he would work out this problem, just as he handled everything else in his life, by tightly controlling the circumstances in a way that precluded any messy emotions. That brought him straight back to Heather, who churned up a whole bundle of messy emotions just by existing.

He glanced up and spotted the woman in question strolling down the street in her trademark flowing skirt, strappy shoes, gauzy blouse and bangle bracelets. Her hair was a riot of flyaway curls that he instinctively wanted to untangle and tidy up, just like their disorderly relationship. In this town that prided itself on down-to-earth people and a no-nonsense lifestyle, she was like a rare species of orchid.

"Isn't she the most beautiful lady you ever saw?" Sissy asked in a faintly awestruck tone. "I hope I'll be that pretty someday."

"You are going to be gorgeous," Todd assured her.

"Do you think I could be an actress?" she asked, regarding him hopefully. "Like Heather?"

"I think you can be anything you want to be. Why do you want to be an actress?"

"Because then you can be somebody else, at least for a little while," Sissy said in a tone that came very close to breaking his heart.

Impulsively, Todd gave the girl a hug. "Don't be so anxious to be somebody else, darlin'. I think you're pretty special just being you."

She gave him a shy smile, then dashed off to meet Heather. He couldn't hear what she said, but Heather's gaze suddenly shot in his direction. So did Angel's. As had become her habit, Angel broke free of her mother's grip and ran toward him, oblivious to everything else.

It all happened in the blink of an eye. One instant she was calling out his name with innocent glee and the next there was a squeal of tires and a thump, then a terrible, terrible silence.

For an instant Todd couldn't move, couldn't

think. He was plunged back into the past. Not again, he pleaded with God. Not again!

Then, heart pounding, he made himself move. He dashed down the steps, reaching Angel at the same time Heather did.

The driver of the car, an elderly woman who was so short she could barely see over the dash, got out and started around the car, then hesitated, all the color draining from her face.

Henrietta, who'd come running from the diner along with several of the customers, cast a frantic look at Angel, then urged the woman back into the car. She sent someone inside to call for help and bring back a glass of water for the driver.

Todd knelt beside Heather, whose complexion had gone ashen. Angel looked so tiny lying there, so fragile, but there was no blood, not even a scratch. He picked up her tiny wrist and felt for a pulse, relieved when he felt the steady beat.

"I've sent for the doctor," Henrietta said, leaning over his shoulder. "How is she?"

"Unconscious," Heather whispered, her voice choked. "Dear God, my baby . . ."

Todd pushed aside his own panic to put his arm around Heather. "She's going to be fine," he said, forcing a note of conviction into his voice. He'd have her flown to the best medical center in the country, if necessary. "Her pulse is strong and steady."

Keeping Heather calm, preventing her from

scooping Angel into her arms and risking further injury as they waited for the doctor required all his attention. He stroked her cheek, then Angel's, murmuring reassurances meant for both of them. The part of him that stayed cool in a crisis surfaced, blocking the emotional agony of seeing his little girl lying there so still and silent, blocking out the flood of memories of another little girl, another accident.

Only when the doctor arrived and shooed them both out of the way to examine Angel did the panic and self-recriminations kick in. She had been running to him, he reminded himself with a sick sensation in the pit of his stomach. It was all happening again, proof positive that he couldn't be trusted with a child's well-being.

Heather clung to his hand so tightly she was cutting off circulation.

"She'll be all right," he soothed, pushing aside his own anxiety and stroking her knuckles until she eased her grip.

"Then why isn't she awake? What if she has a fractured skull? What if there's brain damage?"

"Whoa," Todd said, touching a finger to her lips to silence her. He was quaking enough inside without listening to such wild speculation. "Let's not leap to any conclusions. It's probably nothing more than a concussion. The car wasn't going very fast. It doesn't look like any bones are broken. She probably just hit her head when she fell."

"She's waking up!" Henrietta called.

Heather dashed to the doctor's side and knelt down. "Hi, baby. How're you doing?"

Again Todd hunkered down next to Heather, relieved when he saw Angel blink in confusion, then finally focus on him. "Hiya, Todd."

"Hey, sweetheart. How are you feeling?"

"Head hurts," she whimpered, as tears suddenly pooled in her eyes. She reached out her arms, not for her mother, but for him.

Todd glanced at the doctor. "Is it okay?"

The man nodded. "I'd like to get her to the hospital in Laramie for a CAT scan, but I think her only problem is a mild concussion. Go ahead and hold her. It'll keep her calm."

Todd picked Angel up carefully and cradled her against his chest. His pulse had finally slowed to something approaching normal, but he wasn't sure he'd feel completely okay until they'd been to Laramie and Angel had been checked out.

"Doc, you want the ambulance to take her to Laramie?" the sheriff asked. "I've got Jeter on call. He'll be here in two minutes if you say the word."

The doctor glanced at Todd and Heather. "You two want to take her? I can ride along with you in case there's a problem."

"We'll drive," Heather agreed. "We can take my car. Todd, do you mind holding her? She seems to be doing fine with you."

221

Todd regarded Heather intently, saw the too-bright sheen in her eyes, the lack of color in her cheeks. He might still be uneasy behind the wheel himself, but he knew enough to recognize someone who had absolutely no business being there. He shot a look at the doctor.

"Doc, how about you drive, so Heather and I can ride in the back seat with Angel?"

"Sounds good to me. Unless there's something I missed, we'll all be back here before nightfall."

"You call me the minute you know anything," Henrietta told them as an obviously distraught Sissy clung to her hand.

Todd knew there would be plenty of time spent waiting at the hospital for the CAT scan results for him to wallow in guilt. And maybe it would also be the perfect time to tell Heather all about his past. Combined with today's accident, it ought to be more than enough to convince her to take Angel and get as far away from him as possible.

Heather had never known the real meaning of fear until she'd seen her baby lying in the middle of the street. She felt as if every ounce of blood had drained straight out of her. With her pulse hammering and her skin cold and clammy, she'd been sure she was going to be the next casualty until Todd had put his arm around her and whispered a repeated litany of reassurances. After a while she had finally begun to believe him.

Over the past couple of hours she had drawn comfort from his strength, but she could tell from the way he'd withdrawn ever since they got to the hospital in Laramie that he wasn't nearly as calm and collected as he wanted her to believe. He was pacing from one end of the waiting room to the other, until she was sure he was going to wear a hole in the carpet.

"Todd?"

He was at her side in an instant. "Are you okay? You're not feeling faint, are you? You've had a shock, but Angel's going to be okay. The doc came out after the scan and said everything points to that, right? He's going to release her in an hour or so and send her back to Whispering Wind with us. We have to believe he knows what's best. And you have to admit, she was back to chattering a mile a minute by the time we got here."

"I know," she said. "It's not Angel. It's you I'm worried about."

"Me? Don't be crazy. I'm fine."

"You are not fine." Her gaze sought his, caught it for an instant, but then he looked away. "You're blaming yourself, aren't you?"

"What makes you think that?"

"The fact that you haven't looked me in the eye once since we got here."

His gaze locked with hers now as if to defy her claim. "It was my fault, okay? She came darting

223

across that street to get to me. That's a fact, Heather," he said flatly.

"It's also a fact that I was the one holding her hand. She got away from me. So, is it my fault she got hit?"

"Of course not," he said fiercely. "You didn't do anything careless."

"Any more than you did," she pointed out mildly. "If I could, I would never let anything bad happen to my baby. But there are going to be accidents that even the best parent in the world can't prevent, and that's what this was, Todd, an *accident.* It happened too quickly for either one of us to do a thing to prevent it."

"I still say it wouldn't have happened if she hadn't come running to me."

"And it wouldn't have happened if I had held on to her hand a little tighter," she repeated. "So we're both to blame, okay? For that matter, so is Angel for darting across the street in the first place."

Todd looked aghast at the suggestion that Angel was to blame for anything. "She's just a baby. It's up to us to protect her. Dammit, I should have realized what she was about to do."

"So should I," Heather countered, stubbornly refusing to let him heap all the guilt onto his own shoulders. "I've told her a million times in New York that she is not to cross the street unless I say it's okay. But she is just a baby. Until today, I'm sure she didn't fully understand the possible consequences. She was just excited to see you, the way she always is. And there wasn't a thing you could have done from where you were standing to stop her from running across that street."

He looked more angry than consoled. "Dammit, Heather, we could have lost her."

She touched his cheek. "But we didn't," she reminded him quietly. "Can't we just be grateful for that?"

He pulled away. "I don't know. It's not that simple."

"It is," she insisted. "No recriminations, Todd. Angel is going to be fine and that's all that matters."

He regarded her as if he didn't trust her words. "That's it?"

"That's it," she confirmed. "I mean it. I won't have you blaming yourself for another, single second.

"She loves you, Todd, and she doesn't even know yet you're her daddy. Nothing that's happened today changes that. You saw how she instinctively reached for you when she woke up. She trusts you. She's certainly not blaming you for the accident."

"She's too little to understand," he insisted, stubbornly clinging to his guilt.

Heather stared at him. Why was he so deter-mined to claim guilt? Was this just the excuse he'd been waiting for to try to get rid of them? Or was it something more? Did it go back to that ridiculous claim he'd made that he was a danger to their daughter? Once again she realized how vital it was that she get to the bottom of that. But how, when he refused to talk about it?

"Stop it," she commanded. "What happened was an accident. Stop dwelling on it and concentrate on Angel."

She grabbed his hand and dragged him toward the door of the waiting room.

"Where are we going?"

"To the hospital chapel," she said at once. "We're going to thank God that our little girl is all right and then we are putting this behind us."

She waited for him to balk at her plan, but when she glanced up, she saw an unexpected trace of amusement flickering in his eyes.

"I'd forgotten how bossy you are," he said, his mood lightening ever so slightly.

"Only when it's called for."

"I'll have to remember not to get you riled up too often," he said, his expression relaxing at last.

He slipped an arm around her waist then. Heather paused just outside the chapel door and turned to face him, slipping her arms around his neck and burying her face against his chest. As if a dam had suddenly burst, sobs shuddered through her as the reality of the past few hours finally sank in.

"Hey," he said. "What's this?" He tucked a finger under her chin.

Heather felt more tears welling up, but there was nothing she could do to stop them. "I was so scared," she whispered brokenly.

His arms tightened around her then and his chin rested atop her head as he waited for the storm to pass. "So was I, darlin', so was I."

They stood that way for the longest time, until finally Heather felt the tension ease and the tears begin to ebb.

"You okay?" Todd asked eventually.

"I will be," she said, her voice stronger now. "As soon as we say that prayer and get our baby home again."

14

Everybody in town seemed to be hanging around the Starlight Diner for word of Angel's condition. It was apparent that even in their brief time in town, Angel and Heather had been accepted as part of the community. Todd supposed that shouldn't have come as a surprise. After all, with her spontaneity and her vivacious demeanor, Heather had always attracted admirers.

Tonight, though, Todd wished she and Angel were a little less popular. He had envisioned getting Angel straight up to bed, then escaping to think long and hard about the negligence that had led to the accident. Despite what Heather said, he knew he bore some responsibility.

But rather than heading upstairs, Heather acceded to Angel's plea to see 'Retta and have ice cream before bed.

"Ice cream make me feel better, Mama," Angel said.

"I'm not sure I buy the medicinal powers of ice cream," Heather replied. "But you do deserve a treat for being so brave today."

The instant they entered, the customers immediately clustered around Angel, until Henrietta scolded them and told them to back off.

"Give the child some breathing room," she blustered. "You'd think she was some sort of sideshow at the circus the way you're behaving."

Todd couldn't have agreed more, especially since one of those most concerned seemed to be Joe Stevens, the cowboy who spent an awful lot of time flirting with Heather. Lately he'd taken to paying a lot of attention to Angel, as well.

"You two come right on over here and sit with me," Stevens said, coaxing the pair of them toward the booth he'd abandoned at their entrance. He ignored Todd altogether.

Since the place was packed, Heather sent a regretful glance in Todd's direction, then slid into the booth. Todd just barely restrained himself from shoving in after them. More disgruntled than he wanted to admit, he headed for the last available stool at the counter, instead.

"You okay?" Henrietta asked, pouring him a cup of coffee.

"I've had better days," he confessed. "But Angel's okay. That's what counts. How's the driver? She looked pretty shaken earlier."

Henrietta shook her head. "Josie Warren has no business being behind the wheel of a car. She's been told that by just about everyone, but the fool still has a license, so she insists on driving. 'Just to the store,' she says. Obviously, she'd be a menace just backing out of her own drive-way."

"It wasn't her fault," Todd said. "Thanks to me, Angel darted right in front of her."

"Thanks to you? What is that supposed to mean? The child got away from Heather, the way kids do. Josie should have anticipated it, but the woman's so short I doubt she could even see the child." She scowled at the judge, who was seated at the other end of the counter. "I told Harry time and again he ought to yank her license. Maybe now he will."

Despite his glum mood, Todd chuckled.

"What's so funny?" Henrietta demanded.

"The way you've managed to make this the fault of a man who was two blocks away in the court-house."

Henrietta looked vaguely flustered by the

amused accusation. "Yes, well, most things come down to being his fault sooner or later."

"Is that so?"

She gave Todd one of her sassy grins. "It's certainly best if he thinks so, anyway. Keeps him on his toes."

Todd swiveled slightly to see how Angel was holding up, but his gaze landed on Heather, instead. She seemed to be basking in the attention of that poster boy for the rugged West.

"Jealous?" Henrietta inquired, now regarding *him* with tolerant amusement.

Todd gave a start. "Me? Jealous? Don't be ridiculous. Heather's a free woman. If she wants to make time with that rancher, it's up to her."

"Is it really," Henrietta said, her tone skeptical. "And it wouldn't bother you in the slightest?"

"Not a bit," he said, hoping God wouldn't strike him dead on the spot for the bald-faced lie.

Henrietta shook her head. "Men!" she muttered, and went off to pour coffee for her other, presumably more sensible customers.

After another survey—or two—Todd deliberately turned his back on Heather and Angel and concentrated on his coffee and the piece of apple pie he'd managed to snag on Henrietta's last huffy pass-by. But even as he did his best to ignore Heather, he could hear the tinkling sound of those blasted bracelets, the uninhibited sound of her laughter, which seemed to be counterpointed by Angel's giggles. The whole jolly trio were clearly having the time of their lives not hours after Angel had almost gotten herself killed.

Angel should be upstairs, in her bed, getting some much-needed rest, he thought darkly. What was wrong with Heather, anyway? Had she forgotten all about the trauma the child had been through? Her tears and the prayer of thanks they'd given in the hospital chapel? Was this Stevens guy so fascinating that she couldn't tear herself away? Maybe it was up to him, Todd, to remind her what was important. That wasn't jealousy talking, he assured himself. It was concern for the child's well-being, plain and simple.

Scowling, he was about to stalk over and explain a few facts of parenting when the absurdity of his plan struck him. Who was he to be giving advice to anyone about taking care of a child? Just then, Flo slid onto the vacant stool next to his. He noticed the glance she gave to the scene in that booth; she didn't look one bit happier about it than he was.

Her gaze sought his in the mirror opposite the counter. "I'm real glad Angel's okay," she said sympathetically. "It must have been rough on you seeing her lying in the road like that. I know my heart leaped into my throat when I looked out the window of Jake's office and realized what had happened."

"It was. It was a close call."

She snuck another glance at Stevens. "Joe seems like he really cares about her and Heather."

"Mmm-hmm," Todd said tightly, then something in Flo's tone made him realize that her feelings for the rancher were deeper than he'd realized. "You okay?"

"Fine," she said unconvincingly.

By Todd's assessment, Flo had changed a lot in the months since she'd come bursting into Megan and Jake's life. After abandoning Tess with Megan's grandfather, Tex O'Rourke, Flo had wanted Tess back once she realized that her daughter stood to inherit a big chunk of Tex's wealth. Jake and Megan had put a quick stop to those ideas, but then, in her usual take-command way, Megan had set out to reform the woman. Jake hadn't exactly been overjoyed, either with having Flo around Tess or in his office, but he'd indulged Megan.

Ironically, Flo had proved herself to be more than capable of running his office smoothly. More important, she was trying to form a new bond with Tess. After a lot of years of rough breaks and bad decisions, she was doing her best to straighten out her life, and Todd had to give her a lot of credit for that. A little voice inside nagged that if Flo deserved a second chance after her past mistakes, maybe he did, too.

"Seeing Joe with Heather and Angel really bothers you, doesn't it?" he asked, deciding to focus on someone else's problems. It helped drown out that voice in his head.

"I hardly know the man," she said, denying the truth that was plain on her face. "We've never even been on a real date."

As denials went, it wasn't very effective, not with the way her gaze repeatedly strayed back to Joe's reflection in the mirror.

Todd recalled the way he'd fallen for Heather in less than a heartbeat when they'd met. "Time's not always a factor where the heart's concerned."

She turned her attention back to him. "Hey, you're looking at the queen of love-at-first-sight," she said wryly. "But I'm here to tell you that that kind of romance burns itself out just as fast. You want something lasting, you've got to give it time and you've got to work at it." She gave a little self-deprecating laugh. "Not that I've personally tried that part yet, you understand."

Todd glanced at the rancher in the mirror. He was slouched down in the booth giving Heather a lazy once-over, accompanied by a crooked grin. Obviously some women found that sort of thing sexy. Heather certainly looked as if she was lapping up the attention and Flo looked envious enough to shoot daggers into the competition.

"What is it about the guy?" he muttered. "I don't get it."

"You wouldn't," Flo said. "It's the way he looks at you, the way he listens as if every word you say is important. It doesn't hurt that he's got a butt just made for a pair of tight jeans, either."

Todd rolled his eyes. It was the damned Western mystique, he supposed. Some women were apparently suckers for it. He just hadn't figured Miss Broadway herself would be one of them. She'd always professed to like the sophisticated, smooth, yuppie type. Hell, she'd fallen in love with him, hadn't she? And he and Joe Stevens couldn't be more unalike if they'd come from two different universes.

He cast another disgruntled look at Stevens, then decided it was way past time to call it a night. If Heather didn't have sense enough to know when to take Angel home, he'd explain it to her. Excusing himself to Flo, he crossed the room in three long strides, then had to wait to catch her attention, since she was so busy hanging on to Joe's every word.

"Don't you think it's time Angel went to bed?" he asked when finally he had her attention. He nodded toward the child who was curled up in the corner of the booth, her eyelids at half-mast. Before Heather could respond, he reached across her and gathered Angel up. He considered it a preemptive strike, since Joe looked as if he might be about to volunteer for the task.

With a nod in the cowboy's direction, he headed out the door, figuring Heather would follow, if only to lecture him on his rude behavior. Sure enough, the tinkling sound of her bracelets trailed him up the outside staircase. When they had both reached the landing, there was no mistaking the fact that she was ticked off at him.

He waited while she turned her key in the lock and pushed the door open, then he brushed past her to deposit Angel in her room. For the next few minutes, Heather's attention was focused on getting Angel into bed. Todd couldn't get out of that room with its mounds of stuffed animals fast enough. It reminded him all too vividly of another nursery that had been decorated in a Peter Rabbit theme and crowded with bright toys and a plush menagerie by indulgent parents thrilled to have a second baby after so many years.

While Heather was occupied with Angel, he walked back into the living room, then glanced around at the touches that were purely Heather— the colorful scarf draped over a lamp to create a soft glow, the scented candles, the glass with a bouquet of wildflowers. She had turned the small apartment into more of a home in a few weeks than he had managed with his in months. She had a gift for making a place her own, usually through imaginative and inexpensive decorating such as this. It was a knack that might translate well into a television show, he thought, then dismissed the idea. The last thing he needed was to make a suggestion like that to Heather or Megan. He wanted her gone, not even more deeply entrenched in his life.

He moved to the window and stood staring out at the deserted street below, remembering with a shudder just how dangerous it could turn in the blink of an eye. He was still lost in that awful moment when Heather joined him.

"Would you mind telling me what that was all about?" Heather asked, her tone more curious than angry.

Todd didn't waste time trying to pretend he didn't know exactly what she was asking. Even an idiot would have seen his behavior for the actions of a man driven by jealousy, not concern for his daughter. He turned slowly, prepared to offer some sort of honest response, even prepared to admit that he'd been ridiculously and inexplicably bent out of shape by the attention Joe Stevens had been showering on Heather and Angel.

Instead, his gaze locked on Heather's, his pulse slammed into overdrive, and all he could think about was kissing that sassy, knowing expression off her face.

Hours of stress and adrenaline kicked in as he reached for her and dragged her to him. His mouth claimed hers with deep, dark, drugging kisses that blocked out weeks of sound reason and noble intentions. Her fingers tunneled through his hair and her body molded itself to his.

He didn't hesitate, didn't ask by so much as a glance. He just took what he needed—the heat, the closeness, the passion that he'd been missing for four long years.

They tumbled onto the sofa in a tangle of arms and legs and desperate need, stripping away clothes when they got in the way of the desire to touch bare skin. It was just the way Todd remembered, every uninhibited, urgent caress, every slick inch of her satiny skin.

She was writhing beneath him when he finally paused to draw breath, when he finally stopped to consider her pleasure along with his own. But Heather was impatient, her needs linked to his own, apparently, because she drew him inside her with the same urgency that was rocketing through him.

"Now," she pleaded. "Don't stop. Don't think." She smoothed his forehead as if to coax away the sensible thoughts she knew were suddenly crowding in. "Love me."

Todd couldn't have resisted if he'd wanted to, which he didn't. Her pleas were all he needed to run his hands over sensitive flesh, to pound away inside her until muscles tightened around him and shudders washed over her and then, in a swirl of dark, delicious urgency, claimed him as well.

How had he ever forgotten that it could be like this? How had he blocked it from his mind?

And now that he remembered, how could he ever let her go again?

• • •

Heather came back to earth slowly, resisting the fall, wanting to savor every incredible second. When she finally dared a glance into Todd's eyes, she expected to find them filled with regrets, expected the apologies to start tripping off his tongue in a tumble of words like "sorry" and "mistake" and "never again." She was prepared for that. She wasn't prepared for the utterly lost, utterly hopeless expression she found, instead.

"Don't you dare say you're sorry," she told him, trying to gauge his mood.

"I'm not sorry."

"Don't tell me it's not going to happen again."

He sighed heavily at that. "It probably will."

There was no mistaking the regret in his voice. She frowned. "You don't have to sound so blasted depressed about it. It's not very flattering."

"Nothing good can come of this, Heather."

She refused to be daunted. "I'd say something already has," she said with a satisfied smile.

"If you're talking about Angel . . ."

"I'm not. I'm not looking back or ahead. I'm talking about right now, this second. I am where I want to be, in your arms. I'd forgotten how safe and secure I feel when I'm here. I'd forgotten what it's like to climb clear up to the stars with a man who really cares about me."

"I don't . . ." he said, then, "Okay, I do care, just

not the way you mean, not the way you ought to have a man care about you."

"Todd, if you cared any more, I wouldn't be able to move for a month."

The frown was back, deeper this time. "I'm not talking about sex."

She touched a finger to his lips. "Just this once, just for tonight, could we not complicate this? Could we not analyze it or talk it to death?"

"But—"

"Just for tonight," she repeated.

"I don't see how—"

"Todd."

A smile crept across his face. "Okay, okay. Just for tonight."

"Will you stay with me?"

"I don't think I have any choice, do I? You've got me trapped under you."

He didn't sound nearly as distressed about that as he might have. "You complaining?"

Their gazes locked.

"No way," he murmured, shifting to make the most of the contact. "I know when to give in gracefully."

"Good instincts," she praised, for once without the edge in her voice that had to do with his wasted abilities as an actor. His fingers slid inside her, tormenting her until her breath caught in her throat and her pulse was ricocheting crazily. "Very . . . good . . . instincts."

"Only with you," he murmured as he eased her onto her back and plunged deep inside her again.

Once more the twist of tension, the swirl of heat, tugged her into a rising wave of sensual delight, captured her, lifted her, then dragged her under until she was gasping for breath and crying out with the sheer wonder of it.

Morning would be time enough for rational thoughts and regrets, she thought as she snuggled closer to the man whose most innocent caress could bring her ecstasy.

"Umm, Heather?"

"Yes?" she murmured sleepily.

"We aren't really going to try sleeping on the sofa, are we?"

She didn't see why not. Cuddling was a guarantee in such limited space. One look at Todd's awkward position, however, convinced her it wouldn't seem half so romantic by morning when aches and pains had settled in.

"There is a perfectly good bed not far from here," she conceded.

"Thank God."

He started to get up, but she held him in place. "Just one thing."

"What's that?"

"You'll stay close to me. You won't wander over to the far edge of the bed and drag all the covers with you."

"Are you more worried about getting lonely

or cold?" he inquired with obvious amusement.

"If I'm not lonely, I can almost guarantee there's no way I'll get cold," she told him.

He gazed into her eyes. "Deal," he said solemnly, holding out his hand.

"A handshake is good," she agreed, placing her hand in his. "But a kiss is better."

"A kiss could seriously delay us getting off this sofa," he warned.

She grinned. "Not a problem."

His mouth dutifully slanted over hers.

He was right, she concluded somewhat later. A kiss could be the start of an incredibly worthwhile delay. In fact, if she used the tactic inventively, maybe she could postpone his running out on her and Angel for a long time to come.

15

Exhausted, his emotions in more turmoil than ever, Todd slipped out of Heather's bed in the morning, planning to sneak out of the apartment without waking her or Angel. He wasn't sure he wanted to rehash last night's events quite so soon, and Heather was very big on talking. She was also big on cuddling in the morning and had always been able to fog his brain and lead him astray.

He actually made it out of Heather's room without her stirring, but when he peeked in Angel's room, he found her wide-awake and playing some kind of game with the dolls crowded around her. Her expression brightened when she spotted him.

"Hiya, Todd," she said with delight, reaching for him.

He instinctively picked her up, amazed by the feelings that stole through him as she snuggled close. Instead of the terror he'd anticipated, he felt . . . almost paternal. A little awed. He realized that the sensation was becoming commonplace, that he was beginning to expect—and accept— it.

"What are you doing awake at this hour, cupcake? It's early."

"I not sleepy," she informed him. "I hungry."

Uh-oh, he thought. What was she supposed to have for breakfast? He could manage toast, he supposed. Or maybe cereal. Maybe some juice.

"Let's see what the options are," he said, carrying her into the kitchen. He set her on her feet and began poking into cupboards, most of which were bare, a testament to the intended temporary nature of their stay in Whispering Wind. Once again, awareness of that depressed him more than it relieved him. He simply had to get a grip, he told himself sharply. His control was slipping. He did not want the two of them staying. He did not.

Impatient and knowing the layout better than he did, Angel scooted past him and tugged open a lower cabinet door near the refrigerator. She poked her head inside and emerged happily holding a box of cereal.

" 'O's," she announced.

"Ah," Todd said. "Nothing better than Cheerios."

Angel seemed impressed by his enthusiasm. "You like 'em, too?"

"I love them," he assured her, grabbing two bowls, a couple of spoons and retrieving the milk from the refrigerator.

He dumped the cereal into the bowls and was about to douse it with milk when Heather wandered in and regarded the scene sleepily. His hand froze in midair at the sight of her in a T-shirt that barely came to midthigh and left very little to the imagination thanks to the soft, clinging fabric. His pulse, which should have been resting comfortably after the night they'd shared, kicked into warp speed again.

"Pour that milk at your own risk," Heather said mildly, clearly oblivious to the fact that he'd all but forgotten he was even holding the carton.

"Huh?"

"The milk," she repeated pointedly. "Not on Angel's cereal, unless you want to give her a bath to get the soggy Cheerios out of her hair."

The prospect snapped him back to the moment. He shoved the bowl of dry cereal in Angel's direction. She promptly grabbed a fistful. Apparently table manners weren't yet a part of her repertoire.

"I'm sorry if I woke you," he told Heather, his gaze unabashedly surveying her now that he'd averted the soggy-cereal catastrophe. This was bad, he told himself as he sank onto a chair. Really bad. No one understood the pull of great sex better than he did. Wasn't that at least a part of what had kept them together the first time for as long as it had?

As uninhibited as ever, Heather clearly didn't share his reservations. She moved easily straight into his lap and looped an arm around his neck. Her kiss on his cheek was innocent enough, but his response to it was anything but. From the gleam in her eyes, it was evident that she was fully aware of the effect she was having. In fact, she seemed to be thoroughly enjoying it!

Eventually, though, her expression sobered. "We might have just the teensiest problem," she told him.

Knowing Heather, Todd suspected this was a massive understatement. "What?" he asked.

She nodded toward Angel, then leaned down to whisper, "Not the most discreet kid on the block."

Understanding dawned immediately. "You mean she's going to blab it all over that I was here all night?" he asked in a horrified whisper.

"It's not a sure bet, but there's no way to stop her. She does like to chat with 'Retta."

"Oh, boy," Todd muttered. Not that Henrietta would be all that shocked. It was apparent she already believed that there was more going on between him and Heather than he'd admitted to. She seemed more distressed by his denials than she was likely to be by the proof that she'd been right all along. No, it wasn't Henrietta who would be a problem.

"Just keep her away from Megan," he pleaded.

"Don't want the boss knowing what you've been up to?" Heather inquired tartly. "Is there some sort of morality clause in your contract with her?"

He frowned. "Don't be ridiculous."

"Then what's the problem?"

Todd tried to decide how best to phrase it. "When Megan was being chased by Jake, I more or less encouraged him. She just might get it into her head that turnabout is fair play. Trust me when I tell you that I—we—don't need the pressure."

Rather than being subdued by the warning, Heather looked fascinated. "Pressure, huh? As in meddling?"

"As in making my life a living hell," he said, then regarded her darkly. "Yours, too, for that matter."

"Not necessarily," she said thoughtfully. "For once, your boss and I just might share common goals."

"Such as?" The last he'd heard, Heather's only goal was to involve him in Angel's life, then head east. Had last night changed that? If so, it might turn out that last night was the costliest mistake of his life.

"That's still evolving," she informed him with one of those sassy grins that scared him senseless. "I'll keep you posted."

Todd groaned. He was doomed. No doubt about it, he was totally and positively doomed.

In the end it took precisely two hours for Angel to announce to anyone listening that "Todd slept with my mommy." It took another fifteen minutes for that news to reach Megan. He knew it from her expression when she strolled into his office.

"My, my, my," she murmured gleefully. "Isn't *this* a fascinating turn of events."

"What?" he demanded, praying her upbeat mood had something to do with the major sponsorship he'd just negotiated for Peggy's new cooking show, which all but guaranteed they would be going into production with it by fall.

"A little birdie just told me some absolutely delicious gossip."

"Must be quite a birdie," he muttered. "A vicious parrot, trained by a salty old sailor, no doubt."

"Nope. This little birdie is a blonde."

"Flo," he guessed, growing more despondent by the minute. Flo's spin on this was bound to be colorful.

"Bingo. Seems she stopped by to grab a cup of coffee on her way to work this morning, and guess what she heard being discussed over breakfast at that hotbed of local news, the Starlight Diner?"

"I can't imagine. You shouldn't listen to gossip, especially in a small town like this," he said disdainfully. "You know how rumors get started."

"Are you saying a sweet little girl is capable of starting a rumor?"

Thank heaven Heather had warned him of the possibility earlier. "I'm saying a sweet little girl doesn't understand the implication of the words that come out of her mouth," he said grimly.

"Is there another way to interpret—now, let me see if I have this exactly right—'Todd slept with my mommy'?"

"There are many ways if your mind's not in the gutter," he retorted. "All Angel actually knows is that I was there when she went to bed last night and I was there when she woke up this morning. She's three, dammit. What else could she know?"

"Out of the mouths of babes," Megan taunted. She perched on the corner of his desk. "So, what's the scoop?"

"There is no scoop, as you so delicately put it."

"Todd, Todd, Todd," she said with exaggerated disappointment. "If you can't trust me with the truth, who can you trust?"

"Nobody in this town, that's for sure. It's enough

to make me long for life in the big, anonymous city, where nobody gives a damn about anybody else's business." He scowled at Megan. "I could be on a plane back there tomorrow, you know."

"No, you couldn't," she retorted, clearly unfazed by the threat. "We have a contract. A very long-term contract, I might add."

"Something I will no doubt regret till my dying day."

Megan laughed. "Oh, why don't you just admit it?"

"Admit what? That I slept with Heather?"

"Actually, I was going for an admission that you're starting to love it here, but I'll take the truth about last night instead." Her expression suddenly sobered and she regarded him worriedly. "What exactly does that mean, Todd? Are you still in love with her? Is the old romance starting to bloom again? You're not the kind of guy to fool around with a woman unless it's serious."

He was getting sick and tired of all these people claiming to know him. His life was not an open book, dammit. He had his share of secrets. Well, one, anyway.

"You don't know what kind of a guy I am," he protested, most likely in vain.

"I think I do," she insisted. "*Honorable* is one word that comes immediately to mind. I recognize it—and admire it—because it's so rare in this business."

Todd thought of Heather, wished desperately that she was the only one involved here, but she wasn't. There was still Angel and all those years of quiet resolutions to never put another child at risk.

"Don't get too carried away with the heady praise," he warned Megan. "Before all is said and done, it might turn out that I'm as much of a bastard as the next guy."

"I'll never believe that," Megan declared. "Not in a million years."

Her faith in him, her prompt and fierce defense, should have reassured him. Instead, he simply reminded himself that he knew better and he was the one who had all the facts.

Heather couldn't figure out what was going on with Todd. He loved her. She knew it. She could feel it every time he looked at her, every time he touched her. A few nights ago when they'd made love, it had been about as perfect as any woman could dream of. It wasn't what she'd envisioned when she'd impulsively come to Wyoming, but she wasn't about to turn her back on it. She was beginning to think she owed it to herself as much as Angel to stick around Whispering Wind however long it took to see where that incredible night might lead. Summer might not be nearly long enough.

Of course, Todd seemed equally determined to

avoid a repeat. If he'd steered a wide course around the two of them before, he practically avoided all of downtown now. He hadn't been around since that night. He'd also been avoiding her calls. His secretary had come up with at least a dozen inventive reasons why he wasn't available, but the excuses were wearing thin. Heather had stopped believing any of them after the first three.

Just in case she'd been misjudging him, she tried one more time, then hung up in disgust when the secretary told her that Todd was out of town indefinitely, then refused to say where he'd gone.

"Problems?" Henrietta asked, studying her intently.

"I've been trying to catch up with Todd."

"He's out of town," Henrietta said, then flushed guiltily.

"He is?" she asked, surprised that his secretary hadn't been lying. Then she regarded Henrietta with dismay. "You knew?"

"He mentioned it," Henrietta admitted. "He stopped by yesterday morning just after I opened. He told me he had to fly back East for some meetings."

"Todd is in New York," Heather said, just to be sure she was getting an accurate picture.

"That's what he said."

"For how long?"

"He didn't say." Henrietta gave her a knowing look. "I got the feeling the trip came up suddenly."

"Yeah, right after he and I . . . Never mind. I suppose he specifically told you not to tell me."

"Actually, he said to tell you if you asked. I think that's why he wanted me to know. It's not like he automatically checks in with me before he takes off."

"Isn't that thoughtful of him," Heather muttered. "Secondhand information is better than none, I suppose."

Henrietta motioned toward a booth. "Sit. I think we need to have a talk."

"I don't need to talk. I need to find Todd and wring his neck," she said, but she sat down opposite Henrietta, anyway.

"Is that really what you want to do?" her boss asked, studying her knowingly.

"Right this second, yes."

"That's frustration talking," Henrietta said dismissively. "Seems to me like you're after something else entirely. It started with Angel, but I don't think that's how it's turning out, is it?" This was more a statement than a question.

Heather sighed. "Not exactly, no."

"You're falling in love with him again, aren't you?"

"I don't think I ever stopped loving him," she finally confessed. "It makes me so blasted furious. That was not what this trip out here was all about." She regarded Henrietta despondently. "And what good will it do me? He doesn't want me or Angel. He's living here and I want to work in New York. The whole thing is a mess."

"One thing at a time," Henrietta said reasonably. "You love him. And if I'm any judge of these things, he loves you."

Heather was surprised by the assessment. "Then why did he go running off to New York?"

Henrietta shrugged. "Why do men do anything? Usually it's because they don't want to deal with their feelings. You just have to be patient till he can sort things out."

"How patient?"

"There's no telling."

"Well, isn't that just great," she said sourly. "I'm supposed to put my life on hold until he sorts things out? Well, excuse me for saying this, but as much as I like you and enjoy working here, I want to act, not wait tables."

"Any reason you can't do that right here in Whispering Wind?" Henrietta asked. "The truth is, I've been giving this some thought, just in case the subject ever came up. There's a stage in that big old barn out at the fairgrounds. Hasn't been used for much besides announcing the winners of the pie-baking contest and such, but I'd say for someone who really wants to act, it would do."

Heather's gaze narrowed. "What are you suggesting?"

"Start your own theater company."

Heather stared as if she'd suggested stripping as a hobby. "You can't be serious."

"Why on earth not? Or is the audience around here too unsophisticated for a big New York City star?"

The taunt in Henrietta's voice was deliberate, no doubt about it. The gleam in her eyes proved it. Heather frowned. "I don't think . . ."

"What? You don't think you can hack it? Is that what this is about? Fear? If it is, you're no better than Todd."

Heather didn't like being compared to Todd in that particular way and especially not in that derisive tone.

"I am *not* afraid," she retorted.

Henrietta gave a nod of satisfaction. "Good. You're the professional. You were good enough to be on the stage in New York and on daytime television. Putting together a show out here should be a snap. People will be so grateful for the entertainment, they won't judge you as harshly as those snobby East Coast critics, anyway. You'll be a smash hit. You'll be doing something good for a community that's welcomed you and your daughter. It'll be the highlight of the summer."

"It takes a lot of time to stage a production," Heather hedged. "It's already mid-June."

Henrietta's sharp-eyed gaze challenged her. "You got someplace else you have to be?"

253

She thought wistfully of going back to New York, then weighed that against the stakes right here. "No, but . . ."

"But what?"

"How is Todd going to react? I'll tell you. He'll see it as one more sign that I'm sticking around. He's not going to be happy."

"You think not? If you ask me, the man will be delirious with joy." She grinned. "He just might not recognize it at first."

For the first time in days, Heather chuckled. "Maybe I'll at least go out and take a look at the stage," she conceded. "There wouldn't be any harm in that, I suppose."

Henrietta bounced up. "No time like the present. I'll get my car keys. Sissy's upstairs with Angel. We'll send them over to stay with Janie at the hair salon."

"We're supposed to be open for dinner in an hour," Heather protested. "This could wait till tomorrow."

"No point in putting it off," Henrietta chided. "It won't take that long, and if it does, the customers will just have to wait. Won't kill them to put off their evening meal for a few minutes. A few of them could put it off for days and they wouldn't starve. Who knows, maybe Mack will show some initiative, step out of that kitchen and let them in."

Since Heather didn't believe for a second that

the temperamental Mack was going to set foot out of his kitchen to deal with the customers, she suggested, "Maybe you should at least leave a note on the door. I don't want you losing business on my account."

"Oh, for goodness' sake, all right." Henrietta snatched up an order pad and scribbled a note on the back of a page.

"Back when I get here" it read curtly. Not exactly the apology for any inconvenience that Heather had envisioned, but Henrietta was obviously satisfied. She placed an equally abrupt call to Janie about dropping off Sissy and Angel.

"Now, let's get a move on," she commanded when the two girls were settled.

It turned out that Henrietta drove the way she did everything else, with grim determination and at full throttle. Heather's heart was in her throat by the time they skidded to a stop in front of an old weathered barn that looked as if it might tumble down at any second. It was set beneath a stand of trees on about ten acres of land that were otherwise marked only by what appeared to be an unpaved parking area, a rodeo ring and some bleachers for spectators. It wasn't exactly the sort of fairgrounds Heather had anticipated. Maybe when it was crowded with animals and people and a visiting carnival it would be downright festive; now it merely looked forlorn and deserted.

"This is it?" she asked, not even trying to mask her disappointment over the state of the barn in particular.

"It could use a coat of paint," Henrietta admitted.

Knocking it down and starting from scratch struck Heather as a better alternative, but she kept her opinion to herself. "Is it open? Can we look inside?"

"Of course we can," Henrietta said. "Wouldn't have brought you out here otherwise." She jiggled her massive key ring until she found the one she was looking for. "This ought to do it."

"You have a key for the barn at the fairgrounds?" Heather asked. "Why?"

"Somebody's got to," she said matter-of-factly, already turning the key in the lock. She shoved aside the massive door, which squealed on its hinges. Then she waved Heather inside.

With the sunlight streaming in through the open doorway, Heather supposed there was a certain rustic charm about the place. Rows of chairs had been lined up facing a stage that was certainly big enough for a theatrical production, but the lighting seemed to consist of a single spotlight aimed at center stage. There was no curtain. The stage floor was made of wide planks of wood that had been swept clean, but never polished.

"I don't know," Heather said. "It's . . ." Words failed her.

"I never said it was the caliber of a fancy Broadway stage," Henrietta said defensively. "But for someone with a little imagination, someone with a little grit, it has possibilities." Her gaze seared Heather. "Don't you think so?"

Heather wished she shared Henrietta's vision, but the truth was she was totally intimidated by the amount of work it would take to turn this barn into a home for a decent production. She might be able to direct in a pinch, but . . .

"It would take an awful lot of work," she pointed out honestly. "Would it be worth it for just one play?"

"It would be an investment in the future," Henrietta corrected her. "Not just the future of this old place, but yours and Todd's. Or can't you see that?"

Her penetrating look had Heather squirming. "I suppose."

"You think about it. If you decide against it, nothing's lost except a few hours of wrestling with your conscience."

Heather gaped. "What does my conscience have to do with this?"

There was a mild rebuke in Henrietta's gaze as she replied, "You think about that, too, child. I'm sure you'll figure it out."

16

At Jake's request Todd sat down in New York with the company's entertainment lawyer, along with Dean Whicker and Micah Richards, to see if a settlement could be reached that would preclude a suit. Jake didn't want Megan to go through the stress of a long legal battle. He didn't seem to care how Todd might feel being in the same room with the traitorous Micah.

The woman was as beautiful as ever in a lean, avant-garde sort of way, but for the first time since she'd come on board as Megan's producer, Todd looked at her without interest. In fact, about the only emotion he could muster up was disgust. He felt a similar surge of hostility when he met Dean Whicker's gaze, but the man was still their program's syndicator, so he was forced to hide his reaction.

"I thought all this was settled when I decided not to drop Megan's show," Whicker said.

"It wasn't," the attorney said mildly. "Megan still has grounds for suing both of you for misuse of her studio time. I won't even get into the morality of what you did."

"I imagine not," Micah retorted. "Lawyers are rarely concerned with the morality of an issue."

Whicker shot her a warning look that silenced

her. "What exactly is Megan looking for?" he asked, turning to Todd. "Blood? Money?"

"An extension of the current contract at more favorable terms," Todd said readily. His gaze slid to Micah. "And a written guarantee that you will not enter into any programming agreement with Micah during that time."

"You can't—" Micah began.

"Done," Whicker said, then rose. "Anything else?"

Todd barely hid a grin as Micah stared at him bitterly. "That should do it," he said pleasantly. "I'll leave the attorneys to hammer out the details. I have a plane to catch."

He left the room without further comment. In the hallway, he punched out Jake's number and triumphantly reported that the deal was done.

"Nice work," Jake said. "You okay about Micah?"

"The woman is slime," Todd said. "I can't imagine what I ever saw in her."

He had a feeling it was easier to say that now because he'd been spending time with Heather again. For that much, at least, he was grateful to her for coming into his life again and reminding him of how important kindness and decency were.

But where Heather and Angel were concerned, he headed back to Wyoming with his thoughts still in chaos. And this for a man who prided himself on his ability to remain focused.

Jake's advice that he hire his own lawyer and put an end to the custody issue once and for all no longer seemed as distasteful as it once had. Quickly and decisively, the way he dealt with most problems, seemed like the way to go. Of course, it was awfully late in the game for anything he chose to do to be labeled *quick* or *decisive*.

But when he picked up the phone book at the airport in Laramie on his return and checked the yellow pages for listings of attorneys, he couldn't seem to make himself choose one and dial the number. Nor could he convince himself that the only reason for his hesitance was his distrust of lawyers in general. He tossed the phone book back with an edgy sense of frustration and the grim realization that he wasn't over Heather Reed, not by a long shot. Like it or not, he was going to have to deal with that, because his gut told him that Heather wasn't going to go away until he did.

Maybe brutal honesty would do the trick, he thought desperately. Maybe telling her that he'd made a final decision, that they did not stand a snowball's chance in hell of getting back together, would finally convince her to turn tail and run.

Yeah, right. That night in her bed said otherwise and she was smart enough to know it. He could lie through his teeth and claim it didn't matter, but that wouldn't change anything. Hell, he could already hear the sound of her chuckling disbelief. With one little peck on the cheek, one innocent little caress, she could prove him a liar.

He returned to Whispering Wind dreading the encounter they were bound to have. He imagined she was going to have plenty to say about him running out on her without a word. He could have avoided it for another twenty-four hours or so, but he saw little point to postponing the inevitable. If leaving town for an entire week hadn't accomplished anything, another day's delay could hardly matter.

He drove straight into town and strolled into the Starlight Diner as if he hadn't even been away. Henrietta gave him a quick welcoming hug as she darted past him to pick up an order. To his con-fusion, there was no sign of Heather. His heart thudded dully as he considered the possibility that he'd finally gotten his way, that she had packed up and left town, taking his daughter with her. He didn't like the unsettling feeling of loss stealing over him one bit.

He slid onto a stool to wait until Henrietta had time enough to talk. She eventually breezed past long enough to pour him a cup of coffee and deliver a piece of apple pie, but she was way too busy to linger. Finally, when he could no longer stand not knowing, he snagged her arm.

"Hey, where's your help?" he asked, hoping he sounded no more than casually curious, rather than panicked. "I thought Heather would be working this time of day."

Henrietta gave him a knowing look, then waited in what was obviously an attempt to drag out his torment. "She is usually, but she's tied up this afternoon out at the fairgrounds."

Not gone, he thought with a barely concealed sigh of relief, but out at the fairgrounds. Why? Henrietta escaped his grasp before he could demand an explanation. A sinking sensation in the pit of his stomach suggested he wasn't going to like it, whatever it was.

When she finally paused again to refill his coffee cup, he looked her straight in the eye and asked, "Why is she at the fairgrounds?" He was pleased that he managed to sound calm and reasonable, even though his gut was churning.

"She's overseeing the renovations," Henrietta said as if it was common knowledge.

Renovations? What renovations? And why on earth would Heather be involved? Unfortunately it was clear that Henrietta wouldn't be giving him any details, at least not for another hour or so until the dinner rush died down. He figured the only way to find out was to head for the fairgrounds himself.

He heard the hammering and the sound of rock music being played at full volume before he even made the last turn onto the property. However, he was not prepared for the sight that awaited him. Men were swarming all over the old barn, replacing boards, spreading paint over the parts that were finished.

And in the midst of them was Heather, looking frazzled and dusty and sexy as hell in a pair of denim shorts and a tank top with her wildly curling hair tugged through the back opening of a baseball cap in a makeshift ponytail. She waved distractedly when she saw him, then went right back to her conversation with that damnable cowboy, Joe Stevens.

Before Todd could react to that, he heard a squeal and then thirty pounds of unleashed energy crashed into his legs. He might have tumbled straight onto his butt if he hadn't spotted Angel heading toward him at the very last second and braced himself for the impact. Well, at least one of the females in his life appeared glad to see him.

"Where you been?" she demanded, reaching out her arms to be picked up.

With a gesture that was becoming second nature, he scooped her into his arms, even as his gaze sought out her mother. Heather and Stevens had their heads bent over what looked like some sort of a sketch.

He felt a soft pat on his cheek and turned to meet his daughter's gaze. She grinned in satisfaction at having captured his attention.

"Where you been?" she repeated with single-track determination.

"In New York."

Her expression brightened with apparent recognition. "I been to New York."

Todd grinned back. "You used to *live* in New York."

Only after he'd said the words did the implication strike him. *Used to live in New York,* as if that was no longer true, as if she now lived in Whispering Wind. Had he already stopped thinking of them as just passing through? Was that why he'd balked earlier at calling an attorney in Laramie? Was that why his heart had sunk at not finding Heather where he'd expected her to be—at the diner?

"Sweetie, I need to talk to your mommy," he said, putting Angel down. She promptly grabbed his hand, clearly not understanding his unspoken request for privacy.

"I go with you," she announced.

Todd automatically slowed his impatient pace to match hers. He listened with only a fraction of his full attention as she chattered away, but when she said something about her mommy making a play, his gaze snapped toward her.

"What did you say?"

"Mommy's making a play," she repeated. "I gonna be in it. Sissy, too."

Sweet heaven, Todd thought. That's what this beehive of activity was all about. Heather had somehow gotten it into her head to do some sort of theatrical production out here. What was she thinking? Staging a play took time. She was going back to New York. Not once had she implied otherwise, despite his own nagging sense that he might be just as happy if she changed her mind. Who on earth was supposed to take over when she abandoned the project to go back to her real life?

Those weren't questions Angel could possibly answer, so he stored them up for Heather, who seemed to have vanished, probably with Stevens, who seemed content to trail around after her like an adoring puppy.

Sure enough, he found the two of them at the back of the stage staring up, debating whether there was room enough to install concealed tracks for lighting.

"There isn't," Todd said emphatically, startling them both.

Heather frowned at him. "Since when did you become a lighting expert?"

"Since I had to have sound stages built out here for Megan's television show," he replied.

Her expression brightened as if he'd announced an expertise in electrical engineering. "Good. Then you can be in charge of getting this place professionally lit."

Before he could respond to that, she was on the move again, Stevens trailing after her. Obviously she assumed Todd would fall into step with her plans in the same way.

"Heather!"

His bellow brought her to a halt. She turned slowly, tilting her head quizzically. "Yes?"

"We need to talk." He leveled a look at the rancher. "Alone, if you don't mind."

Stevens regarded him with knowing amusement. "It's up to Heather."

Heather frowned, but finally said, "Okay, fine. Joe, go ahead and check on Parks and Grady. See if they think we need more paint. Those old boards are soaking it up like sponges. Henrietta said if we needed more to go ahead and get it and put it on her account."

He nodded. "Will do."

He took his own sweet time about leaving, though, Todd thought, as Joe paused to bend down to Angel's level. "Short stuff, want to come with me?"

"Okay," she said readily. "I ride on your shoulders?"

"You bet," he said, hoisting her into position before finally going off and leaving Todd alone with Heather.

Todd didn't care to examine the twinge that sight caused him. He focused all his attention on Heather, instead. "What the heck is going on around here?" he demanded.

"What does it look like?"

Chaos? Bad judgment? Danger? She wouldn't like any of those answers. He settled for saying, "You don't want to know."

There was a quick flash of hurt in her eyes before she snapped back, "Thank you for your support. Now, if you're just out here to criticize, I don't have the time. I'll see you around."

She'd taken several brisk strides toward the door before he caught up with her, grasped her arm and whirled her around. Her gaze clashed with his, sparks flying.

"What is your problem?" she demanded.

"I just asked a simple question."

"It didn't sound simple to me. It sounded pretty darned close to an accusation that I was doing something wrong, something you might find a little messy or inconvenient, like sticking around town with your daughter a little too long for your comfort."

Todd raked his hand through his hair in frustration. "I never said that. I—"

Heather cut him off. "No. You never do say exactly what's on your mind these days, do you?"

"That's absurd."

"Is it?"

Todd drew in a deep breath and forced himself to inject a calmer note into his voice. Riling Heather had never been the way to get a straight answer out of her.

"Let's back up a minute," he suggested, wanting desperately to stick to the facts, because he had no idea what to do with the emotions he was feeling right this second. He gestured toward all the activity. "What's going on? Angel says you're making a play."

To his dismay, she nodded. "That pretty much sums it up. Henrietta suggested I start a theater company while I'm here, then she showed me this place. I floated the idea by some people, it took off like a runaway freight train, and here we are."

"Henrietta did this," he said slowly. "This was all her idea?"

"Yep. She pointed out that all an actress really needs in order to work is a stage—it doesn't really matter where it's located. After all, it's laughter and applause we crave, right? Or have you forgotten that?"

He ignored the jibe and lobbed one of his own. "You've lowered your sights quite a bit, then. I thought you had your heart set on Broadway."

She shrugged with an indifference he didn't buy for a second.

"Things change," she said. "Goals shift. People adapt. You might want to keep that in mind. Of course, that *is* what you did, isn't it?"

Todd heard the familiar note of censure and chose once again to ignore it. "We're talking about you. How long is this supposed to keep you happy, Heather? Last I looked, you had a fairly short attention span."

"That's not fair."

"You've said you intend to leave here. Will you stick around long enough to get the first play on stage? Or will you bail out the minute you and I settle this custody issue?"

It occurred to him then that that might be precisely why he was taking so long to reach an agreement with her. It fit with every other piece of evidence he'd discovered since his return. A part of him didn't want her gone, no matter what sort of trouble her staying brought into his life. And maybe, just maybe, he'd been testing her to see if she would stay, if he mattered enough this time for her to stick around for the long haul.

She regarded him with a wry expression. "Since that doesn't seem likely to happen anytime soon, it's a moot point, don't you think?"

Because he wasn't one bit happy about what he suspected his less-than-honest motives to be, he said, "We could settle it today, if you'd just be reasonable."

"Me? You're the one who won't give an inch."

"For good reason."

"Which you refuse to explain."

He groaned. "Dammit, Heather. This is just another example of you acting on impulse without thinking things through."

He could tell that the accusation stung, because of the renewed hurt that promptly registered in her eyes. But her chin went up and the sass in her voice didn't falter when she shot back, "Well, if I'm such a screwup, I'm surprised you ever spent a minute with me. You won't mind if I get back to work. This little play of mine might not matter to you, but it does to me. Contrary to your low opinion, when I start something, I like to see it through."

This time when she stalked off, spine rigid, Todd didn't try to stop her, partly because he didn't know what else to say. He'd already bungled the past few minutes so badly he doubted she'd forgive him. Why was it he could negotiate with some of the most powerful, egocentric people in television without missing a beat, but when it came to carrying on a simple conversation with Heather, he managed to blow it?

Because the stakes were higher, he conceded. Business was just that, business. He might be one of the more dysfunctional men around when it came to relationships, but even he recognized that what he had—or didn't have—with Heather mattered more. In fact, he was slowly becoming aware that it might be the only thing in his life that really mattered. That didn't mean he had to like it.

Sighing, he set off to find her and apologize. Accusing her of being impulsive might be accurate, but it was a low blow, especially when that was one of the things that had drawn him to her in the first place. She was everything he wasn't—carefree, spontaneous, emotionally connected. Acting impulsively wasn't the sin he'd implied; it just went against his thoughtful—okay, plodding—nature. There were times when he envied her spontaneity, her ability to live life with a passion, seizing whatever chances came her way and making the most of them. The expression about turning lemons into lemonade could have been coined for her. He doubted she realized how much he admired that about her.

He found her sitting under a tree, drinking a soda while Angel sat nearby eating a peanut butter and jelly sandwich. He lowered himself to sit beside her.

"I'm sorry," he said eventually when she didn't seem inclined to react to his presence.

"For?"

"Acting like a jerk."

A reluctant smile tugged at the corners of her lips. "Keep talking."

"You just took me by surprise. I thought you intended to head back East. You keep telling me that's the plan. It bothered me that you were jumping into this theater thing with both feet, getting a lot of people I care about all excited about something, when you might not follow through."

"I don't walk away from commitments," she said pointedly.

Todd heard the unspoken accusation in her words and struck out with one of his own. "That's not quite true."

"Oh?"

"You walked away from me."

"Only because you'd already gone," she said, resting a hand against his cheek as if that might take the sting out of her words. "You left me the day you signed on permanently with Megan."

"Not that again," Todd said, impatiently removing her hand because her touch was too distracting. "I took that job to give us some financial stability. I'm not going to apologize for wanting to take care of you."

"Who asked you to? We were doing fine, Todd. We weren't starving or living on the streets."

"It wasn't enough. You deserved more."

"Your choice. I didn't need more."

They had had the same argument a hundred times before she had walked out. They'd both been stubbornly entrenched in their positions. Obviously that hadn't changed. It was also old news.

"We'll never see eye to eye on this," he said. "So there's no point in discussing it."

She regarded him with visible exasperation. "How many times have I heard that? When I won't give in, you just cut off the discussion. How are we supposed to resolve anything if we don't thrash it out, weigh all the arguments and options? Shouldn't we at least listen to each other?"

He regarded her ruefully. "And then what?"

"Compromise?" she suggested. "I've heard it's a great way to settle disputes."

"Your idea of compromise is to talk until I give in," he said.

"That's certainly one way to go," she conceded lightly. "Then again, who knows, you might eventually muster up an argument that gets me to change my mind."

"Are we talking about career planning or custody now?"

"Your choice."

Suddenly the last thing he wanted to do was to discuss either topic. They were too complicated, too fraught with minefields. He turned his head slightly, captured her hand and pressed a kiss to the palm. "How about we don't talk at all?"

"Now, there's a solution," she whispered, seemingly as eager as he to stop all the arguing. She leaned toward him as his mouth came down to cover hers.

The familiar swirl of urgent need and spinning senses took over then, pushing everything else aside. That had been their pattern, letting explosive chemistry solve what logic couldn't. Unfortunately—then and now—when the slow, deep kisses or the magnificent sex ended, the deep-rooted complications were still there and, as far as Todd could tell, there wasn't a realistic solution in sight.

After that kiss, Todd seemed to be in a much more agreeable frame of mind. Heather managed to talk him into bringing some of the experts from Megan's production company out to the barn to consult on lighting and set design. But there was something else she wanted from him, something she feared he'd reject out of hand. She had to get him in exactly the right frame of mind before she tried any sneaky persuasive tactics on him.

"Come to dinner at my place when we finish here tonight," she suggested. "We should be quitting in another half hour or so. I promise I can do better than peanut butter and jelly or macaroni and cheese."

"I don't know. Maybe you should fix those just for old times' sake."

Although there were certain aspects of old times she was hoping to re-create, those Spartan meals weren't among them. "Leave dinner to me. About eight? Or have you gotten used to ranching hours out here? I can have dinner on the table earlier, but Angel will still be awake."

"Eight is fine," he said too quickly, as if the prospect of avoiding Angel appealed to him even more than the lateness of the dinner hour.

For once Heather ignored the reaction. She didn't want to head down that particular path when she had a more immediate problem to resolve. She bounded up, pressed another kiss to his cheek, then called for Angel.

"Come on, sweetie. Let's go see where Joe is," she said, knowing the comment would annoy Todd.

She had seen the way Todd had watched the two of them earlier, frowning just at the sight of them chatting. If only he knew, she thought with amusement. She was trying her level best to get Joe hooked up with Flo. Half of their conversations were spent with her touting the other woman's virtues.

So far, though, Joe had stubbornly resisted the bait. For some crazy reason he had gotten it into his head that Flo wasn't interested in him.

"She turned me down flat not once, but twice," he told Heather. "I can take a hint."

"Maybe you should ask her why," she'd suggested.

"And maybe you should mind your own business."

Of course, she had no intention of doing that. She just had to get the two of them together under the right circumstances. Flo was not the kind of woman that any healthy virile male, which Joe most definitely was, could resist for long.

She found Flo inside, balanced precariously atop a ladder, spreading paint across the frame of a window. Her hair had been tied back with a hot-pink, Western-style bandanna. Her white shorts displayed an awesome length of bare, curvy leg. Joe was standing a few yards away, mouth agape as she reached for a distant bit of trim. The stretch tugged her form-fitting top out of the waistband of her shorts to expose more smooth flesh.

The ladder wobbled, not dangerously, but Heather deliberately let out a yelp of dismay, which startled Flo. Joe sprang forward, just as the ladder toppled, catching Flo in a solid grip against his chest. Her arms instinctively circled his neck. Joe's gaze locked on her literally—and justifiably—heaving bosom.

Watching, Heather gave a little nod of satisfaction. *I think my work here is done,* she said to herself and slipped out of the barn before either of them realized her role in their currently intimate situation.

The conversation she'd meant to have with Joe could wait till morning. Besides, leaving now would strand Flo, who'd ridden to the barn with her. She was pretty sure she didn't have to worry about the woman getting a lift home. In fact, unless she was very much mistaken, it might be quite a while before Joe even got around to putting her down. She knew better than to think that one little incident constituted a relationship, but judging from the way those two had been gazing at each other, it was definitely a good beginning.

Now she just had to get home and find a way to work the same sort of magic on Todd.

17

Naturally Angel chose that night to be difficult. She turned the bathroom into a sea of sudsy water while taking her bath. Once in bed she cried and pleaded for another story and then another, until Heather was almost at her wit's end.

This was the very reason she'd come to Whispering Wind, so Todd could share the burden of these charming episodes. Unfortunately tonight would not be the best occasion for him to see his daughter at anything less than her best. That meant getting Angel asleep well before he arrived, even if she had to bribe her. It was not a tactic she liked using, so she made one last attempt at simple persuasion.

"Sweetie, Mommy has to change clothes and fix dinner."

"Why, Mama? Me ate. P'butter 'n' jelly, remember?"

"Yes, I remember. But I haven't eaten. And Todd's coming over."

Oops! Wrong thing to say. Angel's expression brightened at once.

"Wanna see Todd!" she declared eagerly, even as she sleepily rubbed her half-closed eyes.

"No, baby. It's past your bedtime now."

"Wanna see him!" Angel wailed. "Please, Mama!"

At this rate, Todd might get peanut butter and

jelly sandwiches for dinner, after all, Heather thought despondently. And she wasn't going to be fit company for anyone, much less at her persuasive best.

"Angel," she said firmly. "I want you to close your eyes this very instant."

To her astonishment, Angel blinked rapidly at the unexpectedly sharp tone, then dutifully snapped her eyes shut.

"See, Mama," she cajoled. "I sleeping."

Heather breathed a sigh of relief. "Good girl. Sleep tight. I'll see you in the morning."

She flipped on the night-light, then turned off the overhead and eased out of the room. Outside the door, she leaned against the wall and waited to see if Angel's sudden display of agreeability would last. Not a sound, she thought when several minutes had passed. That was definitely promising.

She grabbed a quick shower, pulled on a long gauzy skirt, a tank top and a pair of sandals. For once she left off her bracelets, because she knew Todd found them annoying. Since tonight was all about persuading him to do something that would likely go against the grain, she figured it was a necessary concession.

Unfortunately he took one look at her bare arms when he walked in the door and eyed her warily. "What do you want?"

She regarded him innocently. "I don't know what you mean."

"No bracelets. That's a sure sign you want something."

She laughed. "I just forgot them after I took my shower," she insisted. "I was running late. If it'll make you feel better, I'll go put them on."

He held up a hand. "No, please. I imagine you were late thanks to the cowboy."

"No, thanks to your daughter. She wanted to wait up for you. It took longer than usual to get her to settle down."

That seemed to distract him from both Joe and the bracelet issue. "I don't understand why she's formed this attachment for me. I really haven't tried to encourage it."

He seemed genuinely bemused and troubled.

"I think she senses the bond," Heather told him. "Kids do."

"Just the way cats seem to gravitate toward people they know are annoyed by them?" he suggested dryly.

She frowned at the comparison. "Would it be so terrible for your child to actually love you?"

"Yes," he said bluntly. "I don't have anything to give back to her."

"Todd, that's absurd," she said impatiently, then tried to temper the response. "You're very good with her."

"No," he insisted. "Just because I don't ignore her doesn't mean I'm good with her."

This wasn't getting them anywhere. Heather figured if she didn't change the topic, Todd would automatically start contradicting everything that came out of her mouth. She'd never get him to fall in with her plan that way.

"Have a glass of wine," she suggested, already pouring his favorite red wine.

His eyebrow quirked when he saw it, but he accepted the French vintage without comment, then followed her into the kitchen where she'd managed to get the salads ready and on the table. The chicken was still baking.

"It will be another half hour or so," she apologized. "I didn't get dinner in the oven until just a few minutes ago."

"No problem. I'm not starving."

"Let's sit out on the steps awhile, then. It's a nice night."

In truth, the temperature had dropped dramatically since sundown. She still hadn't gotten used to the way Wyoming weather could change so drastically from one minute to the next. She sat down beside him and promptly shivered.

"Cold?" Todd asked.

"It's chillier than I expected."

To her astonishment, he inched closer and draped an arm over her shoulders.

"Does that help?"

The contact definitely turned up her inner heat by several degrees. She nodded and snuggled closer. This was going well. Between the wine and the intimacy, he ought to be feeling really mellow in no time at all.

"Spill it, Heather." The light command proved he hadn't forgotten his suspicions that she was up to something.

"What do you—"

"The expensive wine, the lack of bracelets, dinner. Sweetheart, I know you. You're up to something. You might as well spit it out and save us both the suspense."

She considered trying to distract him with a kiss, but concluded that would only rouse his suspicions further.

"I can't imagine why you think I'm up to some-thing."

"History," he said succinctly. "Those bracelets never come off unless you're trying very hard not to annoy me. The only time you care about that one way or the other is when you want something and you're convinced I'm going to say no unless you go to extreme measures."

"Speaking of annoying," she muttered.

"What?"

"You know me too well. And I am definitely not supposed to be that predictable. It's exas-perating. Men are not supposed to be perceptive enough to figure out our tricks."

"Since I have, why don't you cut to the chase? Is this about Angel?"

She shook her head, then smiled at his barely perceptible sigh of relief.

"What then?"

"I told you I'm doing this play." She felt him stiffen ever so slightly.

"Which has nothing to do with me," he said emphatically.

"That's not entirely true."

"Heather, I've already agreed to get you some professional help with the lighting and the sets. I don't know what more I can do."

"It's not much," she assured him. "Just one teensy little favor."

He edged away from her, then stared into her eyes with a steady, penetrating look. Before she could even open her mouth, he was shaking his head. "Oh, no. Forget it."

"I haven't even asked yet."

"Don't waste your breath."

"But it's a great part."

"I don't care if it's Macbeth at the Old Vic in London, I'm not doing it."

"Actually it's Romeo," she said, testing him because she knew he'd always harbored a desire to do that particular Shakespearean tragedy.

His expression never wavered. "No," he said flatly.

"You would turn down a chance to do *Romeo and Juliet* with me?"

"In a barn in Wyoming? You bet."

"Then how about *Oklahoma!?*" she asked quietly. They had done the musical in summer theater on Cape Cod. It had been one of the best summers they'd shared.

The heat in Todd's eyes suggested he remembered every passionate minute of that summer as vividly as she did. The scowl on his lips suggested he wasn't happy about it.

"You really are a sneaky, rotten person, aren't you?" he said, but without any real rancor.

"Does that mean you're tempted?"

"It means I am appalled that I ever had the misfortune to fall for a woman who knows how to zero in on my weaknesses."

"Would that be your weakness for a classic musical that's guaranteed to be a crowd-pleaser?"

"Not exactly," he said, his gaze locked with hers. He brushed a strand of hair back behind her ear.

"Surely not your weakness for a certain co-star?"

"You know damned well that was the summer we first started talking about living together," he muttered. "We'd been dating for a year. We shared that cottage at the beach to save on expenses, then decided we ought to make the living arrangement permanent."

She feigned wide-eyed surprise. "Was that when we made that decision?"

A faraway look crossed his face. "Why would you want to go there again, Heather?"

"It was the best time of my life. Why wouldn't I?" she countered.

"Because no good can come of it."

The regret in his voice told her otherwise. "I'm not nearly as convinced of that as you seem to be," she said, pausing long enough to brush a kiss across his lips before standing up and heading inside. "Just promise me you'll think about it while I get dinner on the table."

"You've had days to dream up this scheme and you're giving me five minutes to think about it?" he grumbled, following along behind her.

"Five minutes is plenty long enough to decide, especially for a man with your decision-making prowess," she insisted as she dished up the chicken and carried the plates to the table, then gestured for him to sit opposite her. "Just this once, go with your gut."

"My gut is telling me to stay as far away from this little production of yours as I possibly can."

"Oh."

He grinned as he speared a piece of chicken. "Still want me to listen to my gut?"

"No. Tell your scaredy-cat gut to go to hell," she said at once. "Jump in with both feet. Do something totally impulsive. Take a risk."

She saw immediately that she'd gone too far. Todd's hand froze halfway to his mouth. Mentioning *risk* had been a bad idea, she realized at once. For reasons she'd never entirely understood, Todd was vehemently opposed to risks of any kind. Phrase it as a dare or a challenge and he'd seize it in a heartbeat, but risks turned his complexion ashen. She was certain there had to be a story behind it.

"I take it back," she said hurriedly. "There's no risk at all. In fact, this will be a breeze. You know the play inside out. You know the songs. We'll barely have to rehearse. You got rave reviews when we did this."

"Rave?" he repeated doubtfully, but he finally took that bite of chicken that had been hovering in midair.

"They were. The critics loved you. They thought I was adequate. I need you to do this play with me. How could I possibly go on with anyone else? They'll fall in love with you and overlook my inadequacies."

He finished chewing. "No one as beautiful as you could ever be described as inadequate."

She waved off the compliment. "I need you," she repeated emphatically. She could see from his wavering expression that she'd finally struck just the right note of desperation. Todd was the kind of man who thrived on being needed. It was why it had been so easy for Megan to seduce him into staying on the job with her company. She had been in desperate need of someone to organize her out-of-control corporate life. He had leaped into the void like Superman going off to save Lois Lane from certain calamity.

"You don't need me," he hedged, taking another forkful of food. "This is good, by the way."

"Thanks. I told you I'd learned a few things in the kitchen. And I do need you. Who else around here has the talent?"

"Maybe you ought to hold auditions and find out," he suggested. "Maybe your cowboy buddy can sing like an angel."

"Joe has already said he'll step onto that stage only after I've taught his prize steer to fly. He sounded like he meant it."

"So how come you've taken his no for an answer and refuse to listen to me?"

"Because Joe is not crucial to the success of this play. You are."

"Maybe you should have taken the scarcity of actors into account before you leaped into this theater project."

"Why would I when I knew that one of the best actors on Broadway was right here?"

He frowned at the flattery. "Speaking of award-caliber acting, you're laying it on a little thick, aren't you?"

"Come on, Todd, if you won't do it for me, do it for the town you claim to have adopted. Think of the fun people will have getting involved with putting on a musical."

"You sound like Mickey Rooney and Judy Garland in some old movie."

"Cute," she muttered. "Okay, then, think of the enjoyment they'll have attending a real theater out here in the middle of nowhere. This could be a big contribution to Whispering Wind and its future."

His gaze narrowed. "A one-time theatrical venture is going to contribute to the town's future?"

She leveled a look straight at him. "It wouldn't have to be a one-time venture," she said quietly, turning the words into a dare as much as a promise.

"Meaning?"

"You're a bright man. You figure it out. In the meantime, I'll get dessert."

Fresh strawberries and mounds of whipped cream, she thought with a smile as she went to retrieve them. If he thought everything that had come before tonight had been sneaky and low-down, this was totally diabolical.

She brought the bowls to the table and watched the quick flare of heat in Todd's eyes as some extremely erotic memories predictably slammed through him, just as she'd planned. He sat back at once and held up his hands in a gesture of surrender.

"Okay, okay, I'll do it."

Heather grinned and slipped onto his lap. She dipped a lush, ripe strawberry into the cream and held it to his lips. "I just knew you'd see it my way."

"Of course you did," he said dryly. "I never stood a chance."

"I hear you're going to star in a production of *Oklahoma!*," Megan said before Todd could even shrug out of his jacket the next morning.

"Excuse me? What grapevine are you tapped into? Or have you left some sort of a bug in Heather's apartment?"

She chuckled. "It is a small town and this is hot news."

"I only agreed to do this last night, after a whole lot of soul-searching," he claimed. And the sight of a bowl of strawberries and whipped cream. To his very deep regret, Heather knew exactly how to push all of his buttons.

"Well, I think it's terrific. I've always wanted to see you on stage. Just don't catch the acting bug again and charge back to New York."

"No chance of that," he assured her. "I'm perfectly content keeping your productions on schedule and under budget."

"Speaking of which, how's Peggy's show coming?"

"Couldn't be better. The sponsors are lined up and I've already started sending feelers out to our current station lineup. It's going to be an easy sell. That woman has the potential to be a gold mine. If you ever get a notion to retire, the money she rakes in will keep you comfortable."

"Just as I told you," she gloated.

"Megan, you are not right about everything all the time."

"Don't spread it around," she advised. "My image depends on everyone else thinking I am."

"I could mention a certain foray into creating homemade dyes for fabrics that got, shall we say, a little messy. I have the stained clothes and the videotape to prove it."

Megan laughed. "Okay, but only the first time around. I nailed it the second time." She gazed idly around his office. "Where is that tape, by the way?"

He laughed. "Someplace you'll never find it. I have plans for that tape. Peggy's show might pay for your retirement, but that tape could pay for mine."

"You would blackmail me?" she asked with feigned shock but little evidence of dismay.

"In a heartbeat," he assured her. "At the very least it will make for a lot of laughs at the production party when we wrap for the season."

Her expression sobered. "Okay, all kidding aside, what's going on with you and Heather? You've avoided answering me every other time I asked. I thought she was just in town for a short visit."

"It started out that way."

"But?"

"I really don't want to get into this."

"Okay, look, I have kept my mouth shut since the day she turned up, because I figured sooner or later you would get around to filling me in."

"You're my boss," he reminded her. "This is personal."

She looked vaguely hurt by the reminder. "I also thought we were friends."

"Yes, of course, but—"

"But you didn't want me to start getting worried that you might take off and abandon me just when we're starting to make this work out here?"

"As you so recently reminded me, we have a long-term contract. I haven't even considered bailing on you."

"You know perfectly well I would let you out of that contract if you really wanted to get married and move back to New York."

Blind terror rolled through him. "Married? Who the hell said anything about getting married?"

"Todd, you love the woman. You have a child together. Naturally, I thought—"

"Well, you thought wrong."

"Meaning?"

He couldn't honestly say what he meant anymore. "I wish to hell I knew."

"Okay, let's back up. What exactly does Heather want out of this? Marriage?"

"Absolutely not. It's never come up," he said fiercely, though he had to wonder if that wasn't behind this theatrical venture that was keeping her in town and the vague hints that it didn't have to be a one-time thing.

"What, then?"

"Child support and some kind of shared custody of Angel. Those are the only issues on the table."

Megan seemed surprised. "That's it? Some men would be ecstatic about that. They want to be a part of their children's lives, but their ex-wives make it impossible."

"I'm not one of them," he declared flatly.

He expected her to regard him with disapproval, but instead, she merely studied him intently.

Eventually she said, "I'm getting the same vibes now that I got when I asked you to be a godfather to our baby."

He'd been very much afraid she might link the two. "That's because you have a vivid imagination," he suggested.

"No," she said. "It's because I'm perceptive and you're not very good at hiding your emotions."

"I had no idea I was so transparent," he said stiffly.

"Oh, you can be all cool and calm in a crisis, but with something like this, the turmoil is right out there for anyone to see. Have you at least explained all this to Heather? Told her why you're so vehemently opposed to sharing custody of Angel?"

"There's nothing to explain."

"I disagree. If you don't want to be a part of your daughter's life, then I think there's quite a lot to explain. You can't just say thanks but no thanks and turn your back on her."

"I already have."

"Heather's not buying it, though, is she? And she never will without a straight answer. You may not owe *me* that, but you certainly owe it to her. And, believe me, down the road you're going to owe it to your daughter."

Because he wasn't crazy about the fact that she was right, he pointed out one more time that this was none of her business.

"Maybe not, but you ought to listen to me, anyway. Remember my history, Todd. I was abandoned on my grandfather's doorstep by my mother. I never saw her again. I never knew my father. No one ever explained a blasted thing to me. You've seen firsthand what that did to me."

"Turned you into the head of a multimedia empire?"

She frowned. "No, it left me unable to trust anybody. It left me with enough self-esteem issues to keep a shrink in a new Mercedes every year. If I'm an overachiever, it's because I was always afraid of not being good enough. Don't do that to Angel. Whatever it is that makes you think you don't belong in her life, rise above it. Get some help. Deal with it. Whatever it takes, don't let your daughter down the way my parents let me down. Tex was the best grandfather he could be and I loved him, but it wasn't the same."

"Megan—"

She held up a hand, cutting off the protest. "I know, I know. It's none of my business. But think about what I said. You're a decent guy, Todd. You won't be able to live with yourself if you don't find some way to be there for your child." She gave him a sly look. "And for Heather."

"Heather is not an issue," he repeated one more time.

She grinned. "Tell that to someone who'll buy it."

She shot to her feet then and exited his office before he could think of a single lie to spin for her. Because the truth was, Heather was turning into an issue. Old feelings were coming back at a dizzying clip. Hormones were kicking into gear with an undeniable ferocity.

And he had absolutely no idea what the hell to do about any of it, because right there in the middle of everything was an innocent little girl who scared him senseless.

That night for the first time in years, Todd awoke from a nightmare in a cold sweat. The sound of screeching tires and shattering glass echoed even after he shook himself awake and reminded himself that it was only a dream. This time, any-way.

Years ago it had been all too real. He shuddered at the too-vivid memory, tried to block it out, but the attempt was as unsuccessful now as it had been for months back then. Every time the memories had dared to die down even a little, his father had been there to fan them back to life.

"Irresponsible."

"Reckless."

And in a drunken rage, "Murderer."

If his father had been right there in the room with him tonight, he couldn't have stirred Todd's guilt any more effectively. It didn't seem to matter that he'd been exonerated by everyone else who mattered—his mother, the legal system, his friends.

His father dished out more than enough blame for all the rest of them combined. Todd knew that until his father drew his last dying breath, he would blame Todd for killing his baby sister.

Worse, Todd had never stopped blaming himself.

18

"You stranded me at the barn last night," Flo accused Heather when she stopped by the diner for her morning cup of coffee. "That was a sneaky, low-down thing to do."

Pleased with her evening's accomplishments,

Heather grinned. "What can I say? I was on a roll last night. Did it work?"

"If you're asking if Joe gave me a ride home, the answer is yes." She didn't sound especially happy about it.

"And?" Heather prodded.

"We talked," she said with a sigh.

"And?"

"That's it. We talked. In the car, parked at the curb. I invited him in for coffee, but you'd have thought I'd suggested we roll around in the mud buck-naked. I'm giving up on him. He's obviously lost interest."

Heather thought maybe the exact opposite was true. "How long did you talk?"

"A couple of hours, I guess."

"About?"

"His ranch, the kind of childhood he had and how different it was from mine. We even talked a little bit about Tess and how grateful I am that she's forgiven me for dumping her with Tex. He brought it up. You were right. He already knew most of the story."

Heather hid a smile at the personal information they'd both shared. "That doesn't sound like a man who's not interested," she observed. "Obviously he didn't cut and run when he heard about Tess, did he?"

"Okay, no. You were right about that, too. He seemed real understanding."

"I'm telling you, the man's interested. He just needs a nudge."

Flo still wasn't buying it. "Most men would have made a pass by now."

"Most of the men you *used* to know," Heather agreed. "Isn't that why you're attracted to Joe, because he's different, more substantial, more of a gentleman? He's treating you like a lady, Flo. He's showing you the respect you deserve. He's not just out for a quick tumble into bed."

Flo's expression brightened as Heather's interpretation sank in. "You think so?"

"I saw the way he looked at you when you fell off the ladder and into his arms last night. I definitely think so. The man wants you so bad it's scared him silly. He's done a fine job of resisting all the other women in town, but you're clearly testing his willpower."

"Funny. I could have sworn it was you he wanted."

There was genuine fear and dismay rather than jealousy in Flo's voice. Heather sought to reassure her. "Oh, I think maybe he thought he did for a minute or two, because I was someone new, but trust me, he has never looked at me the way he was staring at you last night."

Flo grinned. "You mean the way Todd looks at you, like a lovesick calf?"

Heather was startled by the observation. "Todd looks at me like that?"

"You have to know he does. The two of you were an item, weren't you? You must have been for him to be Angel's daddy."

"That was a long time ago." And again very recently, if she was totally honest. She just hadn't thought it really meant anything to Todd.

"Oh, *please*. Talk about delusional. If you can't see that the man is still crazy about you, you're every bit as blind as you claim I am about Joe."

A funny little twinge of hope stirred deep inside her. Was that what she wanted? Was that the real reason she'd worked so hard to get Todd to agree to do the play, because she'd hoped to rekindle the old romance?

She took a good, hard look into her heart and realized that that was exactly what she'd been doing. She might as well face it. She no longer merely wanted Todd to accept a role in Angel's life. She wanted him back in hers.

Heather had pulled together a surprisingly good cast of amateurs, Todd conceded on the first night of rehearsals. Several people had strong, solid voices. They'd also taken the assignment to learn their lines to heart and come to the barn prepared to really rehearse. In fact, they seemed downright eager to have a real Broadway actor as their director. It was entirely possible she could pull this thing together in a month, the way she'd told him she planned to. It was scheduled for weekend performances in August.

Watching her low-key approach with admiration, Todd admitted that Heather had a knack for drawing the best out of the cast, too. Rather than intimidating them, she used praise and encouragement to get what she wanted. And because she was an actress, she could demonstrate exactly the way a line should be delivered for maximum effect. It was an approach that worked well with amateurs who might otherwise be floundering.

As the last of the actors straggled out after that first rehearsal, Todd offered her a mock salute. "My hat's off to you. You're really good at this."

She regarded him with surprise. "You think so?"

He nodded. "I was impressed. Honestly. You got the best out of them. For a first rehearsal, that's amazing."

"Thank you. Coming from you that really means a lot."

"I know we never discussed it, but did you ever consider directing rather than acting?"

She settled into the seat next to him, her legs tucked up with her long skirt billowing around them, bare toes sticking out. She rested her chin on her knees, her expression thoughtful. "Never. I always wanted to be on stage." She turned to him. "Do you think I should reconsider?"

"I just think it's an option you might want to

explore. Get a couple of plays under your belt as a director out here and who knows where it could lead? How did it feel to see things starting to come together tonight?"

"Amazing," she admitted. "I've always been so concerned with nailing my own part before that I never saw the big picture." She grinned. "Did you watch Sissy? It was like seeing a flower open up to the sun. She was good, really good."

"I noticed," Todd said. "I wonder what Henrietta's going to think when Sissy announces she wants to head for Broadway or Hollywood."

"She'll do whatever she can to help," Heather said at once. "That's the way she is. There's not a selfish bone in that woman's body. Just look at the way she took those two kids into her life without batting an eye. I can't help admiring her for that. It must have been quite an adjustment."

"Are you talking from experience?" he asked, not at all sure he really wanted to go down this particular path, but needing to hear the answer just the same. "Was that what it was like for you when you had Angel? A sudden and difficult adjustment?"

She met his gaze evenly, as if trying to determine just how honest he wanted her to be. "I won't lie to you," she said finally. "It was a whole lot harder than I expected it to be." Her eyes lit up and a smile tugged at the corners of her mouth. "Better, too, in other ways." Her gaze caught his.

"You missed so much. Her first word. Her first step. It is so amazing to watch her grow and learn. She's so bright, so curious about everything."

"You don't regret . . ." He couldn't bring himself to say the rest.

"Having her? Absolutely not," Heather said fiercely. "I never considered any other option. I can't imagine not having her in my life."

In the past few weeks Todd had experienced tiny flickers of those same emotions, but they weren't deep enough to combat the fear that was always with him.

"I wish . . ." Again his voice trailed off.

"What?"

He shook his head. "Nothing." He deliberately changed the subject. "How's Henrietta's romance with the judge progressing?"

Heather looked as if she might protest the sudden shift in topic, but eventually—to his relief—she merely sighed.

"He's taken the whole family out a few times now," she said. "That hasn't kept Henrietta from giving him grief every time he sets foot into the diner, but he doesn't seem to mind. I've also noticed that he and Will are getting closer. At first Will seemed scared to death of him, but I suppose that's natural given the way his father was. The judge has been extremely patient, but I saw how his eyes lit up when Will crept up beside him the other night and actually initiated a conversation."

"I wonder if Henrietta and the judge would have come this far if you hadn't come along to intervene," Todd said.

Heather regarded him with surprise. "Me? I didn't do anything."

"Right. Just like you haven't stuck your nose into Flo's relationship with the cowboy. Not that I'm unhappy to find his attention diverted from you. The man was beginning to annoy me."

Heather grinned. "Really? That's quite an admission."

"I just didn't want to see you starting something you had no intention of finishing," he claimed.

"Is that so?" she asked with obvious amusement.

"Yes."

"Admit it, you were pea-green with jealousy."

"I do not have a jealous bone in my body," he protested.

"Liar."

"Am not."

"I can prove it, too."

He regarded her cautiously. "How?"

She beckoned him closer, then cupped his face in her hands and kissed him. She might as well have lit a fire under his feet, given the way the heat shot through him. His body was hard and aching in nothing flat, but just when he would have done something about it, she sat back with a satisfied expression.

"Nobody who kisses with that much passion is going to let another man onto his turf," she announced. "Not that I'm yours, you understand."

"Of course not," he intoned solemnly. "Never thought you were."

He turned to find her looking at him with a worried frown puckering her brow. "What?"

"This is getting complicated, isn't it?"

He considered denying it, but figured there were enough evasions between them already. He nodded. "Yes."

"Any idea what we ought to do about it?"

"Not a one. You?"

She looked as if she might offer one, but then she sighed instead and shook her head. "None."

"Then I guess we'll just have to play it by ear and see where we wind up."

She seemed startled by that. "You can do that? You, the man who has a day-planner for a brain?"

Once he would have chafed at the not-very-flattering but all-too-accurate description. Now he managed to take it in stride. "If I have to," he conceded. "It's better than the alternative."

"Which is?"

"Making a decision we'll both live to regret."

"So I was thinking that when the time comes, I could maybe go to New York with Heather," Sissy was saying to Henrietta when Heather went into work the following day. "What do you think?"

Henrietta frowned, caught sight of Heather and beckoned her over. "You field that one, why don't you."

Heather was afraid she'd heard enough to gather that Sissy had just announced her decision to become an actress. Henrietta didn't seem overjoyed. Or maybe it was the declaration that Sissy wanted to go to New York now that had her looking utterly defeated.

"Sissy, why don't you come over here and tell me exactly what you and Henrietta were talking about?" Heather suggested, gesturing toward a booth.

Sissy slid into the booth, her cheeks flushed with excitement and her eyes shining. "I was telling Henrietta about last night's rehearsal. I told her you said I was really, really good, and that I wanted to be an actress."

"But didn't I hear you also say that you wanted to move to New York with me?"

"Uh-huh." Her expression turned anxious. "I wouldn't be any trouble. I could help out with Angel and stuff."

"Sissy, you're still a young girl. You have to finish school. Maybe even go to college."

"But why? There are kids in commercials and stuff at my age. I could pay my own way, so Henrietta wouldn't have to."

"I don't think Henrietta minds. Besides, it's not that simple. Even when you're good, it takes time to get the right agent, to start getting jobs. It's a tough life. You need time to be a teenager."

Sissy regarded her with a steady, sad look. "I'm not a kid. I grew up a long time ago," she said quietly.

"Oh, baby," Heather said, reaching for her. "You've seen way too much, been *through* way too much, but you are still a kid. I don't want you to squander what's left of those years by putting too much pressure on yourself."

Sissy's lower lip trembled. "You don't think I'm good enough, do you? You were just saying that."

Heather held Sissy's shoulders steady and stared straight into her eyes. "Absolutely not," she told her emphatically. "You're wonderful, really remarkable for someone with no training at all. But there's no need to rush into this. Your talent isn't going anywhere. It will just get better and better."

"How? If you go back to New York, who's going to show me?"

"Who said anything about me going back to New York?"

"You did. That night in the park you told me you were just here for a while."

"Well, maybe I've changed my mind."

Sissy regarded her hopefully. "Really? You're not going away?"

Henrietta joined them just then, looking every bit as anxious to hear Heather's reply as Sissy was.

"Not right away," Heather said carefully, not wanting to make a promise she couldn't keep. Her talk with Todd the night before had given her hope, and a very good reason to consider postponing her return to a life that, despite the occasional acting job, had been nothing but a struggle.

"Then you'll do lots of plays?" Sissy asked. "And I can be in all of them?"

Heather laughed at her eagerness. "Let's just get through *Oklahoma!* before we start thinking about the next play, okay?" She gave Sissy a fierce hug. "I promise you this, though. When the time is right, if this is something you still want, I will do everything in my power to see that you make the right connections."

Sissy's eyes shone. "Really?"

"It's a promise."

"And Heather never breaks a promise," Todd said quietly, slipping into the booth opposite them, his gaze locked with hers. "Isn't that right?"

"Never."

"Thank you," Henrietta mouthed silently as she gave Heather's shoulder a squeeze. Then she clapped her hands together. "Okay, you two, let's get moving. Sissy, fill those salt and pepper shakers. Heather, I'll bring the napkin holders over for you to fill while you talk to Todd."

She moved off briskly, leaving Heather to face Todd, who was regarding her with an odd expression.

"What?" she demanded.

"You. You're fitting right in here, aren't you? Taking on the world's problems, just the way you always did."

"Is there something wrong with that? Aren't we put on this earth to try to make a difference?"

"I know that's what you believe," he agreed. "I just thought you were dead-set on being a big-city girl."

"I've recently discovered that there are certain perks to being part of a small town. I never appreciated that growing up, but now it's nice having a support system, seeing friends every day, instead of once a month for a quick lunch. Even in a few weeks, I feel more connected here than I ever did in New York. You must feel the same way or you wouldn't have stayed here, even for the hefty paycheck you're getting from Megan."

"I haven't really had time to think about it. There's been too much work to do."

Heather regarded him impatiently. "Todd, be honest for once. You bought a truck, for heaven's sake."

"So?" he said, scowling.

"A truck," she repeated. "A pickup truck."

"Yeah. So?" he repeated.

She gave an exasperated sigh. "You could have gotten some trendy sport utility vehicle or a flashy sports car. That would certainly have been more in keeping with your New York image, but you've obviously gotten all caught up in the Western mystique." She glanced down at his feet. "Don't think I haven't noticed those fancy, custom-made cowboy boots of yours, either. You wear them almost as much these days as you do your Italian loafers."

"They're just more practical out here," he said defensively, tucking his long legs out of view under the table, or trying to.

"Of course they are," she soothed. "And you look very sexy wearing them."

An obviously reluctant grin tugged at his lips. "Is that so."

"Oh, yeah."

Before they could pursue that, Roy Nolan from the hardware store down the street came in with one beefy hand cuffed around Will's wrist. Will was flushed and his eyes were red from crying. Henrietta rushed over to the boy and gathered him into a protective embrace.

"What's this all about, Roy?" she demanded as she smoothed the boy's hair back off his face.

"The boy knocked down an entire display," he said. "Did it deliberately, too."

"Did not," Will said, scowling up at him belligerently. "It was an accident."

Henrietta hesitated, clearly torn between wanting to believe Will's denial and knowing that the store owner had no reason to lie. She framed the child's face in her hands and looked directly into his eyes. "Will, tell me the truth," she said firmly. "What happened?"

His lower lip quivered, but he remained stubbornly silent.

"I'll take that for an admission of guilt, then," Henrietta said. "I have to say I am very disappointed, young man. I can't imagine what possessed you to do such a thing. What sort of display was it?"

"Hunting rifles," Roy said, suddenly looking uncomfortable. "Case and all. I've got glass from one end of the store to the other."

Heather exchanged a look with Todd, who was already on his feet. To her surprise, he promptly went over to stand beside Will. The boy turned to him, his expression filled with fear until Todd put a reassuring hand on his shoulder. Relief spread across the boy's face.

Why, she wondered, couldn't Todd see what instinctive parenting skills he possessed? It was obvious that Will knew whatever trouble he might be in, he had an ally.

"Will, why don't you go on into the kitchen and get your lunch?" Todd said quietly.

The boy regarded him with a grateful expression and ran. Todd turned slowly to face Roy. "You have to know what was going through his mind."

"Of course I do," Roy said. "I sympathize with him. No boy should have to live with the fact that guns were always being waved around at the house or that his daddy shot his mama, then died in an exchange of gunfire with the sheriff. I can't have him wrecking my store, though, can I?"

"I'll see that it doesn't happen again," Henrietta promised. "Naturally, I'll pay for any damage and take it out of his allowance. And I'll send Will over there to help you clean up the mess. He has to understand there are costs and consequences to the mischief he got into."

Roy nodded. "That'll do, then. I can't tell you how bad I feel about this, Henrietta."

"Same here," she said, her gaze straying toward the kitchen.

After Roy had left, she sank down on a stool at the counter. Heather walked over and sat beside her. "You okay?"

Henrietta shook her head, shoulders slumped in defeat for the first time since Heather had known her. She gave Todd and Heather a bewildered look. "I thought he was doing okay," she said wearily. "Better than Sissy, in fact, but now . . . I just don't know."

"Do you really think it was about the guns?" Heather asked.

Henrietta's gaze snapped toward her. "Well, of course it was. What else?"

Todd gave a nod of understanding, picking up on Heather's observation. "It was a test, wasn't it?" he said slowly to Heather, then faced

Henrietta to explain. "He wanted to see how you'd react. Maybe even how the judge would react. After all, the judge represents the system that never punished his father for the way he treated his mother."

"Well, then," Henrietta said briskly, rallying. "I suppose this calls for what they describe as tough love. When Harry gets here, I think the two of us will have a talk with the boy. Together we'll think of a suitable punishment, but we'll make sure he knows that we don't love him any less."

She sighed heavily. "Right now, though, I think I'll just go in the back and give him a hug. The poor little thing is probably scared to death. Then I want him over there helping Roy with the cleanup."

"Poor Will," Heather said as Henrietta left.

"Poor Henrietta," Todd said. "I don't envy her having to handle this one. It's going to be a delicate balancing act. If she's too harsh, the boy will just lump her in with all the other adults who've mistreated him. If she's too lenient, there will be no reason for him not to get into more and possibly worse trouble next time."

"I think the person who's really going to have to walk a tightrope is the judge," Heather countered. "Not only does he have to handle this just right for Will's sake, but for Henrietta's. One misstep and she could hold another grudge for another thirty years."

Todd's gaze locked with hers. "Makes you stop and think, doesn't it? One wrong decision and it can change someone's whole life."

Heather could tell he was no longer thinking about Henrietta and the judge, but rather about their own past. What she didn't know was which decision was really bothering him—his to work for Megan or hers to keep silent about Angel.

"Todd, I—"

He touched a silencing finger to her lips, then drew her into his arms. "Don't say anything," he said quietly. "Let's just make a vow here and now to think through whatever decisions we make from here on out."

She nodded, content to let her head rest against his chest, where she could feel the steady, reassuring beat of his heart. For some reason that solemn vow of his gave her more cause for optimism than she'd felt since coming to Whispering Wind.

Todd might not recognize it yet, might even be fighting it, but the fact was he was showing all the signs of being a strong, instinctive father figure in Will's life. Now all she had to do was persuade him that the same talent he had for being a role model for Will could be translated into being a dad to Angel.

19

The judge took the news of Will's misdeed in stride. He didn't seem nearly as distraught about it as Henrietta was. Todd had to admire the way he just stepped in, called Will over to sit with him and talked to him in a man-to-man way that left no doubt how he felt about either the transgression or the boy who'd committed it.

At one point, Will's eyes were bright with unshed tears, but his chin stayed up during the lecture. When the judge finished what he had to say, he opened his arms and Will scrambled into them, tears falling freely. Todd was pretty sure he spotted the sheen of a tear or two glistening in the judge's eyes, as well.

"It won't happen again, will it, boy?"

"No, sir," Will said softly.

"We can't go letting Henrietta down, can we?"

"No, sir," Will chimed dutifully. "Henrietta's the best."

"You'll get no argument from me there," the judge said. His gaze strayed to the woman who was watching the exchange, her expression anxious.

"Now, then, I recommend we cap off this discussion with some ice cream. Henrietta, find Sissy and let's go down the street where someone can wait on *you* for a change."

"I don't know . . ." Henrietta glanced at Heather.

"Go," Heather said at once. "If it gets busy before you get back, Todd can pitch in. He did a stint or two as a waiter. I don't think he'll dump the customers' dinners into their laps."

"Thanks for the recommendation," he muttered, then winked at Henrietta. "Go, while Heather's so eager to volunteer my time. In fact, take the night off. We can handle things around here."

"You don't mind?" Henrietta asked, regarding him worriedly.

"Of course not. It'll be a humbling experience to recall where I've come from."

"And goodness knows the man could use a dose of humility now that he's a hotshot television executive," Heather said.

He scowled at her. "So much for my intention to share my tips with you."

Henrietta looked from them to the trio waiting for her by the door, then nodded. "I believe I will take the evening off and spend it with my family."

The judge overheard the comment and a smile spread across his face. He gave Heather a wink. "Sounds to me like she's coming around. What do you think?"

"Don't go getting carried away," Henrietta warned him.

"Little chance of that, the way you bring me down a peg or two every time you think I'm getting too big for my britches," he grumbled.

Henrietta held him back when he would have walked out of the café with Sissy and Will. Her gaze locked on his. "I wasn't sure you'd stand beside me on this. I'm grateful. I truly am."

The judge's gaze softened. "Don't you know by now that I will always stand beside you?"

She searched his face, then gave a small nod of satisfaction. "I'm beginning to believe that."

They walked out the door arm in arm, leaving Todd alone in the restaurant with Heather.

"Think you remember how this is done?" she asked.

"Of course."

"Good. Then I'll run across the street and get Angel. She's been over with Janie this afternoon."

"Angel's been at the beauty salon?"

"Oh, yes," she confirmed, sounding amused. "Our daughter could have been a central character in that movie *Steel Magnolias*. You know, the one that takes place in a Southern beauty shop."

"She's a little young to be having her hair done, isn't she?"

"Actually, she likes to watch Janie styling hair. Janie seems thrilled to have an appreciative audience. And her customers seem to find Angel a diverting entertainment. She's better than the tabloids, Janie says."

Todd didn't like the sound of that. "Exactly what is Angel revealing over there? The gossip she picks up in here? Or the story of our lives? The last time Angel got chatty, she told everyone who'd listen that I'd slept with her mama."

Clearly unconcerned, Heather chuckled.

"We're talking about your reputation," he said.

"I can weather a little gossip," she insisted, then regarded him pointedly. "Can you?"

His gaze narrowed as he studied her. "Are you thinking if enough people leap to the conclusion that you and I are an item, I'll be forced to make good on it?"

She shot a pitying look at him. "Todd, I am not so desperate that I'd want a man who had to be forced to be with me."

"That wasn't what I meant."

"Wasn't it? Get a grip."

"I meant the whole family thing. Not just you and me, but the three of us."

She regarded him impatiently. "Now, there's a news flash. That's why I came out here, remember? To get you involved in Angel's life."

Nothing was coming out the way he'd intended, and despite her insistence that she still wanted only a custody agreement, he had a feeling Heather's agenda had changed. For a woman who usually prided herself on being direct, she was suddenly being awfully circumspect.

He grabbed her by the shoulders and forced her to meet his gaze. "Spell it out, Heather. What are you really after? It's not just about Angel anymore, is it?"

Her eyes flashed with defiant sparks. "No," she said evenly. "No, it's not. Though why I was stupid enough to fall in love with the most hardheaded man on the face of the earth for a second time is beyond me. You'd think once would have been more than enough."

He'd wanted her to be direct, but he wasn't sure he'd been prepared for such unvarnished honesty, after all.

Before he could gather his wits, she twisted out of his grasp. "Now, if you don't mind, I'm going to get our daughter. Try not to break any dishes while I'm gone."

Stunned into silence, Todd stared after her. By the time he could speak, she was already out the door. "Heather, wait," he called, but she kept right on going. He would have gone after her, but four teenagers chose that moment to barrel into the diner wanting burgers and fries.

Todd placed their orders with Mack, brought their soft drinks to the table, then went back to the door to watch for Heather, who seemed to be taking her own sweet time about returning. The sharp ringing of a bell from the kitchen signaled Mack's impatience when Todd didn't pick up the order the second it was off the grill.

Scowling, he served the four customers, then forced a smile as he seated three of the evening regulars who always sat in the same booth. The three widows ate together every single night, so

Todd had seen them often and knew their ordering habits. He automatically brought them their iced tea and didn't bother with menus.

"Where on earth is Henrietta?" Frannie Milsap demanded, looking him over suspiciously as if she thought he might have locked Henrietta in the freezer.

"And how did she talk you into waiting tables?" Cass Peterson wanted to know.

Daisy Harper squinted at him through her thick glasses. "You haven't lost your job, have you? Can't support that child of yours by waiting tables in a place like this."

The others nodded their agreement. "Absolutely not," Frannie said.

"No, indeed," Cass said.

Todd stared at them. "Excuse me? What child?"

"What's wrong with you, boy? You hard of hearing?" Daisy Harper asked. "I'm talking about Angel, of course."

"You think she's mine?" Todd asked cautiously.

"Well, of course she is," Cass said impatiently. "Looks just like you."

"Knew it the minute she and Heather turned up," Frannie agreed. "It's about time you acknowledged it, don't you think? About time you made an honest woman of that little girl's mama, too."

"Absolutely," Cass agreed. "Heather's a lovely young woman. Very sweet. We've grown very fond of her."

"Now, girls, we don't know all the facts," Daisy cautioned. "Could be there's a good reason why he and Heather aren't together." She gazed up at him inquiringly. "Is there?"

Todd had had no idea the trio had been engaging in such wild—if accurate—speculation. He supposed it shouldn't have come as such a shock, but he was taken aback just the same. Given their outspokenness, he probably should be grateful they hadn't brought the subject up sooner.

"Ladies, I'll go put in your orders," he said, backing away from the table without responding to the probing and far-too-complicated question.

"We haven't told you what we're having yet," Frannie pointed out.

"Meat loaf, mashed potatoes and peas," he countered. "It's the special and you always have the special."

"Well, I declare," Daisy said, looking dismayed. "Are we that predictable?"

"*Boring* is the word for it," Cass declared. "Get back over here, young man. I'll have a cheeseburger, thank you very much. With onion rings."

"You won't sleep a minute all night," Frannie warned her. "You know fried food gives you terrible indigestion."

"I'll take my chances," Cass insisted. "Now, what about the rest of you?"

"I'm sticking with the meat loaf," Daisy said staunchly. "I happen to like it."

Frannie looked torn. "Bring me a BLT," she said finally. She met Cass's gaze and seemed to take it as a dare. "With fries."

"Have you got that?" Cass asked.

Todd grinned, thrilled to have the attention off him and focused on food. "Got it."

He headed for the kitchen where Mack had already dished up three plates of meat loaf. "Sorry," he said. "A slight change in plans. Only one meat loaf."

"No meat loaf for the other two?" the cook said, looking stunned. "Henrietta takes off before the dinner hour. Heather disappears, and I am left with a television person to wait tables. What is going on around here tonight?"

"The times, they are a-changing," Todd said.

If the cook looked vaguely disgruntled by the news, it was nothing to the panic clawing at Todd. He had a terrible feeling that when all was said and done, these changes were going to turn his life upside down.

Heather finally strolled back into the diner about six-thirty, when the dinner rush was well under way. Todd scowled at her arrival, but he was clearly way too busy to pause and tell her what he thought of her little disappearing act.

"Miss me?" she inquired as she sashayed past and grabbed an apron.

"Like chicken pox," he muttered, only to barely

evade Angel's enthusiastic rush toward his legs.

"Hiya!" she called out cheerfully.

"Hi, kiddo," he said, skirting her as he aimed for the kitchen with a tray of dirty dishes.

To Heather's amusement, Angel toddled right after him.

"Whatcha doing?"

"The work your mother should have been doing," he murmured.

"I heard that," Heather called out as she moved on to take the orders of four new arrivals.

"I help," Angel offered, toddling right back into the dining room in his wake.

"No, thanks, sweetie. Why don't you sit down in that booth over there and color one of your pictures?"

"You hang it on your 'frigerator?" she asked hopefully.

"Sure," he said absently as he briskly placed food in front of a group of tourists.

"Okay," Angel said, retrieving her crayons and coloring book from behind the counter and scrambling into the only vacant booth.

Coloring didn't exactly rise to great art when Angel did it. She scrambled right back down three minutes later and handed Todd a picture that was little more than colorful scribbles. "All done," she announced.

"Thanks, sweetie," he said, tucking it under the tray he was carrying.

She regarded him hopefully. "You wants another one?"

"Sure."

"Okay."

Heather had to bite back a chuckle as the scene was repeated several more times. Suddenly Todd glanced down at the handful of papers he'd accumulated without realizing it.

"Enough for a gallery showing," Heather observed. "She's going to be expecting to see the entire display. Your refrigerator must be bigger than I remembered."

Todd shrugged. "I'll put up one or two. She'll forget all about the rest."

Heather laughed. "Obviously you haven't spent a lot of time with a three-year-old. Angel has the memory of an elephant." She glanced at the stack of drawings. "Offhand I'd say there are enough there to paper the whole kitchen. It'll be really impressive when *Entertainment Tonight* comes to do a feature on Megan's hotshot executive."

"Fortunately I'm a behind-the-scenes guy. Nobody cares about me."

"Oh, I think I could see to it that that changed."

He frowned. "You wouldn't."

"Publicity would be good for the show, especially now that you're about to launch Peggy's cooking spin-off." She nodded. "Yes, indeed, I can definitely see the media possibilities.

Maybe I'll have a chat with Megan about them."

She got the first nagging hint that she'd gone too far when he deliberately stepped out from behind the counter, his gaze locked with hers. There was an unpredictable glint in his eyes as he strolled toward her. Heather swallowed hard and backed up a step, then another. Todd kept right on coming, forcing her farther back until she felt the edge of a table against her bottom and realized she was very likely about to settle into the middle of some customer's dinner.

"Um, Todd. Maybe this isn't the best time to get into this," she said.

"Really? You seemed anxious enough to get into it a minute ago."

Heather stole a quick glance over her shoulder into the three upturned, fascinated gazes of Daisy, Cass and Frannie.

"Sorry," she apologized.

"Oh, don't mind us, dear," Daisy said. "We haven't had this much fun in years."

"We'd all but forgotten what it was like to see sparks flying between a man and a woman," Cass added. "It's just not the same in the movies. The real thing takes me back."

"Oh, yes, indeed," Frannie confirmed a little breathlessly.

Todd regarded Heather with amusement. "How does it feel to be the main attraction in an unscheduled floor show?"

"You're enjoying this, aren't you?" she asked, startled.

He winked at Cass. "Oh, my, yes. I'd almost forgotten what it was like to see those old sparks flying myself."

He placed one arm on either side of her and grasped the edge of the table, pinning her in place. Heather's breath snagged in her throat. She heard the faint, collective gasp of the three women in the booth. Her pulse ricocheted wildly. What had gotten into Todd, for heaven's sake? He wasn't an exhibitionist. She was usually the one who initiated any public display of affection.

"Whatcha doing?" Angel asked, peering up at them with obvious fascination.

"I'm preparing to kiss your mother," Todd explained quietly, his gaze never venturing from Heather's face.

"Okay," Angel said agreeably.

Once again, the three widows seemed to catch their collective breath.

Todd's thighs were pressed against hers. The telltale bulge of his arousal was cradled by the heated juncture between her legs. She might have been able to escape by making a sudden, unexpected move, but she didn't want to. Despite their fascinated audience, she wanted to see just how daring he was inclined to be, just how far he would take this. It might turn out that a little provocation was a very good thing.

His mouth settled over hers in a kiss as gentle as a spring breeze, but then the kiss turned greedy and the storm began. His tongue invaded. His teeth raked over her lower lip.

"Oh, my," Frannie whispered.

"I declare," Cass murmured.

Daisy only sighed.

Heather slowly came back to earth as Todd eased away. A little provocation could definitely turn dangerous. She thought the three women had it exactly right. Oh, my, indeed.

Weeks later, Todd still wasn't sure what had come over him that night in the Starlight. He'd all but declared his intentions toward Heather in a very passionate way in a very public place. If he didn't make an honest woman of her after that kiss, he could think of at least three women who would likely tar and feather him. Four, if he counted Heather. Five, if he counted Henrietta. Sweet heaven, what had he been thinking?

Fortunately he didn't have time to think about it, because someone pounded on his office door, then jerked it open without waiting for him to reply. Peggy's husband came barreling in, looking mad enough to spit nails.

"This is your fault," Johnny Blakely accused, hands palm down on Todd's desk, a scowl fixed on his face.

"What?" Todd asked cautiously.

"You're ruining my marriage, that's what. This cockamamie scheme to make my wife into a TV star is turning my life into chaos. I want it to stop."

Todd sighed. He'd been afraid of this. "Does Peggy know how upset you are?"

"Do you think she'll listen to me? You and Megan have dangled this carrot in front of her and she can't stop thinking about it. It's all she talks about. Every time I point out that she has other responsibilities, she about takes my head off."

Todd sympathized with the man, but he had no intention of getting caught in the middle. He reached for his phone.

"What are you doing?" Johnny demanded.

"Calling Peggy. She's the one you need to talk to."

Johnny's anger deflated immediately. "Don't call her," he pleaded. "Things are bad enough without her knowing that I'm down here trying to get her fired."

"Is that what you want?" Todd asked. "You want me to fire her?"

Johnny raked a hand through his hair, which had been mashed flat by his John Deere baseball cap. Now his hair stood up in spikes. His expression was a mix of frustration and misery.

"I just want my wife back, that's all."

"Talk to her," Todd suggested.

"And say what?"

"The same thing you just said to me, that you want her back. Peggy loves you."

"Then why is she doing this?"

"Because she's good at it," Todd said. "You should be proud of her, Johnny, not trying to derail her. Just because she has a career doesn't mean she doesn't want her marriage to you. She can have both, if you'll let her. I'm not saying it won't be difficult, that it won't take some compromises, because it will, but Peggy's worth it, don't you think?"

"Well, of course she is," Johnny replied fiercely.

Todd nodded. "Then tell her that, too."

His door opened again and Peggy stuck her head in. When she saw her husband, some of the color drained out of her face. "I heard you were here, but I couldn't believe it," she said to Johnny, then turned an apologetic look on Todd. "I'm sorry."

"Not a problem," he said at once. "You two talk. Besides, I've got to get into town."

And on the way he had to figure out how to deal with his own relationship problems. It was one thing to reach a rock-solid, logical decision when he was all alone. It was quite another to cling to it when he had to share a stage with the woman in question night after night as they rehearsed a play.

Naturally Heather was never satisfied with a dutiful peck on the cheek or even a chaste kiss on the lips. Oh, no, she threw herself into their on-stage kisses with the same passion with which she'd delivered that kiss in the diner. The woman generated enough heat to keep that drafty old barn warm during a midwinter blizzard. In mid-August they were sizzling. He left the rehearsals each night with his body aching with unfulfilled desire.

He made it a point to be the first one out the door, so he wouldn't be alone with Heather. Resisting temptation was one thing. Sainthood was quite another.

So far, she hadn't challenged him, but he knew the day was rapidly approaching when the questions would start flying.

"Todd," she called out when he tried to make his escape following that night's dress rehearsal.

So, he thought, this was it. He hesitated at the barn door, then turned back reluctantly. "Yes?"

"Could I see you for a minute?"

Refusing in front of the few lingering cast members was not an option. "Sure," he said a little too brightly. He walked slowly back and stood by as she gave Flo some last-minute encouragement.

"I'm so nervous, I'll probably throw up all over the stage tomorrow night," Flo said. "I've never done anything like this. I don't know what I was thinking. You talked me into it. It'll be your fault if I ruin your play."

"You are not going to ruin anything. There's no need for you to be nervous," Heather assured her. "You know your lines. You have a great voice. You're going to be wonderful. You'll knock Joe's socks off."

"It's not his socks I'm trying to get him out of," Flo said, then blushed furiously when she realized Todd had overheard.

"Pretend you didn't hear that," she begged him.

"What?" he asked, grinning at her. "By the way, I think I saw the man in question lurking outside in the shadows. Is he waiting for you?"

Flo nodded. "He's giving me a ride home."

"Still dropping you off at the front door?" Heather asked.

"I got him inside for coffee last night. I have real high hopes for tonight."

Heather gave her hand a squeeze. "Don't rush it, Flo. Let Joe set the pace. Remember the goal —long-term, not a one-night stand."

Flo nodded. "I know. It's just that I've never talked so much in my life, not to a man, anyway. I'm afraid he's going to get bored."

Todd chuckled at her concern. "That expression I caught on his face when you were doing your scenes tonight was definitely not boredom."

Flo regarded him gratefully. "You really think so? I hope you're right. He's the most decent guy I've ever known. He's real sweet to Tess, too. She told me she likes him. When the three of us are together, it makes me realize what I missed not doing things right years ago and having a real family. Not that Tex O'Rourke would have considered marrying me, but I had other chances. I guess I was just too scared to take them. I'll shoot myself if Joe gets away."

She glanced toward the door. "I'd better go before he gets tired of waiting."

"Flo," Heather said, stopping her rushed departure.

"What?"

"Slow down. You're worth waiting for."

A smile spread slowly across Flo's face. "Yes, I am, aren't I. Thanks for reminding me."

Once again Todd was impressed by Heather's uncanny ability to make people feel special, to instill confidence.

"You're a good woman, Heather Reed."

She gazed at him, clearly surprised. "You think?"

"I know it."

Her gaze locked with his. "If you honestly believe that, then why have you been avoiding me?"

20

Now there was a sixty-four-thousand-dollar question, Todd thought as Heather stared at him expectantly. Why *had* he been avoiding her?

Because he was smart? Because it was the right thing to do? Because he was terrified of what would happen if he didn't? It was all of those things and a whole lot more.

"It's complicated," he began.

"Well, at least you're not denying it," she said.

"Did you think I would?"

"To be honest, I haven't known what to think. Ever since the night I told you I loved you, ever since you kissed me senseless in front of God and everyone at the diner, you've acted as if I were contagious. The only reason you get close to me on stage is because you're too good an actor to ruin the play over something personal."

The accurate criticism stung. "I know how important the play is to you," he said stiffly. "I would never do anything less than my best."

"And your best is better than most of the people winning Tony Awards."

"Don't go there," he warned. He wasn't in the mood to listen to another lecture on how foolish he'd been to abandon his art.

"Okay, right. As a topic of discussion that's off limits. You and I are off limits, too, I suppose. That must be why you haven't given me a straight answer yet."

"Like I said, it's complicated."

"It doesn't have to be."

Oh, how he wished that was true. But Angel's mere existence complicated things. He could never make Heather see that without getting into things he hated remembering, much less talking about.

"There was a time when you didn't hide from your emotions," she reminded him.

Ironically, she really believed that, because with her—and only her—it had been true. She would never understand how rare it had been for him to allow himself to be in touch with his real feelings, how he'd closed himself off emotionally from the moment his baby sister had died while in his care. It was as if for a couple of years, he had experienced an incredible, never-to-be-repeated freedom to truly live his life without fear.

"I wish . . ." His voice trailed off.

"Wish what?"

He met her gaze, then looked away. "That we could go back."

"We can."

He touched her cheek, the caress a wistful reminder of all he wanted to do and couldn't because a little girl's safety depended on stopping this here and now. Since nothing else had worked, since Heather was still very much in his life, he knew that drastic measures were called for and he intended to take them. If he couldn't persuade her that they had no future, if he couldn't talk her into going back to New York, then there other ways he could make going back home seem irresistible to her. He'd already put his plan into motion. Just that morning he had made a call that he was pretty sure would change everything. He just prayed she wouldn't hate him when she found out.

"No," he said firmly for now. "We can't."

He was about to walk away, when she asked point-blank, "Todd, do you love me?"

It was the question he'd been dreading. He could have lied and made it easier for both of them, but he couldn't seem to make himself do it. He wasn't a good-enough actor to carry off that particular line convincingly.

"Yes," he admitted quietly, then regarded her with genuine regret. She would never know what it cost him to add, "But it doesn't matter."

"It does!" she corrected him with evident frustration. "Don't you see? It's *all* that matters."

"If only that were true, darlin'. If only it were true."

Heather couldn't shake the image of the despondent expression on Todd's face when he'd finally said he loved her. It kept her awake all night, then nagged at her all day. The contradiction made no sense, not to her, anyway. Apparently, it made all too much sense to Todd. She spent a lot of time that day cursing him and his stubborn refusal to listen to his heart.

That meant she arrived at the barn on opening night exhausted and stressed out. She managed to communicate her own nervousness and anxiety to the entire cast, until Todd stepped in and soothed everyone by reminding them that they were doing this play for fun.

"It's not like we're facing a bunch of vicious critics from New York," he told them. "We're doing this for friends and family. If we flub a line or two or miss a note, the world is not going to come crashing down around us. We'll all go back to our day jobs in the morning."

The cast regarded him with grateful smiles and went off to get into their costumes with a lighter step.

"Thank you," Heather said.

"No problem. What's with the sudden attack of nerves? You're usually the coolest person backstage on opening night."

"This is different for some reason," she said. Maybe because the burden for pulling the production together rested on her shoulders. Maybe because she wanted this play to succeed for everyone who'd helped.

"You've done your part. Now it's up to them to do theirs," Todd reminded her. "Surely you know that, don't you?"

"Yes, but—"

He regarded her knowingly. "This isn't opening-night jitters, is it? It's the conversation we had last night."

"Don't be ridiculous," she retorted. She certainly wasn't about to admit she'd had a sleepless night. He would guess it had been because of him and not about the play at all. He'd left her, clearly satisfied that things between them were settled when the truth had been just the opposite. Since there was no time to get into all that before the curtain went up, she had to postpone that particular discussion for another time.

In the meantime, she would simply cling to his reluctant admission that he loved her. Whatever reason made him think that wasn't enough could be dealt with later.

When she finally made her first entrance, the familiar rush of adrenaline pumped through her and she forgot everything except the play. Her scenes with Todd were some of the best she'd ever performed because every line came straight from her heart, because the simmering passion between them was real.

When the final curtain came down, the audience erupted with applause and cheers. Heather glanced first at Todd, caught his wink, then looked at Sissy, whose face was alight with excitement.

"Did you see?" she asked breathlessly. "They were giving us a standing ovation. They loved it. They really loved it."

Heather gave her a hug. "You were wonderful, honey. Was it as much fun as you thought it would be?"

Sissy gazed at her with stars in her eyes. "It was better. I never believed I could stand up in front of a crowd of people and act, but I did it. It was totally awesome." She spun around, searching the people who were coming backstage. "I have to find Henrietta and Will. Have you seen them?"

"No, but I'm sure they'll be here," Heather said. "They'll find you. And they'll be at the party in the lobby later."

Sissy threw her arms around Heather. "Thank you. Thank you so much." Tears welled up in her eyes. "This is the very best thing that's ever happened to me."

Even if she hadn't known the whole story of Sissy's sad life, Heather would have been touched by the comment. As it was, she felt incredibly moved, and her own eyes filled with tears. "You deserve to have good things happen for you, Sissy. Remember that."

Before the girl could respond, they heard Henrietta calling out to her. The older woman's gaze filled with pride when she finally spotted Sissy and rushed toward her to gather her into an embrace. The judge came along more slowly, but he looked no less proud as he tucked a finger under Sissy's chin and said, "You were magnificent, gal. I intend to be right there when you pick up your first Tony Award in New York."

"You were awesome!" Will declared. "I couldn't believe you were my sister."

"Does that mean you'll stop making fun of me for singing in the shower?" Sissy asked.

"Nah," Will said. "Somebody's gotta keep your head from getting too big."

As the four of them moved off together, Heather sighed.

"You did a nice thing for that girl," Todd said quietly. "You gave her back her self-esteem."

"She didn't need me to do that. She's a strong girl and she has Henrietta. She would have been okay, no matter what."

"Maybe, but I still think a lot of the credit goes to you. And in case no one has thought to mention it—" he smiled "—you were pretty terrific out there tonight yourself."

"For the first time, being on stage was actually fun," she admitted. "The real challenge was the directing."

"Speaking of that," he said quietly, "there's someone here I'd like you to meet. Come with me."

She followed along beside him, an uneasy feeling in the pit of her stomach. When she saw the unfamiliar, well-dressed man he was taking her to see, her uneasiness increased. This was a well-heeled businessman from back East, not some local rancher. She recognized the type.

She hung back a second. "Todd, what's this all about?"

"You'll see in a minute." He grinned at the man. "Peter, this is Heather Reed, who not only starred in tonight's show, but directed it. Heather, this is Peter O'Brien."

The name rang some distant bell, but she couldn't pin it down. "Mr. O'Brien," she said, shaking his hand and accepting his congratulations on the play's opening-night success.

"I gather you pulled this theater together from scratch," he said. "Quite an accomplishment in just a few weeks. I'm impressed."

"I had a lot of help."

"Maybe so, but Todd says you were the guiding force."

Why, she wondered, had Todd been so busy selling her talents to this man? She glanced at Todd, but his expression was blank. He kept his gaze carefully averted.

"Think you'd like to do it again?" O'Brien asked.

She stared at him and her nagging unease turned into full-scale panic. "I don't understand."

"I love theater, Ms. Reed. Unfortunately I have absolutely no talent either for acting or for any of the behind-the-scenes skills necessary to mount a play."

"He's extremely successful, however, at making money," Todd said.

Suddenly Heather knew why she had recognized the name. Peter O'Brien was a venture capitalist. Among other things, he backed theatrical productions, usually smaller off-Broadway shows, but he had been involved in at least one or two major musical revivals.

"I was very impressed with what I saw here tonight," O'Brien told her.

"But how did you even know about it?" she asked, her gaze on Todd, though the question was directed at O'Brien. "I assume Todd had something to do with that."

"Absolutely," the man said without hesitation. "We're both in his debt. One of my companies is a primary sponsor for both Megan's television show and for the new cooking show Todd is producing. We have quite a lot of discussions. He knows I'm always looking for new opportunities."

Heather frowned at Todd. "Is that so?"

Peter O'Brien didn't seem aware of the undercurrent of tension in the air. He went right on singing Todd's praises. "He invited me to come tonight and take a look at one of the most exciting young directing talents to come along. Frankly, I thought he might be exaggerating, but I can see now that he wasn't. If anything, he understated your abilities. If you can stage a production like this in a few weeks with amateurs in Whispering Wind, Wyoming, there's no telling what you could do in New York, given enough time and backing."

Heather knew she ought to be gratified by the praise, knew her pulse should be pounding at the opportunity he was hinting at offering her. Instead, she felt dead inside. Todd had obviously taken extreme measures to see to it that she left

Whispering Wind and returned to New York. It was clearly a last-ditch attempt to get her out of his life, despite the love he claimed to feel for her.

"I don't know what to say," she said, barely managing to get the words out without a display of angry tears.

"Say you'll consider it," O'Brien said. "I know you have celebrating to do tonight, but I'll stick around town. We can talk again tomorrow, hammer out the details. I don't have to tell you, Ms. Reed, this is a once-in-a-lifetime opportunity."

"No, you're right," she said. "You don't have to tell me that." She backed away, desperate to escape before she embarrassed herself. "Now, if you'll excuse me, I'll speak to you both later. Please, Mr. O'Brien, join us for the party, won't you?"

"I'd love to. Thank you."

Heather slipped away without another word, losing herself in the crowd backstage before finally making her way to the tiny, makeshift dressing room, where she locked the door, then leaned against it and let the tears come.

As much as she'd wanted to remain hidden in that dressing room all night, Heather knew she couldn't let the other members of the cast down like that. This was their night and she owed them this celebration. She figured that it would require her greatest skill as an actress to get through tonight's party without betraying her inner turmoil. That meant steering clear of Todd for the next couple of hours. She wasn't sure what to say to him, and anything she said right now was likely to be said in anger.

Fortunately it seemed the whole audience had stuck around for the party, so it was easy enough to lose herself in the throng, to slip away whenever Todd neared. It was only when the crowd was thinning out that he finally caught sight of her. He managed to trap her near the refreshment table that had been set up in the "lobby" they had created at the front of the barn.

"You must be walking on air," he said. "It's an incredible coup to have a man like Peter O'Brien make you an offer like that."

"Yes, it is," she said without enthusiasm.

He gave her a thoughtful look. "Then why don't you seem happier about it?"

The anger she'd kept at bay for the past couple of hours roared back to life. Words failed her.

"Heather?"

"How could you?" she finally asked in a tense undertone, trying not to shout the way she wanted to. "How could you invite him here without telling me, without even asking me if it was what I wanted? Do you want me gone that badly?"

"It wasn't about—" he began, then cut himself off before he could complete the obvious lie.

"Okay, yes, I thought it would be for the best. And I didn't tell you because I didn't want to get your hopes up. I didn't know if Peter would be as excited about this as I thought he'd be."

"Hogwash! You didn't tell me because you were afraid I'd tell you not to invite him." She gave him a pitying look. "I don't understand you, Todd. I really don't. You love me, but you can't wait to get rid of me."

He raked his hand through his hair in a gesture of pure frustration. In the old days, when he kept his hair preppy-short, the gesture wouldn't have mussed it as it did now, causing a stray lock to fall into his eyes. She wanted to reach out and smooth it back but didn't dare.

"It's not that," he said.

"Don't you dare tell me it's for the best," she said, barely keeping a tight rein on her temper. "That's a lie and we both know it."

"Dammit, it *is* for the best. You just don't understand."

"Then explain it to me," she pleaded. "Make me understand why two people who love each other the way we do, the way we always have, can't be together, especially when we have a wonderful little daughter to be considered."

Before he could respond, the last stragglers wandered over to say good-night. Flo gathered Heather in a hug. "Congratulations, sweetie. It was a blast. I can't wait till we do it again."

341

Heather mustered a halfhearted smile. Would she even be here a week from now? Not if Todd had anything to say about it, that was for sure.

"You knocked 'em dead," Joe told Heather.

She squeezed his hand. "Thanks for all your help. The theater would never have been ready without it."

"My pleasure." His gaze shifted back to Flo. "You ready, darlin'?"

"You bet, cowboy." She gave Heather a wink as she added under her breath, "You will never know how ready."

Joe obviously heard the remark. He rolled his eyes. "I keep telling her she is just going to have to wait till she puts a ring on my finger, but the woman is relentless."

"Hopeful," Flo corrected him, linking her arm through his. "Hopeful."

As they wandered off, lost in each other, Heather sighed. "That's the way we should be," she murmured wistfully. Even though she knew what the answer was likely to be, she swallowed her pride and faced Todd. "Let's put an end to all these games."

"I'm not playing games with you, Heather. I wouldn't."

"Okay, call it whatever you want to, but let's just end it here and now."

"You'll go back to New York, then?"

Even though he'd seized on the possibility, it

didn't seem to make him happy. Quite the opposite, in fact. She took heart in that.

"No," she said emphatically. "I have an entirely different ending in mind."

He regarded her warily. "Meaning?"

"Marry me," she said bluntly. "Just do it, Todd. Take the plunge. Go with your heart, dammit, instead of trying to rationalize every little thing."

He looked as if part of the set had fallen and landed on his head. It wasn't a particularly flattering reaction.

"It's not going to happen," he said quietly but emphatically.

She might have taken that as his final word, if she hadn't seen the regret in his eyes. There was something going on here she didn't understand, something tearing him apart inside. Their future depended on her figuring out what it was.

21

Todd knew that he'd handled things badly. He probably should have warned Heather about his invitation to Peter O'Brien, but just as she'd guessed, he had been afraid she'd tell him not to bring the man to Whispering Wind.

Still, he couldn't help thinking that she wouldn't be foolish enough to blow off Peter's offer just because she was angry with him for setting it up.

He just had to make her see that she would be making a terrible sacrifice for all the wrong reasons. He didn't miss the irony of their roles being suddenly reversed. The difference was that his decision to work for Megan had been made logically and for all the right reasons. Hers to stay in Whispering Wind was nothing more than a pipe dream of a future that couldn't happen.

Unfortunately she seemed determined to give both him and Peter the cold shoulder. She managed to avoid a meeting with Peter on Saturday and steered clear of Todd except on stage during that night's performance.

Peter seemed surprisingly unfazed by her rebuff, but Todd was seething. The woman was throwing away the chance of a lifetime and he didn't intend to let her do it.

He walked into the diner on Sunday morning armed with a whole list of solid reasons why Heather shouldn't walk away from Peter's proposal. Unfortunately she was nowhere to be found, but Angel came toddling straight to him, her face alight with pleasure.

"Hiya," she said, holding out her arms.

Todd obligingly picked her up. "Where's your mom?" he asked.

"Cooking," she said matter-of-factly.

Todd stared at her in surprise. "Excuse me? Your mother's actually cooking?" He gestured toward the kitchen. "In there?"

"Uh-huh," Angel said. "Mack's sick."

Oh, brother, Todd thought. The whole town was likely to be just as sick if it were up to Heather to step in as his replacement. Her skills in the kitchen had improved since the old days, but she wasn't up to restaurant caliber.

"Where's Henrietta?"

" 'Retta's cooking, too."

"Thank God," Todd murmured, heading for the kitchen.

Sure enough, the two women were standing over the grill, concentrating on rows of eggs in various styles and stages of readiness.

Heather tried to flip one, only to have it break, then splatter. "Kenny won't mind if his is scrambled, will he?" she asked Henrietta hopefully.

"Kenny will take what he gets this morning," Henrietta said grimly. She regarded Todd irritably. "Don't just stand there, boy. Grab a tray and get these breakfasts out there."

"I have a better idea," he said, setting Angel on her feet and rolling up his sleeves. His planned discussion with Heather would just have to wait. "Move over. I'll take over in here. You two wait tables."

"Not that I'm not grateful for the offer, but do you have any idea what you're doing?" Henrietta asked as he stepped up to the grill and took the spatula from Heather's hand. He noticed she didn't even try to fight him.

"Believe me, I have done my share of time as a short-order cook," he said. "Struggling actors get a wide range of odd-job credentials while they're between roles. I can't do fancy, but I can do fried."

Henrietta gave him a smacking kiss. "Thank you. You're a lifesaver."

It wasn't lost on Todd that throughout this entire exchange, Heather not only hadn't said a word, she had barely looked at him. She'd just backed away eagerly as soon as she'd relinquished the spatula. The instant Henrietta accepted his offer to take over, Heather flew out of the kitchen with a tray filled with overdue breakfasts.

Henrietta gave him a piercing look. "You two have a spat?"

"Not exactly."

"What, then?"

"Henrietta, do we really have time to dissect my personal life?"

"I'll make the time," she said. "Tell me what's going on. She's been acting like a bear with a thorn in its paw for the last two days, when she should be floating on air after that triumph out at the theater. Everyone in town's talking about the play and begging her to do more."

Todd winced, aware that he was now pitted against the whole damn town. "If you're so curious, ask her to explain. I have work to do."

"Those eggs can wait," she insisted. "I'm

asking you for an explanation, since instinct tells me you're at the root of the problem."

"Okay, just to save time, here it is. I invited a major Broadway investor to come to the play on Friday night. He was impressed and he made her an offer. Instead of being grateful, she's furious."

Henrietta regarded him with pity. "And you can't understand why," she guessed. "Men!"

That said, she flounced out of the kitchen. The next time she came in, she scowled at him. "For a supposedly brilliant man, you are dumber than dirt, Todd Winston. I've said it before and I'll say it again. More times if necessary. If you let that woman get away, you will regret it for the rest of your life."

"You have mentioned that," he agreed. "Are you finished now? Can I get to work?"

She gave him an impatient look, grabbed a few more plates and stalked out of the kitchen. When the door swung open again, Heather came through, snatched up her orders without a word and left. Todd had the distinct impression he was still in disfavor, despite having pitched in to help.

For the next couple of hours, the pattern was repeated over and over. He was so busy he didn't have time to dwell on it. On Sunday mornings, people who only drank coffee and ate doughnuts during the week ordered big breakfasts of hot-cakes, eggs, hash browns and sausage or bacon. Then they rushed off to church, only to make way for others who'd been to earlier services and were now ready for a big brunch.

The next time anyone actually spoke to him, it was only to announce that "that man" was sitting at the counter. "He'd like to speak to you," Heather added with a dark look.

"Tell him I can't leave the grill. Send him back here," he said.

When Peter came through the door a moment later, he took one look at Todd's frazzled appearance, then burst into laughter. "When Heather told me you were back here, I didn't believe it. Do you do dishes, too?"

"Not if I can help it. If you don't have anything better to do, roll up your sleeves and help."

To his surprise, Peter looked intrigued. "Really?"

"Why not? It's amateur day around here."

"Hey, I'm no amateur. Read my press some-time. I'm a gourmet chef. My dinner parties are legendary."

"I always assumed you had them catered."

"Depends on the guest list. If I want really terrific gourmet food, I do it myself."

"We don't care about gourmet. Just try not to break the egg yolks. People are getting testy about all the eggs being scrambled."

Peter didn't have to be asked twice. He eagerly grabbed an apron off a hook on the back of the door and stepped into place beside him. To Todd's amazement, he quickly fell into the rhythm of getting the orders ready for the two women.

"Heather turned me down," Peter announced after a while, when the pace had eased thanks to the two of them working.

Todd shot a startled look at him. "She did?" He'd been so sure she would see things his way, once she'd had time to think about it. Then again, hadn't he come over here this morning precisely because he thought she needed to hear a few hard truths? He just hadn't had time to deliver them.

"Did she say why?" he asked.

"She says she's settling here, that this theater group is just getting off the ground and she wants to see it through, since she was the one who started it. There was a whole lot more about commitment, but I got the feeling not all of it had to do with the theater. Any idea what else she could have been talking about?"

Oh, Todd knew, all right. "That's absurd," he said, waving off everything Peter had reported. "This is an amateur group in the middle of nowhere. I'll talk to her."

"Don't," Peter advised. "If she's not fully committed, I'd rather not do it. There are other talented directors who'd kill for the opportunity." He regarded Todd knowingly. "Personally, I think she has another agenda."

"Yeah," Todd mumbled. "She's out to drive me crazy."

Peter chuckled. "If I were you, I'd let her.

You could do a whole lot worse, my friend."

Todd scowled. "The only advice I really want from you, *my friend,* is how we're going to handle the lunch crowd when they come in here expecting roast chicken and mashed potatoes."

Peter seemed inclined to argue, but he finally shrugged. "Whatever you say. As for the chicken, no problem. If there's some rosemary around here and a little olive oil, I'll give these people a Sunday dinner they won't soon forget."

A half hour later, Henrietta came into the kitchen, sniffed the air, then stared at the two of them. "What is that I smell?"

"Lunch," Todd said succinctly. "You can thank Peter."

She rushed over to the oven, opened the door and peered inside at the roasting chickens. "Oh, my," she murmured. "Maybe I'll just close up and we can sit down and have ourselves a feast."

"There's more than enough for us to do that after you feed your usual Sunday crowd," Todd assured her. "By the way, who's helping Heather out there?"

"Heather and I are on a break. She's at the counter drinking a soda. I came back here to start lunch. I put the judge and Sissy to work. That old man is surprisingly quick on his feet, but he has a tendency to stop and chat too long with the customers." She grinned. "I'll break him of that soon enough. I've already told him if he wants to gossip to do it on his own time."

Todd's feet were killing him and his back ached like the dickens by the time Henrietta closed the doors at three o'clock.

He was more grateful than he could ever say that he'd found a profession that allowed him to sit behind a desk and use his brain. Peter seemed equally wrung out, but happily so.

"Haven't had that much fun in years," Peter declared as he slid into a booth with a plate filled to overflowing with the chicken, mashed potatoes and peas he'd fixed.

The judge, Henrietta and Sissy sank into a neighboring booth with their own food. Heather stood beside them with a plate, clearly debating which table to join.

"Sit here," Peter invited, patting the seat next to him. "I promise I won't badger you about directing a play for me."

She looked reluctant, but she finally sat down. For the first time all day, she actually met Todd's gaze across the table.

"You're a mess," she declared. For some reason that seemed to make her happy.

"How kind of you to notice," he said.

"I've got to say, the two of you amazed me today," she said. "Not many big shots would pitch in the way you did."

"You must not know the right big shots," Peter chided. "Any man worth his salt would jump through hoops to help two damsels in distress."

"Now that you mention it, until now, Todd was just about the only big shot I knew, and I was beginning to think I didn't know him very well."

The pointed barb struck home. Todd regarded her levelly. "Peter tells me you turned down his offer," he said. When she scowled at him, he said, "I'm not the one who promised not to bug you about this."

"The offer was very generous, but the timing was all wrong," she said, regarding him with a touch of defiance.

"If you ask me, the timing couldn't have been better," Todd countered.

"For you, maybe," she shot back.

Peter held up a hand. "Hey, you two, it's okay. If things change, Heather can always get in touch with me. In the meantime, let's just enjoy a nice, friendly meal, okay? I didn't spend hours anticipating this food only to wind up with indigestion because of the company."

Heather's scowl indicated there was nothing friendly between her and Todd, but she dutifully fell silent.

Todd and Peter exchanged small talk after that, but they were unable to draw Heather into the conversation. Peter observed her sullen expression with obvious amusement, then grinned at Todd.

"I think I'll be on my way. It's a long drive back

to Laramie and I've got an early-evening flight."

Heather scooted out of the booth to let him leave. "I'm sorry you wasted a trip."

"Discovering someone with so much talent is never a waste," he told her. "I still think we'll work together one of these days."

"Mr. O'Brien—"

"Peter," he corrected her.

"You're very kind, but I know you just did this as a favor to Todd," she said.

Todd was about to deny that, but Peter saved him the trouble.

"If you think that, Heather, then you don't know Todd very well, and you certainly don't know me."

His words and his sharp tone drew a startled look from Heather. Todd could see the apology forming on her lips, but he didn't give her time to utter it.

"I'll walk you out," he said to Peter.

Peter paused to accept Henrietta's heartfelt thanks, then went outside. "You'll get in touch if you think she's wavering?" he asked Todd.

"Absolutely," he agreed. Unfortunately he had a feeling Heather had dug in her heels every bit as deeply as he had. "I just don't expect it to be anytime soon."

"I can always hope. The woman's a major find. For some reason, she can't see that." He grinned. "I guess she's blinded by love."

"More's the pity," Todd muttered. He shook Peter's hand. "Thanks for coming."

"Anytime. I'll be in touch about the advertising schedule for Peggy's show. You keep bringing me talent like her and Heather and you'll make me a wealthy man."

Todd laughed. "You already have more money than Bill Gates."

"Not quite yet," Peter said. "But I'm working on it."

After Peter had driven away, Todd returned to find Heather sitting alone. Surprised that she hadn't opted to join Henrietta and the judge, he slid in opposite her, trying to gauge her mood.

"Second thoughts?" he inquired hopefully.

"You wish."

"My goal wasn't to drive you away. It was to make you see the potential you're wasting on a lost cause."

"My choice."

"Of course, but—"

She cut him off. "Todd, you can't win this argument. I'm staying. Therefore, your daughter's staying. I'm not entirely sure why that terrifies you so, but you might as well learn to deal with it."

"Damn, but you're stubborn."

"Look who's talking."

Her gaze clashed with his, daring him to back down. Since there wasn't a snowball's chance in hell of that happening, he merely sighed.

"Excuse me. I think I'll go deal with the budget for Peggy's show. At least numbers make sense."

She let him get as far as the door before she called out. "How much is one plus one?"

He regarded her with a narrowed gaze. "Two."

"That's the simple answer," she agreed. "Add up you and me and somehow we wound up with three. Keep that in mind while you're crunching those numbers of yours."

This time his sigh was deeper and more heartfelt. It wasn't as if he could forget about Angel. In fact, she was at the root of all his problems. That little girl's image was always with him—laughing, happy and, most of all, safe. But how long would it stay that way?

"The man is tormented about something," Heather told Flo later that night when her friend called to report her own frustration over her inability to get Joe into bed. "How am I ever going to get Todd to tell me what's really bothering him?"

"Have you tried asking him?" Flo asked.

"Of course I have. I've all but gotten down on my knees and pleaded with him to tell me why he's doing this to us. He just says it's for the best."

"What about Megan? Think she knows?"

"I doubt it. Todd's the kind of man who believes his personal life has no business in the workplace."

"But he and Megan are friends, too. I've seen them together. I'll bet she knows things about him that no one else does."

"Even so, he would hate it if I asked her."

"Then I will," Flo offered. "I talk to her all the time when we're conspiring to get Jake out of her hair and back into his office. I can just casually bring it up and see what she says. I owe you for getting Joe and me together." She sighed. "Well, almost together, anyway. The man has the will-power of a saint."

"Think of it as respect and you'll feel better," Heather advised.

"Maybe mentally," Flo agreed, sounding thoroughly dispirited. "But my body doesn't seem to give two hoots about respect. It wants action."

"Look at this another way. Joe's a very virile man. Don't you think he's frustrated, too?"

"I suppose," she said, but she obviously took no comfort in it. "Enough about that. Let's talk some more about Megan. I really think she could help out."

"No," Heather said. "I think we'd better leave her out of this. Let me try going straight to the source one more time. I'd rather hear whatever it is directly from Todd, instead of a third party. That's the honest, straightforward way to get answers.

"Besides," she added candidly, "I think it would bug me no end to discover that he's confided something to Megan that he refuses to tell me, especially when he claims to love me."

"Suit yourself," Flo said. "Keep me posted. I think I'll take another cold shower and head to bed."

"Do cold showers really work?" Heather asked.

"Not really, but it's so hot these days that it's worth taking one, anyway."

Chuckling, Heather hung up, but the light mood faded quickly. She needed to get this situation with Todd resolved once and for all. The only way to do that was to try to force the issue. It was past time for subtlety and polite questions. In fact, there was no time like the present.

Even though it was already after eleven, she knew the kind of hours he kept when he was trying to avoid a problem. She suspected he'd been up past midnight a lot lately. Before she could reconsider, she picked up the phone again and dialed.

"Yes," he barked.

"That's a friendly greeting. Hoping to scare off the telemarketers?"

"Why are you calling so late?" he asked at once, his tone instantly more worried than irritated. "Is everything okay? Angel's not sick, is she?"

She couldn't help being vaguely surprised by his immediate concern for Angel. As far as she'd been able to tell, he tried not to give the child a second thought.

"Angel's fine. But I was wondering if you could come over."

"Now?"

"Is that a problem? Were you already asleep?"

"No, but—"

"It's important or I wouldn't ask."

"Have you been reconsidering Peter's offer?"

"Something like that," she said vaguely.

"I'll be right there."

She hung up feeling thoroughly disgruntled. Even though she knew she should be pleased he was heading over, she still felt irritated that it was only because he thought she'd finally been convinced to leave town.

When he finally walked through the door, she pushed her annoyance aside, offered him coffee, then gestured toward the sofa.

"Relax. This could take a while." She deliberately sat down very close to him. She let her hand "accidentally" come to rest on his thigh, then bit back a chuckle when he regarded her with alarm.

"What are you up to?" he asked.

"I am not *up to* anything."

He carefully removed her hand, then sat back and waited. So did she, as she searched for the right way to get into this.

"Okay," he said finally. "Why am I here? What's the big emergency?"

"No emergency. You're here to talk," she said.

His gaze narrowed. "About?"

She shifted, snuggling close. "Us."

He drew in a sharp breath, then tried to ease away. The end of the sofa kept him right where he was. "Heather," he protested, "this is not a good idea."

She began fiddling with the buttons on his shirt, then drifted lower to the waistband of his pants. "I think it's the best idea I've had in a long time. It kind of cuts right through everything else."

"No. It only complicates it."

"Are you saying you don't want me?" she asked, her hand already seeking the evidence that would blatantly contradict any lie.

Todd groaned. "Dammit, Heather. This is a mistake."

"No, it's not," she said confidently. "Not with you and me. It could never be a mistake."

"A bad idea, then."

She deliberately caressed him through the fabric of his pants. "*This* is a bad idea?"

"No," he admitted. He visibly fought for control, then said, "Yes. A very bad idea."

"You want me to stop?"

"Yes," he insisted, then sighed. "No."

"Which is it?"

"I'm trying to think here. I'm trying to do the right thing. You are making that all but impossible."

"Want me to cut it out?"

He looked torn, but he nodded. "Yes."

She kept her hand right where it was but looked directly into his eyes. "Then tell me the truth. Tell me why you want Angel and me gone when it's obvious to everyone—and you even admit it—that you love me."

He sat back as if she'd touched him with a branding iron. "Dammit, Heather, you don't want much, do you?"

"Just the truth," she said again. "The complete, unvarnished truth. I think if you're going to give up on something this good, you owe me that much."

"And you'll leave if I tell you?"

She sketched a cross over her heart. "Promise," she said, while keeping the fingers of her other hand crossed behind her back.

Todd stood up and began to pace. He looked so thoroughly unhappy that for an instant she almost regretted backing him into a corner. Then she reminded herself of the stakes. This had to be done. Whatever had been weighing on him had to come out in the open so they could deal with it.

He moved to the window and stared into the darkness. He was silent for so long she began to wonder if he was going to tell her even now.

"It happened when I was seventeen," he finally began, his voice so low she could barely hear him. "The year before, after years of trying, my parents finally had another baby, a little girl."

The tormented expression on his face told her that whatever else he was likely to say was going to be heartbreaking. Her pulse pounded slowly as she waited for the rest with a growing sense of dread.

"At first I was embarrassed," he said ruefully. "After all, I was a teenager. To me my parents were old. They had no business having sex, right? But when the baby came, she was so beautiful. I think I was as enchanted with her as my mom and dad. Her name was Alicia."

Todd had never mentioned a sister. In truth, he rarely talked about his family at all. She knew he was estranged from them, or at least from his father, but that was all she knew. She gathered from his expression now that something awful must have happened to rip the family apart. Even though she was no longer certain she wanted to know what that was, if she was ever to understand, she needed to hear this. Even more important, probably, she sensed that he needed to get it out, to share this agonizing secret with someone who cared.

"What happened to her, Todd?" she prodded him gently.

"She died," he said, his expression as stark as his words. "She was with me and she died."

"Oh, God," she whispered, getting up to stand beside him, reaching for him.

He seemed surprised by her touch, as if he'd

expected her to be repulsed, but all she could think about was a young boy—and that's what he'd been, a boy—blaming himself for his baby sister's death, a boy who had grown into a man who feared that the same thing would happen again with any child left in his care. Even without the details, she understood it all now. His fear. His refusal to be left alone with Angel. His need to keep a safe distance between himself and the two of them. It all made a terrible kind of sense.

"How did she die?" Heather asked.

"It was an accident. I'd had my driver's license for a year. I was a good driver. One day I was baby-sitting my sister and a friend called and wanted me to meet him at the mall. I figured what the heck, so I put Alicia in her car seat and off we went. It should have been okay. The mall was only a mile away and I'd never even had a close call before, but it was raining. This guy was driving too fast and the light changed. He tried to hit his brakes, but he skidded right into me, on the passenger side."

He shuddered and fell silent. When he finally spoke again, his voice was barely above a whisper. "Alicia . . . Alicia died right there in my arms."

"Oh, Todd," Heather whispered, tears gathering, stinging her eyes. "I'm so sorry."

He regarded her with a bleak expression. "It

shouldn't have happened. If I'd stayed home like I was supposed to, if I'd been more vigilant, it wouldn't have happened. I was reckless and irresponsible."

"You were seventeen years old," Heather said fiercely. "And unless there was something you didn't say, the accident wasn't your fault."

"She was in that car because of me."

"Were you cited by the police?"

"No, but—"

"Did your parents blame you?"

"Not my mother, no," he conceded.

Heather thought she was beginning to see the real problem. "But your father did?"

Todd nodded. "He was right, too. I should never have left the house that day."

"It was a mistake in judgment, not a crime," she said.

"And it cost Alicia her life. My father never forgave me. He and my mother split up after that. That was my fault, too."

Shocked, she stared at him. "You can't believe that."

"Because of my stupidity, my parents' whole world fell apart."

"And you've spent every minute of your life since heaping more guilt on yourself, trying to control every little detail so that nothing like this can ever happen again," she said.

"Exactly. That day Angel ran into the street, it

363

was like déjà vu. I almost cost our daughter her life, just the way I killed Alicia." His gaze met hers. "Don't you see?" he said with quiet desperation. "I can't risk that happening again. Not ever."

"The blame belongs to that other driver or to fate, not you," she said, but it was evident he couldn't—or wouldn't—hear her.

He had lived with this for years. Believing it, hating himself, was as ingrained as breathing. Todd would go to his grave convinced that he was responsible for his sister's death, that no child would ever be safe with him. How could she possibly prove to him otherwise, especially when he steadfastly refused to listen to reason?

Even now, knowing about that awful, long-ago tragedy, she would trust him with her life. More important, she would trust him with Angel's.

Over the next few days, with Todd avoiding her as if he couldn't bear to see her now that she knew about his past, she realized that drastic measures were called for. Maybe she had to find a way to see to it that he spent time with Angel.

But would a day or a week or even a month alone with his child overcome years of soul-wrenching torment? Her heart told her it was the only chance she had of getting through to him.

Unfortunately she knew if she asked him to keep Angel for her, he would refuse. But what if she virtually abandoned her on his doorstep, gave him no choice except to rise to the occasion?

It was a huge risk, not to Angel, but to their future as a family. She understood that he might never forgive her for it.

But without such a drastic action, what sort of future would they have, anyway?

22

Heather kept her plan a secret from everyone while she worked out the details. She didn't want Flo or Henrietta caught in the middle when Todd went ballistic. She knew it would take him a while to cool down once he realized what she'd done—that she'd deliberately gone off and left him all alone with his daughter.

She figured that a few days hiding out in Laramie would be just about long enough for her to make her point, but those few days weren't likely to be pleasant for anyone in Todd's line of fire.

She also had one other little bit of ammunition left in her arsenal. Up until now she hadn't revealed to Angel that Todd was her father, but something told her the time had come. A pint-size female had persuasive powers that a grown-up couldn't even *hope* to imitate.

By Thursday she was ready to put her plan into action. She waited until the last minute to tell

Henrietta she needed a couple of days off to attend to a personal matter. Being Henrietta, she didn't ask a lot of prying questions, just whether there was anything she could do to help.

"No, this is something I need to take care of myself. Will you be okay here? I know this is really last minute, but it just came up. It's busier than usual with summer tourists in the area. Can you manage?"

"Of course I can. Sissy's still out of school. She can pitch in." A smile tugged at the corners of her mouth. "And I might just give the judge another trial run. He's been making noises about wanting to retire from the bench so we can spend our golden years together."

Heather caught the subtle implication of that and regarded her with delight. "He's proposed? Why didn't you say something?"

"Nothing to say. I haven't said yes."

"Why on earth not?"

"I have my reasons."

"Pardon me for saying it, but aren't your reasons old news by now?" Heather asked bluntly.

Henrietta looked vaguely startled by the criticism. "That's what he said," she admitted. "He said thirty years was too blasted long to keep a man dangling. Said he'd more than proved his love by now, and by gosh, it was time for me to stop sitting on the fence."

"I have to say I'm inclined to agree with him,"

Heather told her. "You sure it's not just a habit you don't know how to break?"

Henrietta waved off the explanation. "Poppycock! This isn't about the past. It's about the future. He has all these big ideas about running off and seeing the world. I'm not ready to give this place up. It's been my life for a long time. I'd miss it if I went gallivanting all over. People are what counts in life, not the places you've seen."

"Haven't you ever yearned to see Europe or Hawaii or New York?"

"Can't say that I have. Of course, if Sissy keeps on about this acting bug you've put in her head, I suppose the time will come when I'll have to go see her star on Broadway. That'll be soon enough."

"Have you explained to him how you feel?"

"The man doesn't listen to a word I say. He says we'll start with a fancy honeymoon to some island in Hawaii. Can you imagine? All that water around." She shuddered. "I want nice, solid land under my feet."

"Did you tell him that?"

"Well, of course I did. When have I ever been shy about stating my opinion to anybody?"

"And?"

"He says if I give in on this one point, I might discover I like it." She uttered an indignant huff. "Giving in is not in my nature."

"So what do you want?" Heather asked,

wondering how on earth these two stubborn people could have known each other for so long —loved each other for so long—and not been able to work out their differences. If *they* couldn't, how on earth could she possibly expect to get through to Todd?

"I want that foolish man to face facts. We're old. We need to stay right here, where we've got people who matter all around us. Plus, he needs to know that if he's not going to be down at the courthouse every day, he's going to be putting in his fair share of hours right here," she said emphatically, then allowed herself a grin. "We'll see how he takes to that notion, and then I'll decide one way or the other."

Heather chuckled. "You're a hard woman, Henrietta."

"Look who I'm dealing with," she said. "He'd have walked all over a weaker woman. Wouldn't have kept his interest for a month."

"So this refusal to give an inch was all a tactic to keep him interested?"

She nodded without the slightest sign of regret or embarrassment. "That, and a test, I suppose. His leaving all those years ago almost broke my spirit. I couldn't chance it a second time."

"Seems to me like he's proved himself over and over again," Heather said.

Henrietta's lips curved into a slow smile. "That he has," she admitted. "But I'm not quite ready to let him know that just yet. Another week or two ought to do it."

"Why another week or two?"

"That'll be the anniversary of the first time he asked me to marry him. I'm wondering if he'll remember. I have to say I wouldn't mind discovering a little hint of romance in the man at this stage of my life."

If he didn't remember the occasion on his own, Heather vowed, she would see to it that a little birdie got the message to him. It was the least she could do.

Her arrangements for time off complete, Heather got Angel all dressed, then sat down with her daughter in her lap.

"Where we going, Mama?"

"I'm going away for a couple of days."

Angel's face clouded over. "Not me?"

"No, you're going to stay here."

"With 'Retta?"

Heather shook her head. "With your daddy."

Angel was silent for a moment as she grappled with that news. "Daddy?" she echoed.

"That's right, baby. Todd is your daddy and you're going to stay with him."

Angel's expression brightened at once. "Todd is my daddy?"

"That's right. Think you can remember to call him that?"

Her head bobbed up and down enthusiastically.

"I call him daddy," she agreed. "We go see him now?"

"You bet," Heather said.

In fact, she could hardly wait. Too bad she wouldn't be close enough to get the full effect of the expression on his face when he heard Angel utter the word for the first time.

Todd opened his front door on Thursday at midmorning to find Angel standing on the steps, a Little Mermaid suitcase beside her. With her Mickey Mouse baseball cap and her Lion King T-shirt, she looked like a walking advertisement for Disney.

"Hiya, Daddy," Angel said, as if she arrived alone every day.

Panic crawled up his spine, and not just because she had addressed him as Daddy. He would deal with that little twist later, once he'd strangled her mother.

"Where's your mama?" he asked, looking up and down the block.

"Gone bye-bye," she said, pushing past him, suitcase in hand. "I stay with you."

Dear God in heaven, what was Heather thinking? Where had she gone? To the grocery store would be one thing, but that suitcase suggested something else entirely. A couple of coloring books in a tote bag hinted at a brief visit. That suitcase probably had clothes in it.

Enough for how long? he wondered desperately.

He scooped Angel up and gazed into her eyes. "Where did your mama go?" he demanded, trying to keep his voice calm.

Angel shrugged. "Don't know."

"How did you get here?"

"Mama."

Then she couldn't have gone far. She had to have stayed nearby to coach Angel to ring the doorbell. That had been no more than a minute or two ago. Or was it? He'd been distracted when he first heard it. It had taken a few minutes for the sound to register, another couple of minutes to tear himself away from the budget projections for Peggy's show. Was that long enough for Heather to have disappeared from the neighborhood? Would she have done that before seeing that he was home and that Angel was safely inside?

Still carrying Angel, he ran outside, circled the apartment building and then the entire block. With every step he took, his panic escalated.

Just as he returned from the fruitless search, the phone started ringing. He snatched it up.

"Heather, if this is your idea of a joke, it's not amusing."

"What's Heather done?" Megan demanded.

At any other time he might have been gratified by her prompt and loyal assumption that Heather had done something to him, rather than the other way around. "She's left Angel on my doorstep and disappeared," he announced, trying not to let his stark terror show.

"As in left town?"

"I have no idea, but you have to get over here. You have to take Angel out to the ranch."

"Why?" Megan asked, clearly perplexed. "Are you going to look for Heather?"

No, he thought, he was not going to look for her. He was going to wait right here, let his temper simmer and then strangle her whenever she returned. His plea was all about protecting his daughter.

"You just have to come, okay? I'm counting on you," he told Megan.

"I'll be there in twenty minutes," she said. "I'm bringing Jake with me. If Heather's in some kind of trouble, we may need him."

"Leave Jake out of this. The only trouble Heather is in is with me," Todd said darkly.

The wait for Megan was the longest of his entire life. He watched Angel as if she might shatter right in front of his eyes. She seemed thoroughly unaware of his turmoil. She crawled up next to him on the sofa, then happily handed him book after book to read to her. Fortunately there were few words and not much plot. She seemed content with turning the pages and telling *him* the story.

When she tired of that after a few minutes, she regarded him hopefully. "Wanna see my dolls?"

His gaze fastened on the front window and his

ears attuned to the arrival of a car, he nodded distractedly. "Sure."

"This one's Leaky," she told him, waving a familiar plump figure wearing only a diaper in front of his face. "She cries. Hear?"

She tilted the doll forward and back, filling the room with plaintive cries that sent chills down Todd's spine. He seized the doll, then placed it gently back against Angel's shoulder. "See?" he said a little desperately. "No more crying."

Angel tossed the silent baby aside, then grabbed a Barbie dressed in an evening gown. "This is Leaky's mama. Isn't she pretty?"

"Very pretty," Todd agreed, barely sparing the doll a glance. Where the devil was Megan?

He finally heard the slam of a car door just as Angel was showing him her "most favoritest," a rag doll with yarn hair and a missing eye. "She was Mama's, a long time ago," she said reverently. "She's very, very old." She shoved her in Todd's arms. "You hold her."

He had the doll cradled against his chest as he answered the door.

"New toy?" Megan asked with an amused smile.

"She doesn't have any trucks," he muttered. "I'm going straight to the toy store and buying her trucks. Maybe a train."

Megan patted his hand. "Good for you." She knelt down in front of Angel. "Hey, sweetheart, how are you doing?"

"I fine. I come to stay with Daddy."

Megan's gaze shot to his. "Is that so?"

Todd shrugged. "A new wrinkle."

Megan studied him intently. "Is everything okay here?"

He regarded her with disbelief. "What do you think? I stay home to finalize the budget and the syndication deal for Peggy's show—which may or may not happen depending on whether Johnny gets his way—and the next thing I know Angel is on my doorstep all alone. Does that sound as if everything is okay?" He raked a hand through his hair. "I swear I have no idea what Heather was thinking. I thought we'd settled this."

"Settled what?"

He gestured vaguely toward his daughter. "This."

"Okay," Megan said slowly. "But I'm not sure I see the problem. Wherever Heather's gone, she'll be back. In the meantime, how big a deal is it for you to keep Angel? It might be inconvenient, but it's hardly a calamity. Get a baby-sitter if you need to go out, or take her with you. You can manage."

"I cannot manage," he said tightly, then drew in a deep, shuddering breath. He had to make other arrangements—now, before it was too late. Once more he told her, "I want you to take Angel out to the ranch with you."

Unfortunately Angel overheard. "No go," she

said, tears welling up. "Stay with you. Mama said."

"I think that settles that." Megan studied him closely. "What's really going on here? This isn't about being a little inconvenienced at all, is it?"

He felt as if he were caught up in some bizarre real-life version of truth-or-dare. He had to come clean with Megan or she would never understand his reluctance to keep Angel.

"No," he admitted finally. "If the circumstances were different, if I were different, this wouldn't be a problem. I cannot keep her here, Megan. I just can't."

"Why?" she asked gently. "What are you so afraid of?"

For the second time in less than a week, Todd explained about his baby sister's death. Like Heather, Megan clucked sympathetically and tried to assure him that the tragic accident hadn't been his fault. Sensing her compassion, he found that the words came easier this time. The pain in his chest wasn't quite as tight.

"That's it in a nutshell," he said finally. "Bottom line, I'd never forgive myself if something happened to her."

Megan took his face in her hands and gazed directly into his eyes. "Nothing is going to happen. You're an adult, not a teenage boy. She's a toddler, not a baby. And you're her father. There's no getting around that. Sometimes you have to take a leap of faith that you can do this scary parenting thing, and just plunge in. Isn't that what you told me when Tex made me Tess's guardian?"

"Tess was eight, not a fragile toddler."

"Believe me, that was no less terrifying. What did I know about being a mother? Absolutely nothing."

"But you've never been responsible for a child's dying," he countered.

"Todd, neither have you. It was an accident, and accidents can happen at any age. Tess was thrown from a horse right after I became her guardian."

"She didn't die," he repeated stubbornly.

"No, but she could have."

"Angel ran in front of a car because of me."

"An accident," Megan insisted. "This baby I'm carrying could choke on its formula. You can't live your life anticipating the worst. You can only do everything possible to guard against an avoidable tragedy. Trust me, Angel is as safe with you as she would be out at the ranch. Probably more so, when you consider all of the horses and equipment out there."

"I don't know . . ."

"Let her stay," Megan urged. "Not just for her sake, but for yours."

On a rational level, Todd knew she was right, could see the value in a trial-by-fire immersion into fatherhood. But in his gut, a million doubts churned.

Then he saw Angel gazing at him so trustingly, thought of Heather's blind faith in him as she'd left their daughter on his doorstep.

Suddenly he saw why she'd done it just this way, why she'd gone off without asking him, without any warning. This wasn't about retaliation at all, as he'd first suspected. She'd wanted to prove in the only way she knew how that she had complete faith in him, that nothing he'd revealed about his sister's death mattered. His father might not have forgiven him, might have taken every opportunity to remind him of his recklessness, but Heather was cut from a different cloth. She knew exactly who he was, and she trusted him with the most precious thing in her life, their daughter.

Maybe, just maybe, he should have as much faith in himself. Maybe it was time to concede that the father he'd respected and loved might be wrong. Maybe it was finally time to put the past behind him where it belonged and live in the here and now, with this child who'd been left so trustingly in his care.

He figured in another million years, if he survived the next few days, he'd be able to forgive Heather for putting him to this test. He wasn't even going to think about the future that might open up for the two of them if he passed the test.

"Okay," he said at last. He scowled at Megan. "But you are on twenty-four-hour call. I'm putting your number and Henrietta's on speed dial. If Angel so much as whimpers and I call you, I expect you to drop whatever you're doing and get over here immediately. That includes taping, sex, anything at all. Okay?"

Megan chuckled. "You'll have to talk to Jake about the sex part, but as for the rest, yes. I'll rush right over if you need me. You're not going to, though. You and Angel will be just fine."

To his astonishment and relief, Todd didn't need a savior to rush in and take over. Thanks to the computer and his fax machine, he was as linked to his office as Megan had been when the headquarters had been in New York and she'd been in Wyoming. He settled in to keep a very close eye on his daughter.

For a three-year-old, Angel was surprisingly self-sufficient. To his undying relief, she was apparently long-since potty-trained. She had very definite opinions about what clothes she wanted to wear, mostly the ones she'd arrived in. That meant doing a load of laundry every afternoon during nap time and again at night, but it was better than arguing in the morning or struggling to put something else on a squirming child who was resisting.

By Saturday afternoon, he had come to savor nap time. He collapsed onto the sofa, exhausted from entertaining a child who apparently had more energy than any aerobics instructor or marathon runner on the face of the earth. She wasn't demanding, but she was definitely not a kid who could be left in front of the TV for hours on end. He took her for endless walks, during which she delighted him with her observations, and after which he was more worn-out than she was.

She needed activities—coloring, reading, dolls—along with someone to talk to, morning, noon and night. She was a very social child and Todd was her only companion. He'd had no idea what kind of pressure that entailed. His admiration for Heather increased tenfold.

He discovered that Angel was almost as opinionated about food as he was, though their tastes varied wildly. After the first two days when he ran out of her favorite cereal and couldn't produce another box, she announced, "We go to 'Retta's. She gots it." No other option would appease her.

Todd had been dreading this moment. It would pretty much make a public declaration that Angel was his. Although to be honest, just about everyone in town had probably long ago guessed the truth. It *would* have to be Sunday, though, when everybody in Whispering Wind was likely to be in and out over the course of the morning.

He consoled himself with the prospect of possibly getting some information on Heather's whereabouts out of Henrietta. She had been surprisingly closemouthed on the phone, which suggested she knew more than she'd let on. He figured she'd be less reticent face-to-face.

"Let's do it," he agreed, suddenly aware that Angel's expression was beginning to cloud up. He'd learned that the quickest way to avoid tears was to give in. He really hated to see her cry. She had waterworks that could bring a man to his knees.

It was the first time since Angel's arrival that he'd attempted to go anywhere in his car. Not until he was ready to go outside did he think about his lack of a car seat. For an instant he considered trying to make do with a seat belt, but he dismissed the notion at once. First thing tomorrow, he'd do a little research on the best ones on the market, then buy a car seat. In the meantime, they could walk. Someone in town with a car seat would give them a ride home.

As soon as the decision to buy a car seat was made, he stopped in his tracks. He realized he was already thinking long-term. When had that happened? When had he started to adapt, to accept Angel's presence? When had he started thinking like a father who was in it for the long haul?

He glanced at Angel, who was toddling alongside him, clinging to his hand and chattering a mile a minute, making nonstop observations about passersby and the world around them. A lump formed in his throat.

When had he stopped being terrified and fallen in love with this miracle who was his child?

23

"Have you seen Todd?" Heather asked Henrietta when she could stand the silence no longer and finally called her boss early Sunday morning hoping for news about Todd's reaction to her drastic measures.

"No, but he has called here half a dozen times a day, asking questions. What do you want me to tell him?" Henrietta asked, sounding more disgruntled than usual. "I swear, if I had known you intended to run off and leave that little girl with him without warning him ahead of time, I'm not so sure I'd have agreed to give you time off."

"This was something that had to be done," Heather assured her. "If you'd said no, I would have quit."

"You aren't running out on the two of them, are you?"

"Absolutely not."

Henrietta plunged on as if Heather hadn't spoken. "Because if you are, then there are a few things you and I need to get straight. I wouldn't be one bit happier about that than I would be if Todd hurt you."

"I'm not running out," Heather promised.

"Then when will you be back?"

"That depends."

"On what?"

She couldn't very well tell Henrietta that it depended on how long it took for Todd to wake up and see the light. She hadn't quite figured out how she would know when that happened. She assumed it was a good sign that he hadn't foisted Angel off on Henrietta or Megan.

"A few more days. A couple of weeks at the most."

"Where are you?"

"I'd rather not say. I don't want you to have to lie to Todd if he asks."

"What do you mean if? More like when. He's walking in the front door now. And I can tell from his expression that he's got more than breakfast on his mind."

"I'll let you go, then. Give Angel a hug for me. She is with him, isn't she?"

"Of course she is. Where else would she be? Looks real cute, too. Of course, her hair's in tangles. Men never did know how to do a little girl's hair right. She probably cried when he tried to brush it and that put an end to that."

Heather grinned at the image of Todd struggling to tame Angel's curls. Suddenly tears stung her eyes at having missed such a moment between father and daughter. She just had to keep reminding herself of the goal.

"I'll be in touch," she promised, and hung up before Henrietta could persuade her to talk to

Todd. If she heard his voice, gave in now and came home, it would ruin everything she'd been trying to achieve.

She'd no sooner hung up than the phone in her motel room rang. Startled, she stared at it, trying to imagine who could possibly be calling. No one knew she was here.

Since the insistent ringing didn't seem to be stopping, she picked up the phone. "Hello," she said cautiously.

"So, you *are* there," Jake said with more than a little exasperation. "Heather, what the devil were you thinking?"

"How did you find me?" she asked, ignoring his question.

"It wasn't all that difficult. A quick trace on your credit card by an investigator. If you're planning to go on the lam, you really need to be better at it. I assume you're hiding out from Todd to teach him a lesson."

It was close enough to the truth. "More or less," she conceded.

"Does that mean you're prepared to give him sole custody of your daughter?"

"Of course not," she said indignantly. "Why on earth would you think that?"

"Because that's the risk you've taken by doing something this rash and impulsive. He could use this in court to have you declared an unfit mother."

In her wildest dreams she couldn't imagine Todd deciding that he would make a better parent than she was. In fact, the whole idea had been to prove to him that he was capable of being a parent at all.

"That's not going to happen," she said, though Jake's fear that it might shook her confidence.

"Well, I hope you know what you're doing, because right this second, I'd have a real hard time defending your actions. You left that child all alone on his doorstep, Heather. When Megan told me, she was furious, even though I think she understood what you were trying to accomplish. I believe 'irresponsible' was one of her kinder descriptions. To be honest, I can't say that I blame her."

"I was right there until he took her inside," she said, defending her actions. "Believe me, Angel was never in any danger and she was never alone, not the way you're implying."

"If you were so desperate for some time to yourself, all you had to do was ask. Angel could have come to the ranch and stayed with Megan and me. Tess would have loved it."

"Jake, it isn't about my getting away. It's about giving Todd a chance to see that he's capable of being a father. I can't explain, but this was the only way I could think of to give the three of us a chance at a future together."

Jake fell silent as he digested that. "I see. Is he going to figure that out?"

"Once the panic wears off, yes," she said. "Jake,

384

I wouldn't have done it if I hadn't believed it was the best thing for Todd, Angel and me. The biggest risk of all was to me. Todd might not forgive me, but he won't take Angel away. I'm sure of that."

Jake sighed heavily, clearly not thoroughly convinced. "I'll take your word on that for now, but don't stay away too long, Heather. A court might not care that much about the reasons you chose to abandon your little girl."

"I did not abandon her," she repeated in frustration. "Why can't you see that?"

"Because right this second, all I can see is that little girl standing outside ringing Todd's doorbell. It sends a chill down my spine."

"She was never out of my sight," Heather repeated. "Please, Jake, you have to stay with me on this. I just talked to Henrietta. Todd and Angel are doing fine. I just need another couple of days for my plan to work. If it fails, I swear to you that the worst that can happen is that I will accept Todd's settlement offer and Angel and I will go back to New York."

"Two days," Jake said, seizing on her self-imposed deadline. "That's it. I'll try to keep Megan's temper in check until then. But if you're not back here by suppertime Tuesday, something tells me all hell is going to break loose."

"I'll be there," she promised. She just had to pray that would be long enough for Todd to grasp the point she'd been trying to make.

• • •

Todd had never before been away from the office for four straight days. He'd barely even taken weekends off the past couple of years. On Monday morning, he had no choice—he would have to go in and deal with all the little crises that had arisen during his absence on Thursday and Friday. Normally he would have slipped in over the weekend and caught up, but with Angel around that hadn't been feasible.

In fact, she'd settled into his apartment as if she'd been there forever. After breakfast on Sunday, she'd insisted on getting some of her toys from the apartment above the diner. They were now scattered around the living room, turning what was once tidy and bland into colorful chaos.

Even so, he couldn't seem to help chuckling at the arrangement of dolls asleep on a footstool in front of the fireplace or the stuffed bear nuzzling a pillow on the sofa. Angel's "babies" had their own nighttime routine, he'd discovered, and they each had to have a bedtime story. It was a wonder he'd gotten to bed by midnight. He had to wonder if Heather caved in to so many demands, or if Angel simply knew that in him she'd found a real sucker.

Monday morning, showered and half-dressed, he brewed himself a pot of gourmet coffee, then sank wearily onto a kitchen chair to savor a few minutes of rare quiet. Before he could truly enjoy it, a wail from the bedroom cut through the silence and had him stumbling to his feet. He stepped on a plastic figure—one of dozens she seemed to have from various fast-food restaurants and movie promotions—then limped toward the bedroom on his sore foot.

He wasn't sure what calamity he expected, but it wasn't the sight that greeted him. Angel was sitting in the middle of the bed, tears streaming down her cheeks as she gazed around the room in sleepy confusion.

"I wants my mama!" she wailed.

Didn't they both, Todd thought wryly as he stared at her helplessly. He sat on the edge of the bed and Angel promptly scrambled to climb into his lap and snuggle against his chest with a tiny sigh.

"Where's my mama!" she asked on a hiccuping sob.

"She's away on a little trip, sweetie, remember?"

A thumb popped into her mouth. Big green eyes swimming with tears gazed at him solemnly. Todd could have cheerfully shot Heather on sight right at that moment.

"You're staying with Daddy," he reminded her, hoping that would reassure her, even if it did precious little to soothe him.

Her expression brightened. "Daddy," she murmured happily. " 'Kay."

He stared at her. That was it? The storm was over?

"We gonna play at the park today?" she asked, already scooting out of his arms and heading for her clothes, which he'd once again washed the night before. "Sissy come, too?"

"No, we're going to Daddy's office today," he told her.

Tangled in the T-shirt she was trying unsuccessfully to get over her head, she had no comment on that. Todd helped her with the shirt, then plunked her on the bed so they could deal with shoes and socks. It was not a quick task. She preferred to do them herself, snapping the Velcro buckles into place with evident satisfaction, but she was usually willing to let him switch them to the correct feet afterward before scrambling down from the bed and toddling off to the kitchen in search of cereal. He'd bought the biggest box in the store after they'd left Henrietta's the day before.

He realized as he tried to gather up enough toys to keep Angel entertained that he should have arranged for a sitter. Finding one now on such short notice would be impossible, though, and he couldn't rely on Henrietta. She had a business to run, too.

After breakfast, he piled Angel into the pickup's borrowed car seat, lent to him the day before. He vowed once again to buy his own before the day was out.

Usually the drive to the production facility was his favorite time of the day. He could spend those few minutes planning his schedule and pondering problems that needed creative solutions. Today, Angel had a thousand and one things to say as they drove. When she wasn't delivering her opinion on something, she was asking questions, most of them questions for which he had no answer.

"Why's the sky blue?" she asked.

"Sorry, sweetie, I have no idea."

"How come?"

"Because I never checked it out. Maybe there's a book on the subject. Or we can look on the Internet when we get to the office."

" 'Kay." She fell silent, but not for long. "Hey, Daddy?"

"Yes."

"Are there boy cows and girl cows?" This as they passed a pasture dotted with an entire herd.

"Yes."

"How do you know which is which?"

Oh, boy. "You can just tell, that's all. Boy cows are called bulls."

" 'Kay." Blessed silence fell. "Hey, Daddy."

"Mmm-hmm?"

"Do you gots a mommy and a daddy?"

"Yes," he said warily. That was definitely not a topic he cared to pursue.

"Are they my grandma and grandpa?"

He hadn't thought about it before, but the relationship was undeniable. He had to wonder how they would feel once he told them. His mother would probably be overjoyed, might even pay him a long-overdue visit, but his father? He would probably rail that the child was doomed.

"Daddy, are they?" Angel prodded.

"Yes."

"Where are they?"

The truth was, he wasn't sure. The last time he'd heard from his father, he'd been living in New England. His mother had been in Palm Beach last winter, but no doubt had moved on. Neither of them stayed anyplace for more than a few months at a time. For the first time, he recognized that they'd found their own ways of hiding from the past.

"I'm not sure," he told Angel.

"In heaven?"

He turned a startled gaze in her direction. "No, not in heaven. Why?"

"Because Sissy's mommy and daddy are in heaven."

Todd suspected that Lyle Perkins was somewhere else entirely, but he kept that opinion to himself. "She told you that?"

"Uh-huh."

Once again, there was silence, but it didn't last more than a minute or two.

"Daddy?"

"Yes."

"I gots to go to the potty."

"Okay. We'll be at the office in just a minute."

"Now, Daddy," she said with urgency.

The next couple of minutes were among the most awkward of Todd's life as he slammed to a stop on the side of the road and helped Angel out of the car to a makeshift and hardly private bathroom in some tall grass.

"Daddy, that cow is watching me," she protested.

"No, he's not."

"I can't go with him watching me."

Todd moved her to the opposite side of the road, where the mission was finally accomplished.

By the time they got to the office, he was so worn-out he could have happily sprawled on the couch and taken a four-hour nap. Instead, he prepared for his 10:00 a.m. meeting with Megan, which was likely to include a whole lot of questions about why he'd dragged his daughter to the office, as well as why he still had her at all. It was not a conversation he was looking forward to.

At fifteen minutes before ten, Peggy stuck her head in. "Got a sec?"

"Sure." She came in, caught sight of Angel and grinned. "New assistant?"

"Don't ask. What can I do for you?"

"Well, actually, I came in here to ask what you'd think about scrapping that segment on summer berries today, but I didn't have anything specific in mind to replace it. Seeing Angel, I think I do. Can I borrow her?"

"You want to borrow my daughter?" He was torn between curiosity and relief.

"Your daughter?" she said slowly. "I see."

It was obvious that she had a lot of questions, but she refrained from asking them. Instead, she merely repeated her request. "Can I borrow her?"

"Of course," he said a little too eagerly, then caught himself. "For what?"

"We'll do something on teaching kids to cook. I'll see if I can get mine over here before we tape, and maybe Tess, too. A lot of moms are probably frantic this time of year trying to think of ways to entertain the kids, especially on a rainy day. Maybe we can give them some ideas for simple recipes."

"Sounds great, but don't you think Angel's a little young to be cooking? So far her only recipe calls for dry cereal in a bowl."

"She may not be much help, but she's too cute to leave out. The audience will love her."

"Okay, if you're sure." He told himself his eager reply was because he trusted Peggy's instincts and not because he was desperate to get a few uninterrupted minutes of work done.

"Absolutely."

"Peggy, before you go, fill me in on whether you and Johnny have resolved your differences over your taking on this new show. We're at a crossroads. I don't want to finalize things if there's any chance at all you're going to back out."

"I won't back out," Peggy said fiercely.

"And Johnny's okay with that?"

A smile spread slowly across her face. "Let's just say I've made it worth his while. I—"

Todd held up his hand. "Don't tell me. I don't need to know the details as long as your marriage is solid again."

"Not yet," she said slowly. "But it's getting there. Trust takes time. It'll be a while before I have complete faith that he won't cheat on me again, and it'll probably take just as long for him to believe that he'll always come first with me, no matter how involved I get in this new career. The bottom line is that we love each other, we have a family and a long history, and we want it to work."

"I'm glad for you."

She chuckled. "You're just relieved that I'm not going to bail out on you."

"That, too," he admitted.

"Is that it?"

He nodded.

Peggy knelt down in front of Angel. "Hey, sweetie, want to come with me to the kitchen?"

"We bake cookies?" Angel asked hopefully.

"Maybe," Peggy said.

Angel promptly tucked her hand in Peggy's and

headed for the door without a backward glance. As they left, Todd breathed a sigh of relief.

Megan wandered in just then. "I gather Peggy arrived just in time to save the day."

"You could say that."

"Jake talked to Heather yesterday," she announced, sitting across from him.

Todd stiffened. "Oh? Where is she?"

"He wouldn't say, but he did say she promised to be back tomorrow."

That should have filled him with more relief than it did. He should be ecstatic that this little trial by fire of hers was almost over, but for reasons he didn't care to examine too closely, he wasn't. In fact, he felt an awful lot like he was about to lose something he'd just barely discovered, something very precious.

24

When Heather got back to town on Tuesday at dinnertime, she headed straight for the diner, convinced she would find Todd and Angel where Henrietta could serve as backup.

"Haven't seen them since Sunday morning," Henrietta announced.

Alarm flickered. "What do you mean you haven't seen them? They haven't been coming here for dinner?"

"Nope."

Vaguely unsettled by that news, she sank onto a stool at the counter. "What do you suppose they've been doing for food?" she murmured. "Surely he's not taking her to the fast-food place outside of town."

"I don't know for sure, but I heard something about Peggy teaching a bunch of kids how to cook during one of those tapings. Maybe they've been eating at the studio."

Todd had taken Angel to work? Heather was stunned. For some reason she'd expected him to hire a sitter or find a local day-care to keep Angel out of his hair. In fact, she had envisioned him going about the interviewing process to make the arrangements in his usual thorough, methodical way. Of course, maybe he had done just that and deemed none of the candidates suitable. She had a feeling if he ever took to the idea of fatherhood, he would be far more compulsive than even Jake Landers.

"You planning on eating, working or what?" Henrietta inquired testily.

The tone was so uncharacteristic that Heather regarded her friend with concern. "Are you still mad at me for running off the way I did?"

Henrietta flushed guiltily. "No. Sorry. I shouldn't be taking my bad temper out on you."

"Has something happened? Are you okay? Has something happened with one of the kids?"

"I'm just plumb out of my mind, if the truth be told." She sighed deeply, then met Heather's gaze. "Last night I told the judge I'd marry him. Frankly, I don't know what came over me. He's been pestering me for so long I guess he finally just wore me down. It didn't seem to make much sense to wait for that so-called deadline I'd set. It's only a few days away, anyway, so what difference does it make if he remembers or he doesn't? He asked, I said yes, and that was that. I must be crazy, getting married at my age."

Heather went to her and gave her a tight hug. "You love him, that's why you agreed to it. Now, stop second-guessing yourself and be happy. You deserve to be."

"What if . . . ?"

"No what-ifs," Heather insisted. "Everything's going to be perfect. You're going to live happily ever after. Did you set a date?"

"A week from Saturday," Henrietta admitted, looking shell-shocked. "Once I said yes, we agreed there was no point in wasting time."

"Good grief, that doesn't give you any time at all to plan a proper wedding. Why so soon?"

"We don't need a lot of fancy foolishness at our age," Henrietta declared, but there was an unmistakable hint of disappointment in her eyes. "We'll be married at the courthouse. A judge from the next county will come over to perform the ceremony."

The thought of such a no-frills ceremony

appalled Heather. She refused to go along with such a thing, not for these two wonderful people who'd waited so long to be together.

"Absolutely not," she told Henrietta indignantly. "You deserve a beautiful dress, lots of flowers, an elegant reception, the works. If you want white doves flying overhead and rose petals scattered everywhere, you should have them. Forget about getting married in a stuffy courtroom. You're going to have a church wedding, just the way you should have had years ago. It'll be followed by a magnificent reception, so that everyone who loves you can be there to tell you how happy they are for the two of you."

"All that at my age? It's a waste of good money," Henrietta declared.

"If it makes you happy, it is not a waste."

Henrietta's eyes brightened. "But the date is so soon. How can we possibly . . . ?"

"Don't you worry about that. I am not letting my best friend in Whispering Wind get married without doing it up right. You leave the details to me. I'll get Flo to help and I'll talk to Todd. He's an expert at making miracles happen overnight. He'll want to help. I know he will. This will be our present to the two of you."

Assuming he was still speaking to her, of course. Then again, this was about Henrietta, and she knew he would move mountains for her. He would even put aside his anger at *her* for as long as it took to pull the wedding together, and he would spare no expense doing it.

She gave Henrietta another brisk, reassuring hug. "If I'm going to pull this off, I'd better get started, but I'll be back at work in the morning, if that's okay."

"The customers will be mighty glad to see you," Henrietta said. She hugged Heather back. "So am I."

Heather tried to think of another time in her life when a homecoming had meant as much, but she couldn't. She was still basking in the warm feelings when she arrived at the studio. Sure enough, Todd's pickup was in the parking lot, even though it was after seven.

She looked for him first in his office, but the room was dark. She thought she could hear childish squeals from down the hall, though, in the studio where Megan's show was taped. The red light above the door was off, indicating they weren't taping at the moment, so she quietly opened the door and slipped inside. Then she stared at the set in stunned silence.

The usually spotless kitchen in which Peggy taped her segments was splattered with what appeared to be spaghetti sauce. Pots and pans were piled haphazardly on every surface. A half-dozen children, Angel among them, were seated at the kitchen table, along with Todd, Peggy, Johnny, Megan and Jake. It looked like some family gathering, except for the surrounding cameras and technicians, who were evidently setting up another shot.

"One last take," the director called out. "Everybody ready on one. Five, four, three, two, one, and action."

A camera light blinked on and he pointed to Peggy, giving her her cue.

"That's it for this week," she said. "This is only for the brave. Or those who have maids to do the cleanup." Then her gaze circled the table. "I take that back. Look at these faces. Not the smudges and smeared spaghetti sauce, but the expressions. Aren't they worth a little extra cleanup? That's it for now. See you next time you come to visit *Megan's World* to see what our budding young chefs can cook up."

"And we're out," the director said, giving them all a thumbs-up. "That's a wrap."

Megan pushed back from the table, looked around the set and moaned. "My God, will you look at this? What have we done?"

"We have taught our children to cook," Peggy said. "I can hardly wait for the next segment. The first two have been terrific."

"But spaghetti sauce," Megan whispered. "We had to be nuts."

Just then her gaze landed on Heather and her expression hardened ever so slightly. "Well, well, look who's decided to come home."

Heather heard the censure in her voice, but she drew herself up, squared her shoulders and stepped into the light, her gaze locked on Todd's face.

"Mama!" Angel shouted with glee, and came running toward her at full speed, holding out her arms.

Heather gathered her up, but she kept right on staring at Todd, whose gaze finally dropped before he turned and moved off to hold a hushed conversation with Megan.

"Chin up," Peggy murmured to Heather. "And don't pay any attention to Megan. You know how protective she is of Todd. All that matters is how you and Todd resolve whatever's going on between you."

Heather gave her a grateful look. "Thanks."

"Now, let me get the rest of these hellions out of your hair. I'm sure you and Todd have things you'd like to talk about in private. Johnny, help me round up our kids. The cleanup can wait till morning."

Peggy cleared the studio in record time. Even Megan succumbed to her urging and Jake's quiet insistence. She didn't leave before casting one last scowl in Heather's direction, however.

Heather stood where she was, listening to Angel's chatter with half an ear as she watched Todd move around the studio doing whatever he could to avoid her.

"Aren't you even going to say hello?" she asked eventually.

His gaze shot to hers. "I have a lot of things to say to you," he said slowly. " 'Hello' isn't on the list."

She drew in a deep breath. "Okay, then, let's get Angel back to my place and into bed and you can get all those other things off your chest."

He shook his head. "You go ahead. We'll talk another time."

"Why not tonight?"

He regarded her coldly. "Because right this second I am so angry with you I'm not sure we could have a civilized conversation. Just take Angel and go."

"Todd—"

"Go," he repeated.

"When will you be ready to talk?" she asked, determined not to let the anger simmer until they couldn't get beyond it. "Tomorrow? The next day?"

"I'll be in touch."

"Make it soon, because I promised Henrietta we'd help her pull off a wedding a week from Saturday."

He regarded her with a mixture of surprise and delight. "She agreed to marry the judge?"

Heather nodded. "They were planning a quiet ceremony at the courthouse, but I convinced her she deserved more. I told her you'd help whip the details into shape. That this would be our present to her." She regarded him with uncertainty. "Is that okay? Will you do it?"

"Of course I will," he said without hesitation.

She should have taken some solace in the knowledge that they would have to spend time together over the next week or so, that perhaps that could bridge the terrible chasm between them as talking might not, but she knew better. Todd would view the wedding as an obligation, maybe even a joy, since it was for two people he cared about. He would behave professionally toward her for as long as it took. After that, there was no telling if he would shut her right back out of his life as he had tried to do moments ago.

"We'll start making plans tomorrow, then," she said quietly.

She turned to go, but Angel raised her head. "Daddy coming, too?"

The words galvanized Todd's attention as nothing else had. For an instant the vulnerability in his eyes tore at Heather, but then his expression closed down again.

"Not tonight," he said quietly. "You're going home with Mama."

"No," Angel protested, struggling in Heather's arms. "Want Daddy." She turned a tear-filled gaze on Todd. "Please."

He looked as if he might relent and reach for her, but then he shook his head. "No, sweetie, not tonight. I'll see you first thing in the morning, though."

Not quite pacified, Angel sniffed and asked, "Where?"

"At the diner, okay? We'll have breakfast and I'll bring you your toys."

" 'Kay," she said, finally satisfied. "You make sure my dolls go night-night?"

"I promise," he said, then cast a defiant look at Heather as if he expected her to remark on his willingness to do Angel's bidding.

She said nothing, but she had to admit she was dying to know just exactly what Angel had cajoled him into doing the past few days. She sensed that putting her dolls to bed was only the tip of the iceberg.

Worn out by the busy day she'd had and her brief tantrum, Angel was asleep in her car seat before Heather pulled out of the parking lot. Heather paused before turning onto the highway back into town, gazing at those tear-streaked cheeks.

"Oh, baby, what have I done?" she whispered. Todd was furious. Angel was upset. It seemed to her right then as if everything was far worse than before she'd left. Only Henrietta's news gave her hope that happy endings were still possible. She just wasn't sure she could wait years for hers.

Todd would have preferred a close encounter with a spitting mad bull to the prospect of seeing

Heather in the morning, but he had no choice. Not only had he promised Angel, but there were Henrietta's wedding plans to consider.

As exhausted as he'd been by Angel's visit, he had expected to sleep soundly with her gone, but instead, he seemed to keep one ear attuned all night long for sounds from the guest room. The silence wasn't nearly the relief he'd expected it to be. The lack of sleep only added to his generally black mood as he approached the diner.

His foul humor improved slightly when Angel caught sight of him and shouted "Daddy!" as if she hadn't seen him in a month.

"You bring my toys?" she asked at once.

"They're in the car."

"Wanna see," she said, as if she feared he might have left one behind.

"Okay, let's get them," he said, using it as an excuse to avoid Heather for another few minutes.

He hadn't realized just how many they had taken from Heather's place until he'd started packing them up for the return trip. The books, stuffed animals and dolls filled two large trash bags in the bed of the pickup. Angel waited impatiently until he'd retrieved the bags, then eagerly began tossing everything out of the first one.

"Sweetie, let's leave them in the bags," he said. "They'll be easier to take inside."

"Have to find my bunny story," she told him.

She poked her little head deeper into the bag, then emerged, triumphant. "Here's the bunny. You read it to me."

"Not right this second. We'll read it later."

"I didn't get no story last night," she said sadly.

"Then I'm sure Mommy will read you two tonight."

"Want you to read this one now."

"No, baby," he said firmly. He was about to reach for her when she jerked away and started howling at the top of her lungs.

"Now! Now! Now!" she chanted between sobs.

"Problems?" Heather inquired lightly, her expression amused.

"Where did you come from?"

"She's been temperamental all morning. I thought you might need backup." Seemingly unfazed, she gestured toward their still-screaming daughter. "So, what's up?"

"I refused to read her a story right this second. She didn't take it well."

"Your daughter is into instant gratification," Heather advised him.

He regarded the still-wailing child warily. "What do I do? She didn't pull this while she was staying with me."

"She saves it for special occasions. If you give in, it will only encourage her."

"Then we just let her scream?" he asked, horrified. Surely all this yelling indicated she was being traumatized for life. Aside from which, people were beginning to stare.

"That's my advice," Heather said. "Of course, you are her father. If you have a better solution, go for it."

He shot a nasty look at her, then gazed at Angel, whose sobs had subsided as she stared at him expectantly. Clearly she thought she was on the verge of winning this round. He might not know diddly-squat about kids, but he knew a whole lot about tactical maneuvers and losses that came because one side weakened too soon.

He reached for his daughter and scooped her up. He took the book she clutched and tossed it back. "Okay, kiddo, we're going back inside. The toys can stay in the truck for now."

Angel stared at him in apparent shock. "No story?" she asked sorrowfully.

"Not now," he said firmly.

Angel seemed to consider that for a minute, then nodded. " 'Kay."

Todd grinned at Heather over Angel's head. "Take charge. Show her who's boss. That's the ticket."

Heather regarded him with apparent skepticism. "If you say so. Winning one tiny battle does not guarantee you'll win the war. Believe me, I know."

In the diner, still basking in the glow of his triumph, he settled Angel into a booth, placed an order for cereal for her and pancakes for himself. Angel managed to steal most of the pancakes.

After breakfast, Janie came in and offered to take Angel, Sissy and Will to the park along with her son for an hour so that Henrietta, Flo and Heather could sit down with Todd and talk about the wedding. Henrietta and Flo conspired to see to it that Heather squeezed in next to him. His only solace was that Heather didn't look one bit happier about it than he was. Proximity for the two of them was not a good thing. Hormones kept getting in the way of reason.

Todd drew a sheet of paper out of his pocket, along with a pen. "I've made a list," he began, only to hear a chuckle from the woman beside him. He scowled at her. "What?"

Heather returned his gaze evenly. "Nothing. I just mentioned to the others that you would surely make a list."

"Well, how else are we going to be sure we don't forget something?" he demanded.

"Todd, you make lists for everything from groceries and chores to life choices," she accused, as if it were some sort of crime, or perhaps merely evidence of a severe obsessive-compulsive disorder. "You probably have one tucked away somewhere on the options you have where Angel and I are concerned."

"Oh, boy," Flo murmured.

"Okay," Henrietta said, standing up at once.

"That's it for me. I've got things to do in the kitchen. The wedding can wait."

"It's a week from Saturday," Todd protested.

"Doesn't matter," Henrietta declared. "You two have things to talk about and I have things to do."

"What things?" he demanded.

"Important things."

"I'll help," Flo said, scooting right out behind her.

Left alone with Heather, Todd swallowed back another surge of the anger that had been brewing inside him for days. "How did we get from planning Henrietta's wedding to you and me?"

"Just bad luck, I suppose," she said, regarding him with a defiant lift of her chin. "We might as well get this over with. You're furious because I went off and left Angel with you. I don't blame you. It was a drastic thing to do."

"It was damned irresponsible, is what it was."

She didn't even blink at the accusation. "Irresponsible how? You're an adult. You're Angel's father. I left her in the best possible hands."

"How can you say that after what I told you?"

"What you told me was a very tragic story about something that happened years ago when you were a kid. It wasn't your fault and it has absolutely nothing to do with the man you are now. I don't know a more responsible, trustworthy man on the face of the earth. Not only that, Angel adores you and you adore her. I can see it whenever you're with her. I want that for Angel." She touched his cheek. "I want it for you."

"But what if something had happened?" he asked, unable to shut off the reel of possible disasters that ran nonstop through his mind.

"Nothing did, did it?"

"No, but—"

"Todd, what-ifs can immobilize a person. That's not living. It's playing it safe."

"It wasn't your choice to make. You should have given me a say."

"You would have said no, correct?"

"Of course."

"Then you wouldn't have had six days with your daughter," she pointed out. "Would you trade those for anything?"

He thought of the discoveries he'd made seeing things through Angel's eyes. He thought of the way she snuggled against him, of her little-girl smell, of the trusting way she tucked her hand into his. Would he have preferred never experiencing any of that? He couldn't honestly say that he would have. Those were memories he could cherish for a lifetime. They would last long after she and her mother went back to New York where they belonged.

"No," he admitted reluctantly. "I wouldn't trade the time we shared for anything."

Just as he wouldn't trade the time he'd spent

with Heather all those years ago and again more recently. The time before she'd come into his life, the time in between when they'd been apart, had been little more than existing, playing it safe, just as she'd described. He hadn't been living at all. He wasn't so blind that he couldn't see that without her his world was gray and with her it was filled with color.

But he wasn't so delusional that he thought he could capture that magic again and make it last, either. He definitely wasn't prepared to take the next step, the leap of faith that what they had once shared could last a lifetime. Even with the example of the judge and Henrietta right in front of him, he wasn't sure that love could conquer all.

Because of that uncertainty, he tapped his pen on the paper still in front of him.

"We'd better finish this list if Henrietta's going to have her perfect wedding," he said. "The logistics aren't going to be a breeze, not in the little bit of time we have, especially since the flowers are going to have to be ordered and flown in, along with just about everything else."

"That's it?" Heather asked, ignoring the monumental task facing them to seize on his avoidance of a more personal topic. "That's the end of any conversation about *us?*"

He lifted his gaze from the paper, met her indignant glare and nodded. "That's it," he said quietly. There was no mistaking the hurt and disappointment that darkened her eyes, but she gave him a curt nod.

"Then by all means let's plan Henrietta's wedding," she said briskly, not quite meeting his gaze. "Somebody around here deserves to live happily ever after."

"Heather—"

"Forget it, Todd. I can't fight you about this, not now. Right now I intend to concentrate on making a week from Saturday the happiest day in Henrietta's life."

Her willingness to let the matter drop bothered him for reasons he couldn't quite explain. He felt suddenly empty inside, as if he'd lost, rather than won.

Even so, he regarded her evenly and asked, "Shall we start with the flowers?"

"Sure. Why not?"

"Any preferences?"

"She hasn't mentioned any."

"What about you?" he asked.

"It's not my wedding."

"But if it were," he persisted.

"Tropical blooms," she said finally, a dreamy expression on her face as if she'd imagined this a thousand times. "The kind from Hawaii that smell so wonderful. Mixed with white roses in the bridal bouquet."

Todd jotted this down, not entirely certain why, since it was Henrietta's preferences that mattered.

Since the bride continued to make herself scarce, he questioned Heather about every other detail until he knew exactly what *her* dream wedding would be like, from the design of her dress to the canapés she would want served at the reception.

Only after he'd left the diner and gone to the office, only as he was making the calls to florists, caterers and dress designers, did he realize that he wanted to give this wedding to Heather someday. He wanted her dream to come true.

Then he tried to imagine her walking down the aisle toward some other man, but his imagination balked at the image. His stomach churned as he saw his daughter scattering rose petals along the path that Heather would walk to reach her groom.

The ringing of the phone snapped him back to the present. "Yes?" he said impatiently.

"Todd?"

His heart plummeted. "Yes, Dad." These rare calls never failed to take him by surprise, never failed to unnerve him.

"I just called . . ." His father hesitated, sounding uncertain in a way he never had before.

"Dad, what is it? Is something wrong?"

"No, nothing," his father said with more vigor. "I just wanted to hear the sound of your voice."

Now Todd knew something had to be *very* wrong. One sort of tension slid away to be replaced by another. "Dad, if something's wrong, you have to tell me."

"It would matter to you, after the hell I've put you through all these years?" his father asked, sounding surprised.

Truthfully, Todd was no less surprised by the reaction. "Yes," he said firmly, thinking of the man he had once idolized before fate had intervened.

"Then it's more than I deserve, son. Much more than I deserve." His voice dissolved into a choking cough.

"Dad, are you ill?"

"Just a bad cold. Nothing to worry about. I have to go, though. Once this cough kicks in, it takes a while to settle it down."

"Wait, Dad. There's something I'd like you to know. I . . ." He sucked in a deep breath before continuing, "I have a three-year-old daughter. She's beautiful and smart and maybe the best thing I ever did."

He waited for a sudden shift in mood, waited for the familiar harangue about his recklessness. Instead, his father merely sighed heavily.

"Are you sure . . . ?" his father began, then coughed. "You're married, then?"

"No, not yet."

"But you're in love with your daughter's mother?"

"Yes, I am," Todd said. The admission made him feel as if a weight had suddenly been lifted from his shoulders. "It's taken a long time, Dad, but I'm finally beginning to realize that what happened with Alicia wasn't my fault, not entirely, anyway."

"No," his father said slowly, "it wasn't. Not entirely."

Another fit of coughing cut off the statement that left Todd stunned.

"Dad, what are you saying?"

"It's not easy for me to admit this, son, but the truth is, I blamed myself for putting you in that position."

A memory began to emerge, but Todd waited for his father to go on.

"I should never have left you that day just so I could go grab a couple of drinks with my buddies. I took my own guilt out on you. I've wanted to tell you how sorry I was for a long time now, but it was easier to keep silent. Your mother knew, though. That's why we split up, because she couldn't forgive me for what I'd done that day and what I kept on doing to you."

Until that moment Todd had completely forgotten about his father being home the afternoon Alicia had died, had blocked the fact that his father had left the house after a call from one of *his* friends. His father was the one who was supposed to be staying home to care for Alicia. Todd's plans to go to the mall had already been made. His friend had called only to see why Todd was late, not to entice him out of a baby-sitting commitment he'd made.

All these years he had gotten it wrong. True, he had been behind the wheel, but the accident had been just that, an accident. Maybe he had made a bad judgment call in leaving the house in the first place, but his father had made a worse one and then spent years taking his guilt out on his son.

"Thank you," he said to his father.

"You're thanking me? For what?"

"For reminding me of what really happened that day."

"Too little, too late," his father said.

"No, Dad, it was just in time. I really hope you'll come for a visit. I'd like you to meet Heather and Angel."

"Angel? That's your daughter's name?"

"Angelique, actually. Will you come?"

His father's response was lost in another fit of coughing.

The awful sound, which he suspected was more than a cold, reminded him of just how short life was. In that instant, he knew he couldn't let Heather get away a second time. He knew without a doubt that he loved her—and Angel—too deeply to ever let them go. Peggy's words came back to him, her insistence that the love she and Johnny shared would triumph over whatever problems came their way.

He reached the first impulsive decision he'd made in years. "A week from Saturday would be a good time," he told his father. "With any luck, you'll be here for my wedding."

25

In all of his thirty-three years, Todd had never really done one single wildly impulsive act. During his years with Heather, he had acted spontaneously on occasion, but always at her instigation. He supposed in a way he could blame her for this crazy idea he couldn't seem to shake, but the truth was it was his and his alone. He didn't even know if she would go along with it. If she didn't, it could be the most embarrassing moment of his life. But a few moments of dramatic uncertainty would be worth it if she said yes.

To pull it off, he needed allies. He needed Henrietta and the judge. After all, what he was planning would affect their own wedding day.

He got the two of them alone in the diner after Heather had left to take Angel upstairs to bed. He locked the front door, just to be sure there were no interruptions.

"What's this all about?" Henrietta demanded as he peered nervously through the window of the locked door. "You're not acting at all like yourself."

"If this is about the birds and the bees, you're a little late," the judge commented dryly.

"Yes, I assumed I was," Todd said. He sat down

opposite the two of them, cleared his throat. "Actually . . ." Words failed him.

"Spit it out, son. Is something wrong?" the judge asked, his concern mirroring Henrietta's.

"Actually, I was wondering how the two of you would feel if I horned in on your big day."

"Horned in how?" Henrietta asked, clearly not grasping what he was asking. "You're right in the middle of it as it is. If it weren't for you, Heather and Flo, we'd never pull it off."

"We're mighty grateful to you for that, too," the judge added. "If there's something you need in return, just ask. Henrietta thinks the world of you and so do I."

Todd didn't consider himself a sentimental man, but the judge's brusque pronouncement brought a lump to his throat. He realized that he'd somehow found himself a family in Whispering Wind, something he'd never expected when he'd come here so reluctantly months earlier.

"I want your ceremony to be a surprise wedding for Heather and me, too," he said in a rush, then sat back while they stared at him in stunned silence. He took hope from the fact that neither of them had barked out a flat no to the unusual request.

"Oh, my," Henrietta finally murmured, eyes shining. "If that isn't the most romantic thing I have ever heard in my life."

The judge looked more skeptical. "If you don't

417

mind my saying so, it sounds a bit risky. Most women prefer not to have something like this sprung on 'em." He glanced at the woman beside him. "They want to take the time to consider a proposal from every which way."

Henrietta frowned at him. "I had my reasons, old man. Heather doesn't have a doubt in the world about Todd. She'll be thrilled." She beamed at Todd. "I say go for it."

"You won't mind sharing the day?" Todd asked. "You've waited a long time for it. If you'd prefer to keep it all to yourselves, I certainly understand."

"A wedding day ought to be unique and memorable," Henrietta said. "This ought to guarantee that. It ought to be about love, and judging from the way you look at that girl, I suppose it is definitely about that, too. I can't wait to see Heather's expression when she figures out what you're up to. Do you have something in mind for springing it on her?"

"She's going to be a bridesmaid for you, right?"

Henrietta nodded.

"Then how about when she's walking down the aisle?"

"Kinda last-minute, don't you think?" the judge asked again. "She could turn right around and hightail it out of there, leaving you and all the rest of us looking like fools."

"She might," Todd agreed. "But I figure it's my best shot at showing her just how serious I am.

The proposal has to be spontaneous and risky. It has to be daring enough to prove that I love her and that I will go to any lengths to show her just how much. That where she's concerned, I'm willing to throw caution to the wind."

The judge turned to Henrietta. "Well? Will it work? Or will we all end up with egg on our faces and our wedding day in ruins?"

"She'll say yes," Henrietta said with confidence.

"I hope you're right," Todd said fervently.

"The girl's not an idiot," Henrietta said. "Though for some time now, I've had to wonder about you." She grinned at him. "You're restoring my faith in your good sense."

"Think we can pull off the legalities without giving away the game?" Todd asked the judge.

"You've come to the right person," he declared, finally getting into the spirit of it, now that Henrietta had given the idea her full-fledged blessing. "I do believe I've got the power to pull this off without a hitch. Might as well be *some* advantages to all my years on the bench. I'll have a word with the minister, too, so he won't be taken by surprise."

For the first time since Heather had appeared in Whispering Wind, Todd had the feeling that he had his life back under his own control. It was ironic, really, since once he married Heather, he doubted he'd have another moment when he felt that way again.

"Do you think there's something odd going on with Todd?" Heather asked Flo a few days before the wedding.

"Not that I've noticed. Why?"

"He's got this look in his eyes. I can't explain it. Every time he catches my eye, I get the sense that he knows something I don't. It's like there's this deep, dark secret and he's just about to pop."

"A good secret or a bad one?"

"Exciting, from the looks of it."

"Have you asked him?"

Heather shook her head. "No. We're not actually speaking, not unless we have to. We're polite for Henrietta's sake, and we're civilized when he picks Angel up to take her on some outing every evening, but that's it."

"He's spending evenings with Angel?" Flo asked.

"Believe me, you are no more stunned by that than I am. He insisted on it. For weeks he wanted no part of custody. Now he's spending almost as much time with her as I am. Angel adores him. You know daughters and their daddies. There's a special bond there."

"You almost sound jealous."

"Don't be ridiculous. I'm delighted. It's what I've wanted all along."

"You just wanted to be a part of the family,"

Flo guessed. Her gaze narrowed. "You're still in love with him, aren't you?"

Heather sighed. "It doesn't matter."

"Why? Because he says it doesn't?"

"It pretty much takes two to do that particular tango," Heather said.

"He's in denial," Flo said. "Believe me, I know all about male denial. Joe is king of it."

Heather knew better. She knew that Joe had every intention of asking Flo to marry him. He was just waiting for her to understand that he loved her because of the woman she'd become, not the sex object she'd always thought herself to be.

"Has it occurred to you that Joe values you as a woman, not just someone to sleep with?" Heather asked, trying to help Joe out by nudging Flo in the right direction. The woman's self-esteem needed a serious adjustment.

Flo's expression turned thoughtful, but then she shook her head. "The two go hand in hand. No man wants a woman unless he also finds her desirable. Joe treats me like his sister."

Heather laughed. "Honey, no man kisses his sister the way Joe kisses you."

Flo blushed furiously. "Okay, that's true, but—"

"No buts. The man is crazy about you. He's just waiting for you to start valuing yourself."

Flo regarded her hopefully. "You think so?"

"I know so."

Flo grinned. "Then how do I go about letting

him know that I think I'm the best thing ever to walk into his life?"

"Just go with the program. Stop trying so hard to get him into bed and concentrate on all the other things you two have in common. Show him what a multidimensional woman you've become, instead of focusing all the time on the one area where you always felt comfortable with men. He needs to know you're not just lumping him in with all those other guys from your past, that you're sharing a side of you with him that no other man ever got to know."

"I get it. Make him see how special he is to me, but not just for the same old thing."

"Exactly. Sex is easy. Love is hard. Nobody knows that better than I do," Heather said with a deep sigh.

"If you ask me, Todd is just being stubborn."

"You ever know a man who wasn't?"

"No," Flo admitted. "But he'll come around, just like you say Joe will. I guess men have to do things at their own pace, so we don't get the idea that we have the upper hand."

"I suppose," Heather said glumly. Given the pace Todd was setting, she'd be Henrietta's age before he got around to forgiving her, much less doing anything about the fact that he loved her.

When Friday night's wedding rehearsal finally rolled around, Heather watched in amazement as

Todd orchestrated the event with the skill of a military tactician. Give the man a thousand little details, and not a single one escaped his notice. Give him a woman who was crazy in love with him, and he couldn't seem to see her at all. It was extremely frustrating.

Worse, with Henrietta and the judge acting like a couple of lovestruck teenagers, and Joe and Flo gazing deeply into each other's eyes and stealing kisses every chance they got, Heather felt completely left out, romantically speaking. Watching so much happiness was stirring up a whole lot of envy, especially when the man who could change all that for her was right in the same room.

Todd seemed oblivious to the fact that out of the entire wedding party, at least among the adults, they were the only pair not connecting. She wanted to smack him and tell him to wake up and smell the coffee.

But she kept silent. She was not about to spoil even a second of Henrietta's big moment with a petty little spat with Todd. If he wanted to hold a grudge, let him. She spent the entire rehearsal dinner pushing food around on her plate and pretending to ignore the mule-headed male at the opposite end of the table who seemed totally captivated by his daughter.

At the end of the dinner, Angel crawled out of Todd's lap and toddled toward Heather. "Night, Mama. I go with Daddy."

Heather's gaze shot from her daughter's face to Todd's. "Excuse me?"

"I thought maybe she could spend the night at my place tonight."

She told herself the reason she found the idea so irritating was that he hadn't discussed it with her first, but the truth was she was flat-out jealous.

"Won't you have too much to do to be worrying about Angel?" she asked.

"Everything's under control. I thought you might appreciate a good night's sleep and some extra time to get all gussied up for the ceremony in the morning. I'm sure Henrietta would like you and Flo on hand early. If Angel's with me, she'll be out from underfoot."

"Yes, I'm sure Henrietta would appreciate the extra help. That's very thoughtful of you," she said grudgingly.

He gave her a sharp look. "If it's a problem . . ."

She sighed. "No, of course not. It's a very sensible plan."

He grinned. "That's me, Mr. Sensible."

"Don't sound so proud of yourself. It's an annoying trait."

"Maybe I'll work on changing it," he said easily. "You never know."

"You?"

"Darlin', your skepticism wounds me. What kind of man doesn't change?"

"Your kind," she said at once.

He didn't seem especially concerned about the accusation. In fact, before she realized his intention, he gave her a quick, hard kiss, then reached for Angel's hand. "Let's go, munchkin. Mama's got to get her beauty sleep. Tomorrow's a big day."

"Big day," Angel echoed, nodding. "Gonna be a wedding."

He winked at her. "That's right, baby. There is definitely going to be a wedding."

Heather watched the two of them walk away hand in hand and wondered why she didn't feel happier about having accomplished the goal that had brought her to Whispering Wind. The answer, of course, was obvious. Even Flo had seen it. Heather wanted more. She wanted the man she loved to want not just Angel in his life, but her. She wanted Todd to be madly, head over heels in love with her the way he'd once been.

But she had to wonder if he would ever let it happen.

Todd cursed the crazy notion that he'd had to bring Angel home with him. He'd wanted Heather to be rested and receptive when he popped the question at the church, but he hadn't realized he was going to be sacrificing his own sanity to accomplish it.

Over the past couple of weeks he had foolishly thought he'd become adept at handling Angel's routine. Unfortunately he was discovering this morning that getting Angel dressed in shorts and a T-shirt was one thing. Getting her all dressed up for Henrietta's wedding to the judge and his own possible wedding to her mother was something else again.

He was soaked from head to toe by the time he had her bathed and into the frilly flower-girl dress Henrietta had delivered for her. The damn dress must have had a million tiny buttons and he was all thumbs.

He had exactly ten minutes to shower, shave and get into his own tuxedo if they were going to get to the church on time. He turned the apartment upside down trying to find the diamond-studded wedding ring he'd bought for Heather, then discovered it was already in his pocket. He was a wreck by the time they finally drove to the church.

As he gave Angel one last survey before they walked inside, he looked into her precious upturned face.

"You remember what we talked about?" he asked.

"Uh-huh."

What had he been thinking trusting his fate to a three-year-old? "Are you sure?"

"I carry flowers," she said.

"And?"

"Mama's ring."

"Exactly. Don't lose it, okay?"

She nodded solemnly.

Todd checked one more time to make sure the ring was securely tucked into the little pocket Henrietta had sewn onto the flower-girl dress. Satisfied, he took Angel to find the bridal party. Unwilling to risk a bad-luck glimpse of his own prospective bride, he turned Angel over to Flo.

"Bye, Daddy."

"Bye, Angel. Not a word, okay? It's our secret."

Flo regarded him intently. "What secret?"

"If I told you, it wouldn't be a secret, would it?"

"But Angel knows?"

"Yes, and if you try to pry it out of her, you are the lowest form of humanity," he said.

"How long will I have to wait to find out what it is?"

"Twenty minutes, tops."

She grinned. "Just within my limit."

Todd went off to find the judge, confirmed that everything had been taken care of, then went to wait just inside the back door of the church. The organist had been warned not to shift from background music to the wedding march until she was cued by a signal from the minister.

Todd heard Angel's excited squeals first, then the rustle of gowns as Henrietta, Flo and Heather took their places in the foyer. The organist hit the first preliminary notes to signal Angel's walk down the aisle with her basket of rose petals. She toddled into view at Heather's coaching, followed by Flo.

Then Heather stepped into the doorway. Henrietta had claimed to want an all-white wedding, so both her bridesmaids were wearing floor-length slim white dresses that could just as easily have passed for bridal gowns. Her bouquet was a smaller version of Henrietta's, just a spray of white tropical flowers, a single white rose and satin ribbons.

Todd gazed at her in awe. She took his breath away. She was so incredibly beautiful, so blasted unpredictable, so outrageously impudent.

And he loved her, never more so than he did at this moment. His heart was filled to overflowing with it. Though he'd given her no encouragement over the past few days for fear of giving away his plan, she winked at him. He took that as a sign from God that this was going to turn out exactly as he'd prayed.

He stepped into the aisle, then stunned her and everyone else by kissing her. He was dimly aware that the music had settled into a solemn holding pattern, that a gasp had rippled through the guests, that Angel was enthusiastically pelting them with rose petals.

When he finally released her, she gazed at him with a dazed expression. "Todd?"

"Will you marry me?" he asked quietly.

"Todd, this isn't—"

"It is the perfect time and place," he said.

"But Henrietta—"

"Knows all about it. We have her blessing. The only thing missing is your saying yes."

She glanced over her shoulder to see Henrietta nodding enthusiastically, then toward the front of the church, where the judge gave her a similar nod of encouragement.

"You're serious? Here and now? Just like that?"

"A double wedding," he confirmed. "I did my best to make it your dream wedding, right down to the canapés for the reception."

"Todd, you don't do things like this."

"I will if I have you by my side. Will you stay right here, keep producing plays for all of our friends, have more of my babies?"

She regarded him with hope shining in her eyes. "And you promise that you won't turn all stodgy on me, that you'll keep taking chances like this?"

"I do."

She laughed. "The words every woman dreams of hearing."

"Is that a yes?"

"If you're sure this is legal, then yes."

"Believe me, I am very sure that this will be legal enough to last a lifetime. I have the judge's word on it."

"Indeed, he does," the judge blustered from the

front of the church. "Now, can we get this show on the road? I'm not getting any younger."

Four people said their *I do*'s that morning. Five, counting Angel, who insisted on being picked up by her daddy so she could chime in.

And as Todd and Heather turned to make the return trip down the aisle as husband and wife, his gaze locked on the tall, distinguished-looking man sitting in the second pew, along with Heather's parents and his own mother. His father, tears in his eyes as he studied Angel, gave Todd a thumbs-up. It was the final blessing Todd needed to begin the best part of his life.